THE BURNS DESTINY

THE FIRE SALAMANDER CHRONICLES BOOK SIX

N. M. THORN

N.M. THORN

THE Burns DESTINY

THE FIRE SALAMANDER CHRONICLES • BOOK SIX

The Burns Destiny

By N.M. Thorn

Cover art design by www.originalbookcoverdesigns.com

Edited by Spirit Editorial

PROLOGUE

* * *

At the dawn of creation.
Somewhere in the heart of Vyraj.

THE GARDENS of Vyraj were beautiful at this time of year. Located far outside of the human realm, at the end of the Milky way, they nestled peacefully on the mighty branches of the World Tree. Sun showered the blooming gardens with its warm rays, throwing playful flairs of light on the colorful flowers bedazzled with morning due.

Amazing, exotic trees grew in the gardens, their hefty crowns a perfect shelter for birds whose sonorous chorus could be heard for miles around. A delicate scent of greenery, wild-flowers and fresh water wafted through the air, and the melody of the creek competed with the gentle song of the birds.

Deep in his thoughts, a man sat in a small clearing next to a huge stone, leaning his back against a thick trunk of an apple tree spangled with golden apples. His long blond hair fell over his face, but he didn't bother throwing it off. As a light gust of wind blew through the meadow, he lifted his face and looked around. His crystal blue gaze stopped on a large black crow sitting on the rock. The bird crowed loudly, its guttural voice traveling far through the gardens, and the man grunted, throwing his hands up as displeasure radiated around him.

"Crow," he said, rising. "What now?"

The crow flew up and then twirled in the air, surrounded by bright sparkles. As the light vanished, so did the bird. A tall man with long obsidian hair dressed all in black, stood by the stone next to him. He lowered down to one knee, pressed his fist to his chest and bowed his head.

"Lord Svarog," he said, his voice pleasantly deep.

"What do you want, crow?" asked Svarog with an exasperated sigh and motioned for him to rise.

"The same as always, my lord," replied the man-crow, rising, his dark gaze lingering on the powerful deity before him. "I'm here to beg mercy for your brother."

"I already told you, crow." Svarog pressed his lips into a stubborn straight line, crossing his muscle-bound arms over his wide chest. "We all have our place in this world. His is in the Nav, and I want to hear no more of his teenage rebellion. He has his obligations, and it's time he grew up."

"My lord, with all due respect..."

The man-crow bowed his head, squeezing his hands together until his knuckles became white. Then he raised his eyes and took a deep breath before continuing.

"Please reconsider. Your father doomed your brother to spend eternity in the darkness of the realm of spirits and demons. Anyone would rebel against that, and if your brother was a regular teenage boy, I would say nothing. But he is one of the most powerful gods of your pantheon, and his rebellion will result in terrible bloodshed." The man dropped to both knees, reaching to Svarog with a trembling hand. "Since Rod has retired, you have the power to change the situation. I beg you, my lord... For the safety of Prav and Yav, please reconsider."

Svarog jumped to his feet, his chest shuddering with furious breaths. "The Nav was supposed to be the realm of spirits and *dreams*. It is his impossible attitude that turned it into the world of demons! He got what he deserved, and I will hear no more of this!" He stomped his foot, and the ground trembled.

The man-crow got up with a low grunt, his arms dangling along his sides. "My lord, I'm not asking you to change his position. All I'm asking is to hear him out. Show him a little kindness." He raised his pleading eyes at the infuriated deity. "Trust me, a little kindness can go a long way—"

"I. Said. NO MORE!" Svarog slammed his massive fist on the stone, and dark clouds veiled the sky. The wind rushed through the gardens, bending the tall trees down to the deep, lush grass, and a few golden apples fell off the branches, dropping to the ground with soft thuds.

"As you wish, my lord." The man-crow bowed low, touching the ground with the tips of his fingers. "Just know that—by abusing and disregarding your brother, you are throwing the world into a war."

"Is that a prophecy, crow? Or is it a curse?" hissed Svarog, his eyes blazing with the light of his mighty power.

The man blanched, raising his arms. "No, my lord, neither. I'm just—"

"I've had enough," hissed Svarog, his terrible power swirling around him like a blazing twister. "You want to be a prophet of doom? So be it. You're no longer the gatekeeper of the gardens of Vyraj. Surrender the key at once."

The man-crow sighed but reached into his pocket and produced a small golden key. "As you wish, my lord," he whispered, his voice deep with sorrow and resignation. "You're making a giant mistake."

Svarog snatched the key out of the man's hand, pocketing it.

"You're no longer welcome in Prav and Vyraj. Leave and never come back here."

The man dropped his head, biting his lip. "How about my daughter? What will happen to her?"

Svarog glowered down at him, the furious light of his power slowly subsiding. "She can remain in the sacred garden as its guardian."

"Thank you, my lord." The man-crow bowed low.

"Since you're so loyal to my brother, from now on your place is by his side, in the Nav. Go serve him as the prophet of doom and calamities." Svarog made a dismissive gesture. "Leave now and never come back."

Bright sparkles surrounded the man as he twirled in place, shifting into his bird form. Carried by his strong wings, he rose in the air and disappeared into the sky above the Vyraj gardens.

For a few long moments, Svarog remained standing, trying to gather his thoughts. He leaned forward, bracing his arms against the warm surface of the large rock. After a while, he slammed his hand on it, swearing under his breath.

"Fire and ice!" he shouted, his voice echoing through the gardens. "As much as I hate to admit it, the crow has a point. Since I can't change the order my father Rod had established, I better get ready." He shook his head, and his shoulders sagged. "Goddammit, brother... why can't you do as you've been told?"

Svarog snapped his fingers, and his appearance started to change. His white linen pants got replaced by darker ones, and his short caftan vanished, replaced by a leather apron of a blacksmith. He pulled a long leather strip out of his pocket and tied his hair into a ponytail on the back of his head. Reaching up, he muttered a short enchantment, and a massive hammer glowing with bright scarlet light materialized in his hand.

Gently, he ran his fingers over the surface of the stone as if he was caressing the face of a woman he loved. Bright light flared from the rock, and rivulets of white gold streamed down to the ground, disappearing into the tall grass.

"Alatyr stone... the heart of the world," he whispered, tones of regret in his voice. "Here we are again." He sighed. "Let's do it."

Svarog swung his mighty hammer, plummeting it down on the Alatyr stone, and a beautiful blade engulfed in dancing flames materialized under his hammer. For a while, he worked in silence, shaping the weapon. Using the power of the Alatyr stone, he endowed the sword with magical energy and power beyond any weapon he had ever forged before. Once he was done, he lifted the sword, observing it with a critical eye.

"I name you the *Sword of the Prav*," he rambled, placing it on the ground next to the rock. "You are the Sword of Justice with the power to rule over the elements."

Turning back to the Alatyr, he swung his hammer again, and the white gold splashed up in a fountain of blazing sparkles from under his tool, blinding him for a moment. When he regained his vision, he saw a blade shining as bright as the sun itself lying atop the Alatyr. He kept working furiously, forging another powerful weapon, and once he was done, he held the most beautiful sword ever known to the world of gods and humans.

"*Sword Kladenets*, I name you," muttered Svarog, running his fingers over the delicate design engraved in the blade. "Your light has the power to destroy anything, magical or mundane."

He placed the second sword on the ground next to the first one and wiped the sweat off his forehead with the back of his hand, nibbling on his lip.

"This weapon is too dangerous," he whispered to himself. Squatting down, he touched the sword with his fingers, channeling his power through the blade made of pure white gold of the Alatyr stone. "I'm giving you the power to hide and disguise yourself as any living or inanimate object." Straightening up, he smirked. "Good luck to anyone who dares to find it without my permission."

He rolled his shoulders and winced, massaging his right arm. Then he swung his hammer once more, plummeting it down on the Alatyr. The last mighty blade materialized in his hands, shining brighter than any star of the Milky way. It was so perfect, he barely had to work on it.

"Your name is *Krest-Sword*," he whispered, lowering it to the ground.

For a while, Svarog worked with the Alatyr stone, creating armor, battle axes, sabers and mazes for the mighty army of the Prav. Once he had enough, he stopped and touched the stone again, extinguishing its light. Staring into the cloudless sky above the Vyraj, he chuckled darkly.

"I'm ready, brother!" he shouted into the heavens. "Bring it on!"

* * *

Somewhere in the Dark Nav

SOMEWHERE IN THE scariest depth of the Nav, the dark god rose from his cold throne. The pain inflicted by his brother's words gripped his entire being, and he clawed at his chest, wishing to tear his aching heart out. As bitter anger seared through him, he thrust his fist in the air, his magical energy wrapping around him like a black cloak.

"Bring it on? Ask and you shall receive, brother!" He threw the challenge into the air, staring at the dark ceiling of his place as uncontrollable fury twisted his face.

Dark mist rose around him, obscuring him for a moment, and when the mist disappeared, a mighty black serpent-dragon with powerful wings took his place, its iron tail shining dimly in the shimmering light of magical orbs.

The serpent hit its enormous wings against the floor and vanished. He flew for what seemed to be forever and didn't stop until he reached the Marabél stone. Black as night, it stood darker than the darkness of the Nav, its powerful magical energy radiating around it. Using his iron tail instead of a hammer, the Black Serpent forged a deadly weapon—a sword that could kill immortal gods. Just like his brother, he worked for a while, forging the weapons for his dark army, raising the scariest demons and phantoms from the lowest levels of the Nav.

Once he was done, the black serpent-dragon spun in place, taking his godly form.

"I'm ready, brother! Bring it on!" he shouted, and his dark army carried his battle cry. "Tell our darling father I am coming for both of you!"

* * *

It's not a fairy tale... It's life...

7

CHAPTER 1

~ ZANE BURNS, A.K.A. GUNZ ~

Coral Springs, Florida
Six months later...

A lonely rider moved slowly along a dark street, the sound of his horse's hooves echoing through the silence of midnight suburbia. His pale face looked almost translucent in the silvery light of the full moon, and his eyes shone with a soft, reddish glow. A light, warm breeze ruffled his long, blond hair, brushing it off his face and throwing it to his back.

Despite the warmth of the South Florida weather, he wore a long leather coat, and his tall riding boots seemed to be out of place in combination with his modern jeans and tight, black shirt. His stallion was just as unusual as the rider, its thick mane and long tail sparkling gold with the reflected glimmer of the streetlights. All in all, the pair didn't fit into the contemporary surroundings, looking strangely archaic and outlandish.

Crouching on the flat roof of a single-story building at the edge of a large corner plaza, Gunz watched as the rider promenaded slowly back and forth along Coral Ridge Drive. He shook his head, pursing his lips. *"Slavik, what the hell are you doing,* man?" he asked, using their blood bond. *"You and Siv stand out like a sore thumb here."*

A wide grin split Yaroslav's face, and even from this distance, Gunz could see the tips of his fangs showing from under his parted lips.

"That's the idea," murmured the vampire, patting Siv's neck. *"Just keep an eye on things and be ready when the time comes. They're still far, but I can sense them already. Can you?"*

Gunz nodded, forgetting that Yaroslav most likely couldn't see him. He inhaled, detecting the barely noticeable salty odor of the ocean and the delicate scents of grass and earth. But together with the freshness of the evening, the reek of demonic essence invaded his senses, and he grunted as his stomach twitched. Sharpening his hearing, he registered the guttural roar of engines somewhere in the distance.

"I can sense them, alright." He stared in the direction of the sound, but the street remained as dark as ever. *"Demons on motorcycles."* He rolled his eyes. *"What a cliché."*

"Yeah, well..." Yaroslav's hand slowly moved down toward the hilt of his katana as he rose slightly on the stirrups. *"Just because they are a 'cliché', doesn't make them any less dangerous."*

Yaroslav was right. It'd been a few weeks since the motorcycle gang, calling themselves *Night's Angels,* arrived seemingly out of nowhere. One day, everything was fine, and the next day, all hell broke loose. The Night's Angels invaded the streets, robbing people, burning houses, abusing and raping residents without much care for their victims' age or gender. They were equal opportunity destroyers, and since they showed up, people were afraid to sleep at night or step out of their homes after sunset.

The gang had spread around the area like a plague, and the police and national guard were helpless, all their efforts ineffective against the powerful supernatural assailants. The demons, even though they weren't pureblood abominations of Hell, seemed to be impervious to modern fire weapons. Besides, some members of the gang were rogue vampires, upirs, and even werewolves, which was quite uncommon since lycanthropes preferred to keep the company of their own kind, obeying no one but their Alphas.

Reports about similar problems flooded Jim's desk, and the FBI Headquarters turned to him, expecting him to find a silver bullet solution to the quickly spreading wave of violence and chaos. Soon, it became clear that there were only two ways of killing members of the demonic gangs—decapitation and fire. Since neither police nor national guard walked around armed with swords and incendiary devices, and exposing the World of Magic to humans wasn't an option, Akira's company had to step in.

At first, Akira refused to let Yaroslav get involved in the situation on the streets. His last disappearance had awakened motherly instincts in the ancient vampire with new strength, and like a true helicopter parent, she spread her wings over him, afraid to let him out of her sight. Unable to disobey his maker, Yaroslav stuck in the *EverSafe Security* building and no amount of begging and pleading from his side could convince Akira to change her mind.

However, after Gunz and Agent Andrews cornered her in her office, explaining why they needed Yaroslav's help, she had no choice but to agree. Reluctantly, she allowed her son to leave the building with them but not without some stipulations— Gunz was supposed to be Yaroslav's personal bodyguard.

It'd been a while since Gunz and Yaroslav had begun fighting on the same side, facing the followers of Chaos and other supernatural creeps. They knew each other's strengths and weaknesses; they had a blood bond, which allowed them to communicate telepathically, and they trusted each other with their lives and beyond.

As far as Gunz was concerned, agreeing to be Yaroslav's

bodyguard wasn't going to change much in their normal dynamics, and if his promise would give Akira some peace of mind and Yaroslav his freedom, it was worth it.

Angel, Uri and Svyatobor came and went, showing up only when Gunz summoned them in extreme situations. However, they couldn't remain in South Florida on a constant basis, as they were trying to contain outbursts of chaos all over the world. Aidan had never come back from the Otherworld, helping Gwyn ap Nudd reinforce the defenses around his realm and the Isle of Legends—one of four magical nexuses on Earth. Tessa had returned to the Guardians Order, and Mrak Delar remained in Kendral. So, it was up to Gunz and Yaroslav to deal with the Night's Angels and protect the city.

The short blast of a police siren ripped Gunz from his thoughts, and he leaned forward slightly, ready to jump off the roof and get involved if needed. The red and blue lights sliced through the darkness, reflecting in the windows of the vacant units of the plaza as a single police cruiser approached Yaroslav, signaling him to stop.

He halted and inclined his head respectfully, giving the police officer a tightlipped smile. "What can I do for you, sir?" he asked softly, carefully covering his katana with the side of his coat.

The policeman, a stout man in his late fifties, walked out of his vehicle, his right hand trembling slightly over his gun holster in the best traditions of western movies. Gunz snickered. He knew perfectly well that Yaroslav could rip this man apart with his bare hands before he could even think about pulling his gun out.

"Sir," said the policeman sternly, "step out of your—" He cut himself off and cleared his throat uncomfortably. "Just, um"—he twirled his hand in Siv's direction—"get off your horse. Hold your hands where I can see them."

Yaroslav dismounted and raised his arms. "License and

registration for my vehicle?" he asked in all seriousness, but the wild twinkles of suppressed laughter danced in his eyes. Siv snorted loudly in a very un-horse-like manner. Gunz made a move to get off the roof, but as if sensing his intentions, Yaroslav glanced in his direction and gave him a tiny shake no.

"Don't get smart with me, son," grumbled the policeman, his face red from either annoyance or the lights of his car. He lowered his hand on the handle of his gun, ready to give another command, when Yaroslav tensed and looked to his left, his hand reaching under his coat for his sword automatically.

"Yaroslav, get ready. They're coming... Many of them," said Gunz as a wave of demonic essence assailed his senses with new strength. *"You need to get rid of this cop."*

"Officer," said Yaroslav, turning back to the policeman, his voice friendly but firm, "I'm sorry to cut the entertainment short, but I need you to get back into your car and leave. It's not safe for you to be here."

The older man's jaw dropped, and he all but hopped in place. Pulling his gun out, he pointed it at Yaroslav's chest and shouted, "Turn around slowly. Hands behind your head. Let's see what you're gonna sing after a night in jail, smart-ass punk."

Yaroslav sighed. Still holding his arms up, he reached with his right hand and pulled the sleeve of his coat down, exposing a thick, leather bracelet on his left wrist. It was bright red, and the black logo of *EverSafe Security* was clearly visible even in the unsteady light of the surroundings.

The officer's eyes widened, and his eyebrows climbed up as he stared at the red bracelet. "Are you an employee of Ms. Ida's company?" he managed to say, putting his gun away.

"I'm Yaroslav Potemkin, part-owner of *EverSafe Security*, sir," replied the vampire, lowering his arms. "I'm sorry, but shit is about to hit the fan here, and you're not equipped to handle what's coming. Please, allow me and my team to do what has to be done without endangering human lives. I need you to leave."

The policeman stared at him, flabbergasted. "But you're alone. Where is your backup, your team?" he mumbled, staring around wildly. "You're just a boy…"

The bright headlights of the upcoming motorcycles lit up the air at the far end of the street and the roar of their engines became louder. In one swift motion, Yaroslav mounted Siv and pulled his katana out.

"I'm a dangerous boy," he hissed, pointing the blade in the direction of the police cruiser. "I'll be all right if you let me do my job. Leave now, sir."

As the policeman hopped into his car, shut down the lights and left, Gunz switched his attention to the approaching gang. Being in the middle of South Florida suburbia, he couldn't use his elemental energy, and knowing what was coming, he needed all the help he could get. He channeled his magic and connected with the Dark Codex. As the instant headache blinded him for a split second, he grunted, planting his fist against the warm metal roof.

"*Slavik, I'm ready,*" he growled. "*I can see them.*"

Before he finished his statement, the silence exploded with the thundering of engines, and the darkness shied away from the blazing beams of the motorcycles' headlights. Gunz couldn't quite count how many gangsters were in the group. They barged into the area, laughing and screaming profanities, but as soon as they saw Yaroslav and Siv, they slowed down and surrounded them, swarming around like a bunch of vultures.

"*Gunz, stand down and watch the road,*" hissed Yaroslav. "*There are less than thirty of them here, but judging by the amount of negative energy I can sense, there should be a lot more. Something is not right. Once I get them off their bikes, I can deal with them on my own.*"

"I know. Try to get them off the road and into the plaza," murmured Gunz, an intense feeling of unease spreading through him, making his shoulders ache. Both Akira and Jim had directed them here. Each of them had stated that they received intel placing Night's Angels in this neighborhood at this time. They wanted Yaroslav and Gunz not only to protect the residents and vanquish the demons but also to learn what they were searching for.

The bikers came to a screeching halt, and the demonic energy spiked around them to a new high, permeating the air with its suffocating stench. Brandishing their chains, clubs infested with metal spikes, swords and knives, they got off their bikes and moved closer to Yaroslav. The vampire didn't blink an eye, staring down at them calmly.

"What can I do for you, gentlemen?" he asked softly, relaxing his posture as he lowered his sword arm.

A large demon, dressed in leather pants and a vest with the gang's name on the back, stepped forward, planting his feet wide apart. With his long, overly muscled arms, and massive chest and shoulders, he was living proof of Darwin's theory of evolution. His narrow forehead with a low hairline just added to his resemblance to an ape.

He halted next to Siv, taking in Yaroslav's appearance, and his thick lips stretched into an ugly sneer. Tapping his metal club on the palm of his hand, he turned to his gang, flicking his bushy eyebrow.

"This one is a vamp, yah know?" He jerked his chin at Yaroslav and pointed his club at one of the gangsters. "Your kind, Dick. Wanna have a word with him before I tear him a new one?"

A vampire, presumably Dick, stepped forward, followed by at least ten more vampiric members of the gang. He cocked his head, his uneven smirk exposing his dangerous blade-like fangs.

"Long, blond hair," he hissed, his eyes shining scarlet. "Katana. I bet you anything, this is Yaroslav Potemkin. If I'm right, he stopped being my kind when his maker, the Scarlet Queen, sided with humans, fighting against us."

Yaroslav smirked and waved his hand at the vampire lazily. "Bell bottom jeans, obnoxious polyester shirt... Hmmm, let me guess?" He tapped his finger against his lips. "At the beginning of the seventies, you were turned accidentally by a drunk vampire who was getting high on your LSD-spiced blood?"

The vamp howled in anger and launched himself at Yaroslav. The katana swooshed through the air, and flakes of gray ash fell to the ground in the place where the vampire Dick had been standing just a second ago. The rest of the gang shouted and shifted closer, their weapons at the ready.

"Slavik, if you and Siv step away, I can turn them all into ashes before they know it," projected Gunz, ready to spring into action.

"Something is not right, Gunz. I was expecting a lot more of them. Keep your strength. I'll deal with them on my own," replied Yaroslav, switching his attention back to the gang.

The rest happened so fast that Gunz could barely follow their movements. Yaroslav laughed and gave Siv a light kick in his sides. The horse reared and neighed angrily, smoke and fire coming out of his ears and nostrils. He pushed off the ground and jumped over the heads of the monsters, landing onto the pavement of the empty plaza. The demons shouted all at once and followed them, surrounding the vampire.

One moment, Yaroslav was still on his horse, and the next moment, he had vanished. The vampiric gang members followed him, becoming nothing more than a blur. The sound of metal on metal, cries of pain and curses rose in the air, but all of that lasted no longer than a few seconds. The remaining group of gangsters stood back to back in the center of the plaza, staring around with wide eyes as they searched for Yaroslav, the weapons in their hands trembling. Both the horse and the rider were gone, leaving behind piles of dust and ashes.

Straightening to his full height, Gunz scanned the plaza but couldn't see his friend anywhere. Bright flares of light a few blocks away attracted his attention, and he sharpened his

CHAPTER 2

~ ZANE BURNS, A.K.A. GUNZ ~

unz watched Yaroslav and Siv move away stealthily, and once they were far enough, he walked toward the demons with his sword ready in his hand. Suppressing his fire energy as much as possible in the given situation, he kept in the shadows for as long as he could. Despite his efforts, the gang noticed him sooner than he intended, and the carnivorous light ignited in their eyes. As their battle cry rolled over the area, they charged forward, waving their weapons. Their demonic essence washed over him, making his stomach lurch, but he didn't slow down.

"*Ignius!*" he shouted, and the steady stream of fire escaped his blade, blasting the approaching demons.

The flames engulfed the front line, and they spun in place, howling in pain, their arms flailing. Keeping his elemental energy under control, Gunz allowed the fire to take him over. With his body ablaze, he didn't wait for his enemies to recover and shouted, "*Ignius Amplio.*"

His second blast was a lot more potent than the first one. Quickly devouring the demons' bodies, the flames ate their way through, creating an opening to the other side of the street. Without slowing down, Gunz entered the passage he created and as expected, the attackers closed their lines, surrounding him. He weaved between his formidable enemies, setting as many demons ablaze as he could. Moving almost as fast as Yaroslav, he cut and stabbed with his flaming sword, slicing and burning his way through.

Fighting in a confined space against opponents who were a lot taller and heavier than him, he knew he wouldn't make it out unscathed. But while both the fire and adrenalin were pumping through his system, the only thing he cared about was staying alive. Injuries he could deal with later. However, dying in a highly populated area wasn't an option because the elemental blast created at the moment of his death would wipe out thousands of humans.

The clatter of metal, the cries of pain, the shouts of anger, and the continuous stumping of heavy boots against the asphalt turned into an overwhelming racket, and he couldn't help but wonder why no one from the local residences called nine-one-one. Somewhere in the distance, he heard Siv's neighing and Yaroslav's laughter. They were alive, and they were getting closer. He needed to move faster.

Spreading the last deadly blast of physical fire around him, he rose to his full height. Making sure that none of the monsters survived the confrontation, he observed the area and stopped, his chest rising and falling with laborious breaths. The pavement was covered with dead bodies, and the last flames were still burning here and there, spreading waves of heat around him. Dirty swirls of smoke rose in the air, carrying the nauseating stench of burnt flesh.

"Cease," he shouted, moving his hand over the street that was now resembling a medieval-style battlefield, and the fire died out.

Yaroslav walked toward him with Siv by his side. Holding his blade in his hand, the vampire was covered in blood from head to toe, his long hair hanging in long, scarlet strands. The stallion's mane was more red than gold, white smoke still pumping from his nostrils. In combination with his large, rotating eyes and flattened ears, he looked fearsome.

"Gunz, you're bleeding," hissed the vampire. Turning his head to the side, he pressed his hand to his lips.

Gunz smirked at the vampire's reaction, recognizing the familiar gesture—Yaroslav didn't want him to see his natural response to the smell of his blood. Just now noticing the pain in his left arm, he ran his hand over it, feeling the sticky wetness under his fingers.

"I'll survive." Slowly moving his head from left to right, he flexed his shoulders. As his body responded to his movement with aches and pains, he grunted, realizing that the cut on his arm wasn't the only injury he sustained. Nevertheless, nothing seemed to be serious enough to prevent him from moving forward, so he waved his hand dismissively. "Just a flesh wound. I'll revert later. We need to get going."

"There are more of them..." Yaroslav sucked in air and closed his eyes for a moment. Then he pointed up the street. "I can smell them, and they reek of death and hatred. Demons and vampires mostly, but there are some other creatures I don't recognize."

"I know," replied Gunz at length, biting his lip. "It feels like someone is..." He choked on his last words and frowned, staring into space. "It doesn't matter. We have no choice. We need to see what's going on and clear the streets."

He narrowed his eyes, staring at the darkness gathering no more than a city block away. Like a sinister, stormy cloud, it accumulated over the houses on the right side of the road, slowly rotating counterclockwise. Electrical discharges zigzagged through it, illuminating the roofs and the tops of the palm trees with purplish flares of light.

At this point, he was sure that whoever was in charge of the demonic gang knew about their presence, so there was no reason in hiding. They walked briskly forward without giving a thought to why they were rushing toward a clear and present danger from which any normal person would run away screaming. As they moved, the air became thicker with the energy of dark magic mixed in with a hellish amount of demonic essence. The streetlights were off, and the area was submerged under the cover of night.

Gunz stopped in front of the entrance into a small gated community and probed it with his Salamander senses. Yaroslav halted by his side, standing still like a statue. Siv reared back slightly, shaking his head, his golden mane flying around.

"Nu-huh," he neighed fearfully, his ears pressed down, his eyes like two round plates. "I ain't going there. Nu-huh."

Gunz and Yaroslav exchanged a quick look and headed toward the gate.

"Hey, you! Two idiots!" yelled Siv. He reached them in one hop and blocked their way in, regarding them with a furious gaze. "Are you out of your friggin' mind?" He pushed Gunz on his shoulder and stomped his hoof down. "I can understand him." He glared at Yaroslav. "He's defective. His brain is just as silent as his heart. But what's your excuse, firetwat? Wanna die much? And kill every single human in a mile radius while you're at it?"

Gunz and Yaroslav shrugged and moved around Siv without saying anything.

"Fire and Ice and all the beautiful mares!" yelled Siv behind them. "This is ludicrous! The amount of dark energy in this area is so thick you can cut it with an axe. Don't you feel it? The vampire may survive it—he is a demon after all. But you, Fire Salamander... It will render you powerless!"

Gunz sighed and stopped, turning around. "Maybe it will, but maybe you need to give me some credit. I'm the Great Fire Salamander—the ultimate weapon against demons and vampires." He winked at the stallion, sadness squeezing his heart. "Listen, Siv, Yaroslav and I must go on. It's our duty, you know. But you don't have to go with us. Why don't you leave, my friend?"

Yaroslav approached the horse and patted his neck affectionately. "If we need your help, we'll summon you."

"Promise?" Siv's eyes narrowed at the vampire. He sighed and lowered his massive head on Yaroslav's shoulder, stilling for a brief moment.

"Cross my silent heart." The vampire flashed his toothy smile and stepped back.

As Siv turned around and galloped away, muttering something under his breath, Gunz and Yaroslav headed toward the small booth at the entrance into the gated community. The bar was down, but the lights were off, and Gunz couldn't detect the warm presence of a human soul inside.

He bent down and slipped under the bar. Carefully, he approached the gatehouse and peeked inside. A young man in a security guard uniform lay on the floor, his head twisted at an impossible angle, his dark eyes still reflecting the horror he felt at the moment of death.

Yaroslav glanced inside over Gunz's shoulder, and his eyes lit up with a bright red glow, a growl rumbling deep in his chest. He waved forward, gesturing for Gunz to follow. Fast and silent, the vampire moved through the dark neighborhood. With his mind on high alert, Gunz followed him, his fingers squeezing the grip of his sword as though it was his lifesaver.

All houses stood dark, not a spark of light behind black windows. As they kept moving, following the main road, the silence became so heavy it was pressing on Gunz's ears, giving him a slight headache. Even though the crowns of the trees were moving ruffled by a light breeze, there was no rustling sound associated with it. He couldn't hear the familiar noise of the distant traffic or the screeches of ducks and birds that normally never shut up, not even at night.

"Slavik," he called, but no sound came out from his dry throat. *Silencing spell...* A thought spiraled through his mind, and cold shivers ran up and down his spine.

"This entire area is under some kind of enchantment," projected Yaroslav through their blood bond, slowing down a little.

"Silencing spell," replied Gunz, grateful that their blood bond was still active.

"More than that." Yaroslav shook his head. His lips parted, showing his fully expanded fangs. *"Silencing spell is just a small fraction of whatever this is."*

As they came to a roundabout, Gunz halted and surveyed the neighborhood with both his Salamander senses and his other sight.

"To the left." He took the main road leading left and switched to a light jog.

The farther they progressed, the heavier the presence of dark magic became. As Yaroslav had suggested, it wasn't only the silencing spell, and soon, Gunz started to feel the lack of elemental energy. Since there was no other reasonable explanation, he assumed it had been drained by the same malevolent spell. Feeling lightheadedness and shortness of breath, he came to a sharp halt and bent forward, bracing his hands against his knees. As much as he hated the pain, he connected with the Dark Codex, getting ready for pretty much anything.

Cringing from the increasing headache, he felt a burst of energy rushing through his body as the powerful magic took him over. His eyes lit up with a bright, white light, and he straightened, squaring his shoulders.

"Your eyes are like high beam headlights." Yaroslav halted by his side, observing him with concern. *"Can you dim them down?"*

"I don't think it would make any difference," Gunz projected, pointing with his blade forward.

The street opened up into a spacious cul-de-sac at the far edge of the development. A large, two-story house stood silent and dark like the rest of the homes, and the sinister cloud of dark magical energy slowly rotated over it. The entire space of the cul-de-sac was taken by the black silhouettes of demonic gangsters looking like a shapeless, malevolent mass. They stood shoulder to shoulder, but what struck Gunz as strange was that none of them had their weapons at the ready. It seemed like someone had just thrown a pile of bodies in their way to stop them from entering.

Slowly, he headed toward the house, wondering what it was about this expensive home that attracted such undesirable attention. He lowered his sword, dragging its tip over the pavement. A few weak sparks erupted from under the blade, but there was no sound accompanying it.

"No fire?" Yaroslav's question appeared in his mind, and he shook his head, halting at the entrance into the cul-de-sac.

The air here seemed to be uncharacteristically cold, and the drop of temperature was so abrupt that even Gunz could feel it. He shivered, and his chest tightened with dread. Catching a movement in his peripheral vision, he saw Yaroslav unsheathing his katana.

The crowd of demons parted soundlessly and stepped aside, revealing a line of humans—men, women, and children. The monsters pushed them forward, hiding behind them. Gunz scanned these people with his other sight and cringed inwardly. Every single person standing in front of the gang was a pure-blood human, their souls shining with white or golden light.

"Goddammit... Now what?" Gunz bit his lip, unable to take his eyes off the innocent people whose only fault was that they were in the wrong place at the wrong time. A young girl dressed in pajamas with kittens imprinted on them stood next to a

young woman, clutching her leg with both hands. Her face was contorted as large tears were escaping her round blue eyes, but no sound came out from her trembling lips.

"I know the fire is suppressed here, but can you use your magic?" asked Yaroslav.

"We're about to find out," replied Gunz. He averted his gaze, forcing the flow of his magical energy away from his eyes to dim down their brilliant glow. "The only problem is that we will expose the World of Magic."

"That's what their bosses are counting on," replied Yaroslav through gritted teeth. "They're sure that we wouldn't dare break the rules, putting ourselves under the Destiny Council's scrutiny. What they don't know is that the Destiny Council is supporting us."

"True, but—"

"No buts, my friend. It's obvious, they knew you were coming," continued Yaroslav, his lips set into an angry, straight line. "They suppressed fire energy as much as they could, and to ensure that you won't use your elemental power, they brought forth these humans."

Gunz laughed soundlessly. "Clearly, they underestimated me." He arched his eyebrow at his friend. "We proceed with caution?"

"Don't worry about exposing the World of Magic. Let's just do whatever needs to be done to save these people and clean this demonic mess. I'll distract them, and you try to get the humans out of the way in one piece," growled the vampire, rising in the air with his arms wide opened.

The monsters upturned their heads, watching his every move, and people's eyes widened in shock. Yaroslav disappeared, moving at his usual blinding speed, and soon the commotion in the back of the demonic lines suggested that his katana was doing its job, wreaking chaos and devastation among the enemy forces. A large part of the demons turned around, endeavoring to deflect the vampire's attacks, but they didn't seem to be successful as one by one, the gang members started to fall.

Gunz gathered his magic in his hands, and his body exploded with the brilliant white light that could rival Aidan's magical energy. He walked forward, and the ground shook with every step he took. Halting just a few feet away from the line of humans, he searched the Dark Codex, and his lips stretched into a cold smirk as he found what he was looking for. Dropping his sword, he moved his arm from left to right, repeating the words presented by the Codex in Dragon tongue.

As he continued chanting soundlessly, the wind picked up, rustling the large leaves of queen palms. A shield of bright, white light surrounded the humans, glowing brighter with each second. The demons jerked but couldn't move their feet, frozen in place by the spell. Soon, the light became too bright to handle, and the demons closed their eyes, shying away from it. Feeling the lack of magical energy on the outside, Gunz tapped into the magic within. As he kept channeling his own energy into the shield, his arms started to tremble, and the headache increased to the point where he had a hard time dealing with it.

Don't give up... Almost..., he thought, channeling more of his magic into the spell he was casting. Unable to tolerate the pain any longer, he screamed, his eyes watering, but the sound died out in his tortured vocal cords. The world swam around him in nauseating circles, and he fell to one knee. With a last effort, he threw all he had into the spell, and the white light flooded the area, making it impossible to see anything.

When the light dissipated, the humans were gone, and only stupefied demons stood in front of him with their mouths agape.

"*Slavik... I need help...,*" he managed to project before collapsing to the ground. He didn't know if the vampire was still alive. He couldn't hear him fighting and the only thing he could see was the wall of demons surrounding him, their lips distorted into carnivorous snarls.

He wasn't unconscious, but he felt drained magically as he

had never felt before. The stench of the demonic essence flooded his senses, and his stomach heaved, making him turn to the side, curling into himself. He saw his sword lying just a foot away and reached for it, but a heavy motorcycle boot stepped on his hand, crushing it. A terrible blow to his back made his body arch, and his mouth opened, the muscles of his neck and chest bulging in a silent scream.

As the demons proceeded to kick him, he curled into a tight ball, wrapping his arms around his head.

"Slavik... are you... alive...?"

When the vampire didn't reply, a terrible thought originated in his mind, and an unimaginable fury shook through him, giving him a new burst of energy. As fire flooded his entire being, bright scarlet flames broke through his skin. The demons cowered back, which gave him a moment to regroup. With a torturous groan, he rose to his knees and spread his shaking arms wrapped in the blood-red flames. His chest shuddered with ragged breaths as an unusual energy boiled up within his battered body, searching for release.

"Slavik, if you can hear me," he growled through their blood bond, fighting to control the rising wave of fire, *"take cover now!"*

He leaned back, his body arching as the physical fire spread around him like an atomic blast. In the last moment, he thought he saw a giant horse with two riders zoom past him through the air, moving above the flow of his fire blast, but he wasn't sure it wasn't a figment of his imagination.

With his vision flooded red, he saw scarlet flames feasting on the demons, devouring them with incredible ease. Dirty swirls of smoke and the reek of burnt flesh polluted the air. The coldness got replaced with unbearable heat, and black clouds of demonic essence escaped into the ground before the hosts' bodies disintegrated into piles of dust and ash.

Drained magically and physically, Gunz fell on his back,

staring straight up into the starless sky where the disgusting cloud kept circling above the house.

"*Slavik...,*" he projected, barely able to move his head to the side. "*Please tell me you survived...*"

CHAPTER 3

~ ZANE BURNS, A.K.A. GUNZ ~

Gunz coughed and winced at the pain in his ribs, his hand going down of its own accord. He tried to move, but the dizziness took hold of him, and he just dropped on his back, pressing his palm to his side.

"Slavik... please be alive..."

"Gunz, I am fine. I am here." Yaroslav's voice broke through the haze in his mind, and he sighed with relief.

He felt two pairs of hands seize his shoulders and gently move him into a sitting position. He moaned softly and opened his eyes. Yaroslav was on his knees by his side, strands of his long hair plastered to his face covered in blood. His leather coat was shredded to pieces, and Gunz could see a few deep lacerations on his arms and chest quickly closing as the vampire's self-healing kicked in.

Clad in his medieval armor, Raoul de Beaumont kneeled on his other side, an expression of bewilderment on his face.

"Raoul, how the hell—," he started to say but cut himself off when he realized that the silencing spell was still active, and Raoul couldn't hear him.

His eyes fell on Siv, who was dancing impatiently behind

the Warden, and understanding dawned on him. He had always considered Siv to be one of the most self-centered creatures of magic he had ever met, so now, he couldn't believe that the stallion had troubled himself with finding the Warden and coming back with him despite the possible danger.

Leaning heavily on Yaroslav's shoulder, Gunz got up and surveyed the area just to make sure that the demons were gone and their path to the house was unobstructed. The entire area of the cul-de-sac was covered in a thick layer of ash, and nothing was moving in the surrounding darkness. A few stray flames danced on blackened bushes, creeping up closer to the smaller decorative palms, but amazingly none of the buildings had suffered any damage from the fire. He stretched his arm toward the flames, ordering them to cease, and they responded to his silent command, dying out immediately.

Raoul picked up Gunz's sword, offering it to him. Gunz took it with his right hand and almost dropped it, staring down at his crushed, bleeding fingers in shock. Sucking in a sharp breath, he moved his sword to the left hand and slowly headed toward the entrance, carefully probing the path ahead with his Salamander senses. Even though the demonic gang was incinerated, the dark spell still dominated the neighborhood, and the black cloud swirled slowly above the house, illuminating the area with flashes of electrical discharges.

He reached a short driveway and halted, raising his hand. The entire house was encapsulated in a dense layer of dark magic. Raising his sword, he touched it and whispered a short spell soundlessly. A large dome of undiluted magical energy lit up with a sinister, purple glow, vibrating and emitting tiny bolts of electricity.

"What the hell?" projected Yaroslav, backing away from it.

Raoul tapped Gunz's shoulder, making him flinch and snap around. Then he moved his hand and a single word glowing with the white light of the Warden's magic materialized in the air—*wards*.

Gunz nodded, and a lopsided grin appeared on his face. He touched his chest and snapped his fingers, igniting a tiny, weak flame at the tip of his thumb. Then he shrugged and pointed at the house, giving the Warden an arched stare.

"*Yeah, yeah... we know,*" grumbled Yaroslav, rolling his eyes. "*You're the fire, you are everywhere, and you know everything.*"

Gunz chuckled and shook his head. "*Not that one... The other one. About the Fire Salamander portals that can burn through the fabric of reality itself.*"

Taking a deep breath, he focused on whatever elemental energy he could gather from nature and from within and waved his hand. A heat wave rushed through him, and the flaming curtain of his portal unraveled before him. Raoul gasped and grabbed Gunz's shoulder, pointing at the blood-red flames burning at the edge of the portal. Gunz just shrugged and gestured for him to go through.

Crossing himself, the Warden mouthed a quick protection spell and passed through the flames, walking out on the other side of the buzzing wards. Gunz turned to Yaroslav, remorse and worry tightening his chest.

"*Slavik, I can't carry you through,*" he said, touching his friend's arm. "*I don't think I have enough magic in me left to protect you from the purifying energy of my portal. I'm sorry.*"

"*That's okay.*" A sad smile touched Yaroslav's pale lips. "*Someone needs to keep an eye on the things out here while you're inside. Siv and I will stay behind.*" He winked at Gunz and easily rose into the saddle, patting the stallion's neck. "*Just be careful.*"

* * *

GUNZ PASSED through his portal and joined Raoul on the other side. Throwing a quick glance back at Yaroslav, he sighed, wishing with all his heart he didn't have to leave his friend behind. But since taking the vampire through his portal without any protective magic wasn't an option, there was nothing he could do. With a sigh, he walked up the steps, stopping in front of the door. For a moment, his eyes halted on a crushed tricycle lying next to the steps, and his heart gave a painful jolt.

Gunz scanned the threshold with his other sight, but since he couldn't detect any presence of dark magical energy, he put his hand on the door handle and pushed it down. To his surprise, the door opened silently and remained ajar, its black rectangle looking ghastly and daunting. Feeling the small hairs on the back of his neck rising, Gunz threw a troubled gaze at Raoul and passed into the dark lobby.

The lights were off, but his sharp Fire Salamander vision allowed him to see clearly. A tall vaulted ceiling was disappearing into the darkness, and a large window took most of the space on the opposite wall. Elegantly arranged panels were partially opened, presenting a view of the dark backyard, complete with a large swimming pool area.

Two marble staircases on either side of the lobby led up to the second floor. A baby grand piano was positioned in the center of the area, and a couple of leather sofas stood by the wall. A folded newspaper and a bunched-up fleece blanket lay on one of the couches. A few pages from the newspaper were scattered over the marble tiles and a pair of slippers was left behind, as if someone had to leave in a hurry, barefooted.

Two hallways leading in either direction were even darker than the lobby. Raoul touched Gunz's shoulder and pointed up at the second floor, a silent question reflected in his eyes. Gunz held his hand up and quickly scanned the house with his other sight. Just like before, he couldn't sense any malevolent presence inside the building, so he focused on searching for the owners of the home. He didn't know why, but somewhere on the level of intuition, he was positive they were still inside.

Carefully checking every square foot of the building, he couldn't detect anything out of the ordinary at first. He took a deep breath and blocked everything around him, focusing all his senses and magical energy on the task at hand. As he checked the hallway on his right, he noticed a barely visible glow. Even though it was weak and flickering, he had no doubt—it was the light of a human soul, possibly more than one. Sharpening his senses, he waved for Raoul to follow and slowly moved toward the light.

He passed through the dark corridor lined with photos of the family and halted in front of a heavy door made out of dark wood. Mouthing the word *humans*, he glanced at Raoul over his shoulder and put his hand on the doorknob.

As soon as his skin came in contact with the cold metal, a sting of dark energy surged through him, throwing him back like an electric shock. He hit the opposite wall with his back and fell to the floor, gasping for air, struggling to fill his lungs with oxygen. His fingers unlocked, and his sword fell to the marble tiles without producing any sound.

What the hell? I couldn't sense any magic here...

Gunz grabbed his sword and scrambled to his feet with an effort, the hallway swimming around him. He exchanged a quick look with Raoul and judging by the expression of bewilderment on the Warden's face, he had no idea what was going on either. Gunz closed his eyes and ran the unbending fingers of his right hand over his face, giving himself a moment to gather whatever strength he still had left in him.

When he lowered his hand, his sword lit up with the soft glow of the fire energy and a few dancing flames rushed up and down his arms. Raoul gasped and his eyes widened as he pointed at one of the flames. Just like the fire of his portal before, this little flame was too bright to be normal, shining a vivid red.

Gunz shook his head, frowning, and raised his sword, channeling the fire energy entwined with his magic through it. Carefully, he touched the doorknob with the tip of his blade, ready to fight the dark magic blocking his way in. Before he could do anything, the floor quaked, almost unbalancing him, and the entire building shook like it was nothing but a flimsy house of cards. A wave of dark energy swept through the hallways, howling like a gusty wind, and all sounds returned at once, overwhelming his overly heightened hearing.

Gunz staggered back, struggling to keep his balance as the house kept shaking, screeching, grinding and moaning, unleashing a hellbent pandemonium. Raoul fell, an expression of horror changing his handsome features. Suddenly, all the walls, the ceiling and floors lit up with deep purple symbols and runes Gunz didn't recognize. The runes swirled into a raging, purple vortex and then stilled, forming three glowing words on the surface of the door, written in all caps.

WE SEE YOU...

The noise seized, and the house stopped shaking. Raoul scrambled to his feet, all the color gone from his face. He pointed at the writing with his sword. "Do you know what it means?"

Gunz nodded, swallowing hard. "Yeah," he whispered, biting his lip. "It means the calm before the storm is over, and we're about to get slammed by a category five magical hurricane."

As soon as the writing dissipated, the electric lights turned on with a soft click, illuminating the hallways and the lobby. The soft thud of the closed entry door sounded through the house and a heartbeat later, Yaroslav was standing by his side.

"Did you break the spell?" asked the vampire, carefully surveying the hallway.

"No," replied Gunz. "The enchantment was lifted on its own." He sighed and carefully put his hand on the doorknob again. Nothing happened. "Let's see what lies behind door number two."

He pushed slightly, and it opened up with a soft squeak, revealing a large office space. The room looked like it was vandalized by a local gang, which it probably was considering all the Night's Angels they'd had to deal with leading to this location. Three walls out of four were lined with bookshelves, but all the books were thrown down and now lay on the floor in a large pile.

The wall on the left had multiple display frames with dried out plants and herbs inside, and a door leading into the adjoining room stood open, hanging on one of its hinges. The glass in most of the frames had been shattered. Some frames were ripped off entirely and thrown carelessly on the marble tiles. Shards of glass were scattered all over the floor, sparkling with reflected electric lights.

A large desk was pushed against the wall next to a window, the contents of its every drawer dispersed all over the room. The computer monitor, cracked and dark, lay on its side over the keyboard, and a few documents were spread over the tabletop.

"Someone was searching for something," mumbled Raoul, staring around the room.

"No shit," muttered Gunz, examining the walls on his right for a trap door. Now that he was inside the room and the effects of the dark magic were gone, he could sense the presence of human souls loud and clear.

"Three heartbeats," whispered Yaroslav. He walked up to the bookshelf on the right, placing his hand on one of the empty shelves. "I can hear them... I can smell their fear and"—he cleared his throat and averted his glowing eyes—"their blood."

His long fingers quickly explored the bookshelf, pulling out the remaining books and pushing on every bump and indentation he could find, but with no results.

"There is a hidden room behind this shelf," he murmured,

throwing a quick glance back at Gunz. "I just need to find what triggers the door."

Gunz squatted and moved the papers and glass out of the way, carefully examining the floor. He found a few dark splatters, undoubtedly blood, and raised his eyes at the vampire. Yaroslav nodded silently, confirming his suspicion. A few more brown stains had accumulated right by the desk. Gunz got up and pulled the office chair closer, lowering himself into it. With his fingers, he examined every drawer and every shelf until he felt a small, round bump under the desktop. He pressed it, feeling the resistance of a spring under his fingertips.

With a soft click, the bookshelf slid open, revealing a reinforced metal door behind it with a small computer display embedded on the left of the entrance. Gunz approached it and noticed the circle of a digital camera above the display.

"A panic room. Smart," he muttered. Turning his sword back into a knife, he placed it into his pocket and pulled out his leather wallet with the FBI consultant badge.

He knocked on the door and lifted his badge to the camera, hoping that whoever was inside was watching the monitors.

"FBI," he shouted. "Please open this door."

He heard a few soft steps and the loud click of the locking mechanism. The door slid to the side, and he saw a young woman standing in front of him. Her hands and her pale face were covered in dark stains of dried out blood, her brown eyes swimming with tears. Without saying a word, she threw her arms around Gunz's shoulders and hid her face into his chest, crying.

CHAPTER 4

~ ZANE BURNS, A.K.A. GUNZ ~

G unz winced as her fingers touched the laceration on his arm and pulled away, giving her a quick once-over.

"Are you okay, ma'am?" he asked, looking over her shoulder.

A man sat on the floor by the opposite wall. His head was bowed down to his chest, and his hand clutched his thigh, dark red blood flowing between his fingers. A small girl, no more than five-years-old, sat by his side, her little, trembling arms wrapped around his. Her large hazel eyes were filled with tears, and her puffy lower lip quivered.

"I'm fine, thank you," she replied, throwing a careful glance at Yaroslav and Raoul. "But my husband is hurt."

Gunz scratched the back of his head, just now realizing how odd the three of them probably looked to her. Between Yaroslav with his long hair soaked with blood and his tall riding boots, and the Warden sporting his Templar armor and a medieval sword, they looked like a historical fantasy movie castaway.

"Are they gone?" asked the man without lifting his head, his voice barely audible.

"Yes," replied Gunz. "You're safe now."

He glanced at a growing puddle of blood under the man's leg

38

and frowned, throwing a warning glance at Yaroslav. Averting his glowing eyes, the vampire nodded and walked away from the door, settling in the office chair. Raoul followed him and perched on the edge of the desk.

Walking around the woman, Gunz approached her husband and squatted. He moved the man's hand aside gently, ripped his pants on his thigh, and quickly examined an ugly laceration. It looked like a knife stab wound and even though he couldn't see how deep the cut was, judging by the dark color of the blood and its even flow, he suspected that one of the deep veins in his leg was damaged.

He took the man's hand and placed it over the wound. "Keep the pressure on," he said, rising.

"He's been keeping the pressure since we got here," said the woman, approaching them. Her voice trembled with concern, and her eyes filled with tears. "The blood isn't stopping."

Gunz nodded. "First, call nine-one-one. Tell them you were attacked by a motorcycle gang, and your husband has a stab wound to his thigh with venous bleeding."

Noticing the woman's desperate stare as she opened her arms, he realized she didn't have a phone. Reaching in his pocket, he gave her his cell phone. She took it and dialed the emergency service. Once she had walked out of the room, he turned to the man and kneeled by his side.

"You don't happen to have a tourniquet in your panic room, do you?" he asked.

The man chuckled and raised his head, wincing from pain. His face was bruised and swollen, and a small cut above his left eyebrow was still bleeding, thick red drops sliding down his cheek.

"No, that's one thing we don't have here," he managed to say, barely moving his bleeding lips. "Sorry."

"I didn't think you would," muttered Gunz under his breath and ripped a strip of fabric from the bottom of his shirt, wincing at the pain in his injured hand. Noticing a large bunch of keys on a massive carabiner hooked to the belt hoop of the man's pants, he pointed at it and asked, "Can I borrow that?"

Without waiting for his response, Gunz unhooked it and took the keys off, throwing them on the floor by his side. Working mostly with his left hand, he wrapped the strip of his shirt around the man's thigh above the cut and tied it, creating the second knot an inch above. Placing the carabiner under the knot, he kept twisting it until his makeshift tourniquet was tight enough to stop the bleeding. Since there was nothing else he could use to secure the tourniquet, he ripped another strip off his shirt and fixed the carabiner using it. Then he got up with a groan and looked around. On a small table at the side of the room, he noticed a coloring book and a few markers.

He grabbed the blue marker and kneeled at the man's side again.

"Daddy, it's mine," the little girl whispered, staring at Gunz with round eyes.

Gunz smiled at her, thinking how scary he looked in his torn, dirty clothes with his face and hands covered in blood and ash. "May I borrow your marker, sweetie?" he asked, trying to sound as friendly as he could. "I'm trying to help your daddy."

The girl exchanged a terrified look with her father and nodded. Gunz glanced at his watch and wrote the time on the man's leg, using the marker. Lowering himself down next to him, he rested his back against the wall tiredly.

"What's your name, sir?" he asked, throwing a sideways glance at the man.

"Eric," the man replied faintly. "Doctor Eric Parker."

"Doctor?" Gunz gave him an arched stare, his eyes darting to the makeshift tourniquet he created.

"Not a medical one," he replied, his hand landing on his thigh above the wound. "I am a plant biologist. Botanist, you know?"

"You study plants and flowers," murmured Gunz, his thoughts scattering away from him. "What would the dem—" He cut himself off and cleared his throat. "What would a motorcycle gang want from a plant biologist?"

Eric rubbed his chin, leaving streaks of fresh blood on his skin. "Not the bikers per se, but they had a woman with them." He lowered his hand, staring at his skinned knuckles uncomfortably. "Tall, with long blonde hair. Stunning... in a cold and terrifying way. She was bossing them around like they were nothing more than dirt under her high heels, and these giant men obeyed her every command."

He fell silent, listening to his wife's distant voice as she was talking to someone on the phone.

Aoife? A blood-chilling thought flashed through Gunz's mind and disappeared, swallowed by hundreds of other questions.

"So, what did she want from you?" he asked, turning slightly to face Eric. "What was she looking for?"

Eric waved his hand in the direction of his office. "In my office, I have a collection of rare and exotic plants and flowers," he said, his speech slightly slurred. "I tried fighting them..." He closed his eyes and swallowed with an effort, his face contorted with pain. "They took Melany and Gracie, and I had to give in." He stopped talking, and a haunted expression darkened his eyes. "That woman... she tortured me until I gave her what she wanted."

"What did she take, Eric?" asked Gunz, cold sweat covering his forehead.

"A flower... the rarest one of them all." He met Gunz's eyes just for a moment before averting his gaze, his face ashen. "I'm going to tell you something, Agent..." His voice trailed off as he waited for Gunz to introduce himself.

"Burns," said Gunz quietly, feeling his heart beat somewhere in his throat. "Not an agent. I'm an FBI consultant. My name is Zane Burns."

He nodded. "Mr. Burns, please don't think I'm delusional," Eric continued, raising his eyes again. "I'm going to tell you what I think, and it will sound strange, so try to keep your mind open."

Gunz chuckled, shaking his head. "Trust me, there is nothing you can say that I won't believe. Go on."

"My team and I were on one of my research trips in the Ukraine," he started. "I remember most of it as if it happened yesterday. It was a late evening on June twenty-third—*Kupala Night*, and a local botanist invited us to experience the celebration." He fell silent, his eyes growing distant as he traveled through the memories of that night. "I don't know how it happened, but somehow I wandered away from the meadow where the celebration took place and found myself in the forest, alone. I don't even remember how I got there..."

He rubbed his forehead with a half-shrug and continued, "Anyway, as I was trying to find my way back, I noticed a light flare in the grass. It was just a tiny glowing dot, but I swear it was calling to me." He threw a quick look at Gunz, and a guilty smile crossed his battered face. "Please don't think I'm crazy."

"I don't," said Gunz. "Trust me. I've seen things a lot weirder than a glowing flower."

"When I separated the grass, I saw a tiny pink flower. Its leaves looked like that of a four-leaf clover. But it was the actual flower that was glowing, emitting a soft pink light and tiny sparks."

Eric swallowed, reached into his pocket, and then exhaled with the disappointment reflected in his eyes. "Oh... that bitch... Forgive my language, Mr. Burns. She took all our cell phones. I had a picture of that flower. Anyway, I took out my pocketknife and tried to uproot this flower, but as soon as I touched the roots, the blade shattered as if it were made of glass or something. I had never seen anything like that. I don't know why, but I touched the stem with my fingers. Now, looking back, I think it was a dangerous and stupid move, but at the time I felt compelled to do so. Once my skin came in contact with the flower, it just..." He shook his head, his eyebrows slowly climbing up. "I can't explain it, but as soon as I touched it, I found it lying in the palm of my hand."

"It chose you... You found—," Gunz started but cut himself off. After so many years of walking the World of Magic, he still couldn't help but feel shocked every time something he thought was just a legend ended up being the truth.

"Yes, Mr. Burns," replied Eric, giving him a stare filled with curiosity. "I see you're not a stranger to Slavic folklore." Gunz nodded. "I found the *Raskovnik* flower. Some Slavs call it *Rasriv-trava*. I don't know why, but at the time, I didn't show this flower to my colleagues. When I returned home, I did some substantial research and learned that according to lore, this flower can find anything hidden and unlock it."

He stopped talking, his fingers tracing the shape of the carabiner absentmindedly. Gunz watched him, thousands of thoughts crowding his mind.

"Do you think this woman is searching for a hidden treasure?" asked Eric, disbelief clear in his words. He huffed, and a weak smile graced his face. "That sounds ridiculous, doesn't it? No one in their right mind believes in the supernatural."

"You'll be surprised," replied Gunz. "Did she take anything else?"

"She didn't, but I don't know if her bikers stole anything else," replied Eric. "She took the box with Raskovnik and left, ordering her gang to search my collection for another specimen and kill us after they were done. I thought that was it... The end, you know? I was terrified... Not so much for myself, but for my little girl... for my wife..."

He swallowed, his face getting almost translucent either from the pain and blood loss or from the thought of what could have happened.

"But then something strange happened." He furrowed his brow, his voice a hoarse whisper. "As soon as she walked out, silence enveloped the house. I couldn't hear anything. I couldn't say anything. All of us, including the bikers, were deaf and mute. I don't know how she did it, but at the time, I didn't care —it worked in my favor. Occupied by destroying my house, the gangsters didn't pay any attention to me and my family, and since they couldn't hear anything, I was able to move the shelf and unlock the safe room with them being none the wiser. This strange silence saved our lives."

The sirens of emergency vehicles approaching the house grew louder, and Gunz got up. "Take care of yourself and your family, Eric," he said, looking down at the botanist with a sad smile. "That woman got what she wanted. I don't think she'll be coming back here again."

"Do you think I should tell the police about Raskovnik?" asked Eric, discomfort lingering around him. "They'll think I'm crazy, and I can't blame them."

Gunz shrugged. "Most people don't believe in the supernatural. You can tell the police the truth, but don't try to prove that the legend has some kind of factual basis behind it. If you're lucky, they'll think you're suffering from PTSD."

As Melany rushed back to her husband, he collected his phone from her and walked out of the room to meet the police and the first responders.

As HE WALKED onto the driveway lit up by the porch lights, the pleasantly cool night air enveloped him, and he sucked in a deep breath. With relief, he noticed that Yaroslav and Raoul had left before the first emergency vehicle had arrived and they had taken Siv with them. It would be hard to explain Raoul's outfit, and if on top of it, Siv would decide to exercise his freedom of speech, the situation could have escalated into a magical disaster of major proportions.

He barely remembered answering all the questions and taking care of the formalities with the police and paramedics. His thoughts were focused on Aoife and the flower she stole, but no matter how he twisted and turned it, he couldn't come up with anything that would remotely make sense. He remembered a paramedic offering to check his injuries, but all he wanted was to go home.

As soon as he could, he walked away from the cul-de-sac, searching for a dark, secluded area where no one could see him. As he stepped into the shadows, away from the brightly illuminated street by the entrance, he noticed the same group of people whom he had teleported out of the area earlier, walking back in through the gates. They were shaken and confused, but they didn't look harmed in any way. He sighed with relief and circled the dark house at the edge of the development. Once he was sure that he was alone, he waved his hand, unfolding the fire curtain of his portal.

* * *

GUNZ WALKED out of his portal in his backyard and stilled, noticing two people sitting on the ground next to his backdoor. He smiled tiredly and headed toward them. Just now he realized how truly exhausted he was, every muscle in his body painfully sore. He made it all the way to the house and slid down to the ground between Yaroslav and Raoul.

"Did you hear the story?" he asked, his speech slow and his voice dull.

Yaroslav nodded, his hands brushing dirt off his pants absentmindedly as if these pants were still good for anything else other than garbage. "Aoife?"

"Who else?" asked Gunz with a weak shrug. He waved over his shoulder at the door and asked, "Wanna come in?"

"No, *mon ami*," replied Raoul, sounding just as tired as Gunz felt. "You need rest and so do we. Besides, I need to notify Grand Master Collins about all this." He twirled his wrist, a deep frown settling on his face. "Dammit... I knew they would show their ugly faces and start acting sooner or later, yet when it happened, it still came as a shock."

"I need to tell Akira," said Yaroslav. He thought for a moment and added, "Gunz, you should probably talk to Kal. Everyone in Kendral needs to know as well."

"While you talk to Kal, ask him about your fire." The Warden leaned forward slightly and glanced at Gunz sideways, wrapping his arms around his bent knees. "I was watching you fight and there was something off about it. Almost as if your fire wasn't elemental by nature." He turned away, staring into the darkness of the backyard. "Your last fire blast burned the demonic gang into ashes. I know you weren't using your elemental energy, so how was it possible? A regular physical fire doesn't burn that hot. No matter how potent your strike was at least some bones would have been left behind."

"I know," replied Gunz. "I already asked him about that a while ago. He just told me that I have nothing to worry about and all is fine. It's not like he was lying, but I had a feeling he wasn't telling me everything." He rubbed his face, barely able to keep his eyes open. "To make a long story short, he told me that there is something I need to know and when the time is right, he'll tell me."

Yaroslav rose to his feet effortlessly, offering his hands to Gunz and Raoul. Gunz took his hand and got up. For the first time, he was almost envious of his friend—it took a lot for him to get tired, and his injuries healed instantaneously, whereas Gunz felt as if a train had run over him. His every muscle buzzed with exhaustion, and the wounds responded to his every move with a sharp pain.

I need to revert... And a hot shower would be nice...

After saying his goodbyes to his friends, he opened the backdoor and walked into his kitchen. His eyes darted toward the refrigerator, and his stomach rumbled.

"Maybe after I take a shower," he mumbled, looking down at his dirty hands, skinned knuckles and bloodstained skin.

He walked through the dark living room and headed to the second floor, silently cursing the stairs as not only his legs but his entire body protested against this unwelcome physical strain. Once in his bedroom, he turned the light on and took his cellphone, Swiss army knife and wallet out of his pockets. He placed them on the bedstand and then quickly stripped all his dirty, destroyed clothes, throwing them on the clean tiled floor.

Feeling the cold touch of the cool air to his skin, he took a deep breath and let go of his control, reverting into the natural state of the Fire Salamander. As he dissolved into the smoldering flames, everything disappeared—the pain and soreness, the heavy thoughts and worries. The human in him was no more. He was the Fire, free and powerful, and there was nothing he wanted more than to stay this way forever.

It took him almost a physical effort to return to his human form. He rested his back against the wall and then slid down to the floor. He knew he needed to take a shower and get in bed. It had been a while since he had a full night's rest, but the words of the Warden still sounded in his mind, spreading a wave of unease through him.

Gunz held out his hand and reached for the elemental fire. Without the need for magic and spells, the wave of his element traveled through him, setting his hand ablaze. It was a normal, red-orange flame. It danced on his hand, traveling from finger to finger as he willed it.

Closing his eyes, he extinguished the fire and blocked the

elemental energy. He thought back to his fight with the Night's Angels and anger spiked within him, bringing the fire forward. The flames broke through his skin, rushing up and down his arms. He moved his hand closer, staring at the blood-red flames engulfing his fingers.

"War," he whispered, glowering at the scarlet fire wrapping around his arms. "I don't understand."

He had returned the ring to Viggo Warrington six months ago, and with that ring, his connection with the Horseman was supposed to have gone. But here he was, staring at the flames of War arisen by his command.

Gunz sighed, extinguished the fire, and got up, supporting himself against the wall. Barely moving his legs, he made it to the shower and opened the water, turning the handle all the way to the left. When steam filled the bathroom, he stepped under the hot jets of water and leaned forward, bracing his hands against the wall.

The hot streams ran down his skin, relaxing his muscles and making his already worn-out body weaker. For a few minutes, he just stood, silently watching dirty rivulets flowing across the tiles toward the drain. He didn't think. He wasn't sure he could, but the painful tightness wouldn't leave his chest.

He slammed his hand against the wall. "What aren't you telling me, Kal?" he whispered, staring at his feet. "A few months ago, you came to Alliandr's palace to see me. What were you going to tell me and why did you decide against it, old man?"

He stopped talking, half-minded to summon the Fire Elemental now and demand an answer, but then changed his mind and straightened, grabbing a bar of soap and a loofah from the shelf.

Twenty minutes later, Gunz shut down the shower and walked out into his steam-filled bathroom. He quickly toweled himself and pulled his pajama pants on. As he opened the door, the cold air embraced him, and he shivered, wrapping his arms around himself.

Crossing the bedroom in two strides, he pulled the comforter off and lay down, covering himself to his chin. Turning to his side, he grabbed his cell phone. The screen showed three thirty-three in the morning. He threw the phone on the bedstand and turned on his back, folding his hands on his stomach.

I'm sure Yaroslav and Raoul will notify everyone about Aoife and everything that has happened earlier, he thought, feeling the even buzz in his feet. *I need to get some sleep. Jim better not be calling me at some ungodly A.M....*

His thoughts faded into the darkness of his frazzled mind, and he was dead to the world a moment later.

CHAPTER 5

~ ZANE BURNS, A.K.A. GUNZ ~

The shrill ring of the cell phone sounded on the outskirts of his mind still fogged by exhaustion and restless sleep. Gunz barely lifted his head off his pillow and squinted at the ringing and vibrating device. With a grunt, he moved his arm and grabbed the phone, bringing it closer to his face.

The photo of Jim on the screen in combination with the time showing six in the morning made him moan and fall on his back. As much as he wanted to propel the device across the room, he answered the call and tapped the speaker button.

"Hello?" he said, cringing inwardly at how raspy and weak his voice sounded.

"Mr. Burns," said Agent Jim Andrews dryly and at the sound of this salutation, Gunz pressed his hand to his eyes, expecting nothing good. "I'm glad to see you're getting your beauty sleep."

"What beauty sleep?" grumbled Gunz. "You're calling me at some stupid A.M. and expecting me to be bright-eyed and bushy-tailed?"

"No, Mr. Burns," growled the agent. "Today is Monday, and I expect you to remember that on Mondays we have an early team meeting. I also expect to have a report on my desk about last night's encounter with Night's Angels."

Gunz sighed and massaged the back of his neck, feeling groggy and slightly sore. "Jim, I came back home past three in the morning," he said softly, unable to suppress a sigh. "I was... a little tired. I barely got any sleep, and I didn't eat anything since yesterday morning. Can I—"

"I'll see you in thirty minutes in my office," Jim interrupted him, the tone of his voice allowing for no objections. "Since you're whining like a little girl, I'll get you some coffee."

Jim hung up the phone, leaving Gunz staring at the dark screen. Gunz sat up and lowered his feet on the cold tiled floor. Rubbing his face tiredly, he felt the roughness of the stubble under his fingers and sighed. Tired and sore, he didn't want to go anywhere, but he barely had thirty minutes to get ready and leave.

He got up and swayed as the room spun around him. *Overused my magic yesterday?* he thought, moving slowly toward the bathroom. He did feel more drained than usual, and the lack of sleep and proper nutrition didn't help either. By the time he finished showering and got dressed, it was already six-twenty-five—no time to eat.

Making sure that his Swiss army knife was in his pocket, he waved his hand and unfolded the flaming curtain of his portal leading into the designated place of the FBI building. Throwing a last look at his bedroom, he stepped through the flames.

* * *

As THE ELEVATOR door opened with a light swish, Gunz stepped inside, grateful that there was no one following him. He pressed a round button with the number eight on it and leaned against the wall, folding his arms over his chest. He was positive that

Jim had a valid reason to demand his presence, but in his current condition, he doubted he would be of any use to him.

The memories of last night's fight with the Night's Angels flashed before his eyes, and a deep shudder rushed through his body. He still couldn't wrap his mind around everything that had happened. There had just been too many demons there for the two of them to handle. And then there was that spell—the one he had used to teleport that large group of humans outside the affected area. He was experienced enough to know that with the lack of elemental energy, it was supposed to drain him completely, yet it hadn't.

After I'm done here, I'm summoning Kal.

The elevator dinged softly, coming to a stop, and he pushed away from the wall. Gunz crossed a small lobby and opened the large glass door leading to the main office. He walked inside and headed toward Jim's office, but before he reached it, a young woman in a business suit, whom he had never seen before, stopped him. She gave him a quick once-over and smirked.

"I assume you're Agent Andrew's consultant," she said dryly.

"Yes," replied Gunz, reaching for his wallet with the badge and ID.

"Leave it. Don't care." She rolled her eyes and pointed at the glass door into a small conference room. "He's expecting you there." She turned around and sauntered away, her high heels clicking loudly on the tiled floor.

Too drained to feel annoyed, Gunz shook his head and moved toward the conference room. Besides Jim, four more agents were inside, sitting around a long conference table with coffee cups in their hands and an expression of boredom permanently glued to their faces. Gunz knew all of them, and he greeted them with a sharp nod.

"Mr. Burns," said Jim, rising. "We feel blessed you finally showed up."

Gunz stifled a sigh. "I'm sorry, sir," he said quietly, pulling a chair out to sit down.

Jim pursed his lips, shaking his head. He bent down and grabbed a small paper bag with the logo of a local bakery and a cup of steaming coffee. He walked around the table and placed everything in front of Gunz.

"You have fifteen minutes to eat," said the agent. "After that, be ready to report on all the events of last night."

"Thank you, sir," replied Gunz as his stomach spasmed painfully.

He wrapped his fingers around the cup, inhaling the bitter-sweet aroma of the burning-hot beverage. He barely listened to the reports of the other agents, knowing perfectly well what they would say—chaos and riots igniting all over the city, loss of civilian lives, property damage.

From the time when he came back from Kendral six months ago, the situation had deteriorated significantly. With dark magical forces in play, the lowest representatives of the human race had reared their ugly heads, and the worst personality traits in people had broken to the surface, the thin layer of civilization gone. Night's Angels and the likes of them were a big problem for the city and for the entire state, but it wasn't the only problem, and Jim had no idea how to handle the situation.

"Are you ready, Mr. Burns?" Jim's voice ripped him out of his thoughts, and Gunz rose to his feet, placing the empty cup on the table.

"Yes, sir—," he started to say, but cut himself off, taking a sharp breath as the elemental fire energy tripled inside the conference room.

A burning curtain of the Fire Salamander portal, blazing with unbearable heat, unfolded at the end of the room behind Jim. Kal and Viggo Warrington walked through the fire and halted, an identical expression of urgency imprinted on their faces. The agents jumped to their feet, shying away from the flames, their eyes round, their hands lowering to their holsters automatically. Only Jim got up slowly without a sign of nervousness and inclined his head just a little, greeting Kal with what he believed was an appropriate bow.

To his shock, Gunz realized Kal didn't have Mrak Delar with him, and the Great Salamander was suppressing his elemental Fire on his own.

"Father?" he mumbled, forgetting to bow. His eyes darted to Viggo Warrington, and he felt a strange jolt in his chest as his heart thudded heavily against his ribcage. He swallowed and bowed to both of them. "War, my lord."

"War?" echoed Jim, staring at the Horseman, flabbergasted. "As in the War? One of the Horsemen?"

A cold, lopsided grin spread on Viggo's face, and he inclined his head in Jim's direction. "The one and only, Agent."

"We need to talk, my child," said Kal softly, but small flames broke through his skin, dancing on his shoulders. "Now would be a perfect time."

"I'm at work, Father," said Gunz, throwing an apologetic glance at Jim. "After—"

"My lord, Agent Andrews," said Kal, interrupting him. "I need to borrow Gunz for a few hours. It is quite important, and I promise to deliver him back to your chambers as soon as we're done."

Gunz? Gunz winced, noticing that Kal didn't call him son, and a thick lump stuck somewhere in his throat in an expectation of upcoming trouble. "Father...?"

He made a move to approach the Great Salamander but before he could, something changed, and he halted, pressing his hand to his chest, gasping for air. The temperature dropped and even the sunlight blasting through the windows dimmed down. Kal froze in place, his hand clutching at his throat. Viggo Warrington's eyes widened. He reached for Gunz but was too late.

A portal, black and malevolent, opened up behind Gunz, sucking the light and warmth out of the room. Dark tendrils sprouted out of the rotating darkness, embracing him in its asphyxiating grip. They wrapped around his chest and face, gagging and immobilizing him. Their icy touch burned his skin, and he screamed, the sound of his voice coming out muffled and weak. He jerked powerlessly as the tendrils pulled him back into the venomous grip of the portal, and the portal closed above him, leaving him helpless and alone in absolute darkness.

CHAPTER 6

~ ZANE BURNS, A.K.A. GUNZ ~

As Gunz started to fall, the darkness around him thickened, and now, he could feel its touch with his skin. It pressed on his chest, squeezing his neck, cutting off his air. He pressed his hands to his throat, struggling to breathe in with his mouth open, and panic spiked through him, clouding his mind. Yet, somewhere far, a small voice whispered that he knew where he was. It wasn't the first time he experienced this terrible fall into the gloomy, hopeless reality filled with pain and despair at the end of the void.

The Dark Nav... A thought flashed through his mind, breaking the hold of the panic. He knew where he was, and he knew what to do to break the fall. All he had to do was stop fighting, stop struggling and give in to the inevitable.

He closed his eyes and dropped his arms, allowing them to hang limply at his sides. *Take me... I am yours...* He stopped struggling, relinquishing himself to whatever was coming.

As soon as he let go, his back hit the ground hard, the impact expelling whatever little oxygen he still had in his tormented lungs. Gasping for air, he opened his eyes, but the surrounding darkness was just as thick as before, and he could see absolutely nothing. He pushed himself up into a sitting position, feeling even weaker than before. His arms trembled, and he fell back with a soft moan. The Dark Nav had no elemental powers, and this fact alone was making him weaker. On top of that, he was still drained from last night's fight.

The crippling fear returned with a vengeance, gripping at his heart with its iron claws, and he grunted, struggling to suppress the quickly rising wave of panic. There was only one person—or rather a god—who could open a portal into the human realm and pull him here. And this god was a bit upset with him at the moment.

Gunz pressed his hand over his tattoo, calling to Mishka, but when the wyvern didn't respond to his call, he dropped his arm, his last hope gone. He tried to connect with the Codex, but he couldn't feel its presence and wondered if the Dark Nav somehow suppressed that too. Chills went through him, making his stomach twist. He was powerless, alone, and at the mercy of Chernobog.

As a last desperate attempt, he called to the fire of War. A weak, barely noticeable wave of heat spread through him, and a tiny, scarlet flame rose in his palm. It flickered a few times, illuminating a small area around him just long enough for him to see a large boot with a metal spur inches away from his face. He cried out as it connected with his jaw, and his mind went blank, falling into blissful unconsciousness.

A DOWNPOUR of freezing water brought him back with a start, and he screamed, jolting to his feet, only to realize he had neither the strength nor the ability to get up. He was sitting in a metal chair, and his ankles were attached to its legs with iron manacles. His arms were stretched wide apart, and heavy chains connected his wrists to large iron rings embedded into the stone floor. He couldn't really see his surroundings as the only weak light was coming from glowing white runes engraved into the cuffs on his wrists and ankles.

The sharp movement made him nauseous, and weakness spread through him, turning his muscles into mush. He moaned, his skin burning at the touch of the cold water filled with icicles.

"Chernobog!" he yelled, but his voice came out in a hoarse whisper. "I know it's you. Show yourself!"

The god of Destruction didn't respond, and he closed his eyes, dropping his head to his chest. He didn't know how long he sat like this. As Voron, Chernobog's righthand man, had pointed out once—time moved differently in the darkness. The feeling of weakness grew with every moment he spent here, and he was positive that it wasn't only the Dark Nav's fireless environment that affected him so brutally.

When the next dose of water mixed with crushed ice hit him, he had no strength to scream. His head jerked back and fell to his chest, a feeble groan escaping his lips.

"Chernobog," he called, his words no more than a raspy whisper barely audible even to his ears.

"Hello, Salamander." The icy voice of the god of Destruction sounded right in front of Gunz, and he made an effort to lift his head but couldn't. "Welcome back to the Dark Nav."

"What do you want?"

"The same thing I wanted when we met the last time," replied Chernobog, anger making his deep voice shake. "I want the Dark Codex, and I know you have it."

Gunz chuckled and winced as bile rose in his throat.

"I know you have it because the useless crap you and Ivan gave me was fake!" Chernobog thundered, and the next wave of half-frozen water washed over Gunz, eliciting an agonizing scream out of him. "If you torture people—or spirits—long enough, they give in. Everyone breaks, Salamander. Sooner or later. Ivan told me what he did. What I don't understand is how you were able to merge with the Codex. You're not a god."

The soft rustling of leather and metal clunks of spurs sounded in front of him and a bright circle of white light flared up around him, illuminating the massive frame of the King of the Dark Nav squatting about a foot away.

"The God's snare," whispered Gunz, barely able to speak. A bitter smirk curved his lips before he could stop it. "Now I understand why I feel so drained."

Chernobog laughed—a cold and sinister sound that cut painfully through Gunz's hearing. "You're learning," he said, pressing his fingers to the glowing circle, and it lit up brighter.

Pain twisted Gunz's insides, and he screamed, his body arching within the restraints like from an electric shock. Chernobog got up with a grunt and brushed his palms together, satisfaction reflecting in his black eyes. With the only source of light coming from beneath, his hard, unyielding features looked more villainous and ominous than ever.

"Nifty little spell the God's snare is," he continued, putting his hands on his hips as he stared down at Gunz. "I always wondered how that would work on a Fire Salamander. You can't die other than in Black Fire. As soon as your physical body is damaged beyond healing, the Fire Salamander in you will take over and restore it, reassembling you cell by cell."

He cocked his head, and his lips stretched into a malevolent smirk. Shivers ran down Gunz's spine, and small hairs rose on the back of his neck.

"So," continued Chernobog, his mocking stare sliding up and down Gunz's body as if measuring him, "since there is no power or magic within the circle of the God's snare, if I kill you, what would happen then? You still won't die, of course. So how would the restoration process work?" The King of the Dark Nav unsheathed his enormous sword, showing it to Gunz. "Shall we try? For the benefit of science, of course?"

He pushed his blade through the circle of light, positioning its tip at the small hollow at the bottom of Gunz's neck. Feeling nothing but endless exhaustion, Gunz raised his face, meeting Chernobog's eyes.

"Go ahead," he whispered, straining to keep his voice flat and emotionless, "do your worst."

Chernobog pursed his lips and lowered his sword. He placed the tip of the blade on the stone floor and folded his hands over its pommel, shaking his head.

"I have to give it to you, Salamander," he muttered. "You're stupidly brave. Or maybe just plainly stupid." He huffed, shrugging. "I am the god of Destruction, one of the first gods of the Slavic pantheon. I know what will happen if I pull on your tail, little lizard. But let me educate you, so you know what you should expect if you disobey me."

He stopped talking, drilling Gunz with his heavy gaze.

"Please, enlighten me, oh mighty god," whispered Gunz. "I'm all about proper education."

Chernobog smirked. "You know the moment when the Fire Salamander takes over?" he asked with a light flick of his wrist. "The few seconds of excruciating, debilitating pain you feel?"

Gunz nodded, averting his gaze. He already knew where Chernobog was going with all this, and he didn't need a lecture on all the possible torture techniques in the dark deity's arsenal.

"Now imagine this moment of pain stretched over the course of two-three days. How would you like that, brave, little Salamander?" Chernobog arched an eyebrow at him. "Even within the circle of the God's snare, the Fire Salamander in you is alive. You can't access its powers since there is no elemental energy, but it is still there, and if you're killed, it will do its duty, trying to bring you back to life. However"—Chernobog raised his index finger, giving him a pointed stare—"since the magic and power are suppressed, it will take the Fire Salamander at least two to three days to restore you. In the meantime, you'll be suffering unimaginable torment, and I wonder if at the end you'll come out with your mind intact."

Chernobog shuddered exaggeratedly and raised his sword again, resting the blade on his shoulder. Gunz locked eyes with the god and gave him a barely noticeable shake of his head.

"Why don't you give me what I want," offered the King of the Dark Nav, sounding peacefully, as if he hadn't just threatened him with torture. "Give me the Codex and I swear, I will help you deal with the rising threat." He sighed, his black eyebrows gathering over his blazing eyes. "I don't want to torture you, Salamander. I do respect bravery and honor, and you have both. But needs must, and I'll do whatever it takes to get what I need."

"Do you really hate your twin-brother so much?" asked Gunz. "Seems like you're going way too far for the sake of old sibling rivalry."

"Sibling rivalry?" shouted Chernobog, throwing his free hand in the air. "Is that what you think this is, boy?"

Gunz nodded with a half-shrug that sent the next jolt of weakness through his body.

"I..." Chernobog grunted and stomped his massive foot with a loud thud that sent a hollow echo, reverberating over and over. "I would love to destroy my brother," he hissed, anger spiking the deadly energy of the Dark Nav around him. "There is nothing that would give me more pleasure than to see him drawing his last breath along with my dear old dad. But this"— he pointed at Gunz—"has nothing to do with my family. This is not the reason I need the Dark Codex. I swear!"

"You swear?" Gunz huffed, an uneven smirk appearing on his face. "Why should I believe anything you say after what you did to me in the City of Gold!"

"Because—!" Chernobog yelled but then cut himself off and took a deep breath, staring at Gunz without blinking. A chain of emotions rushed over his face, and his shoulders slumped. "Because I need you just as much as you need me."

"I don't understand—"

"What don't you understand, Child of Fire?" Chernobog snapped his fingers and a large chair materialized next to him. He sat down and placed his sword across his lap, exhaustion suffusing his harsh features. "We have a common enemy, and I prefer to join you and your crazy friends rather than face what's coming alone."

Gunz's jaw dropped as he searched Chernobog's face for any sign of deceit and could find none.

"If it's not to kill your brother," said Gunz, thousands of thoughts rushing through his mind, "then why do you need the Dark Codex?"

For a moment, Chernobog remained silent, stroking his thick, black beard with his fingers, the white glow of the God's snare reflecting ominously in the obsidian ring on his middle finger. Then he got up, sheathed his sword and snapped his fingers, whispering something. Hundreds of glowing light orbs materialized high in the air, illuminating the area with their shimmering, bluish light. They moved slowly, weaving between the tall columns on the left and right of a spacious hall, and the shadows shifted, growing darker and then melting into the surroundings, following their progress.

Fighting weakness, Gunz swiveled his head slowly, and his eyes widened as he recognized where he was. He remembered Chernobog's throne room as if he were here just yesterday. Everything in this gloomy place seemed to remain unchanged, yet it was different.

The last time he had been here, the giant room had been flooded with light. Now it stood dark and grim, barely illuminated by the weak glow of the magic orbs. The heavy window treatments, which seemed to be unnecessary since there was nothing outside the castle except infinite darkness, were covered in a layer of dust. The large, marble tiles of the floor had lost their shine and now looked like regular, unpolished stone.

But what shocked Gunz the most was the throne area at the end of the room. Chernobog's giant seat was untouched, standing out in its loneliness like a sore thumb. Morena's was demolished, and only a pile of wooden chunks remained in its place as if someone chopped it with a giant axe. The human skulls that had been used as the base of her throne were scattered around, crushed, and the scythe lay broken next to the pile of wood.

As Gunz kept staring at the sight of the destruction with his jaw dropped, Chernobog chuckled darkly. "What can I tell you," he said. "I got carried away a bit."

"You may say so," muttered Gunz.

Chernobog threw a haunted stare at the demolished throne and then yelled at the top of his lungs, "Voron!"

A small door in the back of the room opened up soundlessly, and Voron walked inside. Dressed all in black, he was barely visible in the darkness. Moving briskly, he crossed the hall and took one knee before his master, bowing his head.

"My lord," he said calmly, throwing a quick, veiled gaze at Gunz.

"Rise, Voron," said Chernobog, tapping his righthand man on his shoulder impatiently. "I want to take our mutual friend for a guided tour of the Dark Nav."

Voron got up, a spark of hope igniting in his eyes. "Are you ready to do the right thing, my lord?"

"The right thing? In whose books?" The god of Destruction stared down at Voron, folding his arms over his chest. "Most of the time, our perception of that is quite different." He jerked his thumb at Gunz, unconcealed contempt twisting his lips. "I need you to get him up to his feet." He folded his arms again, tapping his fingers on his elbow. "Sorry, Voron, but I'm not going to let him regain his strength and his magic, so walking on his own isn't an option for him. Not until he gives me what I want, that is. I'm afraid you'll have to drag him all across the Nav."

Voron sighed and approached the circle of the God's snare. Gunz raised his eyes at him, silently pleading for help. Even though he knew that the old warrior was loyal to Chernobog through and through, he couldn't help but hope that Voron's sense of honor would prevail over the blind loyalty of a servant to a master. For a brief moment, a pained expression crossed Voron's features, but he didn't say anything.

"What are you waiting for?" barked Chernobog, his loud voice echoing through the empty throne room. "Get him up already."

"Apologies, my lord, but I can't," replied Voron calmly. "I can't cross the circle of the God's snare."

"Oh, yeah…" Chernobog scratched the back of his head and chuckled. "Right. Let me take care of that."

He squatted next to Voron and whispered something, touching the circle of light. Slowly, it dissipated, leaving the room darker than it had been before. Gunz shifted in his restraints, expecting to feel stronger after the magic-draining spell was removed, but to his shock, he felt just as weak and queasy as before.

Chernobog noticed his move and clucked his tongue, narrowing his eyes. "Not so fast, little Salamander," he muttered under his breath. "You didn't think I'd let you run free, did you?" He cocked his head, smirking. "Aw, you did… how cute."

He reached forward and touched the chains connecting Gunz's wrists to the floor. The chains unlocked, but instead of falling, they became visibly shorter and fused together, binding his hands in front of him. After that, Chernobog freed his legs but left the iron cuffs on his ankles.

Tracing the shape of the glowing runes with his finger, he lifted his head, regarding Gunz with scorn. "You see these runes?" he asked, rising. "Consider them a pocket version of the

God's snare. They have almost all the wonderful features of the main spell with a few tiny limitations. So, don't get any ideas, boy. You can't run. You can't channel your magic. And the Fire Salamander in you is securely locked. Inside my domain, I can squish you like a bug."

His arm snapped forward, and his fingers wrapped tightly around Gunz's throat, eliciting a strangled yelp out of him.

"My lord!" Voron exclaimed, warning in his voice. He lifted his hand but didn't dare touch the god of Destruction.

Chernobog unlocked his fingers, raising his arms in a peaceful gesture. "Get him up, Voron," he ordered. "First stop—my upper dungeons."

CHAPTER 7

~ TESSA ~

Surrounded by a pile of books, scrolls and manuscripts, Tessa sat on the floor dressed in her pajamas. Holding one of the books in her hands, she quickly scanned through the opened page and snapped it shut, throwing it on top of the others, a groan of disappointment escaping her lips. It had been close to a week since she locked herself in her room, leaving it only to make a quick trip to the Guardians Library or to grab a bite to eat in the cafeteria.

Hours upon hours, she searched for any written word she could put her hands on to find at least a mention of her father—the Slavic god of Thunder, Perun. So far, all her hard work had yielded no results and frustration was slowly building up inside her. She got up and sat on the edge of the bed, grabbing her cell phone. Pressing the home button, she sighed—no messages, no missed calls.

She threw her phone on the bed and rubbed her eyes tiredly. Both Aidan and Zane seemed to have disappeared from the face of the Earth. She knew Aidan was still in the Otherworld, and there was no cell service there. Even though she desperately wanted to hear his voice, she didn't want to bother him with her summons, realizing how important his and Gwyn ap Nudd's tasks were. As far as Zane, she knew he was in Florida, and it was pissing her off that he couldn't pick up his phone and say a quick hello just to let her know that he was fine—at least as fine as he could be in the wake of the rising wave of chaos.

Her eyes fell on the stack of old diaries sitting on the nightstand next to her bed. She took the top one, gently caressing the leather surface of its cover with her fingers. Unwanted tears gathered in her eyes, and she swallowed, forcing them back. With the diary in her hands, she lay down on her back and opened it at a random page.

The small letters of her mom's even handwriting covered the paper, and as she read it, she could almost hear her voice. Tessa re-read a few pages and found herself staring at a blank one in the middle of the diary. She'd seen this page so many times before, but she could never figure out why her mom, who was organized by nature and meticulous about doing things the right way, would leave a blank page in her diary.

Running her fingers over the empty page, she felt tiny indentations. She had felt them before as well, and she'd always assumed that it was nothing but imprints left by a pen when her mom had written on the other pages. Now, however, something captured her attention, raising a red flag in her mind. She sat down and put the book on her lap. Gently moving her fingertips over the surface of the paper, she closed her eyes and opened her other sight.

A large rune, glowing with a barely noticeable white light, was imprinted on the page. The rune didn't look complicated and it felt familiar, even though for the life of her she couldn't remember where she'd seen it. She opened her eyes and grabbed a clean piece of paper and a pen from the nightstand. Quickly, she drew the rune and stared at it, frowning.

"What are you trying to tell me, mom," she whispered,

tracing the thin lines of the drawing with her finger. "I know I've seen it before. Where, though?"

Maybe Missi would know what it is?

Making a split-second decision, Tessa put the page on her bed and quickly got dressed. As she turned around to grab it, she peered at the picture, nibbling on her lip. Now that she looked at the rune from a different angle, it looked even more familiar.

"Oh, my God," she whispered, pressing the paper to her chest. "I know where I've seen it before."

Tessa stormed out the door and into the brightly lit hallway of the Witches' Wing. It was eight in the morning and all the hallways were busy with young witches and wizards getting ready for their lessons or leaving on their assignments. She pushed through the crowd, barely paying attention to those who got in her way and didn't stop until she reached the spacious lobby in front of Archmage Allerton's office.

She halted by the heavy oak door with her hand up, ready to knock, but then hesitated, lowering her arm. The Archmage's voice, deep and slightly throaty, flowed through the door. Even though she couldn't make out his words, the tones of urgency were unmistakable.

Tessa blushed at the thought that she was eavesdropping and headed to the opposite end of the lobby where she leaned her back against the wall, squeezing the page in her fingers nervously. A few minutes later, the door opened, and Archmage Allerton's wide frame filled the doorway. His eyes quickly searched the lobby and halted on Tessa, a warm smile lighting up his face.

She hadn't seen him for a while and the change in his appearance almost made her gasp. His eyes were surrounded by dark circles, and his hair probably hadn't seen a comb for a while. His clothes were wrinkled, and it looked as though he had spent quite a few hours in his office without leaving it. As if hearing her thoughts, he rubbed his chin covered in a thick, black stubble and sighed.

"Come in, Therasia," he said softly. "What brought you here?"

He stepped aside, moving lethargically slow like a person who hadn't slept for a few days. She passed into the office and sat down on one of the chairs, waiting for him to settle in his. Leaning forward slightly, he propped his arms on the desk and arched his eyebrows, giving her a short nod.

Tessa unfolded the page and offered it to him. He took it from her hand and squinted his eyes, leaning back slightly to increase the distance. Then he grunted and opened one of the drawers, pulling out a case with reading glasses.

"I hate using these things, but one can't use magic for personal gain," he muttered irritably, putting the glasses on.

"Contact lenses?" suggested Tessa, unable to hide the amusement.

"Yeah, I need to order a new set," mumbled Archmage Allerton, peering at the paper. A moment later, he raised his eyes, staring at Tessa above the frame of his glasses. "Where did you see this rune?"

"In my mother's diary," she replied, quickly explaining how she found it. "Do you know what this rune means?"

Archmage Allerton took his glasses off absentmindedly and put them on top of the desk, his fingers folding and unfolding the paper.

"There should be a second part to this rune somewhere else," he said at length. "I've seen runes like this before. It's a lock. The second rune would look very similar to this one. All you need to do is bring them together to unlock whatever is hidden."

Tessa's eyes widened, her heart thundering in her chest. "I think I know where the second rune is," she whispered breathlessly. "I remember where I've seen it before."

"Oh?" The Archmage gave the page to Tessa, staring at her with curiosity.

She took the paper and got up, stuffing it into her jeans' pocket with trembling hands. "I need to go back home to Florida," she said, excitement and concern swirling within her. "Would you grant me permission to leave, my lord?"

The Archmage leaned back in his chair and nodded, looking up at her with interest. "Permission granted, Ms. Donovan. If you need, feel free to take Melissa with you for protection."

"Thank you, my lord." Tessa inclined her head in a slight bow. "Missi is busy with her latest assignment, and I think I'll be fine on my own. Besides, I'm going home, and if I need assistance, I can always ask Zane Burns."

"Yes, of course," mumbled the Archmage, a tired smile appearing on his face. "He's something else, this young man, isn't he? Well, you may go now."

Tessa bowed and headed toward the exit, but as she was ready to open the door, Archmage Allerton stopped her.

"And Therasia," he said with a quick flick of his wrist, "don't forget to report daily."

"I won't forget," she promised and walked out of the office.

Tessa ran through the long hallways of the Guardians HQ into the Mages' Wing, but just as she suspected, Missi's door was locked. Without wasting more time, she turned around and rushed back to her room. She didn't care about taking any of her belongings except for her mother's diaries. As she placed them carefully inside her backpack, she cast a last look, quickly surveying her room. An unexpected tightness constricted her throat, and a feeling of unease spread through her, but she shook it off and walked out the door.

* * *

TESSA TELEPORTED STRAIGHT into her apartment. The blinds were tightly shut, and the living room was dark and quiet. She opened her other sight, quickly surveying every room for any sign of a supernatural presence, and once sure that she was alone and safe, she relaxed. A barely noticeable scent of Aidan's cologne touched her senses, and she stifled a sigh, wishing with all her heart he were here.

Making her way to the door, she found the light switch on the wall next to it and flipped it on. Everything inside was just the way she had left it a while ago. An iPad lay on the coffee table, and a thin layer of dust coated its slick screen unprotected by the black leather cover. Aidan had loved starting his mornings with a cup of coffee in his hand, reading the news on his tablet. Most likely he had been in a rush. Otherwise, he wouldn't had left it lying like this. Tessa sat down on the couch and placed her bag next to her feet on the floor. Taking the iPad, she brushed the dust off with the bottom of her shirt and covered it, locking the case.

"Aidan," she whispered, a weight of sadness settling in her heart. "I miss you. I hope you're okay."

She put the device back on the table and got up, throwing her bag over her shoulder. The short path to the den seemed to be endless, and by the time she halted in front of the bookshelf, she was a ball of nerves with her heart beating in her throat. Just like a few years ago when she had just discovered her mom's secret for the first time, she wasn't sure what she was going to find there, or what other dangerous secrets her mother had hidden in this tiny room.

Tessa took a deep breath to calm her ragged nerves and reached for the thin book with a blank cover. As she pulled on it, the locking mechanism clicked softly, and the shelf moved forward, creating a small opening. She grabbed the edge of the shelf with both hands, forcing it to open wider, and slipped inside the hidden room. Moving her fingers along the wall, she found the string of a wall lamp and tugged on it. A soft yellow light illuminated the already familiar view, and her throat tightened with sadness.

Pushing all the distracting thoughts away, she headed toward the table and put her bag on top. She opened it with trembling hands, brought the diary out and found the blank page. Then she raised her eyes and carefully observed every single rune and sigil her mother had inscribed on the wall. As expected, right above the desk, she found a small rune that was almost identical to the one she'd seen in the diary.

"This is it," murmured Tessa, her voice raspy and shaky. She channeled her magic and touched the blank page, whispering, *"Latentius revelare."*

The rune on the page lit up with a bright white light, becoming clearly visible. In response, the rune on the wall shimmered with a soft cerulean glimmer, and now Tessa had no doubt she was doing the right thing.

"Here goes nothing," she muttered and placed the page of the diary against the rune on the wall.

As soon as the runes connected, a light vibration spread through the drywall, and the ground trembled under her feet, making her plant her feet harder and lean forward to keep her balance. Something clicked under the diary, and the lamp flickered on and off. A bright white light erupted from under her hands, blinding Tessa for a moment.

When the light dwindled down, and the red spots stopped dancing in her vision, she lowered the diary, placing it on the table. A small, rectangular opening, no larger than the size of an average book, replaced the rune. Except for a white envelope, there was nothing else there. With her heart thudding against her ribcage, she reached forward and grabbed it.

"Therasia Reagan Donovan" was written on the envelope in her mother's beautiful handwriting.

The room around her spun, and she grabbed the table,

leaning forward heavily. Slowly, she lowered into the only chair in the room and placed the envelope on her lap. For a few long moments, she just sat there, staring at the white rectangle, unable to bring herself to open it. The disarray of thoughts ceased, and her mind was blank and silent.

Finally, she took a deep breath and slipped her finger under the corner of the envelope's flap, carefully moving it to the left. It opened easily, exposing a piece of yellow notepad paper inside. She pulled it out and unfolded it. As she glanced at the first words of the letter, tears filled her eyes.

"My dear Tessa. If you're reading this letter, it means I've failed."

Tessa dropped the paper onto her lap and pressed the heels of her palms to her eyes, a soft sob escaping her lips. Squaring her shoulders, she picked it up again and continued reading.

"I failed to protect you from the World of Magic, and now there is no way back for you. You know what you are and what lurks in the shadows beneath the reality accepted by a human's mind. So, I'm writing this letter in the hope that it'll help you protect yourself from what's coming since I can't.

As you probably know now, I'm a Guardian Mage assigned to guard you and shadow your powers. At first, protecting you and concealing your magical energy was nothing more than another assignment, but soon I realized that you were the only thing that truly mattered to me. From the first time I saw your smile, and I heard you calling me 'mommy', you stopped being my assignment and became my life.

As an experienced Mage, I understood that without knowing the truth about your biological parents and the origins of your magic, you would always be in danger, and I couldn't have it. So, I devoted my entire life to protecting you and unraveling the secrets behind your birth.

In a short while, I'll leave this house, most likely forever. I bear no illusions, my little sweetie, the Followers of Chaos are coming for me. They've been tailing me for the last few months, and I'm not sure what has changed, but they've become too aggressive and too bold, no longer hiding their presence and their malignant energy signatures. I can see them everywhere, and I know I won't be able to fight them alone.

They've penetrated the walls of the Guardians Order and there is no one I can trust with the knowledge I have, not even my diaries. So, while I still write down everything, meticulously reporting all the events to the Guardians, not everything you'll read there is the truth.

I hope and pray that the Wardens Order isn't compromised, but I can't be sure. Father Collins is my last hope for survival and your protection. Even though I have some doubts, I need information and help, so I have no choice. I must have faith...

I'm sorry, my little sweetie, I failed you."

Tessa's vision became blurry, and a large drop of water hit the page, slowly spreading through the ink. She closed her eyes, struggling to suppress the pain and grief tearing at her chest. Swallowing her tears, she read the last words of her mother's letter.

"Since you were able to find the rune, I believe you've discovered and learned how to use the power of your father, the Slavic god of Thunder. I'm so proud of you, my sweetheart. Now, I want you to use the power that comes from your biological mother—the reaper. Use it and find me behind the veil. We must talk. Your life and the safety of the human realm depends on it.

I love you.

Your mother, always.

Reilly Donovan

R.D."

Tessa put the letter on top of the diary, staring at it with unseeing eyes, everything inside her numb with grief. Then she folded her arms on the desktop and rested her forehead atop her folded arms. For a short while, she just sat like that. She wasn't crying. She wasn't thinking either. She just needed a moment of absolute quietness—no words, no thoughts, nothing.

After a while, she got up, placed her mother's last letter

inside the envelope and put it in her pocket. Channeling her power, she drew a glowing rune in the air and pressed her palm against it.

"Gwyn ap Nudd, I summon thee," she whispered the summoning spell and stilled, holding her breath.

A few minutes of silence stretched into eternity. The rune still glowed in the air, emitting a soft, white light, but the King of the Otherworld wasn't in a rush to answer her summons. She stood, staring at the rune as if it were the center of her universe, and when it was finally replaced by an oval communication window, she flinched, taking a small step forward involuntarily.

The massive frame of Gwyn ap Nudd emerged from the darkness. He threw his long, black hair off his chiseled face, tucking a loose strand behind his pointy ear, and a tiny smile touched his lips.

"My lord," she greeted him with a respectful bow.

His glowing, angled eyes lingered on her for a moment but then settled on something behind her, and his lips parted, an expression of shock imprinted on his face.

"Who wrote that?" he asked, pointing at something above her head.

"My mom," she replied, surprised by Gwyn's reaction. "All these runes—"

"These are not runes," Gwyn interrupted her, urgency making his voice sound deeper and raspier than normal. "These words were meant for my eyes only."

Tessa twirled around, and her jaw dropped. She knew by heart every single rune and sigil her mom had drawn on the walls of this small room. Now, a new message she had never seen before shone above the desk, just below the ceiling. A few lines of hieroglyphs glowing with bright white light didn't look like any language she'd ever seen before. Her knowledge of magical languages was still limited, but she knew it wasn't

Dragon tongue or Celestial. Also, it didn't look like Sumerian, Aramaic or any other of the ancient human languages.

"What language is that?" she asked breathlessly, unable to tear her eyes off the glowing letters.

"Elvish," replied Gwyn ap Nudd quietly. "This is one of the oldest languages of magic. It predates the Dragon tongue."

A soft knock brought her back, and she turned around to face the King of the Otherworld. "My mother wrote it," she said. "There is no one else who could've done it. Why did you say that this message was for you only?"

Gwyn ap Nudd sighed, the light slowly dimming down in his eyes. "The message appeared after I answered your summons, responding to my energy signature," he explained, his eyes still gliding over the strange words. "It's written in the language only elves and a very few ancient beings of magic can read. Even Aidan isn't fluent in this language, despite the years I've spent teaching him. Besides, right there"—he pointed to the top left corner—"it says my name." A sad smile touched his lips. "Either your mother had a gift of sight, or she was one clever mage."

"What does it say?" she asked, stepping closer to the communication window.

"Your mother tells me that you will need my help," he replied, "and she also tells me what I need to do to help you."

"My lord, I summoned you because—"

"I know why you summoned me." He chuckled darkly, pointing at the wall. "It's all in your mother's message." He fell silent and braced his arms on either side of the communication window, leaning forward slightly. "Don't leave this room, child," he said at length. "I'm going to send Aidan to bring you to the Otherworld."

He snapped his fingers and the communication window closed, leaving Tessa alone. She glanced up at the wall and gasped. The message her mother had written for Gwyn ap Nudd was gone.

CHAPTER 8

~ TESSA ~

Tessa wasn't sure how much time had passed from the moment Gwyn ap Nudd left, but to her, it seemed like an eternity. When a door of shining white light ignited next to her, she got up to her feet, a wave of relief spreading through her. Aidan emerged through the light and halted in front of her, his glowing eyes slowly returning to their normal blue color.

"Tessa," he whispered, the sound of his voice disappearing into the silence of the room.

She took in his appearance, and her heart gave a painful jolt. With darkness surrounding his eyes and a deep crease etched between his eyebrows, he looked beyond exhausted. His blond hair had grown longer, falling to his shoulders in wavy strands, and his normally light complexion was gray.

"Aidan, I missed you so..." She covered the short distance between them in one step and pulled up on her tiptoes, encircling his neck with her arms.

A low growl rumbled in his throat as his arms wrapped around her, pulling her into a tight embrace. Hiding her face against his chest, she stilled, inhaling his familiar scent. She felt his hand moving up her back and pulled away just enough to see his parted lips and his foggy eyes just inches away from her face.

With a soft moan, she stretched up just a little and met his lips. His hands trembled, and his entire body responded to her kiss with such hungry eagerness that it stole her breath, turning her knees into jelly. Before she knew it, her fingers were unbuttoning his shirt, moving down to the waistband of his pants.

"No, Tessa," he breathed out and staggered backward, pressing the back of his hand to his lips, his eyes dark with desire. "We don't have time, my love—"

"A few minutes—"

"...would make all the difference in the world," he interrupted her, his voice regaining normal firmness. "This time, sweetheart, every minute counts. Let's not make Gwyn wait. We must go."

Aidan waved his hand and the white rectangle of his door materialized next to him. He took her hand into his, raising it to his lips. As he planted a soft kiss on her knuckles, she noticed him closing his eyes, and a warmth spread through her, lifting the corners of her mouth into a dreamy smile.

* * *

THEY WALKED THROUGH THE LIGHT, materializing in a dark cave she'd never seen before. As the musty, chilly air touched her senses, Tessa spun around, taking in her surroundings. The relatively small cave had a low ceiling, and a couple of narrow passages led away into the darkness.

"Where are we?" she asked. "What is this place?"

"The underground labyrinth under the Glastonbury Tor," replied Aidan. "This is the only place where Gwyn can open a door to the Otherworld for us."

He murmured something, drawing a rune in the air, and as if to prove his words, a door glowing with a brilliant white light materialized before them. He pointed at it with a slight bow, and a tired smile crossed his face.

"After you, my lady."

Tessa glanced at him, and somehow, voicing her usual displeasure with the archaic salutation she disliked so much seemed to be inappropriate. As she walked past him through the door, she gently caressed his cheek, feeling his fingers brushing her hand.

As the brightness of the door dwindled down, Tessa found herself in the middle of a sizable room and looked around in awe. She didn't know what she had expected to find, but whatever she expected, this wasn't it. Gwyn ap Nudd's house was as modern as it gets—a glass and concrete building, furnished with contemporary furniture and equipped with a big-screen TV and Xbox gaming console. A large crystal chandelier that resembled delicate branches of a willow tree streamed down from the tall ceiling. Instead of electric lights, hundreds of tiny light orbs shimmered inside, illuminating the area beneath with a soft, silvery light.

But what shocked Tessa the most was that everything around her was either white or a light shade of gray. Large, white marble floor tiles were polished to such perfection that she could see her own reflection. A white leather sectional and armchairs were positioned around a small glass-and-metal coffee table. Even the Xbox controllers lying on the table were white.

"Hello, Therasia."

Gwyn's voice brought her back, and she gave a start, turning in the direction of the sound. She'd seen the King of the Otherworld before, but most often than not it had been through a communication window. On the few rare occasions, she'd seen him in person. However, every time it was from a distance or during a battle, and she'd had no time to truly look at him.

Craning her neck, she stared at a tall man with wide shoulders who towered almost two feet over her. His long black hair framed his chiseled features, accentuating the paleness of his skin. His eyes, positioned at a sharp angle like that of a feline, were glowing white, just like Aidan's, but even as the light of his magic subsided, they remained an unnerving silvery white. He stood barefoot, dressed in jeans only, and his naked torso was ripped with anatomically perfect muscles worthy of any *Men's Health* magazine cover.

A wide smile stretched his sensual lips under the thin line of his perfectly manicured black mustache, and he bowed ceremoniously to hide the amusement dancing in his eyes at her initial reaction.

"My lady," he said, his deep voice reverberating against the ceiling. "Welcome to my modest home."

"My lord," mumbled Tessa, reaching to the side where she expected Aidan to be. Feeling his fingers squeezing her hand, she took a deep breath, clearing her mind.

"Father!" hissed Aidan, pulling Tessa closer. "Tone down your charm."

Gwyn ap Nudd laughed open-heartedly, throwing his head back. "Jealous, baby-boy?" He tapped Aidan on his shoulder and winked at him.

"Ugh." Aidan shook his head, wrapping his arm around Tessa's shoulders protectively.

Gwyn sighed, sobering up quickly. "Game over," he muttered under his breath, his black eyebrows gathering over his silvery eyes. He gestured, offering Tessa to sit down. "Let's get to business, then."

Tessa walked to the white couch, her stomach twisting with sudden anxiety. Before sitting down, she reached into her pocket and pulled out her mother's letter, offering it to Gwyn ap Nudd. He took it and quickly read it before passing it to Aidan. Then he sat next to her, the couch bending down under his weight, and his frown deepened. Slowly, he ran his fingers over his mustache and sighed.

"Tessa, in a minute, I am going to summon your mother's spirit," he said softly. He took her hand, giving it a gentle squeeze. "I need you to be ready. You're not going to have a lot of time with your mom. Just a few minutes... I can't even imagine how that will make you feel, child, but I need you to control your emotions and let your mother give you all the information. Do you understand me?"

Tessa met Gwyn's heavy gaze and nodded, her throat too dry to speak. Both Gwyn ap Nudd and Aidan got up, and the King of the Otherworld started to sing, weaving a complicated enchantment in his ancient language. As a portal swirling with shimmering blue lights opened in the center of the living room, Gwyn whispered her mother's name and fell silent.

With her heart thundering in her chest, Tessa slowly got up, barely realizing what she was doing. A woman, glowing with the warm, white light of a human soul, walked out of the portal and halted. Her semi-translucent body flickered, coming in and out of focus, but even though Tessa still couldn't see her clearly, she knew it was her mother.

"Mom..." The words stuck in her dry throat, and tears spilled from her eyes, running down her cold cheeks despite her efforts to keep her emotions under control. "Mommy..."

"Hold on, sweetheart," mumbled Gwyn. He approached the spirit and touched it, infusing it with the bright light of his power. "Now you can talk."

As he stepped back, Tessa gasped and pressed her hands to her mouth. Happiness welled up in her heart, fighting a battle with overwhelming sadness. Her mom was here. She was real, corporeal, and her kind, blue eyes were glistening with tears of joy. With a strangled moan, Tessa rushed to her mother and pulled her into a tight hug.

"My little sweetie. Oh, God... you're so beautiful... all grown up..." Reilly Donovan cupped her face, covering her wet cheeks with kisses.

Tessa closed her eyes, sobbing quietly on her mother's shoulder. "Mommy, I miss you so much..."

For the briefest of moments, she forgot where she was and why she was here. She was back with her mom—safe, protected and content, and nothing bad could ever happen to her. She was that little girl again, thinking about her future, upset about school bullies, and worried only about homework and making it to her martial arts lessons on time. There was nothing supernatural about her life. There was no World of Magic. There was no pain and loss. Her life was simple, and she was happy.

Hot, unruly tears spilled from her eyes, falling into her mom's rich, auburn hair, and she tightened her embrace, afraid to let go.

"My little girl," whispered Reilly, stroking her back and shoulders. "We must talk. Even though we're in the Otherworld, I don't think I can remain in this realm too much longer, and there is much to be said."

She pulled away, wiping Tessa's tears with her fingers. Then she bowed to Gwyn ap Nudd, and a warm smile lit up her eyes as her gaze fell upon Aidan.

"Aodh mac Lir," she said as she approached him and took his hand in hers. "Thank you for taking care of my girl when I couldn't."

Her voice shook as she tried to contain her tears, and she inhaled a deep breath before continuing.

"From the moment I met you at your martial arts school, I knew what you were, even though you were suppressing your energy signature quite skillfully. Watching you take care of my daughter gave me the idea to leave that message for Gwyn ap

Nudd on the wall of my study." She threw a guilty look at Tessa and shrugged. "I knew you would never leave her. You wore your heart on your sleeve, god of the Otherworld."

"I could never leave her," said Aidan, his voice tight with emotions. "I will never leave her. Even if she doesn't want me around anymore."

Reilly nodded, letting go of his hand. "Anyway, the reason I asked you to bring me back, my lord," she said to Gwyn ap Nudd, "was because I discovered the possible location of Tessa's father, the Slavic god of Thunder." She glanced around, as if measuring everyone's reaction to her words, and since no one said anything, she continued, "When the Followers of Chaos found and cornered me, I chose to die rather than to be captured. I just couldn't take the chance…" She lifted her shoulders in a half shrug. "I couldn't take the chance of them breaking me."

Then she shook her head, and her brow creased, bitter wrinkles materializing around the corners of her mouth.

"I remember…" She cleared her throat and continued, her voice dry and hoarse. "I remember that moment when I realized that with all my magic, I stood no chance against them. The only thing I could think of was my daughter and what would happen to her without me…" Her voice wavered, and she stopped talking, swallowing tears.

Gwyn nodded, sympathy and respect reflected on his hard face. "Thank you, my lady," he said, touching her shoulder gently. "The fact that the Followers of Chaos went through so much trouble to capture you makes me believe you were on the right path."

Tessa glanced at her mom, noticing that her body started to shimmer with soft white lights as the pull of the veil was increasing with every moment she spent here. They had a few more minutes at the most. She took a ragged breath and squeezed her hands together, feeling the clamminess of her own skin.

"You said *possible* location," she said, stressing the word 'possible', her words coming out in a hoarse whisper.

"Perun spent years in hiding," replied Reilly. "He's one of the most powerful gods of his pantheon. In his position and power, he's probably equal to Zeus or Odin, and if he doesn't want to be found..." Her voice trailed off, and she lifted her shoulders in a half-shrug. "Anyway, I spent over ten years trying to locate him. And when I finally did—" She chuckled bitterly, shaking her head.

"Where do I find him, mom?" asked Tessa, taking her mom's hand into hers and giving it a light squeeze.

Reilly peered at her daughter, and a chain of emotions flashed across her face, starting with pride and love and finishing with a shadow of concern. Her eyes darted from Tessa to Aidan and back, and she asked, "Have you heard of the Angel Oak Tree on Johns Island in South Carolina?"

"Oak," mumbled Aidan, throwing his hands up, "of course."

Reilly smiled. "Yes, seems obvious, doesn't it? Ancient Slavs used to worship oaks as Perun's trees."

"There are a few ancient oaks around the world," said Gwyn. "Why this one?"

"This particular one has a reputation. It was the combination of the local lore and the fact that Tessa's biological mom was a reaper that made me research this oak. They say this tree is protected by ghosts." She threw a meaningful look at Gwyn ap Nudd, and he nodded, encouraging her to continue. "Also, there is something unusual about the way this tree grows. Normally, oak trees grow out, not so much upwards. The Angel Oak is more than sixty-five feet tall and its branches are growing in all directions... even down, going underground."

"It has to be his tree," whispered Tessa more to herself than to anyone else in the room. She raised her eyes at her mother and added, "I'll go to South Carolina and check it out—"

"You're not going anywhere alone," Aidan interrupted her, taking a step closer to her. "I'm going with you." He glanced at Gwyn, his eyes pleading for permission. "Father, I know we're not done reinforcing the veil, but I can't let Tessa go alone. This mission is too dangerous and too important."

"I can finish the preparations on my own," agreed Gwyn ap Nudd. "Besides, it's been a while since you walked the realm of humans." A tiny, lopsided grin lifted the corner of his lips as his silvery gaze twinkled with humor. "You should get out of the house. Get some sun. Your human body needs vitamin D, you know? You look like a ghost yourself."

Tessa turned to her mother, and her heart skipped a beat. The white sparkles surrounding Reilly Donovan grew thicker, and her body was slowly becoming translucent.

"Oh, no." She reached to take her mom's hand, but her fingers slipped through. "No, no, no..." She spun around and grabbed Gwyn's hand instead. "Please, my lord, please..." She spoke fast, her feverish mind in a wild frenzy, her words barely making sense even to her own ears. "I'm begging you... please... Just a few more minutes. Just one more hug... please... She's my mom... I need to tell her... I've never..."

Her voice broke, and tears flooded her eyes, flowing down her face.

"I love you, my daughter," Reilly whispered, her translucent hand rising in a final farewell. "You don't need to tell me anything. I know you love me. Just be careful, my little sweetie." Her fading gaze darted to Aidan. "Protect her, Aodhán."

"With my life." Aidan placed his hands on Tessa's shoulder and pulled her closer, pressing her back against his body.

Reilly smiled and vanished, dissolving into the mist of the shimmering white lights.

For a moment, Tessa just stood, cold and numb, her limbs

filled with lead as sorrow hollowed her out. Tears kept running down her face, but she didn't bother wiping them. Aidan turned her around, and she encircled his waist with her arms, hiding her wet face in his white shirt.

He lifted her effortlessly, and she didn't object, feeling too tired and despondent. She wrapped her arms around his neck, placing her head on his shoulder as he carried her upstairs. He kicked the door of his bedroom with his foot, walked inside and gently lowered Tessa on the bed.

He didn't sit down but lowered down to one knee in front of her, taking her hands into his. His blue gaze found her eyes and there was so much love there that it stole her breath away.

"I love you," he said simply, a tentative smile lingering on his lips. Reaching up, he wiped her tears with his fingers.

She closed her eyes, his tender touch dimming down the overpowering sadness and pain tormenting her soul. Then she took his hand and pulled him up. As he sat down next to her, she cupped his face with her hands, gazing into his eyes.

"I love you, my ancient god," she said softly. "I don't know… No, I do know. I can't live without you, Aidan. My life—no matter how long it might be—makes no sense without you in it."

Before she finished speaking, his mouth covered hers, his arms wrapping tightly around her waist. As desire whispered through her, she moaned softly, and her lips parted, responding to his kiss. Her fingers threaded through his hair, seizing it on the back of his head. His hands traveled up her back to her chest, and she felt him halting there as if he wasn't sure if he should be touching her.

Tessa pulled away and quickly unbuttoned his shirt, sliding it off his shoulders. Barely touching his skin, she brushed the wide muscles of his chest with the tips of her fingers, moving down his sides. Goosebumps rose on his skin as she continued on her way down, and his breath hitched. She leaned forward, her lips following the progress of her fingers.

"Tessa," he exhaled her name. His breath quickened, and his lips opened just a little.

She got up and pushed him on his chest, forcing him to lie down. Then she sat on the bed next to him and unbuttoned his jeans, yanking the zipper down. He moaned softly and folded his arms under his head, desire emanating around him. Every inch of her body craved him, but she slowly moved her fingers down his stomach, watching his muscles contract under her touch.

He exhaled with a moan, and that was enough to send a wave of fire through her. She got up and seized the waistband of his pants. Happy that just like Gwyn he was barefoot, she pulled them off together with his underwear. His arms jerked down instinctively, but he bit his lip and brought them back up, allowing her to do whatever she wanted.

She took the edge of her shirt, ready to pull it off, when a loud knock on the door stopped her, making her twirl around. Grabbing the side of the silk bedspread, Aidan covered himself as much as he could.

"Gwyn," he growled, his voice deeper than normal, "what do you want?"

"Aidan, you need to come downstairs," replied Gwyn ap Nudd urgently.

Aidan grunted but got up. Wrapping the bedspread around his hips, he headed toward the door and opened it. Gwyn's attentive eyes took in his state of undress and then darted to Tessa.

"I'm sorry to interrupt your"—he twirled his wrist without actually saying the words—"but it's urgent. We have two visitors, and I suggest you get dressed, son, before you go downstairs to see them. You don't want to be caught with your pants down, do you?"

He winked at Tessa and walked away. Stopping by the stairs, he turned around and added, "I suggest not to make them wait since both of them have very short patience and flaming personalities. You know, fire and patience are mutually exclusive."

As soon as Gwyn left, Aidan rushed back into the room, picking up his pants on the way. "He's right," he muttered under his breath, struggling to pull his tight jeans on quickly. "It's Kal and one of the Horsemen, and whatever brought them here, can't be any good. Kal is so furious, his fire energy is about to explode."

CHAPTER 9

~ ZANE BURNS, A.K.A. GUNZ ~

Voron approached Gunz and helped him to his feet, offering his shoulder for support. As the dark hall spun around him, he leaned heavily on the ancient warrior's arm, wondering if he'd be able to walk at all. But as he took an unsteady step forward, all his doubts vanished. His stomach heaved, making him double over as he fought the nausea. He would've probably fallen if the old warrior hadn't held on to him.

"My lord," said Voron. He lowered Gunz to his knees gently and let go. "You need to lighten up your spell at least a little. We have a tough journey ahead of us. Without the protection of his magic, the Nav is feeding on his life forces, making him ill. I can carry him if that's what you wish, but I'm not sure his human soul would survive the trip in this condition."

Chernobog grunted, throwing his hands in the air. Not even attempting to hide his displeasure, he bent down and seized Gunz's hair, jerking his head up.

"You have no idea how much it pleases me to see you on your knees, fireworm," he hissed through his teeth.

He let go of his hair, and Gunz dropped his head, everything

inside his powerless body quivering with indignation. Chernobog took one knee next to him and pushed his chest. Unable
to keep his balance, Gunz fell on his back and hit his head hard
against the stone floor, blacking out for a brief moment. He
came to almost immediately and sucked in a sharp breath,
stifling a cry of pain.

The god of Destruction smirked icily and touched the cuffs
on his wrists, whispering something under his breath. The glow
of runes dimmed down slightly but didn't disappear completely.
Then he repeated the same procedure with the cuffs on his
ankles and got up, glowering down at him with disdain.

"Better?" he asked dryly.

Gunz nodded. As the toxic hold of the God's snare lighted
up, the room around him stopped spinning. But staring into the
black abyss of hatred that was Chernobog's eyes, he wasn't in a
rush to move.

"Why are you still on your back, fireworm? Get up and walk
on your own," Chernobog ordered, pushing him on his side
with the tip of his boot. "And don't get any bright ideas. Even
though I relieved some of the effects of the God's snare, your
magic is still blocked, and the Dark Nav is still feeding on your
elemental powers. In my domain, you're less than a human."

Gunz scrambled to his knees and with Voron's help was able
to rise to his feet. He still felt weak and drained of his magic, but
at least the nausea was gone, and he could move without the
fear of falling. Giving him a scornful once-over, Chernobog
pivoted on his heels and headed toward the backdoor of the
throne room, irritation prominent in his every move.

Accompanied by Voron, Gunz followed him out the door
and found himself in an endless, dark corridor with a low ceiling. The shimmering light of the magical orbs conjured by
Chernobog reflected in the wet surface of the walls where water
mixed with something black and slimy ran in disgusting rivulets

down to the floor. The unclean odor assailed his nostrils, and he held his breath, keeping away from the walls.

Pressing his chained hands over his mouth and nose, he walked as fast as he could muster in his condition until they reached a low door reinforced with thick strips of iron. Chernobog touched a massive, half-rusted padlock, sending some of his magic through it, and it fell open with a loud click. Then he grabbed the shackle, removing it from the hasp, and threw the lock on the ground, his every move infused with unconcealed aggravation. Pulling the door open, he bent down and passed through the threshold without looking back to make sure Gunz and Voron were following him.

Gunz crossed into a small, empty room with the dark hole of a spiral staircase at the end. As he moved down the squeaky wooden steps, the only thing he could think of was the walk back up. With heart palpitations and the shortness of breath the God's snare gifted him, he couldn't see himself making it all the way up these steep stairs.

As if hearing his thoughts, Voron leaned closer and whispered into his ear, "Don't worry. We're not going to return to the palace the same way."

"Splendid," grumbled Gunz, all but rolling his eyes.

The staircase ended in another dark corridor with a low ceiling and multiple reinforced doors on both sides. As they kept walking, the ceiling gradually became lower, and both Chernobog and Voron had to bend down slightly. The glow of the magical orbs seemed to be subdued by the darkness, and without his sharp Salamander senses, Gunz could barely see where he was placing his feet.

The air was stuffy, and the putrid smell of unwashed bodies and human waste hung in the air, making it almost unbreathable. Gunz swallowed, keeping his hands pressed over his nose and mouth. He'd never had a fear of confined places, but now he started to feel claustrophobic, his blood running cold at the thought of people locked behind these heavy iron doors.

"What is this place?" he whispered and shrunk back as Chernobog came to a sharp halt and turned to face him, animosity permeating the fetid air around him.

"These"—he waved his hand around—"are the upper dungeons." He seized Gunz's shoulder, pulling him forward roughly. "This is where my brother Veles imprisoned my wife, Morena."

I hate to think what the lower dungeons look like, thought Gunz, struggling to keep up with the infuriated god as he dragged him forward without giving a thought to whether Gunz could move fast enough in his condition.

Chernobog stopped sharply, and his fingers dug deeper into Gunz's shoulder, eliciting a grunt of pain.

"What do you see, fireworm?" hissed Chernobog, pointing forward at the place where another heavy dungeon door once was.

Gunz squinted his eyes, trying to make out anything in the dark, but all he could see was a tiny cell with rough stonework walls and a bare floor. The door was shattered into a pile of splintered wood and warped strips of iron, and he was terrified to think of what could possibly have done that. Even with his magic suppressed, he could sense the traces of a malevolent energy signature, and there was so much ill-intent in it that his skin crawled. Even Chernobog's dark energy felt like a ray of sunshine compared to this one.

"What the hell is it?" he exhaled, involuntarily taking a step back, but Chernobog held him in place.

"It's not Hell, reptilian. Hell would be our next stop," growled Chernobog mockingly, a crooked smirk curving his lips. "This was Morena's dungeon. As you can see, someone broke her out. Someone—"

His voice shook with anger, and his teeth squeaked as he

clenched his jaws. He raised his hands as if trying to calm himself down and took a deep breath before continuing.

"All these doors have no locks and no keys. I personally placed wards and locking spells on every goddamn cell here, and no one except me and Voron can unlock or remove these spells. Yet, someone was powerful enough to break *my* magic." He glowered down at Gunz, and his chest shuddered with strained breaths, the misty tendrils of the Nav's dark energy swirling around him like baleful serpents. Then he punched the air with his fist and yelled, his words echoing through the dark corridor, "I *am* the Nav! I *am* the ultimate power here! This is *my* domain!"

Gunz threw a quick glance at Voron, but the old warrior didn't return it, his horror-filled eyes glued to his master.

"Do you know who did it?" asked Gunz, carefully inching away from the fuming god.

For a few long seconds, Chernobog remained silent, visibly struggling to get his burning fury in check. Little by little, his anger dwindled down, and the energy of the Dark Nav dissipated. He dropped his head, and his shoulders slumped, making him look tired and broken. Raising his hands, he pressed his fingers to his eyes, and a strangled moan tore from his lips. There was so much torment in this short sound that Gunz cringed inwardly.

"I know who and I know how," whispered the King of the Nav, slowly getting in control of his emotions.

He moved his arm in a wide arch, and the dark shimmering glow of his magical energy followed his move. A weak, red light ignited beneath his fingers, and even though Gunz wasn't experienced in anything to do with the Dark Nav, he knew it didn't belong here.

"You see this?" asked Chernobog, pointing at the flare of crimson light. "It's the energy signature of the Raskovnik flower..."

The last few words he said in a harsh whisper, and it seemed like saying these words pained him. He huffed, and a bitter smirk appeared under his thick mustache.

"I'm sure it wasn't easy to come in possession of the Raskovnik flower," he continued at length, "but it was the only way to find Morena, break into my prison and set her free. Someone went through a lot of trouble to get her out of here."

"Dammit," muttered Gunz. "That was fast. I know who has the Raskovnik flower. Most likely, Morena is with—"

"This is the least of my problems, Salamander," growled Chernobog, interrupting him. "I'll deal with my wife later." He twirled his wrist dismissively. "This was just the first part of my show and tell presentation. And compared to the second one, it was a walk in the park." He turned to his righthand man and added, "You know where we're going next, Voron. Follow me." Then he grabbed Gunz by the scruff of his neck and snapped his fingers.

THE ENERGY of the Dark Nav surrounded Gunz, lifting him in the air. Here, he was defenseless and vulnerable, left at the mercy of the dark magical forces. He jerked involuntarily and felt Chernobog's fingers digging deeper into his neck. A few seconds later, it was over. Chernobog let go, and Gunz collapsed to one knee, bracing himself against the cold, rocky ground with his fists.

"Get up, Salamander," whispered Voron, pulling him up. "You don't want to stay in this place longer than necessary."

"Where are we?" he asked, rising.

The world around him was an obscure nothingness, and there was no end to it. The dark, starless sky looked like an infinite, lifeless void. The land beneath his feet was a black desert covered in sharp rocks, barren of any life. Flat and dreary, it spread for miles as far as he could see.

"Nowhere," replied Chernobog. "Move it, or I swear, reptilian, I'll leave you here to wander in darkness for all eternity."

For a while, they moved in silence. The scenery kept being the same, but with every next step, the presence of the Dark Nav grew heavier, feeding on Gunz's life forces like some bloodthirsty vamp. Every next step he took came with more effort. His heart was beating somewhere in his throat, and he could barely breathe, cold sweat soaking his shirt through. Bearing heavily on Voron's arm, he kept moving, realizing that in this place Chernobog had him over a barrel, and he didn't doubt for a moment that the dark deity would take pleasure in abandoning him here to suffer.

At first, a weak flare of scarlet light appeared far on the horizon, but as they progressed, it grew stronger, spreading strange waves of heat through the cold desert of the Nav. It seemed to be produced by a fire, but it wasn't elemental in its nature, and as such, it gave Gunz neither energy nor strength.

As they came closer, the line of the red light stretched wider, an even scarlet glow illuminating the dark horizon in both directions as far as Gunz could see. Despite the presence of fire, the magical energy here was even darker and more ominous than anything he had ever experienced in the Dark Nav.

"Keep moving. We're almost there," Chernobog said flatly. He didn't look angry anymore, and the slight modulation in his voice made him sound fearful and desperate.

Gunz glanced at the god with curiosity but said nothing and kept walking toward the strange light. The waves of heat grew stronger with each passing minute, making it impossible to breathe, but just like the fire energy before, it provided neither warmth nor comfort. Soon, they reached a giant pit in the ground. It was so wide that he could barely see the other side, and a flaming sea, emitting a blinding light, unfolded at the bottom.

Gunz came to a sharp stop at the brink of the pit, raising his arm involuntarily to protect his vision. Chernobog halted next to him, an uneven smirk distorting his lips, leaving his black eyes cold and distant.

"Ready, fireworm?" he asked, pointing down.

Gunz leaned forward slightly, looking over the edge of the pit. He had no idea what this place was, but unease spread through him, making his blood run cold. Even though his magic was suppressed, he closed his eyes, focusing on the energy the pit was producing. A wave of dread and despair enveloped him, draining whatever hope he had out of his soul. He grunted, staggering backward, away from the pit.

"What the hell is this place?" he asked quietly.

"Hell? I think not." Chernobog laughed mirthlessly. "Your Christian Hell is a child's play compared to this place." He narrowed his eyes at Gunz, his lips pulling into a ferocious snarl. "This is *Peklo*, Child of Fire, my lower level dungeons. The souls of the worst scum of the human realm are suffering here." A deep frown settled on his face, making his hard features look sinister. "And not only human scum. This place is the prison for the darkest, most dangerous supernatural beings—the kind of creatures that could destroy the Yav and the Prav should I lose control over them." He shook his head, a shadow of sadness crossing his black eyes. "My father turned me into nothing more than a glorified prison guard."

The god of Destruction fell silent and bowed his head, his massive arms dangling powerlessly along his sides.

"Why did you bring me here?" asked Gunz.

Chernobog flinched and snapped around at the sound of his voice as if awakened from a deep sleep.

"As much as I wish I could imprison you, you're not here to be punished. I brought you here because—," he started but cut himself off and grunted, shaking his head. "When the time comes, you'll understand why I brought you to this place. The flames of *Peklo* are not going to kill you—this is not the Black Fire—but you're not going to enjoy your trip either." He pointed at Gunz's shackles and added. "Your hands, Salamander."

Gunz raised his arms, and Chernobog touched his cuffs, muttering something under his breath. Then he took one knee and placed his hands over each cuff on his ankles, repeating the procedure. The glow of the runes dwindled down, and Gunz sucked in a sharp breath as a weak wave of his magic rushed through his body, restoring some of his strength. Even though the God's snare spell was lifted completely, the Dark Nav was still feeding on his elemental energy, making him weaker and suppressing the Fire Salamander in him.

"Thank you," muttered Gunz before he could stop himself.

Chernobog peered straight into his eyes—even standing on one knee, the King of the Nav was slightly taller than him.

"Don't thank me, little Salamander," he said as he rose, brushing dust off his knee. "The only reason I removed the God's snare is because I don't want you to be vulnerable down there, where everything and everyone will try to feed on your human soul." He sighed. "Without the protection of your magic, you'll be a sitting duck there, and I still need you alive and kicking. Just remember, I'm still the Dark Nav. Everything here obeys my command. I can warp the reality of the Nav, bending it to my will. Even with the Codex in your head, you can't escape me. So, don't get cute with me."

Gunz shook his head and shrugged, the corners of his mouth lifting in a bitter smirk. "Cute? Me? Never."

For a moment, Chernobog held his gaze, doubt reflected on his face. Then an expression of icy contempt changed his features, and he grabbed the chain connecting Gunz's wrists.

"You think you're the only one who can be funny?" he asked quietly. "I'm a born comedian." He turned to Voron, yanking

Gunz closer to him. Then he thrust the chain into the old warrior's hands. "Voron, while we're in *Peklo*, the Fire Salamander is your responsibility. If he decides to do something"— he twirled his hand, arching his eyebrow at Gunz—"unseemly, it's your head."

"Gunz, please," whispered Voron, leaning closer to his ear. "Don't make him angrier than he already is."

Chernobog approached the fiery pit and gave Gunz an arched stare. "Ready to jump?" he asked, pointing into the flaming inferno.

"You're kidding," muttered Gunz.

"I told you. I'm a born comedian." The god of Destruction laughed icily. Grabbing both Voron and Gunz, he then pushed them off the cliff.

CHAPTER 10

~ ZANE BURNS, A.K.A. GUNZ ~

Gunz couldn't suppress a scream as he started to fall into the pit. He felt Voron's hand squeezing his elbow but couldn't see him, his eyes watering from the blazing light. The fire surrounded him like an impenetrable wall. Cold and unfriendly, the flames licked his skin, doing him no harm. The reek of sulfur and smoke invaded his senses, and his already tormented stomach twisted into a tight knot, responding to the putrid smell.

The fall ended as abruptly as it started, and Gunz found himself lying sprawled on a floor paved with rough cobblestones, gasping for air. Noticing Chernobog's boots right next to his nose, he coughed and scrambled to his feet before the god of Destruction decided to motivate him by kicking him in the face.

He stood in the middle of a large square in front of an enormous iron gate, the top of which disappeared behind the swirling clouds of dark-gray smoke. The iron railings, pickets and ornaments of the gate shone with white, orange and red shades as though they were heated to a high temperature.

"Let's go," said Chernobog grimly, jerking his chin toward

the entrance into *Peklo*. Before Gunz could react, the God of Destruction grabbed his chain and shoved it into Voron's hands. "Keep him on a short leash, Voron. For his safety and your own."

The King of the Dark Nav approached the gate and raised his leather-gloved hand, his dangerous energy spiking around him to a new high. But before he could do anything, something clicked, and the gate opened slowly, revealing a fiery veil behind it. Three short men, no taller than five feet, emerged through the smoldering flames and headed toward them. They were dressed in identical long, red caftans with a crimson sash wrapped around their waists, and Gunz couldn't get rid of the feeling that he'd seen them somewhere before.

All three approached them and bowed low, pressing their right hands over their hearts. As their curly tails went up in the air and their curved, little horns almost touched the ground, Gunz grunted, cursing under his breath.

"*Bieses*," he grumbled through gritted teeth. "My day just keeps getting better and better."

The *Bieses* raised their ugly faces with pig-like snouts, and their lips stretched into identical smirks that looked more like ferocious snarls than greeting smiles. The taller one in the center stepped forward and made a welcoming gesture.

"Your All-destroying Majesty," he said, bowing to Chernobog again, his voice as sweet as honey. "It's a great honor to see you and the mighty *Chernij Voron* back so soon. How can we assist you?"

"*Chernij Voron?* Black Crow?" Gunz whispered, turning slowly to Voron, shivers running down his spine. "You're the prophet of grief, wars and calamities? You?"

A pained expression crossed Voron's face, and his dark eyebrows lowered over his eyes, a deep vertical wrinkle crossing his forehead.

"Be fair, Gunz, I've never lied to you about who I was. My name—Voron—means Crow. You knew it, and you never asked for details," he said, speaking in a fast whisper. "I've never hidden from you that I'm a loyal servant of Chernobog and the Kingdom of the Dark Nav, and that will never change. However, a lot has changed since the time of the original great battle between the Light and the Darkness. I'm not the same person I used to be. Just because you learned my—"

"My lord *Chernij* Voron, your feathery mightiness," sung the *Bies*, interrupting Voron. His squinty, shifty eyes fell on Gunz, and his black lips stretched even wider, a terrifying smile splitting his face from ear to ear. He seized the chain and pulled it out of the old warrior's hands before he could stop him. "To which level would you like us to escort your prisoner?"

He jerked the chain with unexpected strength for such a tiny creature, making Gunz stumble forward, almost falling. The two other *Bieses* appeared at his sides, each seizing his arm in a vice-like grip, their sharp claws digging into his skin.

"Unhand him," growled Voron, partially drawing his sword, but Chernobog got ahead of him.

The god of Destruction placed his hand on Gunz's shoulder and wagged his finger at the *Bieses* warningly.

"As much as I wish to welcome him into one of the dungeons of the lowest level of *Peklo*, for now, the Fire Salamander is my guest," he announced, a vibe of authority in his words. "No harm should befall him while he's in my care. Am I clear?"

"Of course, Your Malevolent Ferociousness, we understand. You're unconditionally clear as always." The *Bies* smiled carnivorously and dropped the chain, pointing at the gate into the *Peklo* with another low bow. "Please, follow us." Passing by Gunz, he pushed him in his side and muttered under his breath, "The one who got away. Again."

"Excuse me?" Gunz made a move to stop the obnoxious *Bies*, but Voron shook his head, a warning in his eyes.

The *Bies* glanced at Gunz over his shoulder, flashing his

sharp teeth at him, and snickered. "Nothing, Your Flaming Lordliness. Just saying we're on the way."

Following the *Bieses*, they passed through the gate and neared the veil of flames. Gunz stalled for a moment and looked up, craning his neck. The waterfall of fire was flowing down continuously, coming from nowhere and disappearing into the ground. Sensing the strange nature of this fire, he pulled against his restraints, halting Voron.

"What is this?" he asked, jerking his thumb at the fiery veil.

Voron smirked darkly. "The point of no return. Once you cross it, there is no way back. You know that saying about abandoning all hope?"

Gunz nodded, small hairs rising on the back of his neck.

"Well, this is it. The *actual* gates into the *Peklo*," Voron said flatly. "The gates will feed on your soul, extinguishing all that's human, and it's not going to be fun for you. There's nothing I can do about that, but I swear on my power, I'll protect you with my life from anything thereafter. Trust me."

"Am I supposed to trust the *Chernij Voron* and Chernobog?" muttered Gunz.

Voron winced as if Gunz had slapped him, but quickly regained his composure. "Do you see anyone else here you can rely upon?" he asked. "Brace yourself and let's go."

Not sure what to expect, Gunz took a deep breath and stepped through the wall of fire. As soon as the flames touched his skin, a raw anguish struck his soul. Everything good and light, all hopes and dreams, and everything that kept him going was extinguished, hollowing him out. Hopelessness and despair took hold of him, infusing his body with the kind of torment he'd never felt before.

He screamed, fighting Voron's grip. The fire burned brighter, and he could no longer see. It was as if someone placed a thick cloak over his face. Images of his past—the most painful moment of his life, his mistakes and sorrows, his deepest regrets—flashed before his eyes. He heard someone screaming, but he couldn't recognize his own voice in this desperate howl of endless agony.

He felt someone's hands on his body, tugging at his arms, pulling him forward. Somewhere in the back of his mind, a weak thought flashed, urging him to fight, but it disappeared almost immediately, suppressed by the flames of *Peklo*. The Dark Codex reacted to his state, adding an excruciating headache on top of everything else. A weak wave of its magical energy rushed through him, partially clearing his frazzled mind, but it was too late. The light dimmed down, submerging him under the weight of darkness.

* * *

"Gunz!"

Like through a wall, Gunz heard Voron's voice, followed by a light slap on his cheek. He shifted away and opened his eyes. At first, he could see nothing—everything around him was shaky and blurry. He raised his arms, but as the weight of the chain seemed to be too much to handle, he dropped his hands on his stomach and closed his eyes again.

"Gunz, are you okay?" demanded Voron's voice. "Gunz! Look at me!"

Someone's fingers squeezed his chin, forcing his head up. He didn't fight. A heavy palm covered his eyes, and suddenly, the weakness and the emptiness he felt were gone.

"Open your eyes, Child of Fire." Chernobog's voice, shrill and unwelcome, sounded right above him.

Gunz moaned and cracked his eyelids open to find both Chernobog and Voron kneeling next to him. A smile of relief lit up Voron's face, and he exhaled, his breath coming out like a gasp. Chernobog sat back on his heels, pursing his lips. He wiped his hands on his pants and picked up his leather gloves from the floor, placing them across his lap.

"You were right, Voron," said the god of Destruction, rubbing his forehead tiredly. "With the Nav blocking the Fire Salamander in him, his soul is too human to survive the trip through the *Peklo* unscathed."

"I'm begging you, my lord, do the right thing," said Voron, his voice pleading. "Stop torturing him and treat him with the respect he deserves. I swear, the young Salamander will do what's right if you give him the chance. He will give you access to the Codex once he understands."

Chernobog regarded his righthand man calmly. "You're taking your life in your hands, Voron. Do you realize that?"

"I do, my lord. And I stand by what I said." He threw a quick glance at Gunz and pulled out his sword.

"No, Voron! I can't give him the Codex!" Gunz tried to scream, but no sound came out from his constricted throat.

Voron placed the tip of his sword onto the cobblestones and rested his hands on the pommel. "My lord... My King, I've been loyal to you from the time of Creation. I swear on my life that you can trust the young Salamander. Protect him from the Dark Nav, and he *will* do what's right when he understands the gravity of the situation."

Dammit, Voron... what did you do? Gunz exhaled, closing his eyes for a brief moment, cursing the gates into *Peklo* that had disabled him completely.

Chernobog grunted. "I wish you didn't swear, my friend," he whispered.

For once, I agree with you, thought Gunz, grief shredding his insides.

Chernobog tapped his shoulder, making Gunz flinch. "Salamander," said the dark deity. "My best man..." His voice trailed off, and he shook his head. "No. My best friend just swore for you. He believes you to be a man of honor, and he's willing to bet his life on this assumption. I disagree with him, but I will do as he said. I will shield you from the energy of the Dark Nav and from the influence of *Peklo*. Don't disappoint me, or it may cost Voron his head."

He spread his arms and started to chant, the words of an unfamiliar language flowing through the air. They wrapped around Gunz, caressing his skin as if they were material. He could feel Chernobog's magic warping the reality around him, changing and reshaping it with every word he said. The fire came to life within him, and his body arched, responding to the flow of his element. Small flames broke through his skin, dancing on his arms, and together with the elemental fire, the scarlet flames of War sprung to life.

Chernobog stopped chanting and froze, staring at him in awe. "I'm not going to ask you," he muttered, rising to his feet. "Ask no questions and hear no lies."

"Good idea. Especially since I have no idea what's going on with my fire." Gunz pushed himself up to a sitting position and then got up.

"You don't know?" hissed Chernobog, and for the first time, Gunz saw a shadow of fear reflected in the dark deity's eyes.

"No, I have no idea. I know these are the flames of War, the power of one of the Horsemen of the Apocalypse," he said, touching the scarlet flame on his arm, willing it to dissipate. "But I'm not supposed to be able to control them. Not anymore."

"Heaven and Earth," breathed out Chernobog, his eyebrows rising in shock. "That's an unexpected twist. Even if I knew, it's not my place to tell you, Salamander. When you see your father, ask him." He chuckled darkly. "Assuming you will ever leave the Dark Nav, that is." He moved to walk away toward the *Bieses* but halted and glanced back at Gunz. "Until you talk to Kal, do not use the power of War. You're not going to enjoy the consequences." He laughed icily and walked away, muttering something under his breath.

Gunz exchanged a troubled look with Voron and followed Chernobog through a tall double door the *Bieses* held open for them. As they passed through the doorway, Chernobog turned around and raised his finger to his lips, asking for silence.

The next room reminded Gunz unpleasantly of the Destiny Council trial chamber, and he shivered, expecting for things to get exponentially worse from here. The round hall had no other source of light aside from a few magical orbs lingering above a giant, black-marble platform at the far end of it. Four massive armchairs that looked like they were carved out of a solid piece of rock were positioned on top of the platform.

A giant man in black armor sat in the armchair on the right. With his elbow propped on the armrest and his legs crossed at the knee, he looked bored and indifferent. Long, bushy hair surrounded his hard face like a mane, and with his wide shoulders and muscled arms, he resembled a lion. A terrible scar cut across his left eyebrow and his forehead, disappearing under his hairline, and his eyes shone with a bright, orange light. As he noticed Chernobog, he rose to his feet and folded his massive frame into a low bow.

"Your Majesty," he greeted him in a deep, rumbling voice.

His appearance flickered for a moment as though he was a hologram or an illusion. His human head disappeared, replaced by that of a lion with a thick black mane and burning orange eyes. His lips stretched into a semblance of a smile, displaying sharp white fangs.

"Radogast," said Chernobog, gesturing for him to rise. "You're alone? Where is Vij?"

"Yes, my lord, I'm alone," replied Radogast, slowly regaining his human form as he straightened to his full height of at least seven feet. "It's been turbulent in the Yav lately, and unfortunately, the unrest has reached even the farthest corners of the Dark Nav. The time of peace is over, and Vij does his duty, patrolling the lowest levels of *Peklo* and reinforcing the bridge over the river *Smorodina*. We can't afford another monster breaking out."

He bowed his head, his black mane falling over his face, but the despondent tone of his voice said it all. Gunz swallowed hard, fear twisting his gut into a heavy, pulsing knot. If a fierce warrior like the afterlife judge Radogast felt desperate, something was seriously wrong here. He glanced at Voron, but the warrior just frowned, giving him a tiny shake of his head.

"That's fine, don't stop what you're doing on my account," said Chernobog with a light wave of his hand toward the other end of the chamber.

Gunz followed his motion with his eyes, and just now noticed a man kneeling before the platform. In his humble position, he looked miserable and insignificant, especially compared to the enormous judge. His semitransparent body was twisted in fear, and his head was bowed low to his chest as he waited for his final judgment.

"As you can see, I have a guest today, Radogast," continued Chernobog, placing his hand on Gunz's shoulder. "This is the young Fire Salamander, and I'm going to take him to..." He didn't finish his statement and waved his hand. "You know. I need him to see. I want you to communicate with Vij. We should have no interruptions, and no one should attempt to feed on his human soul."

"Yes, my lord," replied the judge. His glowing eyes darted to Gunz, settling on his chest. Gunz gasped, feeling as though Radogast was gazing into the depths of his soul. A slow smile stretched the judge's lips, and he nodded. "Despite the terrible power he harbors within this tiny body, he does reek of humanity."

Chernobog smirked, staring down at Gunz. "That he does," he muttered under his breath. "At least for now."

He gave a curt nod to Radogast and pushed Gunz forward.

They circled around the platform where the *Bieses* opened a small backdoor for them.

"Stay here," Chernobog commanded them, leaving the *Bieses* behind to their utter displeasure. Then he turned to Gunz and smirked. "Watch your step, Salamander."

Following the King of the Dark Nav and Voron, Gunz walked through the small door and came to a sharp halt. He stood on a tiny mountain plateau—no more than three feet wide. Looking over the edge, he swallowed, barely able to breathe. A deep trench stretched in both directions as far as his sight could reach. A stormy river flowed at the bottom of it, dark swirls of dirty gray smoke partially obscuring it.

Through the screen of smoke, he could see that the waters weren't clear. Bright red streams, the color of arterial blood, rushed at the bottom of the trench, and even from this distance, he could detect the vibes of wrath, torment, and despair emitting from the river. His own soul resonated with pain, and he staggered away from the edge, pressing his hands over his heart.

With his chest shuddering with ragged breaths, Gunz looked up and his jaw dropped, his eyes widening. The sky above the trench was veiled by low, stormy clouds, and purple lightning bolts were forking through the darkness without stop, illuminating the area with their ghastly flares like some nightmarish fireworks. A flock of phantoms flew over the gorge, soundless and malevolent, ready to plummet down at whoever dared cross the river.

Tearing his eyes off of the swarm of phantoms, he squinted at the other side of the trench where a shapeless, dark mass kept moving and shifting. Gunz sharpened his Salamander senses and immediately regretted doing it. A malevolent wave of demonic essence overpowered him, invading his entire being with its poisonous miasmas.

Fighting the uncontrollable, chilling waves of fear, Gunz closed his eyes and took a deep breath, allowing the elemental fire to flow through him freely, clearing his mind. He took another step back, running straight into Chernobog's stomach.

"Enjoying the view?" murmured the god of Destruction snidely.

Gunz stepped to the side, not sure he could produce coherent words. With his heart still beating somewhere in his throat, he raised his eyes at Chernobog, breathing hard.

"My lord," said Voron, "you promised to do the right thing. Don't make him cross the river on his own. His soul will be scarred forever. Just seeing the *Peklo* while he's still alive is damaging for him."

"Regrettably, he's immortal," grumbled Chernobog. "Anyway, I don't have time to play cat-and-mouse games with him. As much as I wish to teach him a lesson, there's more at stake here than my personal grievances. I'll do as I promised, Voron."

"Thank you, my lord." Voron bowed, relaxing his tense shoulders.

Chernobog seized Gunz's elbow and pulled him closer. Wrapping his large arm around Gunz's chest, he pinned him to his side. Then he leaned down slightly and whispered with tones of regret in his voice, making Gunz wonder what the god of Destruction was regretful about. "Close your eyes, boy. Voron is right, you shouldn't witness all this. It's too much for any living soul. I promise it'll be over soon."

Gunz closed his eyes, unable to contain a deep shudder running through him. Chernobog's hand covered his face and suddenly, he felt as if he was lifted by a powerful gust of wind. The silence became absolute, and all he could hear was his heart beating desperately in his chest and the rush of blood in his ears.

A moment later, Chernobog removed his hand, releasing him. "You can open your eyes, but stay still," he ordered, his voice echoing strangely as if they were in a forest. "This is what I wanted you to see."

Gunz opened his eyes and froze in place. Even if Chernobog hadn't warned him about not moving, he didn't think he could, his limbs filled with lead. They stood in a dark hallway, running endlessly in both directions. Multiple cells, void of light and gloomy, lined both sides of the corridor. Each cell had a see-through front wall, showing who—or rather what—was inside.

After the fight on the Dark side of the Destiny Council's realm, Gunz thought he had seen it all. He had no idea how wrong he was. Never, not even in his worst nightmares, had he seen monsters like these locked up in the lower dungeons of *Peklo*. But worse than the pureblood demons inside the cells was the way they were tortured. He couldn't hear their screams, but their repulsive faces were contorted by unimaginable pain, and the expression of undiluted torment in their inhuman eyes spoke louder than any screams.

"What is this?" he whispered, his mouth dry.

"Monsters," replied Chernobog, shuddering. "There are no human souls here. The lower levels of *Peklo* is the only prison strong enough to suppress their powers and keep them imprisoned. If they break free"—he chuckled, his laugher, sinister and dark, sending the next wave of chills down Gunz's spine—"say goodbye to the Yav, little Salamander. I am the only one who stands between all this darkness and the realm of the light." He waved his arm around as if to prove his point.

"Fire Almighty," muttered Gunz, wiping cold sweat off his forehead with the back of his hand. "Why did you bring me here? What did you want to show me?"

Chernobog's face became a stone mask, his lips pressed into a firm line. He grabbed Gunz's arm and pulled him forward, walking so fast that Gunz had to switch to a light jog to keep up with him. They passed a few large dungeons when Chernobog stopped and pointed to a cell on his left.

"I wanted you to see this," he said in a soft whisper even though no one could hear them.

The see-through wall of the cell was gone, piles of glass-like material and rocks barricading the corridor in front of it. It appeared to be ripped by an explosion of enormous power, but Gunz was positive that no mundane weapon could blow up these walls. Reaching forward, he closed his eyes and opened his other sight. The traces of Black Fire touched his senses, and he gasped, pulling his hand back.

"Black Fire," he said, opening his eyes to meet Chernobog's steady stare.

"Think, Salamander," said the god of Destruction. "You have a reputation for making... reckless decisions, but one thing I have to give you—you're not an idiot. Tell me what you think."

"It's not the Black Fire. It's the Living-Dead Flame," whispered Gunz, afraid to voice his worst fear. "I thought they needed it to lift Veles' curse and free Skiper-Zmey."

Chernobog shook his head silently. Gunz glanced at Chernobog and then at Voron. The old warrior's face was so pale, he looked almost green.

"Who was in this cell, Chernobog?" asked Gunz. "What kind of demon did they set free?"

"Not a demon," objected Chernobog, his voice a hoarse whisper, and there was no doubt in Gunz's mind—the mighty god of Destruction was terrified. "A god..."

CHAPTER 11

~ ZANE BURNS, A.K.A. GUNZ ~

"A god?" echoed Gunz, swallowing a thick lump stuck in his throat. "A god?? What kind of goddamn god?"

"The kind that doesn't need the Living-Dead Flame to break Veles' curse." Bending down, Chernobog seized the shirt on Gunz's chest and lifted him slightly, a sinister smirk distorting his face. "The kind of god that even I can't fight on my own. Thousands of years ago, he was locked up here by the mighty Svarog for his crimes against humanity and against the pantheon." Chernobog took a deep breath and then yelled, slamming Gunz against the floor, forcing a grunt of pain out of him. "Nobody! Do you hear me, Salamander? Nobody in the Slavic pantheon could fight this god alone and get the best of him. Originally, this entire level was built just to contain his powers. He was imprisoned here millennia ago and forgotten by all… All except me."

Chernobog loomed over him with malice, the energy of the Nav swirling and wrapping around him like black smoke. Expecting the infuriated god to strike him, Gunz held his breath and raised his arms to cover his head.

"It's your fault, Salamander. He runs free because you

assumed you could play a god," hissed Chernobog. Seizing Gunz's wrist, he yanked him to his feet. "I needed the Dark Codex so I could find a way to contain his rebounding powers, you worthless fireworm!"

Gunz jerked his arm out of Chernobog's iron grip, and smoldering flames surrounded him, his chest rising and falling with short breaths. As the dark corridor spun around him, he took an unsteady step back, running into Voron, and froze.

"Get me out of here," he hissed through clenched teeth, staring at Chernobog with wide eyes. *The evil triad... The dark deity that worked alongside the air demon and the Lord of Chaos... All these years... It was... How could he...* His thoughts rushed in a wild stampede, tripping over each other, and he could no longer think clearly. Fury entwining with anxiety rose within him, fueling his fire. "I said... GET! ME! OUT! OF HERE!"

The fire exploded around him, and the flames of War surrounded him, lifting him a few feet off the ground. Gunz threw his head back, spreading his flaming arms wide, and a wild howl tore from his lips. The ground trembled, dust and dirt falling down from the ceiling. He heard Chernobog scream something about controlling the power of War, but for the first time in his life he wasn't in control at all, and he had no idea what to do.

He felt someone's hands grab his legs, pulling him down, and he thrashed, fighting against their hold. He thought he saw a giant, black serpent-like dragon wrapping its webby wings around him, but he wasn't sure if it was an illusion created by his frazzled mind. Chernobog's voice invaded his ears, and a heartbeat later, the darkness surrounded him, slowly draining his fire and his strength. He moaned and fell into its terrifying embrace.

* * *

A WATERFALL of icy water washed over him, ripping him out of blissful unconsciousness. He screamed and jerked weakly, once again finding himself tied to the same iron chair in Chernobog's throne room, surrounded by the bright circle of the God's snare.

Chernobog stood outside the circle, his arms folded over his chest, an empty bucket lying next to his feet. Voron sat on the floor, holding his burned hands up. Gunz pulled against his restraints, but gave up right away, realizing that within the circle of the God's snare, he had no strength to fight.

"Did you calm down, boy?" asked Chernobog snidely. "Are you in control?"

Gunz nodded. "Release me. I'm in control."

"It would be almost fun to watch your ignorant ass send the realm of humans back to the stone age," he said, a crooked smirk on his face. "The power of War in the hands of a village simpleton. Tsk-tsk-tsk." He shook his head.

"Release me and let me out of the Nav," Gunz repeated quietly. "Kal and Gwyn ap Nudd must know. Mrak Delar and Alliandr must get ready—"

"The Dark Codex," the god of Destruction interrupted him icily. "Now you've seen it with your own eyes, and you know why I need it. Give me the Dark Codex, Salamander. I'm the only one who stands a chance of fighting against him. None of your friends can do it. Not even Gwyn ap Nudd. It has to be me."

"Why you?" asked Gunz calmly. "How about Svarog or the Brothers Svarozhich? Or Rod himself? Can't they fight him?"

"My father? My brother and his kids?" He laughed, but cut his laughter off abruptly, sucking in a few deep breaths. Anger swirled around him, and his eyes flooded with the darkness of the Nav. "My father and my brothers," he muttered, slowly pulling his gloves off. "One big, happy family."

He threw them to the floor and started to unbutton his shirt with stiff fingers. The buttons wouldn't budge, so he just ripped his shirt open, exposing the powerful muscles of his chest and stomach.

"What are you doing?" yelled Gunz, struggling against his restraints, but to no avail.

Chernobog didn't reply. He yanked his shirt out of his pants and took it off, throwing it to the floor next to his gloves. Then he turned his back to Gunz and flexed his massive shoulders.

"This is my father's and my brothers' handiwork," he said quietly, twisting his arm to touch his back. "Both my father and Svarog believed that it was my duty to keep the Dark Nav and all the monsters within it under control. It was my job to punish and destroy." He dropped his arm powerlessly and lifted his shoulders in a short shrug. "Yes, I rebelled against him once. That's true. But who wouldn't? He damned me to spend all eternity here, in the darkness, alone. And my dear brother Svarog didn't have the balls to object the order..." His voice trailed away, and he continued in a harsh whisper, "He said he would teach me a lesson... and he did, alright. With his hammer."

Gunz glanced at Chernobog and averted his gaze. The entire space of his back was disfigured by old scar tissue. He'd seen the scars left by a whip or a belt, but these looked a lot worse. These were the scars left by magic. The god turned around and smirked.

"Hard to look at?" he asked softly, slightly cocking his head. "Imagine how it felt." He bent down and picked up his shirt, putting it back on, his movements sharp and awkward. "I've never shown that to anyone, Salamander. Only Voron and my wife have seen it. But I need you to understand... I've learned my lesson. I have no choice. I'm a prison guard, and now that one of my prisoners is on the loose, it's my duty to bring him back. Mine and no one else's." He stepped closer to the circle of the God's snare and repeated, speaking slowly, pronouncing one word at a time. "Give. Me. The Codex."

"Gunz, please, listen to him." Gunz heard Voron's voice and glanced down. The old warrior sat on the cold floor, his damaged hands resting on his lap. "He's telling you the truth, my friend."

Feeling torn, Gunz bit his lip, thousands of thoughts flashing through his mind. On one hand, he realized Chernobog couldn't be trusted. But on the other... *What if the dark god is telling the truth? But what if he uses the Codex to capture the evil god and then turns against his twin brother? Or Svarog and the Bothers Svarozhich? What if...*

"What's his name?" asked Gunz, looking up at Chernobog.

"Whose?" Chernobog narrowed his eyes, frowning.

"The evil god who escaped your dungeon," replied Gunz. "What's his name? His position in the pantheon? Who is he?"

"Oh, that?" Chernobog smirked, but his gaze remained dark and heavy. "He is almost as ancient as creation itself. In old Russian, his name means just that—evil. He's the original, primordial darkness. The god of perpetual torment and wickedness. His name is Zlebog."

"Never heard of him," muttered Gunz.

"For a good reason, too." Chernobog shrugged. "He's been imprisoned for more years than you can count, boy. Trust me, I'm the only one who stands a chance against him. Give me the Codex, and I'll put him back where he belongs. After that, I'll help you and your friends deal with the Lord of Chaos and the air demon." He thought for a moment, and then added, visibly cringing, "And with my darling wife, of course."

"You've been searching for the Dark Codex for months," said Gunz quietly, staring down at the dusty floor, his brain working on overdrive. "You've made a deal with Ivan the Terrible and manipulated the situation to bring me to the City of Gold and force me to break into Ivan's Golden Library. Ivan told me that you stood behind all that. So, you've known for months that Zlebog was on the verge of breaking free." He raised his eyes to

Chernobog, meeting his steady gaze. "Goddamnit! Why didn't you say something?"

He expected Chernobog to blow up, but the god of Destruction just shrugged. "Say what exactly? And to whom? My Father? My brothers? They don't give a damn about my problems and they don't want to have anything to do with me." He wrapped his torn shirt around himself, tucking it into his pants. "I didn't need my father to teach me another lesson."

He lowered down to the floor next to Voron and sighed, looking somewhere behind Gunz into the darkness of the throne room.

"You're right, Salamander," he said at length. "I knew something had been going on for a while. Even before the day we battled Skiper-Zmey and Morena, I noticed my wife's unusual interest in the lower dungeons. Normally, I couldn't talk her into walking farther than the Judgment Hall." He sighed and shook his head, crestfallen. "I never could imagine she would betray me. I..." His voice trembled, disappearing into painful silence.

"You loved her," Gunz finished for him, and the King of the Dark Nav finally looked at him.

"No, I didn't just love her. I was in love with her. She was my heart and my soul, my life force," he objected quietly, his fingers fidgeting with the edge of his ripped shirt. "I'm still in love with her, despite my better judgment. Her betrayal hurt me worse than my father's hammer."

"She betrayed you in the worst possible way, Chernobog," said Gunz with a sigh. "She betrayed you as a man, as a god and as the King of the Dark Nav."

"Don't you think I know that?" said Chernobog without looking at him, his voice trembling with barely contained torment. "And yet, when Veles imprisoned her, I was in so much pain, I almost got in a fight with him about it." He sighed again and pressed his fingers to his eyes, a muscle twitching in his jaw.

"Anyway, it doesn't matter now, does it? Zlebog walks the realm of the living, and I can't allow it. I know I can't do it on my own, but I would rather die than ask my family for help. This is why as soon as I noticed that something was off, I started searching for the Codex."

"You could have talked to me," said Gunz, shaking his head. "You could have asked Mrak Delar or Gwyn ap Nudd. You didn't need to go to your family. But you chose to keep quiet until it was too late."

"You're right," agreed Chernobog, sounding flat and cold. "I could have, but I didn't. Even when I realized that some of the magic and wards of my dungeons started to fail, and Zlebog could move around the Nav and the Yav in his incorporeal form, using some of his powers, I still believed I could contain him. My bad." He shrugged indifferently as if he was talking about making a typo in a high school essay.

"My bad?" Gunz parroted, anger slowly boiling up in him. "That's all you have to say?"

Chernobog chuckled, derision shining through his black eyes. "My dear little Salamander," he said, mockery lacing his voice. "Those who live in glass houses shouldn't throw stones. You've made a mistake which led to dire consequences as well."

A low growl rumbled in Gunz's chest as he pulled against the chains, but Chernobog just laughed, staring at him with narrowed eyes.

"You didn't think I knew about that?" He laughed again, slapping his hands on his thighs. "I already told you—everyone breaks, dear boy. Rasputin told me about the potion he gave you. The potion that allowed Skiper-Zmey to communicate with his followers despite Veles' curse. You didn't say anything to anyone either, did you?"

"No," replied Gunz and fell back in his chair, the anger slowly simmering down in him. "Why didn't you tell anyone about my mistake then?"

"Because..." Chernobog smirked, running his fingers over his thick mustache. "I knew how you made this mistake. You did it hoping to save the woman you loved. You wanted to see her face, to hear her voice, to feel her touch... Just one more time." He raised his hand, stopping Gunz from interrupting him. "You're more human than you can imagine, and I'm an ancient god, but I felt your pain... I understood you, and this is the reason I kept my mouth shut."

"If you understood me," said Gunz, a cold, lopsided smirk on his lips, "then why did you leave me blind and helpless, at the mercy of the evil king?"

"Blind—yes. Helpless—not so much," objected Chernobog icily. "Just because I understood your pain, didn't mean I forgave your disobedience and insolent behavior. I believed you needed a lesson in humility, and King Alexander taught you this lesson perfectly well."

"I had no idea the potion would jeopardize Veles' curse." Gunz averted his gaze, the memory of that day in the cave under Mount Karasova still fresh in his mind. "I didn't even follow Rasputin's instructions. It was an honest mistake. You, on the other hand, knew that your dungeons were failing."

Chernobog tilted his head and leaned forward slightly. "Be that as it may." He waved his hand nonchalantly. "But let me ask you and be truthful with me for once. What would you do to keep your Angelique safe?"

"What wouldn't I do," muttered Gunz, pain tearing at his soul. "I would give my life to keep her out of harm's way."

"And so would I," growled Chernobog, darkness surrounding him. "I would give anything to keep Morena safe. It was she who weakened my locking spells and wards that kept Zlebog incarcerated. I knew it. I recognized her energy signature. She'd done it before Veles imprisoned her. But we all, including myself, were so busy dealing with Zmey and his followers that when I noticed the problem, it was too late to do anything. And if I had told anyone in my family, they would have killed her…" He swallowed and added, his voice a hoarse whisper. "They would destroy the only woman I had ever loved. I couldn't have it."

"She is the goddess of Winter and Death!" hissed Gunz, his hands clenching into fists. "Immortal goddess! She can't be killed."

"Your ignorance is just as endearing as it is infuriating, Salamander," grumbled Chernobog snidely. "There is no such thing as perfect, unconditional immortality, you dumbass. An immortal Fire Salamander can be killed by the Black Fire. A vampire can be killed by a wooden stake through the heart or by fire. Gods can be killed too, given the right tools and circumstances. Mind you, it's not easy to destroy a god, and it takes a being of equal or higher power to do that, but it's possible. And when it comes to Morena, I would *not* take that chance."

Chernobog fell silent, and Gunz dropped his head, biting his lip. There was no point in explaining to the ancient god that by saving his wife, who had betrayed him in the worst possible way, he had brought the world to the brim of destruction. Now, because of his actions, they were facing a war—the next battle between the forces of Darkness and the army of Light, the kind of battle this world hadn't seen since the moment of Creation. The King of the Dark Nav had made his choice, knowing the consequences perfectly well, and arguing with him was as pointless as it was dangerous.

Gunz glanced at Voron and his chest tightened with pain, numbness spreading through his arms. *Chernij Voron* or not, the old warrior proved to be a man of honor. Despite his loyalty to his master, Voron had never let him down, and right now his life depended on Gunz's decision. *An impossible decision…*

"Chernobog," called Gunz, leaning forward as far as his restraints would allow him.

The god lifted his face and smirked, looking straight into his eyes. "Did you make your choice, Salamander?" he asked, getting up. He offered his hand to his righthand man and pulled him up to his feet.

"Yes." Gunz bit his lip, casting a veiled gaze at Voron.

Chernobog noticed it, and an arrogant smile appeared on his face. "So, what is it going to be?"

"Release me," Gunz continued through gritted teeth. "As Voron said, I'll do the right thing. And right now, giving you access to the Dark Codex is the right thing to do."

Chernobog crossed his massive arms over his chest and tapped his foot impatiently.

Gunz sighed reproachfully. "I can't kneel, being restrained and all, but I swear, I'm not stupid enough to fight you in your own domain. Release me and remove the God's snare. I need access to my magic to learn how to complete the transfer." He thought for a moment and added, "My lord."

Chernobog laughed and took one knee, placing his hand on the circle of magic. He whispered a few words, and the God's snare disappeared. Then he approached Gunz and removed the spell from his restraints. However, he left his arms chained and his ankles wrapped in iron manacles.

"Come on..." Gunz raised his arms connected by a short chain. "Give me at least some range of movement. How am I supposed to wield my magic?"

"It's not like I don't trust you, Salamander," murmured Chernobog, the corners of his lips quirking up, "but I just don't trust you."

Realizing that arguing with the dark deity was a waste of breath, Gunz closed his eyes and connected with the Dark Codex. As the magical book presented him with a few possible spells, a blinding pain spiked through him. He grunted, pressing his hands to his eyes, but kept searching through the book, looking for a single spell that would allow him to execute the plan he had in his mind.

A few minutes later, he let go and leaned forward, propping his arms on his lap. Breathing laboriously, he dropped his head low, sweat dripping down his back.

"So?" asked Chernobog, tapping on his shoulder impatiently.

Gunz raised his head and looked up at Chernobog, wiping the perspiration off his forehead with his hand.

"I need you..." He stopped talking and straightened up, taking a deep breath. "I need you to take me to the World Tree."

"Are you taking me for a fool, boy?" hissed Chernobog, taking a step closer to him as darkness gathered around him. "You want me to take you to the center of the Slavic realm, the epicenter of all magic, where you'll regain your full power and will be able to summon Kal or Mrak Delar?"

"And being the almighty god of Destruction, why would you be afraid of a Master of Power or a Fire Elemental?" asked Gunz calmly. "Anyway, you have no choice. This is the only place where I can complete the transfer, my lord. I swear, I'm not going to attempt to summon Kal or Mrak Delar or anyone of my friends. But I need the power of the Alatyr stone. That's the only way I can do it."

"I'm not afraid of them," growled Chernobog. "I can't be bothered." Reaching forward, he seized Gunz's neck and put his other hand on Voron's shoulder. "Don't disappoint me, you won't like the consequences."

Chernobog laughed, his laughter bouncing off the tall ceiling of the throne room, and the darkness rose around them, swirling faster and faster, until Gunz could see nothing but a swirling black mass of air.

CHAPTER 12

~ ZANE BURNS, A.K.A. GUNZ ~

They materialized in front of the World Tree right next to the Alatyr stone, and Gunz held his breath, intoxicated by the amount of magical energy in the nexus. He leaned forward, bracing himself with his arms against the stone, its rough, warm surface pleasant to his skin after the coldness of the Nav.

The World Tree had rejuvenated after the demonic invasion, and even though it was late evening, the dayside of the tree was bright with flowers, its green and young leaves reflecting the warm light of the sun. The tender aroma of wildflowers, the scent of the fresh greenery and a barely noticeable odor of the sea invaded his senses, making him take a deep breath and close his eyes. A crescent moon surrounded by myriads of stars gazed down upon him from the nightside of the tree, and everything looked so beautiful and peaceful, that for a moment he forgot why he was here.

Feeling a soft touch to his shoulder, he turned his head. Voron stood by his side, a mix of emotions reflected on his face hardened by age and battles he had survived over the years of his long life. Gunz read the silent question in his eyes and bit his lip, a deep crease etched between his brows.

"Gunz," whispered Voron, the light of hope slowly vanishing from his gaze. "You are going to do the right thing, aren't you?"

Gunz nodded, straightening up. "I am, Voron," he said, dread tightening his chest. "I will do what I have to do for the good of the realm."

"Is that my death sentence?" Voron dropped his head, his lips twisting into a pained smirk.

"I hope not." Gunz put his hand on the old warrior's shoulder, giving it a tiny, reassuring squeeze, but everything inside him was crashing in unbearable agony.

He turned to Chernobog, his movements slow and heavy. "My lord, are you ready?" he asked, cringing at how lifeless he sounded. "May I proceed?"

Chernobog gave him a curt nod and waved his hand, gesturing for him to continue. Gunz placed his hands against the rough bark of the World Tree and whispered a short spell Kal taught him a while ago, channeling his magic and his thoughts into a summoning call. Realizing clearly that in his position this was the only appropriate course of action, he knew exactly what he had to do, but this knowledge provided him neither comfort nor confidence.

Kal, I wish you were here... I need you, Father... He understood that the Fire Elemental couldn't hear him, but any time he found himself in a tough situation, Kal was the only person he prayed to, asking for help, even though the Great Salamander wasn't a god.

A warm breeze ruffled the hefty foliage of the World Tree as two large birds lowered down gracefully, landing on the massive bottom branch. Before they could say anything, Gunz raised his arms and said the second spell. Alkonost spread her white wings, her snow-white feathers reflecting the brilliant light of the day. She hugged her sister, pulling her closer. Sirin's dark plumage gleaming with the colors of the night looked stark next to her.

Their attentive gazes settled on Gunz, and their tender faces of young maidens fell, their beautiful eyes shining with gathering tears. Even Alkonost, who always looked on the bright side of life, appeared to be perturbed.

"Are you sure this is what you want, Great Fire Salamander?" they asked in unison, tears slipping down both their pale faces.

"Yes," replied Gunz, unsure he could say anything else.

Both birds nodded and started to chant, their clear voices sounding like the best music he had ever heard. A single tear dropped from Alkonost's eye and froze in midair before her. She moved her wing over it and the drop of water started to grow until it reached the size of a tennis ball. Both Sirin and Alkonost touched the orb, and two feathers—silvery-white and midnight-black—materialized inside it, shimmering with a brilliant white light.

"This is the power you asked for," said Sirin. "Take it. It's yours."

Gunz brought his arms up, and the orb lowered into the palms of his hands. As soon as it came in contact with his skin, it dissolved, getting absorbed by his body. As always, when dealing with magic and powers, he expected some pain, but it didn't happen. A soft white light surrounded him, and a wave of warmth bordering on physical pleasure spread through him. He closed his eyes, and his mouth opened slightly, a soft moan escaping his lips.

The heatwave dissipated, and he felt the ancient magic of Slavic gods surging through his veins, giving him the strength he needed. He opened his eyes with effort and saw both birds gazing down at him, transfixed. Soft smiles played on their lips, but the deep lakes of their eyes remained dark with sadness.

"Young Salamander, you look breathtaking when you enjoy —," started Alkonost, but Sirin threw a scorching stare at her and she fell silent.

As always, Gunz expected a snarky retort from Miss Negativity Sirin, but it didn't follow. "Farewell, Great Fire Salamander," she said instead, despair flooding her large blue eyes with the next wave of tears. "We're not going to stick around to see what's coming next. We already know." She sighed, ruffling her feathers. "Sometimes, I hate my gift of sight."

The birds exchanged a distressed look and spread their wings. Despite their size, they rose with ease and disappeared in the heavy canopy of the leaves.

Gunz swallowed and slowly turned around to face Chernobog, raising his chained hands. The god of Destruction arched his eyebrows at him, the corners of his mouth lifting just a touch under his black mustache.

"What do you want now, Salamander?" he asked, a considerable layer of sarcasm in his voice. "You better not be playing games with me."

"No, my lord," replied Gunz calmly. "Not at all. But as I mentioned before, I need a wider range of motion to cast this particular spell. The chain is too short, and I can't spread my arms."

"Fine." Chernobog cursed quietly but approached Gunz and seized the chain.

At his touch, it grew long enough for Gunz to spread his arms wide, but it also became increasingly heavier, pulling his hands down.

"It's too heavy," he murmured, staring down at the thick, rusty links.

Chernobog seized Gunz's upper arm, his long fingers probing his bicep. "You should have some strength in all this meat." He snickered, dropping Gunz's arm. "Deal with it like a man and not like the puny lizard you are." He folded his arms over his chest, staring at him derisively. "And oh, Salamander, just wanted to remind you. Should you believe for a moment that you're smarter than me, the manacles still have the God's snare spell on them. All I have to do is say one word, and you're a powerless little boy again. I don't even need to touch you. Am I clear?"

"Crystal," muttered Gunz. "I wouldn't dare…"

Chernobog smirked and nodded toward Voron. "My best man swore for you on his life. It'd be a shame if I was forced to kill him."

Gunz clenched his teeth, stifling the desire to do something he would definitely regret later, like trying to fight the god of Destruction. Instead, he turned to Voron, meeting his haunted gaze.

"Voron, stand behind me. I don't want you to get affected by the spell I'm about to cast." He waited for Voron to step between him and the Alatyr stone and channeled all the magic and elemental powers he could gather in his body. As he connected with the Dark Codex, pain spiked through him, making him clench his fingers into tight fists.

He gathered some of his magic in his right hand and quickly drew a rune shining with a blinding white light in the air. Before Chernobog could do anything, he touched the rune with his fingers and whispered a summoning spell. As the portal, shining with eye-watering brilliance, opened next to him, Gunz started to chant softly, stepping between Chernobog and the portal.

A tall man with long silvery hair dressed in all white stepped out of the portal. He was as tall as Chernobog, and his entire body emitted the brilliant light of his magic. Even though they looked like a strange reflection of each other, everything that was dark about Chernobog was light about the newcomer. His eyes halted on the god of Destruction, and a feral growl rumbled in his throat.

"Hello, brother," he said, mutual hatred radiating between them.

"Belobog," replied Chernobog through gritted teeth. His

hand slipped down to his hip, his fingers wrapping around the grip of his giant sword.

Without waiting to see what would happen next, Gunz whispered an enchantment, making a circular motion with his hands, and the bright white circle of his magic materialized around each god. He entwined some of the Codex magic with the godly powers Sirin and Alkonost had provided and bent down, sending it through the circles.

"You!" shouted Belobog as his eyes darted to Gunz. "How dare—"

"Be quiet," hissed Gunz, channeling the rest of the borrowed power, infusing it with his own magic and elemental energy.

Standing between the twin-brothers, he placed his hands on their chests and started to chant. Knowing perfectly well that both gods were imprisoned by his spell, he allowed himself to focus on the flow of the magical energy. From the corner of his eye, he could see that Chernobog was burning with rage, the energy of the Dark Nav spinning around him inside the circle like a swarm of tiny, angry hornets. Belobog, however, was calm and relaxed. There was no anger or animosity in the gaze of the god of Light and Creation, just interest and a touch of sympathy.

Ignoring the pain, Gunz kept chanting, feeling the energy of the Dark Codex moving and weaving through him, slowly gathering in both his hands. As the pain became more than he could handle, his arms started to shake with the strain, and his eyes watered, making everything blurry and unsteady.

"Hang in there, boy." He heard Belobog's voice and raised his eyes, struggling to see the face of the god through the veil of tears. He wasn't sure if Belobog knew what he was attempting to do, but those unexpected words of support gave him some hope. He stopped chanting, letting the energy of the Dark Codex flow through him freely.

"Protect Voron," he whispered to the light deity, barely

moving his lips. Belobog's eyes darted to the old warrior, and an expression of surprise changed his features, but he gave Gunz a short nod.

Gathering whatever strength he had left in his body, he let go of the Dark Codex, completing the transfer. Both gods screamed. The darkness surrounded Chernobog, lifting him a few inches off the ground as he spread his arms, throwing his head back. A blazing white light enveloped Belobog, and his body, sprawled in the air, arched.

"Done," exhaled Gunz, and his knees buckled. *The balance is preserved...*

He fell to the ground, drained physically and magically, and his fall seemed to be endless. When his back finally hit the dirt, he barely felt it, all his senses dimmed down. The long blades of grass caressed his face as his head lolled to the side. He tried to move his arm, but with the heavy chain still attached to his wrists, he had no strength to lift it.

As both gods returned to normal and lowered to the ground, he clenched his jaw and held his breath, expecting for their wrath to come. Feeling vulnerable and helpless, he glanced at Belobog and mouthed, "Save Voron, please."

Belobog frowned, and his gaze darted to Chernobog. "Brother, what's going on here?"

"I'll let you know as soon as I find out." Lowering down to one knee, Chernobog wrapped his fingers tightly around Gunz's neck. He lifted him slightly, and then smashed him hard against the ground, causing him to lose his breath. "What have you done, fireworm?"

Gunz opened his mouth, struggling to fill his lungs with oxygen, his fingers gripping at the grass. "I did what I promised I would do," he said quietly once coherent speech returned to him. "I gave you access to the Dark Codex. I no longer have it. But I also did the right thing—you can't use the Codex against your twin-brother."

Belobog took one knee next to him. "What kind of magic did you use, young Salamander?" he asked softly. "I felt your magical energy surging through me, settling in my heart and my head. What was it?"

"Not *my* magical energy," whispered Gunz, fear constricting his throat. "The Dark Codex. I split it between you and Chernobog. Now only by working together as one can you use its power. Talk to your brother, my lord, and be kind to him. He needs your help more than he knows. We all do."

"You—!" Chernobog's voice broke off as anger contorted his face into a terrifying mask, making the ground shake slightly. "You did what? How dare you defy me!"

"Brother!" Belobog growled warningly, but the god of Destruction wasn't listening.

Rising to his full height, he turned to Voron. "You swore on your life that he wouldn't disobey me!" he shouted, and the old warrior cowered back, raising his arms. Unsheathing his sword, the god took a step closer to his righthand man and commanded, spitting the words through his clenched teeth, "On your knees!"

Voron sighed and lowered to his knees, dropping his head low. "I swore on my life that the young Salamander would do the right thing and give you access to the Dark Codex, my lord," whispered Voron, keeping his eyes down. "And so he did. It is not my fault that he interprets right and wrong differently than you."

For a heartbeat, Chernobog just stared down at the man who had stood by his side from the moment the army of the Nav was conjured, his chest rising and falling with angry breaths. Without warning, he backhanded him with his left hand, and when Voron fell to the ground, he pressed the tip of his sword under his jaw, drawing blood.

"Do it, master," said Voron, closing his eyes. "My life belongs to you, anyway."

"No..." Gunz made a move to get up and fell back.

Chernobog raised his sword, but as he swung it down, his blade met another, sparks flying in the air as metal hit metal.

"Stand down, brother!" shouted Belobog, his body glowing brighter as the magical energy of the Dark Codex mixed in with the glow of his godly powers. "Don't do something you will regret later. Voron is loyal to you. He has proven his loyalty over the centuries."

The two brothers turned against each other, the mutual hatred between them almost palpable. The darkness that gathered behind the god of Destruction was met with the blinding light of his twin brother. The ground trembled and even the day side of the World Tree got darker. The wind picked up, and lightning split the dark sky.

But as their swords collided again, a blazing ball of light originated between the blades, locking them together. It hung there for a brief moment and then exploded with a thunderous bang, throwing both gods a few feet apart. Chernobog jumped to his feet first, staring at Gunz in shock.

Gunz caught his flabbergasted stare, and uncontrollable laughter bubbled up in his chest. Maybe it was the stress talking, or maybe he was too exhausted to think straight, but all of a sudden, this entire situation seemed to be hilarious to him. He didn't know why he was laughing, but he couldn't stop.

Covering the distance between them in one long stride, Chernobog pulled his leg back and kicked Gunz in his side. Gunz choked and coughed, curling in on himself. But as soon as he was able to breathe in, the wild laughter erupted from his lips again. Chernobog growled as his fist connected with Gunz's jaw. Gunz cried out, splattering blood on the grass, and this time fell silent, tears running down his face.

"I'll deal with you later, fireworm," rumbled the god of Destruction, and the tone of his voice promised nothing good.

He touched the chain on Gunz's arms, and it got shorter,

locking his wrists together. The runes of the God's snare lit up on the cuffs, draining him of all his magic and blocking his elemental power completely.

"Don't go anywhere," added Chernobog mockingly. Then he stepped over Gunz and headed toward Voron with his sword in his hand.

"No…" Gunz moaned, trying to grab Chernobog's leg, but his weak fingers didn't bend, his hands falling limply to the ground. *Voron, fight for your life because I can't fight for you…*

A wave of magical energy rushed through the field, and the brightness of the daylight replaced the darkness Chernobog left in his wake. Time seemed to stop, and all sounds ceased. Chernobog froze in place, standing with one leg up like some terrifying statue. Feeling a gentle touch to his cheek, Gunz raised his eyes. The god of Light and Creation squatted in front of him, his blazing eyes staring at him with sympathy.

"Fire Salamander," he said softly, "I can't hold my brother in the time bubble long. We're equal in strength and now that you locked us with the Dark Codex, fighting him is no longer an option. I can either save *Chernij Voron* or I can save you. The choice is yours."

Gunz raised his eyes at the Slavic deity, and a sad smile ghosted his bleeding lips. "It was never a choice for me, my lord," he whispered. "Save Voron."

Belobog frowned but didn't object. He straightened and approached Voron, placing his hands on the warrior's shoulder. Giving Gunz a quick nod, he snapped his fingers, and both vanished from the Isle Buyan.

As soon as the god of Light and Creation was gone, time resumed its motion, and the sounds rushed back in. Chernobog lowered his leg and came to a sharp halt, twirling in place, searching for Voron. As understanding dawned on him, he punched the air angrily, cursing in old Russian mixed in with modern-day profanities.

When his initial spike of anger subsided, he sheathed his sword and strolled back to Gunz. He stopped next to him and pushed him slightly on his chest, turning him on his back. Then he lowered to one knee next to him and seized his chin, forcing him to look into his eyes.

Gunz met his stare—dark with scorn—and sighed, cringing inwardly. Chernobog unsheathed his dagger and pushed its tip into Gunz's chest. Gunz groaned, feeling the warmth of the blood spreading under his shirt, soaking it through.

"Well, it's just you and me, little lizard," said the dark god and twisted his dagger a little, drawing out a strangled gasp out of Gunz. "My brother left you behind, so I can do with you whatever I please."

Gunz didn't reply and closed his eyes, but Chernobog squeezed his chin harder, jerking his head to the side.

"Open your eyes, fireworm, and face me, or I swear, I'll cut your eyelids off," he demanded, his voice a dangerous growl.

Gunz opened his eyes, meeting Chernobog's furious gaze. He was so weak and tired that at this moment he wasn't sure he had the strength in him to be scared. "Do whatever you want with me," he whispered. "I don't care."

Chernobog laughed. "You will care. Later on, that is," he said, releasing his chin. "You see, my first desire was to take you to the lowest level of *Peklo* and let all the scum there feed on your soul—forever, of course, since you're an immortal Fire Salamander."

Gunz shuddered involuntarily at the idea of spending eternity in the darkness of the Nav, and his eyes widened as fear spiraled through him. An uneven smirk made Chernobog's face look darker and more sinister as the god of Destruction stared down at him with unconcealed contempt.

"I see this prospect scares you, fireworm," he murmured, pleased with his reaction. "As well it should. And I only wish I could do it, but I can't. My brother Belobog knows me well enough, and he will know where to look for you. So, no, I'm not going to do that."

He forced his dagger down, and Gunz cried out, feeling the cold steel slithering its way between his ribs.

"Instead, I'm going to send you to a place where no one would ever think to look for you," continued Chernobog. "So, enjoy the obscurity while going through a few days of infinite death."

"Do your worst," growled Gunz, a cold smirk appearing on his face before he could control it.

Leaning forward, Chernobog pushed down on the dagger, and Gunz screamed, his body arching like a tight bow as the blade penetrated his heart.

CHAPTER 13

~ AIDAN ~

Aidan got dressed a lot faster than he had undressed a few minutes ago. With Tessa following him, he rushed out the door and ran downstairs, skipping steps. As he walked into the living room, he halted by the stairs, taking in an unusual view.

Kal sat on the couch, leaning forward with his arms resting on his lap. With his head bowed down and his flaming hair falling over his face, he looked unusually distressed. Viggo Warrington, better known as War, stood by the wall next to the TV with his hands in the pockets of his stylish pants. His face was a stone mask, and it was hard to say what was on his mind. Gwyn ap Nudd was pacing the small space between the TV and the coffee table, exuding nervousness with his every move.

It was obvious that whatever Kal and Viggo had told him in the short period of time when Aidan was getting dressed had set Gwyn's nerves on edge. Aidan walked inside the living area and bowed.

"My lords," he greeted them with a light smile, but everything inside him twisted with the expectation of trouble.

"Aidan." Kal got up, the elemental fire energy swirling

around him like a fiery whirlwind. "Please tell me you've heard from Gunz."

Aidan frowned, just now realizing that it wasn't anger that set the Fire Elemental ablaze. It was fear. For the first time since he'd met the Great Salamander, this formidable, ancient being of magic showed signs of distress, and that made him freeze in place, unable to make a sound.

"Aidan!" shouted Gwyn ap Nudd. "Have you had any communications from Gunz in the last twenty-four hours! You still have the psychic link with him, don't you?"

Aidan flinched and cleared his throat. "I do, Father," he replied. "But I haven't heard from Zane for a while. I've been in the Otherworld for the last six months. You're better off asking Yaroslav or Agent Andrews."

Kal waved his hand impatiently, stopping him. "We just met with Agent Andrews." In so many words, he told Aidan everything that had happened in the FBI Office.

"I believe Chernobog has him. I'm positive that the black portal that pulled Gunz in was a door into the Dark Nav. It has such a distinct energy signature that it's hard to mistake it for anything else," said Viggo Warrington. "Neither Kal nor I are welcome there, and since Gwyn ap Nudd is bound to the Otherworld, we were wondering if you could take a quick trip to the Slavic world of demons and spirits?"

"A quick trip," echoed Aidan and slowly lowered down to the couch where Kal had been sitting just a moment ago. Tessa sat down next to him, her hand squeezing his elbow gently. He glanced at her but couldn't say a word, thousands of thoughts crowding his mind. Carefully, he opened himself to the flow of magic, searching for Gunz through their psychic link. But no matter how hard he tried, his friend remained silent, a dark void taking the place of their usual connection.

"Dammit, Zane..." He pressed his hand to his eyes, chills spreading through him. Then he glanced at Viggo and slowly shook his head. "I wish I could. The Dark Nav is a locked-down realm. Not even all gods of the Slavic pantheon can travel there. Besides, once you get there, you're at the mercy of Chernobog. None of us can enter the Dark Nav and find their way back. Not even Angel, despite the fact that the Nav is one of his domains." His mind traveled back to his last visit to the Slavic realm of spirit and demons, his fingers fidgeting with the Guardians' pendant absentmindedly. "We need to summon Veles—the Slavic god of the Three Realms," he added at length. "I believe he's our only hope."

"Fine," grumbled Kal. "Gwyn, lift your wards. Let's summon Veles."

Gwyn turned to Kal, doubt written all over his face. "Kal, I'm sorry, but you'll have to leave to do that. I can open the door into the labyrinth, but I can't lift the wards around the Other-world. It's too dangerous." He frowned, his silvery eyes glowing brighter. "Who is to say the evil triad didn't arrange this situation just to get me to remove the wards? The veil is weak as it is, and I can't leave the Otherworld and the Isle of Legends unprotected."

"Fire Almighty," muttered Kal, exchanging a quick look with War. "You're probably right. But I have to do something. Open your door, Gwyn, I'll go back into the labyrinth—"

"Kal..." Viggo Warrington groaned and bent forward, clutching his chest with his hand, his fingers almost tearing through his white shirt. The blood-colored flames of War surrounded him, wrapping around his arms, flowing through his hair. "Kal," he repeated breathlessly, grabbing the Great Sala-mander's arm. "It's Gunz. He is using my power. It's violent, I can feel it from here... Oh, God... I'm not sure he even knows he's doing it."

Aidan's eyes darted from Kal to War and back. "How is that possible?" he asked, rising. "He gave you the ring back, Viggo. He can't be connected to the power of Four."

Releasing Kal's arm, Viggo Warrington straightened and readjusted his suit, throwing a desperate look at the Great Salamander. Kal sighed, fire igniting in his deeply set eyes.

"I have to, Viggo," he said softly. "I'm sorry. It was my mistake, but now I have no choice but to bring your secret out into the open. This is the only way to deal with this situation. They must know the truth."

"Weren't you the one to give me the lecture on the importance of always telling the truth to those you love?" grumbled Viggo Warrington bitterly. The color had drained from his face, and his lips formed a tight, straight line.

"Viggo, I'm deeply sorry—," Kal started, throwing his hands up, but War interrupted him, gesturing for him to proceed.

"What's going on here?" asked Aidan, tension settling in his shoulders, making his heart race. "What mistake are you talking about, Kal?"

Kal reached into his pocket and brought up a small jewelry box, offering it to Aidan. Unsure what he was going to find there, he took it, but before he lifted the top, his fingers lingered over it, trembling slightly. Slowly, he opened the box and held his breath as the undiluted energy of War assailed his senses.

A beautifully crafted ring with a large red stone shone dimly against the black lining of the box. Even embedded into the *Ardenium* steel, the power of the stone was overwhelming. Aidan lifted the ring gently with two fingers, and his eyes flashed to Viggo's right hand where he saw another ring with a red stone that looked like a copy of the one he was holding.

"The second jewel of War," he whispered more to himself than to anyone else. "But why? No one except War can wear it, anyway." He placed the ring back into the box and closed it, giving it back to the Great Salamander. "Kal, I'm too tired to play the twenty-questions game. Just explain. Please."

"It's my fault," said Kal, remorse hiding in his deep voice. "After I told Viggo I would never make a stupid mistake like this…" He threw another glance at War and shook his head, a desperate look in his flaming eyes. "I just couldn't bring myself to tell Gunz the truth. I couldn't tell him that…" His voice trailed off, and he rubbed his forehead, deep lines etched around his tightly pressed mouth.

"Tell them," growled Viggo, "or I will do it myself."

Kal nodded but remained silent.

"Gunz is my biological son," said War, sounding flat and emotionless. "Once he put my ring on, assuming the mantle of the Horseman, he activated the power of War given to him by birth." He slammed his hand on the wall. "Goddamnit, Kal. I was positive that you'd told him by now and given him the ring. It's been over six months! I was the one who wanted to wait a little to give Gunz a few days to recover after everything he'd been put through. But not half a year!"

"Whoa… hold your horses!" Tessa got up, making a time-out sign with her hands. Her eyes darted from Kal to War, confusion written all over her face. "Gunz is the son of War. He's one of the Horseman? How the hell is that possible?"

"Do you need a step-by-step explanation on how it happened?" asked War and as drained as he looked, tones of sarcasm sounded in his voice.

"Ugh," muttered Tessa, rolling her eyes. "I mean, how is that possible as far as magic goes. I thought he is a Fire Salamander?"

"He is," replied Kal, slowly getting back to his normal self. "Years ago, Mrak Delar discovered the Fire in him, awakening the Fire Salamander part of his nature. Wearing the ring of War brought forth the power that had been bestowed upon him as his birthright." He dropped his head to his chest, biting his lip.

"And neither of you"—Gwyn ap Nudd pointed at Kal and then at War—"had enough brains to realize how dangerous this power was? Gunz is a good man and you two put him into a situation where he can destroy the world without even knowing that he's doing it!"

"This ring will help him keep the destructive part of my power under control," said Viggo Warrington quietly, barely meeting Gwyn's furious gaze.

"This ring? The one you failed to give him?" Gwyn ap Nudd punched the air, his body lighting up with the brilliant light of his magic. "What the hell is wrong with you? You, Kal, should have told him about his heritage and given him the ring. And you, Viggo, should have warned him of all the dangers this power presents and about the terrible consequences of using it." Gwyn stood, his chest shuddering with heavy breaths, his hands clenched into tight fists. "Damn you both! You should have taught him how to control it!"

"I wanted to tell him right away, Gwyn," said Kal apologetically, taking a step closer to the King of the Otherworld. "As soon as I learned the truth, I went to find him. He was with Yaroslav at the time and the idea of coming back to the realm of humans was devastating him. He was so tired and resigned that I just couldn't bring myself to add to his misery."

"Heaven and Earth!" yelled Gwyn ap Nudd, and the walls of his glass house trembled, the branches of the crystal chandelier jingling softly. "Both of you have been around for thousands of years and now you decided to spread your wings over him like you're human fathers instead of—" He cut himself off, shaking his head.

Aidan's eyes moved from his father to Kal and then to Viggo as he lowered himself on the couch, the horror of the situation settling heavily in the pit of his stomach.

"Stop it," he whispered and then added, almost shouting, "Stop arguing! Who cares! Pointing fingers and placing blame never helped anyone solve any problems. And we have a ginormous one!" He slammed his hand on the couch. "Now, we need to think about how to get Gunz out. Chernobog didn't summon him for a cup of coffee. He's been furious with Gunz since the battle for the City of Gold, and as far as I know, he's not one of the gods who forgives and forgets. If he's holding him, God knows what he is doing to him. If Gunz accidentally taps into the power of War..." His voice trailed off, and he held his breath, staring at Gwyn ap Nudd with wide eyes. "We need to summon Veles." He threw a scorching gaze at Kal. "Now would be a good time."

Kal smirked tiredly and nodded at Gwyn ap Nudd. "Go ahead, Gwyn. Let me out into the labyri—"

He didn't finish speaking and froze in place with his mouth open, heat rising around him, making the air shimmer and swirl like a mirage.

"Kalidus!" Gwyn took a step closer to his friend, deep worry reflected in his silvery eyes, but Kal raised his hand, stopping him. Gwyn ap Nudd muttered a quick spell, and a dense shield of his power enveloped the Great Salamander, keeping the smoldering heat inside.

A moment later, the fire energy spiked to a new high, and Kal threw his head back, spreading his arms as smoldering flames enveloped his body. A strangled growl thundered in his throat, and he brought his hands together, interlocking his fingers.

A flaming wall expanded inside the power shield as Kal reverted into the natural state of the Fire Salamander. When the fire dwindled down, Aidan saw Kal kneeling with his hand braced against the floor. With a strained groan, the Fire Elemental got up and raked his flaming hair with his fingers, tucking a few loose strands behind his ears. Still breathing strenuously, he brushed his shoulders, extinguishing the last tiny flames.

"Something's wrong," he said quietly, meeting Viggo's puzzled gaze. "It felt like..." He didn't finish and shook his head, averting his eyes.

"He can't die," whispered War. "He's a Great Fire Salamander and the son of War. It's impossible."

"Yes, he can," objected Kal, catching his breath. "We all can die, including you, Viggo. There is no such thing as unconditional immortality. The Black Fire can kill a Fire Salamander, but that's not what I was going to say."

He walked back to one of the armchairs and dropped into it heavily as if his massive legs could no longer hold the weight of his body.

"I was going to say that as the Fire Elemental, I can sense when my children are in distress," continued Kal. "I'm almost sure Gunz just died the human death. At least, that's what it felt like to me." He leaned forward and squeezed his head with his hands, his fingers digging into his scalp. "I felt him dying before. Hell, I killed him myself a few times during training, just so he would know what to expect... But this?" He lifted his shoulders in a half-shrug and threw his hands up, dropping them back down on the armrests with a soft thud. "This didn't feel right. There is something seriously wrong, and I just can't figure out what it is."

Gwyn ap Nudd frowned, and the light of his magic became brighter, reflecting off the white walls and polished floors. "Something tells me we're about to find out, my friend," he said softly and closed his eyes as if listening to something only he could hear. "Two Slavic deities are at the gates into the Otherworld, demanding an entry. One of them is the god of Fire."

CHAPTER 14

~ AIDAN ~

Gwyn ap Nudd opened the door, and two tall men emerged through the brilliant white light. One of them was as tall as Kal, and the powerful energy surrounding him was as potent as that of the Fire Elemental. He was clad in ancient Russian armor, and a giant sword in a leather scabbard sheathed at his belt looked just as intimidating as its owner. His bright red hair fell to his back and shoulders in long waves, and his beard and mustache, shining with red and orange shades, competed with the brightness of real flames.

The second man was taller, but even with his wide shoulders and muscled build, he looked refined and almost delicate next to the first man. With his shoulder-length white hair and white clothes, he blended in perfectly with Gwyn's décor. He wasn't armed—at least he appeared unarmed—but his mighty energy signature suggested that this powerful, ancient god didn't need any weapons to be dangerous.

Aidan just threw one glance at both of them, and he knew who they were right away—Semargl, the Slavic god of the Fire and Belobog, the god of Light and Creation, Chernobog's twin brother and arch frenemy. There was no love lost between the twins, and the presence of Belobog here set Aidan's mind into an entangled frenzy of thoughts and worries.

The man in white met Aidan's troubled gaze, and although a crooked smirk appeared on his lips, his deep, blue eyes remained sad. Despite his mighty appearance, there was something in the set of his shoulders and in the way he moved that made Aidan think the Slavic deity wasn't at his best at the moment.

"Well, hello there," said Belobog quietly, sounding just as exhausted as he appeared.

He inclined his head just a little, and it wasn't clear whether he was trying to show them that while he respected them, he was still above them in the food chain, or he was just too tired for appropriate ceremonial bows. His attentive gaze stopped on Viggo Warrington, and his mouth opened slightly as if he was ready to say something but then changed his mind.

"*Goy esi, dobri molodtsi,*" Semargl rumbled an ancient Russian greeting, rolling his R's generously. He pressed his hand to his chest and bowed low, almost touching the ground with his fingers.

"Welcome," said Gwyn ap Nudd, waving at the couch. "Please sit down. Tell us how we can be of assistance?"

"Thank you, Lord Hunter," said Semargl. He lowered on the couch with a grunt, making it moan under his weight, but Belobog just nodded to Gwyn ap Nudd and remained standing.

"Kalidus, my brother," continued Semargl, turning his massive torso toward the Fire Elemental. "Tell me you felt it? Your child's suffering?"

Kal nodded, staring down at the Slavic deity. "I did," he said, his fingers curving into fists. "Can you tell me what happened, Semargl?" He wiped perspiration off his forehead with the back of his hand and dropped his arm powerlessly.

"I do not know much, brother." Semargl readjusted the position of his sword and shifted uncomfortably. "Luckily, I happened to be in the Land of Dreams when I detected a spike in the fire energy field and recognized the young Salamander. His energy signature was suppressed almost immediately, but his cry of pain was so powerful, I had no doubt it was him." He stopped talking and sighed, running his hand over his long beard. "Anyway, by the time I got there, it was too late. Chernobog forced his dark blade through your boy's heart and teleported him somewhere outside my reach. That's all I know, brother, but Belobog has more information for you, yes?" He turned to Belobog, cocking his copper eyebrows.

Everyone turned to the white deity. He smirked and leaned his back against the wall, folding his arms over his chest. Tilting his head to the side a little, he regarded Kal calmly, and his gaze glided from one face to the next, lingering on Tessa a moment too long. For a split second, his blue eyes narrowed, but he didn't say anything and returned his attention to the Great Salamander.

"Your boy is truly something else, isn't he?" he said so softly that Aidan had to strain his hearing.

"One of a kind pain in my neck," grumbled Kal, throwing a warning glance at Viggo. "Just tell me what happened."

"Yeah," murmured Belobog, rubbing his chin absentmindedly. "Your boy did something none of us expected. Neither my brother nor I." He chuckled, shaking his head.

"What did he do?" asked Kal, his voice a hoarse whisper.

"From what I understand, my brother held him in the Dark Nav, restrained inside the God's snare. He wanted your son to give him the Dark Codex." He fell silent for a brief moment, his gaze growing slightly unfocused. "I don't know how, but Chernobog convinced the young Salamander to transfer the Codex to him."

"Wait... What? No! Gunz would never do that," started Kal, but Belobog raised his hand, asking for silence.

"Your boy didn't give me the impression of someone who

breaks easily," continued Belobog. "My guess—and this is just a guess—Chernobog showed him something, convincing him that he needed the help of the Dark Codex." Aidan moved, ready to ask a question, but Belobog raised his hand again, stopping him. "Don't ask me what that was because I have no idea. Anyway, he complied with Chernobog's demands, but not exactly in the way my brother expected." He smirked. "Instead of transferring the Codex to Chernobog, he summoned me and split the Dark Codex between us."

"You don't say," muttered Gwyn ap Nudd, staring at the Slavic deity in disbelief. "Clever boy. He killed two birds with one stone."

"Exactly," agreed Belobog, a faint smile ghosting his lips. "Now, my twin brother and I are bound by more than our blood. The only way Chernobog can use the power of the Codex is by working together." He smirked at Kal, giving him an arched stare. "Your son achieved something our father has been trying to accomplish for centuries and failed miserably. My brother and I can no longer fight. The Dark Codex doesn't let us raise weapons against each other."

"Something tells me Chernobog wasn't pleased," mumbled Aidan.

"You got that right," agreed Belobog. For the next few minutes, the god of Light told them everything that had happened on the Isle Buyan. He spoke slowly as if every word took a significant effort and when he finally finished, a heavy silence engulfed the living room.

"So, he chose to save Voron. He saved Chernobog's right-hand man instead of himself," said Viggo Warrington quietly, lowering his head to hide the shadow of pain crossing his face.

"That's Gunz for you, Viggo," huffed Gwyn ap Nudd, gazing heavenwards, but the corners of his lips lifted a little in a soft smile. "The Ancient Master used to say that his instinct of self-preservation is below zero. As you can see, he was right."

"So, how can we find him?" asked Aidan.

"That's going to be challenging," replied Belobog. "When I was leaving, Gunz was completely drained, both magically and physically. It took all he had to complete the enchantment that split the Codex. But that's not the worst. I noticed that the manacles Chernobog had placed on him had the God's snare runes engraved into them. I wouldn't be surprised if my brother activated them before killing your son, Kal." He threw a glance full of sympathy at the Great Salamander. "We both know what that means, right?"

"No..." Kal froze in place, his face a silent mask of horror. "No, please tell me he didn't do it to my boy." His voice shook, and he swallowed, his skin turning a sickly greenish-yellow color. "That's beyond cruel..."

"I'm sorry, Kal," said Belobog, remorse making his voice sound deeper. "Even though I knew that the Prav is off-limits for Voron, I took him there because the gardens of Prav is the only place where he would be safe from my brother's wrath. I returned to the World Tree almost immediately to see if I still could help Gunz, but I was too late." He glanced to the side, his lips twisting with silent anger. "I was too late to help him, but I had a few unpleasant minutes alone with my brother before Semargl arrived and interrupted us. Your son told me I should be kind to my brother because he needs my help. And I tried..."

He bit his lip and looked up at Gwyn's white ceiling. The pregnant silence took over the room, but no one made a sound, waiting for Belobog to continue.

"I swear, I tried," he said at length, returning his gaze to Kal. "We couldn't fight each other. Not anymore. The only thing we could do was talk, but my brother was too angry and too upset to be reasoned with. He returned to the Dark Nav before I could get anything out of him. One thing I know for sure though, something is seriously wrong, and since Chernobog refuses to talk to me, the only person who can tell us what's going on is Gunz. We must find him as soon as possible."

"My question still stands," said Aidan. "How do we do that? Chernobog could've sent him to any corner of Creation. Any world. Any time. Any place. How can we find him?"

Belobog smirked. "No, young god, he couldn't," he objected softly. "He was too drained after the Dark Codex transfer. To be honest, I have no idea how Gunz survived the merging process in the first place. It's draining, intense and the pain is"—he shuddered, opening his arms—"more than anyone who's not a god could handle. How did he survive it with his mind intact? He's not a god after all."

It was Kal's turn to smirk. "Let's say there's more to my son than meets the eye," he said, gesturing for Belobog to continue.

Belobog frowned but didn't push the matter.

"What I was trying to say," he continued, "was that after the transfer, Chernobog was too tired to send him far or to warp the fabric of time and reality to transport him in time." Belobog moved his hand up and down, pointing at himself. "Look at me. I can barely speak, I'm so drained. Chernobog was in an even worse condition. Anyway, after my brother left, I tried to search for Gunz, but to no avail. However, I am sure he's not in the Dark Nav. That would be too obvious. So, knowing how my brother's mind works and his magical and physical limitations at the time of the event, I'm positive, Kal, your son is some- where within the boundaries of the nexus."

Aidan observed the room. Everyone remained silent, deep in their own thoughts, and the atmosphere was beyond general concern or fear.

"I'm going to the Land of Dreams," he said, throwing an apologetic glance at Tessa. "I can't leave Gunz when he needs my help the most."

"No, you are not," objected Gwyn ap Nudd calmly, raking Aidan with a heavy gaze of his silvery eyes. Leaning forward in his armchair, he set his palms down flat on the table. "I agree, we must recover the young Salamander as soon as possible, but you're forgetting that you and Tessa have a quest which is just as important if not more so. I believe we have options other than you or Therasia for this mission."

"Who?" asked Aidan. "As far as I know, the Master of Kendral asked Mrak Delar to stay in the realm of Magic until they were done reinforcing all the entry points. If Mrak and I are out of the picture, who else is powerful enough to search the Land of Dreams for Gunz? You're stuck here until the next Samhain. Besides, you and Kal should remain in the Otherworld to defend the veil in case the situation with the evil triad escalates."

"If I may suggest," rumbled Semargl, raising his hand in a thick leather glove. Gwyn ap Nudd gave him a short nod, and he continued, "It is not going to be easy to find the young Salamander. Even after the restoration process is over, his energy—"

"Restoration process?" whispered Tessa, her eyes wide. "That doesn't sound good. What does it mean?"

Semargl glanced at her, and his lips twitched slightly. "I am sorry, my lady, Kalidus will have to give you a detailed explanation later. In short—the Fire Salamander is immortal. When Chernobog's sword pierced your friend's heart, he died the human death, and the Fire Salamander in him took over, restoring his body back to life."

Kal grunted, the fire energy spiking around him, but he nodded to Semargl to continue.

"The biggest problem is that even after the restoration process is completed," said Semargl, "it will be impossible to detect his energy signature because it is suppressed by the God's snare. And since the enchantment was placed by the god of Destruction, I can assure you it is quite potent. So, even if you find your friend, it is not going to be easy to set him free." He glanced at Kal and pressed his fist to his chest. "My apologies, brother, but I cannot offer my help. My lord Svarog demands my presence elsewhere."

"Then I'm the only god available," said Aidan.

"Forgive me, my lord." Semargl bowed slightly, hiding a smirk under his flaming mustache. "You are a Celtic demigod enhanced by Gwyn ap Nudd's powers. I do not doubt your capability, but for this quest, you should send someone who belongs to the Slavic pantheon and has the full power of a god. Only a Slavic deity stands a chance of breaking Chernobog's God's snare." He looked around the room and added, "Since Belobog must return to the Prav, I'm referring to my little kinsman, Svyatobor. He is well acquainted with the young Salamander, and he knows every tree in the nexus. If anyone can find your friend and bring him back, it is him."

"I second that," said Kal, leaning back in his chair.

Aidan sighed, unease spreading through him, but there was no reason to argue Semargl's point. Besides, Gwyn ap Nudd was right. Finding Perun was important not only because of the upcoming war with the evil triad, but also for Tessa.

"Fine," he replied. "I'm going to travel back to the human realm and talk to Svyatobor."

"Why can't you summon him here?" Tessa got up and approached him, her fingers interlacing with his.

"I can, but I prefer not to," he replied, gently covering her hand with his. "It's late, but I want to take a quick trip back to the human realm before we leave in the morning." He turned to Gwyn ap Nudd before continuing. "It's been a while, and I want to assess the situation. Talk to Svyatobor, Uri and Angel and see what's going on."

"Good idea," muttered the King of the Otherworld. "The reports we've been receiving from the local Master Warden and Lord Agent Andrews are troubling. I wish you'd done it a while ago, but better late than never." He tapped Aidan's shoulder. "Be quick. The sooner Svyatobor starts his search, the better."

Aidan hugged Tessa, pulling her to his chest. "Two-three hours," he whispered into her ear, planting a tender kiss on her cheek. "I'll be back before you know it." He straightened and added louder, "Don't let my father harass you in any way." He sent a threatening gaze to Gwyn ap Nudd.

The King of the Otherworld laughed, placing his hands on his hips. "I wouldn't dare, son." He waved his hand and opened the door.

Semargl got up, straightening his armor and readjusting his scabbard. "I must go. Duty calls," he said with his usual low bow. "If you need my assistance, do not hesitate to summon me."

Belobog muttered quick goodbyes and headed toward the doorway. His moves were slow and heavy, and he seemed to be more drained than he was when he arrived. "I must go back to the Prav," he said softly. "It's not easy for me to stay in the realm of Death. My apologies."

Aidan threw one more glance at Tessa and walked through the blazing rectangle of light, following the two Slavic deities. As he emerged in the darkness of the underground labyrinth, he found Belobog standing by the wall with his arms crossed behind his back. The soft glimmer of his power partially illuminated the cave, making shifty shadows slither away, hiding in the dark passages.

Aidan halted, his brows slowly rising. Semargl was gone, and seeing the god of Light standing alone, waiting for him, set his mind on high alert.

"Aodh mac Lir," said Belobog, taking a step closer. "As drained as I feel, I'm not going back to the Prav right away. I'm going to go back to the World Tree and see if I can summon my brother for one more heart-to-heart conversation."

He touched Aidan's pendant and sent a touch of his magical energy through it. A soft ping sounded in Aidan's mind, and he gasped, taking a step back involuntarily.

"Guardians," murmured Belobog. "They found a way to put a

leash on the god of the Otherworld. Creative little bastards." He chuckled darkly. "Anyway, for once their toys would serve for the greater purpose. If you feel that ping, it's me summoning you. Come to the Isle Buyan. I don't want to use open summoning calls. They can be traced and with everything that's going on, I don't know who I can or cannot trust."

"Yes, my lord," replied Aidan with a light bow.

"Wish me luck." Belobog snapped his fingers and vanished.

"Yeah... good luck.... Something tells me we are all going to need it," muttered Aidan and teleported out of the labyrinth.

CHAPTER 15

~ AIDAN ~

Aidan manifested in a dark alley behind a desolate building that used to be occupied by a large supermarket before it went out of business. Now it stood empty with its doors blocked by metal shutters and its parking lot vacant. Somewhere in the distance, the low rumbling of motorcycle engines ruptured the silence, followed by piercing screams, heavy thuds and loud bangs that sounded like gunshots. The harsh smell of smoke touched Aidan's senses, and he sped up his already quick pace, heading toward the exit from the plaza.

As he reached the intersection of two major streets, bright orange flares illuminated the horizon, and he halted, sharpening his senses. The screams and shouting accompanied by the sounds of shattered glass grew louder, and soon Aidan could see the heavy mass of a raging mob moving along the road.

A few men on black motorcycles rode slowly in front of the frenzied crowd. Dressed in leather and wrapped in chains, they brandished their spiked clubs, baseball bats and maces, fueling violence and egging on already frantic people. The mob crashed the store displays, threw torches inside and set on fire the few cars parked on mostly empty parking lots.

The demonic essence, the energy of Chaos, and the vibe of hatred and violence they exuded were so heavy, Aidan didn't need to use his other sight to know that the riot was driven by supernatural forces. After reading the reports sent to him by the Guardians, he knew what to expect. However, now that he was finally back in Florida, watching the turmoil with his own eyes, it looked a lot worse than he imagined. He shuddered inwardly, cursing himself for spending almost seven months in the Otherworld and leaving his friends and his city unsupported.

The shrieks of police sirens rose above the racket of the crazed mob and rumbling of the motorcycles, and Aidan knew that he had a few minutes at the most before local law enforcement agencies would arrive. He wasn't sure how he was going to deal with the riot and the demonic motorcycle gang. Demons had to be vanquished, but he couldn't kill humans infected by demonic essence. They were innocent in all this.

He lifted his hand ready to teleport closer, but before he could snap his fingers, a new group of people materialized out of thin air, blocking the street. A tall man in the center of the group raised his hand, the bright flares of fire reflecting in the mass of his long, golden hair. The mob halted about a hundred yards away, glowering at the people standing in their path.

Yaroslav... Aidan snapped his fingers and teleported, materializing behind the group of Akira's vampires.

"Are you here to help, my lord, or just to observe, working in mysterious ways as all gods do?" Yaroslav's voice was quiet and full of sarcasm, but a glimmer of happiness shone in his glowing scarlet eyes, and a wide grin split his face.

"You got that right," muttered Aidan snidely. "I'm not here for this"—he flicked his wrist at the yellow-eyed crowd breathing with the energy of Chaos—"demonic bullshit. But since you prayed so fervently for my help, I may as well get involved. What do you want me to do, Slavik?"

"You see these leather-clad, stinky assholes on bikes?"

Yaroslav pointed at the gangsters surrounding the mob like shepherds would a flock of mindless sheep. "There are maybe ten of them at most. You don't need to fight. Let my team take care of them. After the demonic influence is eliminated, all you have to do is purify those people's minds and they're good to go home. I'm sure you'd do it much faster than Jim's newly hired wizards would."

"Jim hired wizards?" asked Aidan, but then waved his hand, narrowing his eyes at the fire flares that were growing brighter with each passing moment. "Never mind that. I'll take care of the fires once we are done, too. I hope no one is going to drive through this area while all this is going on. Humans and their smartphones with cameras..." He shuddered. "Exposing the World of Magic and getting innocent bystanders hurt—that's all we need."

"Well, there is never a guarantee that someone isn't filming us from one of the windows right now." Yaroslav glanced around, listening to something intently. "But Jim's team and police have this area surrounded and blocked, so we don't expect any new humans coming in. And the Destiny Council promised to take care of any possible exposure. Let's deal with this little riot swiftly and then we can talk."

He stepped forward, unsheathing his katana. Without saying a word, Yaroslav glanced back at his team, and they all vanished, moving so fast that even Aidan couldn't follow their movements. A short pause got replaced by the mayhem of a battle as the demons hopped off their bikes, trying to resist the attack of Akira's vampires and upirs.

While demons who possessed human bodies were stronger and faster than any average man, they were no match for trained vampires and upirs with their lightning speed, agility and super-strength. Weaving in and out through the crowd, the vampires singled out the demons, destroying them before they could fight back while keeping humans out of harm's way. With only ten demons driving the crowd, the fight was over before it started.

Yaroslav came to a screeching stop before Aidan, making him flinch.

"All yours." He flashed his open-hearted smile that exposed his long fangs and pointed at the crowd of people who were no longer shouting, breaking stores and setting cars on fire. They stood, staring around wildly, their wide eyes filled with confusion. But Aidan could still sense the energy of Chaos permeating the air above the crowd, and there was still a slight yellow glimmer in their irises.

He channeled his magic and made a circling motion, whispering a quick spell. For a brief moment, the glowing dome of his shield lingered in the air, emitting a soft, white light, but then quickly dissipated. He walked through it and started to chant. As his voice got louder, sounding like the most beautiful song, all other sounds disappeared and people froze in place, transfixed. Slowly, the yellowish light vanished from their eyes and the energy of Chaos disappeared.

Aidan waved his hand, removing the shield and glanced at the stunned people. "Go home," he said softly. "I'm sure your families are worried about you."

As the crowd of confused people started to disperse, he connected with the elemental energy of Water and walked down the street, extinguishing the fires. Thick clouds of dark smoke rose high above the destroyed neighborhood, veiling the already starless sky, the reek of burned plastic and wood polluting the air.

Once sure all the fires were extinguished, he turned around and found that Akira's vampires were gone. Yaroslav was standing alone on the dark, empty street, holding his cell phone in his hands. The vampire dialed a phone number and brought the device to his ear.

"Jim?" He raised his index finger, gesturing for Aidan to wait.

"Yes, all set." He fell silent, listening to Jim, a scarlet glimmer gradually melting into the blue depth of his eyes. "No, all demons are dead. Send your people to clean up the dead bodies. No civilian casualties." He nodded, listening to whatever the agent was saying, but then shook his head and sighed. "No, I haven't heard from Gunz. I'll let you know if anything comes up."

He hung up and put his phone in the inside pocket of his leather coat. "I assume you're here because of Gunz," he said, meeting Aidan's eyes.

"You know?"

"Jim told me," replied Yaroslav, sheathing his katana beneath his coat. "He said Kal and some other man he had never met before were there when it happened. Do you know anything about it?"

Aidan nodded, an unusual tightness in his chest making it hard to speak. "Do you have a few minutes to talk?" he asked after a moment.

"Of course."

"Let's talk somewhere more private." Aidan placed his hand on Yaroslav's shoulder and snapped his fingers.

* * *

THEY MANIFESTED inside Tessa's apartment. It was dark and quiet, but Aidan didn't need light to find his way around. He walked to the wall and quickly found the light switch, flipping it on. His iPad still lay on the coffee table. The memory of him spending time with Tessa in this small apartment surfaced in his mind, and his heart skipped a beat. He swallowed, suppressing the longing, reminding himself that in a few hours he would return to the Otherworld where she was waiting for him.

"Can I get you anything?" he asked Yaroslav, gesturing for him to sit down.

The vampire took his coat off and threw it over the armrest of the couch. "Unless you have a bag of B negative somewhere, I'm good." He sat down and leaned back, folding his arms on his lap.

Aidan hesitated for a moment, but then decided against coffee and sat down on the couch next to Yaroslav. The vampire glanced at him sideways but didn't say anything.

"I'm sorry," started Aidan.

"About?"

"Not being here to help you and Gunz, and the rest of the team."

Yaroslav shrugged. "You had your hands full in the Otherworld. We're handling it."

Aidan leaned forward and took the tablet. With habitual movements, he turned it on and opened the local news website, quickly browsing through the headlines. It seemed like every article he could find on the first page was about riots, vandalism, drive-by shootings, and other criminal activities in the area. Yaroslav glanced at the screen and leaned back, crossing his legs at the knee.

"It's a lot worse than they show it in the news," he said quietly.

"Really?" Aidan glanced back at him. "How so? Usually, news likes to paint with darker colors."

"The reporters have no idea who, or rather what, stands behind all this mess." Yaroslav waved in the direction of the screen, his entire demeanor showing just how much he cared about the local news. "If they knew the whole truth..." He trailed off and chuckled softly. "Can you imagine the headlines? *Demonic motorcycle gang keeps terrorizing local neighborhoods.*' Or *Vandals infected by the energy of Chaos destroyed local magic shop.*' Or my personal favorite *24/7 Demon summoning services. Limited time offer—summon one demon, get one free!*'"

Aidan smiled at his friend's undying, dark sense of humor but quickly sobered up and put the tablet back on the table.

"Slavik, Gunz is in serious trouble," he said at length. "Let me summon Svyatobor first, so I don't have to repeat everything twice."

"Svyatobor?" asked Yaroslav, his eyebrows climbing up. "I don't even know in which part of the world he's in now. Haven't seen him here for a while."

"It doesn't matter where he is. He'll hear my summoning call. I need him," Aidan sighed and bit his lip. "Apparently, I'm not enough of a god for this mission. To make a long story short, I don't have what it takes to find Gunz and bring him back. Out of all of us, Svyatobor is the only one who can do it."

"Damn, that sounds promising," muttered Yaroslav darkly, but then waved his hand. "Go on, summon him."

Aidan channeled his power and drew a glowing white rune in the air, infusing it with his magical energy. He touched the rune with his fingers and whispered a summoning spell. For a while, everything remained the same. Aidan exchanged a troubled look with Yaroslav and was about to increase the potency of the summoning call when the air in the middle of the living area shimmered, and a slim young man dressed in a motorcycle jacket and leather pants manifested in a cloud of bright, green sparkles.

His wavy blond hair was matted with sweat, and his face was pale bordering on green. The front of his jacket and pants was coated in something slimy, and his boots were covered in dark brown splatters that looked like dried blood. Breathing laboriously, as if he just ran a few miles, Svyatobor spun around, taking in his surroundings. But as the gaze of his velvety, green eyes halted on Aidan, joy softened his features.

"Aodh." He sighed with relief and took a step toward him, his eyes darting from Aidan to Yaroslav and back. "Thank the gods, man. You're okay."

"I'm fine," replied Aidan, rising. "Sorry, I should've stayed in touch with all of you, but I was a little busy reinforcing the veil and the boundaries of the Otherworld."

Svyatobor, the Slavic god of Nature, or as they used to call him—Sven, had always been a lot slimmer than him, but now he looked almost fragile. Aidan pulled his old friend into a fast embrace, accompanied by a light tap on his back. "I'm glad to see you, Sven," he added softly, gesturing for him to sit down, "but I don't have time for small talk. Zane needs your help."

"Zane?" asked Svyatobor. "What did that Fire Gecko get himself into now?"

"For once, it's not his fault. It may take a few minutes to explain."

Once Svyatobor settled on the love seat, he told him and Yaroslav everything he knew about Gunz's disappearance and his current situation. They listened without interrupting and when he finished, both remained motionless and silent for a few long minutes. Then Svyatobor scratched the back of his head, ruffling the soft curls of his light hair.

"Blasted Chernobog," he muttered, shaking his head. "Do you know how enormous the nexus is? It may take me years to find Zane. Especially if his magical signature is suppressed."

"I know, but the nexus is your domain. If anyone can do it fast, it's you," replied Aidan. "So, the sooner you get started the better. Visit Lady Gatekeeper. Perhaps she or her guarding spirit, Darling Lily, can shed some light on this situation."

Svyatobor nodded and got up, shaking the dust and dirt off his pants. Aidan glanced down at Tessa's used-to-be-clean floor and sighed, worry gnawing at his heart.

"Are you going to take my place in this realm while I'm playing detective? Someone needs to help Uri and Angel," said Svyatobor, giving him an arched stare. "It's a jungle out there."

"There is something else I must do before I can return here," replied Aidan, rising from his seat. "But I'll be back as soon as I can."

He extended his hand to Svyatobor, and the god of Nature squeezed it in his. "Once I'm in the nexus, we won't be able to communicate." He dropped his arm, looking just as troubled as Aidan felt. "With Chaos ruling the human realm and the god of Destruction on the path of war, I don't want to use any magic that can be traced. I think it would be better if neither Skiper-Zmey nor Chernobog knew that I'm out there, searching for Zane."

"Dammit," muttered Aidan, rubbing his shoulder. "So, if you're in danger, you have no way to call me for help."

The old wound he'd received a long time ago while he traveled through the infected nexus started to ache. It was healed and there wasn't even a scar left to remind him of the old injury, but whenever he felt troubled, a dull pain throbbed in his shoulder, resonating in his chest.

"I'm a god. Besides, like you said, the nexus is my domain. Every tree, every lake, every creature in the forest obeys my command." Svyatobor shrugged, his usual mischievous smile making a brief appearance. "What could go wrong? Everything is going to be fine, Aidan. If anything, I can try to summon Semargl. The old man loves me. He'll never say no if I ask for help."

"Yes, you are a god, but we are all old and experienced enough to know that even gods can be killed when given enough hard work and perseverance," Aidan objected softly.

"Come on, my friend, you have nothing to worry about." Svyatobor glanced at him reproachfully. "I'll be in my own realm, in my element. I'll be fine."

Aidan listened to Svyatobor's voice overflowing with confidence but felt none of it. Feeling a touch to his shoulder, he snapped around and saw Yaroslav standing next to him.

"Listen, Aidan, I think Svyatobor is right. The nexus has

been purified and demon-free, but as Mrak would say, it's better to expect the unexpected. So, I have a solution," said the vampire, putting his coat on. "I'll go with Svyatobor. You and I are still connected. I can communicate with you at any time."

Aidan frowned, nibbling on his lip. Letting Yaroslav go with Svyatobor would take two powerful fighters out of the human realm in this dark time, but letting Svyatobor go alone was risky too. Besides, it was Gunz's life on the line. He couldn't risk it.

"Akira is going to kill me," he mumbled.

"I'm not going to tell her if you won't," suggested Yaroslav with a sly wink. "I'll be back before she knows."

"Somehow, I doubt it." Aidan sighed, giving up.

"I'll check in every day," promised Yaroslav, placing his hand on Svyatobor's shoulder.

The god of Nature snapped his fingers, and a thick mist of green sparkles surrounded both of them. When the mist dissipated, both Yaroslav and Svyatobor were gone.

For one last time, Aidan looked around the empty room. As his eyes halted on the large clock on the wall showing three in the morning, he sighed and headed toward the entrance door. Only three hours left before Tessa and he would have to leave the Otherworld and travel to the Angel Oak Tree, searching for Perun. He couldn't even imagine how the idea of possibly meeting her powerful and mysterious biological father could be making her feel.

This time, we are doing it together, my love, thought Aidan. *I will never leave you...*

He turned the light off and snapped his fingers, teleporting out of the dark apartment.

CHAPTER 16

~ TESSA ~

When Aidan quietly opened the door into their bedroom, Tessa wasn't sleeping, but she didn't turn, waiting for him to undress and get into bed. She didn't know what time it was. Gwyn's house had no clocks, and she didn't wear a wristwatch, relying on her cell phone. Since the Otherworld didn't have cell service, she didn't have much use for it and had left it on the small table at the other end of the room.

With the kind of lifestyle they had, time didn't make much of a difference to her—she was always worried about him no matter what time it was. The only thing she cared about was that he was back with her and safe. The current situation in the human realm was beyond alarming, and she caught herself thinking how relieved she felt listening to his soft steps across the bedroom floor.

Aidan got undressed and slipped under the blanket, careful not to wake her up. As he draped his arm over her shoulder, her lips formed a blissful smile, and she shifted closer to him, feeling the coolness of his firm stomach and chest against her back. He buried his face into her hair, kissing her head softly.

"I love you," she whispered. His embrace tightened as he

pulled her into his chest, purring something into her hair like a large cat. "We should get some sleep, Aidan... leaving early in the morning and all..."

She closed her eyes, and a moment later she was asleep.

* * *

THE MORNING PASSED by in one continuous blur of events and conversations. To her surprise, Gwyn ap Nudd behaved like any normal father would, worrying about Aidan and trying to make sure he had everything he might need during the trip. But instead of asking if he had his driver's license, cell phone and some cash in his wallet, he was worried about Aidan's sword and who he was going to summon in case of emergency.

Like through a fog, she heard Aidan and Gwyn ap Nudd ask her something, but she could barely comprehend their questions, answering in single-syllable words. Soon they let her be, most likely realizing her state of mind.

After the conversation with Kal and War, her concerns about Zane's situation surfaced with a new strength, setting her nerves on edge. Even though Aidan did his best to explain why Zane was the one destined to face the Lord of Chaos sooner or later, she couldn't understand why it had to be him. Alone. So, finding Perun and getting him involved was the only way she could help her friend, and that fact alone made the success of her mission increasingly important.

No matter how much she tried, she couldn't think about Perun as her father. She didn't know this man. He abandoned her on the steps of a church the moment she was born and had never made his presence known or even attempted to contact her. The only thing she knew about him was that he was one of the most powerful gods of the Slavic pantheon, and the only god who had fought Skiper-Zmey before and won. Whether he accepted her as his daughter or not, she couldn't care less. All she wanted was his support in the fight against the Lord of Chaos and the other two monsters.

By the time Tessa finally walked through the shining door Gwyn had opened for them, she was a ball of nerves. Aidan halted in the dark cave under the Glastonbury Tor and turned her around, lifting her chin with his fingers. She looked up at him and smiled tentatively, basking in the warmth of his blue eyes as he gazed down at her.

"Everything is going to be fine," he said, raising her hand to his lips and kissing her knuckles softly.

"I know," she replied, her jaw clenched with jitters.

He squeezed her clammy hand with his fingers, and a kind smile lit up his face. "Ready?"

She nodded. He flicked his eyebrow at her slyly and snapped his fingers, his eyes never leaving her face. The musty cave melted into the rotating darkness and disappeared.

* * *

They manifested in the middle of some thorny bushes surrounded by tall trees. Thorns and dry branches dug into Tessa's skin, leaving bleeding red gashes on her arms, and she cursed, struggling to push her way out of the thickets, but Aidan grabbed her elbow, halting her progress.

"Tessa, shh." He pressed his finger to his lips, frowning.

"Where the hell did you teleport us?" hissed Tessa irritably, yanking her arm out of his grip.

"Charleston, South Carolina. Angel Oak Park," whispered Aidan.

"And you couldn't teleport into a place without thorns?" she grumbled, running her finger over a particularly nasty scratch to wipe a few drops of blood. "Now I need to get a tetanus shot or something."

He chuckled, shaking his head. "First of all, you're a demigod with active powers. I don't think you need to worry about tetanus," he whispered into her ear, his warm breath caressing her flushed cheek. "Second, no, I couldn't. I've never been here before—"

"You've never been here before?" she gasped. "How did you know where to teleport then? We could've wound up inside a tree."

"Well, we didn't, did we? I know Johnson Island well enough, and YouTube filled in the blanks." His lips brushed her ear, sending a chain of shivers down her spine. "Sorry about all the thorns, my love."

"Why are you whispering," she exhaled, trying to catch her breath. "There is no one here."

"We're a little early, and the park isn't open yet. But the park employees are on the grounds, so try not to make too much noise. We need to stay down until the park opens and there are other people here, so we can blend in." He pulled her in the opposite direction toward a tall fence. "Come here."

Leaning his back against the metal net, he sat down on the ground under the cover of the bushes and stretched his legs. Tessa lowered down next to him and wrapped her arms around herself, shivering. Despite it being late spring, the morning air was colder than in Florida, and the skin of her exposed arms got covered in goosebumps.

Aidan wrapped his arm around her shoulders, pulling her closer to his side. She turned slightly sideways and lowered her head onto his chest, enjoying the warmth of his body.

"Why did you decide to come here early in the morning?" she asked, running her finger down his forearm toward his wrist, tracing the shape of a thick blue vein. "Wouldn't it be better to come at night, when there is no one here?"

"It would be if we knew what to expect," murmured Aidan. "But since we don't, jumping into the unknown doesn't sound like fun. I thought we'd come here in the morning with other tourists and give ourselves a chance to explore the Angel Oak and the surrounding areas in daylight." He pulled a blade of fresh spring grass, twirling it between his fingers. "Most likely, we'll have to come back at night, anyway."

Tessa closed her eyes and took a deep breath, inhaling the smell of the morning dew, damp dirt and spring greenery. She didn't notice when she slowly drifted asleep, and when Aidan woke her up, she was surprised to learn that he let her sleep for almost a full hour. The sun was shining brightly in the cloudless sky overflowing with the chirping of birds, and the air had finally warmed up.

They made their way through the park toward the famous Angel Oak. Despite the early hour and the day of the week, the park already had a few visitors. Promenading slowly along the paths, they were chatting, taking pictures and videos with their cell phones and cameras, all of them none the wiser that one of the most powerful ancient gods was possibly hiding here, in plain sight, right in front of their eyes.

They hadn't reached the old oak yet when Tessa detected a strange presence. While its energy signature felt vaguely familiar, she couldn't recognize it. She pulled on Aidan's arm to stop him, staring at a wall of greenery a few yards ahead of them.

"Aidan," she whispered, pointing ahead, "is that the Angel Oak?"

"Yes," he replied. "Do you sense something?"

She nodded, her mind on high alert. Opening her other sight, she scanned the area and held her breath. The giant tree was surrounded by a circle of powerful magic. Unlike any magical energy she had ever encountered before, this one was shining with darker shades of blue, mixed in with the occasional inclusions of red.

"Use your other sight," she whispered breathlessly. "It's powerful, Aidan… We're definitely in the right place."

He pulled a pair of sunglasses out of his pocket and put them on. Beneath the dark glass, his eyes lit up with the glow of his magic, and he frowned, taking her elbow.

"Death. I sense death," whispered Aidan, sounding hollow and distant as if he were talking to himself. He shuddered visibly, his eyebrows gathering over his eyes. "You're part reaper, Tessa, don't you recognize..." He trailed off, staring at something intently.

She followed the direction of his gaze and froze in place, blood running cold in her veins. Through the young foliage of the giant oak, she could see its massive branches spreading in every direction, weaving in and out of the ground. Craning her neck, she looked up at the branches stretching high into the sky, squinting at the brightness of the morning sun.

The world around her flickered, turning into a negative image of the surroundings for a brief moment. When her vision returned to normal, she saw at least ten shadowy figures standing on the thick branches, their semi-transparent bodies fading in and out of focus. Their dark faces were calm and composed, but their eyes shone dimly against their ebony skin, and to her horror, Tessa realized that these burning eyes were staring directly at her.

A tall man jumped to the lower branch, quickly and soundlessly moving toward her, his bare feet barely touching the tree bark. She'd seen ghosts before—spirits of the dead people who needed her help to cross the veil and vicious specters, dark and malefic—but never had she seen anything like this.

While she had no doubt all these people were dead, their behavior wasn't that of ghosts. They conducted themselves as though they still had corporeal bodies and this place belonged to them, which it probably did if she could believe the local urban legends.

Instead of floating like a ghost would, the man hopped from one branch to the next until he reached the very end of the last one. He halted there and stretched his translucent arms toward Tessa, glaring at her with narrowed eyes.

"Leave... You do not belong here..." His voice was soft and dull as if it was coming from beneath the ground. A wave of whispers rose in the air as the rest of the ghosts spoke at the same time, their voices blending into a continuous hissing noise.

Aidan squeezed Tessa's elbow tighter, and she was positive he could hear the ghosts too. She checked the area, but the tourists kept strolling around as though nothing out of the ordinary was going on. They moved between the oak branches, nearly touching the spirits, merging through the glowing circle of magical energy as if it wasn't there.

Aidan's eyes lit up brighter under his glasses as he touched his forehead and held out his hand to the spirit. His voice, deep and clear, sounded in Tessa's mind over the whispers of the ghosts.

"We mean you no harm," he said peacefully, addressing the man on the branch. "All we want is—"

"Leave!" hissed the ghost louder, warning prominent in his voice. "Leave and never return, god of the Otherworld. You are outside of your domain and you do not belong here." He turned his attention to Tessa. "You both... you reek of magic! Do not cross the line or suffer the consequences!"

Tessa took a step forward, allowing the energy of the reaper to rise within her, but before she could do anything, the man rose high in the air. With his arms spread wide, he looked like he was flying.

"We are the guardians of this sacred place." He wasn't shouting, but his voice invaded every corner of her mind, morphing into a throbbing headache in her temples. "No one with magic is allowed here."

A few more ghosts followed his example. For a moment, they lingered in midair and then suddenly vanished.

"Tessa," whispered Aidan, his bloodshot eyes watering, "we should leave now. There are innocent people here. We can't risk their safety."

"Hold on, Aidan." Tessa twirled around searching for the missing ghosts. "I don't think they're evil. I don't sense any negative energy in them. I think they're just doing their job. We need to—"

A gust of cold wind rushed through the area, ruffling the leaves of the oak, and Tessa fell silent, listening intently. The whispers ceased, taking away the headache, and a heavy silence engulfed the park. The tourists froze in the middle of whatever they were doing, and the entire scene looked like a frame of a paused movie. The air became significantly colder, and a small, white cloud formed in front of Tessa's lips as she exhaled.

A heavyset, middle-aged man in jeans and a checkered shirt slowly turned around. His movements were stiff and unnatural, his large stomach jiggling with his every move. Slowly, he lifted his face, flat and void of emotions, and stared directly at Tessa. As she met the gaze of his milky white eyes, she shuddered, chills running down her back.

He waved his arm in a wide arch and the sunlight dimmed down, replaced by a soft, blue glow. Four more people turned around and came closer, halting behind the man, their eyes glowing with a bone-chilling white glow.

Tessa looked around and gasped. The Angel Oak and its surrounding area were encapsulated in a dome of magical energy, not unlike the one she'd seen earlier when they approached the tree. Seemingly unaware of anything that was happening inside the dome, the tourists on the outside were walking and probably talking, but she couldn't hear their voices through the thick layer of protective magic. The few people locked inside it, however, were still frozen.

She turned back to the man, but before she could say anything, he moved forward, followed by the other four men.

Even though she didn't feel hostile intent in these ghosts, she jumped back, giving herself a moment to regroup and get ready to defend herself if the need arose.

Detecting a movement on the right, she snapped her head to the side and saw Aidan standing with his icy sword in his hand. His glasses were gone, and his body emitted the energy of his godly power, shining too bright in the dim blue light within the dome. The ghosts possessing the tourists halted, narrowing their glowing eyes at him, and for the first time since they met them, these unusual spirits showed signs of aggravation.

"Leave." The man pointed toward the exit of the park. "We do not want to hurt anyone, but we cannot allow you to go any farther either. Do not make us choose violence." He spoke slowly, pronouncing one word at the time, loud and clear.

They're the guardians of the sacred oak. What if... A thought flashed through Tessa's mind, and she put her hand on Aidan's sword arm.

"Aidan, lower your sword," she said quietly. "I think I know what I need to do. Give me a moment."

"Are you sure?" muttered Aidan, sounding uneasy. He straightened, lowering his blade, but his eyes remained focused on the man possessed by the ghost, his fingers squeezing the grip of his sword so hard that his knuckles became white.

She nodded. "I'm positive."

Raising her arm, she whispered a quick spell, channeling her power. The air around her shimmered, sparkling with hundreds of electrical discharges, and the Axe of Perun materialized in her hand. Enjoying the feeling of power coursing through her, she looked up, and a smile crossed her face. Bright lightning spliced the unblemished blue sky and disappeared into the axe.

She twirled the deadly weapon in her hand and reached up again. Another cloud-to-ground lightning bolt forked down, and she raised her other hand toward it. As millions of volts of electricity rushed through her, she opened her arms wide, her body arching slightly as she rose a few feet off the ground supported by her power—the power of the god of Thunder. Her dark hair fanned around her face, electricity charging the surrounding air, and the low rumble of thunder rolled through the park.

Still levitating, she lowered the Axe of Perun and looked down at the ghosts. Under her steady gaze, they bowed their heads and pressed their hands to their chests, showing their respect.

Tessa lowered herself down, stepping on the ground softly next to the man. She placed her hand on his arm and smiled as friendly as she could, looking up into his face. Inwardly, she wondered if her touch would expel the ghost out of the human body and send him across the veil, but when it didn't happen, she just added it to her list of mysteries surrounding the dead guardians of the Angel Oak.

"My name is Therasia, and I'm the daughter of Perun, the Slavic god of Thunder," she said calmly and waved toward Aidan. "This is Aodh mac Lir, the god of the Otherworld and my friend. I know my father made the Angel Oak his home. All we want is to visit him."

For a heartbeat, the man remained still, his face strained as if he was listening to something only he could hear. Then his full lips twitched in a tightlipped smile, and he inclined his head slightly.

"My lady," he said softly. "Where did you acquire this weapon?"

Tessa raised the Axe of Perun and ran her finger over the gold inlays. "What?" She shrugged with an innocent smile. "This old thing? It kinda found me."

Channeling her powers, she moved her free arm aside and a tiny bold of electricity erupted from her fingers, disappearing into the axe. The man glanced back at the other four ghosts possessing human bodies and they took a step closer, curiosity shining in their unnatural eyes.

Tessa cocked her head, narrowing her eyes at the ghost. "Since you asked me this question, it's safe to assume that you know what this weapon is," she continued coldly. "This is the Axe of Perun, a powerful weapon that belongs to the god of Thunder, and only he and his descendants can use it." She snapped her fingers, and the Axe vanished. "Given that you just witnessed me using it, I don't think I need to prove anything else. Please escort me to my father at once."

"As you wish, my lady," replied the ghost.

He waved his hand, and the winds spun around them in a wild carousel, seemingly blowing from every direction. Raised by the howling winds, the leaves and debris danced in the air, making it impossible to see anything. She grabbed Aidan's arm for support, lifting her hand to shield her face. A sense of weightlessness assailed her, and for a brief moment, she felt as if the ground disappeared, leaving her hanging in the air, helpless at the mercy of the raging elements.

She opened her mouth, ready to scream, when everything stopped. Once the winds dissipated and leaves and dust settled down, she found herself standing next to the massive trunk of the Angel Oak. She let go of Aidan's arm and spun around, taking in her surroundings. While they were still in Angel Oak park, it didn't look normal. At least not from a human perspective.

Just a moment ago, the sky had been bright blue without as much as a single cloud. Now, it looked as if a five-year-old child had drawn it without much care for the colors of the crayons they used. Instead of blue, the sky was a light purple overlaid with fluffy clouds of which the shades varied from yellow to red. Once in a while, a blue lightning bolt, followed by a low thunder, forked through the freakish sky.

The grass under their feet and the leaves on the tree were

emerald green, and the bark shone with the reflected light of the sky's colors. Even without using her second sight, Tessa could see the magical energy flowing around her, weaving through the hefty crown of the tree, fading into the sky.

She touched the trunk, feeling the roughness of the tree bark under her skin and held her breath as the pure energy of the god of Thunder enveloped her. She'd never met him, but as soon as his magic touched her senses, she knew what it was. It surged through her body, giving her a burst of energy and making her feel like she truly belonged here. Glancing over her shoulder, she held the drunken gaze of Aidan's eyes.

"The magical energy here is just as intoxicating as in the Land of Dreams," he whispered.

Slowly, she turned around and leaned her back against the oak, expecting to see the possessed human—or the ghost—who had brought them to this strange place. She didn't find him. Instead, a tall man stood a few feet behind Aidan, his arms folded over his bare chest. The strange yellow-red light of the clouds played on his chest and shoulders, outlining his muscular build, and his white linen pants looked stark against his ebony skin. He was no longer possessing a human, but he wasn't an incorporeal spirit either, his bare feet planted firmly on the ground.

"Where are we?" asked Tessa. "What is this place?"

The man's eyes—now a normal brown color—met Tessa's gaze without blinking, and his full lips quirked up into a smile. He touched his chest with his hand and inclined his head respectfully.

"My lady, about twenty years ago, your mother created this place"—he waved his arm around, gazing heavenwards—"a plane of existence, for lack of a better word," he explained. "My family and I had been guarding the ancient oak for centuries, so she gifted us some extra powers, charging us with keeping this place safe from the prying eyes of humans and the dangerous magic of supernatural monsters."

"My mother?" parroted Tessa, realizing a moment too late that he was referring to her biological mother. "My mother was a police officer. She was—"

"She was a powerful reaper." The man smiled. "One of the ancient ones. She predicted that one day, a young lady with the power to control lightning and quake the earth would come here, searching for her father, Perun."

Tessa exchanged a quick look with Aidan, getting over the shock. There was too much at stake, and she couldn't allow herself mistakes, wrong words, or a waste of time.

"I need to see my father," she said calmly. "It shouldn't be a problem now, should it?"

The man laughed, his laughter a deep, guttural sound that echoed through the empty magical park.

"No, my lady, it is not a problem." Just now, Tessa noticed that he had a light accent, but she couldn't place its origin. "I will be delighted to open the door for you." He fell silent but didn't move.

Tessa raised her eyebrows, cocking her head slightly. "Now would be a good time, then. Could you please open the door for us?" she asked, trying to suppress the tones of impatience in her voice. "We need to see him as soon as possible."

The man's smile stretched wider, his teeth pearl-white against his dark skin. "I would, my lady, but unfortunately, I cannot open the door. It opens on its own, but only once a month."

"Eighteen," muttered Aidan, shaking his head. "Why didn't I think about it earlier?"

"That is true, god of the Otherworld." The man bowed slightly in Aidan's direction. "Every eighteenth day of every month, the door into Perun's realm opens, and it is my duty to protect it." He waved at the tree and folded his arms again.

"Eighteen?" yelped Tessa, throwing her hands up. "And today is…?"

"In less than three days, my lady. You're welcome to stay here and wait," the man replied and vanished.

"Three days in some alternate plane of existence," murmured Tessa, sliding to the ground with her back against the tree. "Do you think they have a McDonalds here?"

Aidan chuckled, lowering down next to her. "It's less than three days and usually time flows differently in places like this. We'll be fine."

"Oh, goodie," murmured Tessa, pushing her hand through the crook of his arm. *Only three days in some weird realm created by my biological mother. What could possibly go wrong in such a short time?*

CHAPTER 17

~ ZANE BURNS, A.K.A. GUNZ ~

Chernobog was right.

The process of restoration wasn't just painful. It was devastating. Liquified anguish filled his veins, replacing his blood. It rushed through his body as it was taken apart cell by cell. For a brief moment, he ceased to exist, his tormented body becoming one with infinity, but his mind was still alive—hurting, screaming, twisting, and struggling in search of salvation.

He wanted to shut down his mind. He wanted darkness and oblivion. Death even. He would welcome it with an open arms if only he could die. He couldn't. He knew it, and this knowledge just intensified the anguish, showing him that there was no way around it. The only way out of this terrible place was through it.

Fire surrounded him, elemental energy wrapping around his arms and legs, and slowly, he transformed into the flaming, golden lizard. He was no more. He didn't exist. There was only the Fire. And he was okay with that.

Kal... I need you...

The fire burned brighter, and soon, the scarlet flames of War broke to the surface, surrounding the golden Fire Salamander in a smoldering circle, running up and down his back and long tail.

Chernobog was wrong.

The restoration process didn't take two-three days. It just took a few hours that felt like two-three years.

Father... please...

* * *

SOMETHING PUSHED AND SHOVED HIM. The movement wasn't strong, but it was annoying. He didn't want to be moved. He didn't want anything.

"Leave me alone!"

Did he just say that? This wasn't his voice. This hoarse, dry squeak—it hadn't come from him. It didn't even sound like coherent words. Gunz tried to clear his throat, but his vocal cords resonated with a fierce pain, and he sucked in a sharp breath, exhaling with a soft gasp.

His hand jerked up to his throat but fell back powerlessly, every inch of his body responding with soreness.

I survived... I'm still alive...

He cracked his eyelids open. A blinding yellow light flooded his vision, and he shut his eyes tight again.

"Dayori!" A loud girlish voice rang right above him. While it was pleasant and musical, for his overly heightened hearing it sounded painfully jarring, and he winced. *"Dayori!"*

Stop screaming, please... I can't understand... Wait... What language is that? Where am I?

He tried to open his eyes again. This time, a strange dark spot shadowed the yellow brightness, but its edges were blurry and fuzzy, and he couldn't figure out what it was. He blinked a few times, readjusting his vision, and gradually, everything came into focus. An unfamiliar young woman kneeled next to him, partially obscuring the brilliance of the sun shining from the unblemished blue sky above him.

She stared at him without blinking, her brown eyes filled with curiosity. Catching his gaze, she tucked a long strand of her black hair behind her ear, displaying a large hoop earring with a tear-drop red jewel attached to it and smiled tentatively. A ray of sunlight reflected in the stone, blinding him again for a moment, and he shut his eyes.

"*Aj, chavoro, nat-nat,*" she yelped, gently slapping his cheek with her hand.

Gypsies... As realization struck Gunz, he slowly opened his eyes, and with recognition of who he was dealing with, the small amount of internal magic he didn't know he had in his body kicked in, allowing him to understand the foreign language.

"Zara, leave him alone." A second voice—this one cracked and dry like the voice of an elderly woman—sounded next to him. "Let him rest, child. And don't call him *chavoro.* He's not one of the Romani people."

Gunz felt a gentle touch to his wrist as someone lifted his arm, tugging at the iron manacles. Struggling to move, he turned his eyes to the side, shocked that even such a tiny motion required so much effort. An elderly woman kneeled next to him, carefully tracing the shapes of the runes on his restraints. Her head and shoulders were covered with a large flowery kerchief and a *manisto*—a necklace made of pearls, silver coins, and beads—responded to her every move with a soft jingling.

A few unruly strands of her gray hair fell on her weather-beaten, wrinkled face, and she pushed it back under the kerchief, shaking her head, crestfallen.

"Aj, Zara, this boy has a serious problem," she muttered, jerking her chin toward the rusty chain connecting his wrists.

Which one do you have in mind? The corners of Gunz's lips quirked up just a touch. *Try to be more specific.*

The old lady peered down at him, and a web of crowfeet materialized around her pale, honey-colored eyes.

"Aren't you a feisty one," she murmured not without amusement, patting his cheek softly. "Well, if you want me to be specific, I can do it. I was talking about your manacles with the God's snare runes."

Gunz gasped, his eyes opening wider, and a thought flashed through his mind before he could stop it. *She can hear my thoughts...*

She just shook her head, pursing her lips. "Of course, I can hear your thoughts. I am a *shuvani*, you know? A witch." She turned toward the young woman and said, "Zara, I don't think I'll be able to take these manacles off without help, but at least we can try to take the chain off. Can you get the blacksmith here? Tell him to bring the tools."

The young woman got up and took off running, lifting her wide, colorful skirts with her hands.

"My name's Lala. What should I call you, *chavoro?*" she asked, turning back to Gunz. She opened his torn shirt and carefully explored his chest with her fingers.

Zane, he replied, wondering if she could hear all his thoughts. *My name is Zane Burns. I thought you weren't supposed to call me chavoro since I'm not a Romani?*

She raised her eyes at him and returned to her work, quickly hiding the amusement in her gaze. "Zane, eh?" she murmured. Turning around, she pulled a small bucket with water and a rag to her side. "Well, Zane, your chest and stomach are covered in blood as if someone drenched you with it, and your shirt and pants are soaked through, but I see no injuries. Whose blood is that?"

Mine... Gunz shuddered as the memory of Chernobog's dagger piercing his heart resonated with pain in his sore body.

She threw a curious stare at him, frowning, but then turned toward the bucket and dipped a rag into the water. As soon as she moved the rag dripping with cold water over his chest, his muscles tensed, responding to the new assault of pain. His eyes widened and his mouth opened in a silent scream.

Stop, please! I swear I don't need more pain...

"Water hurts you?" The old lady threw the rag back into the bucket.

Cold water does. He sighed, closing his eyes for a moment. *I'm a Child of Fire...*

"I figured that after the way you appeared here." The old lady put her hand into the water and whispered a few words. "Almost started a forest fire, you know?" A few minutes later, white swirls of steam rose above the bucket, and she pulled her hand out. "This should be warm enough for you." She dipped the rag into the hot water again and wrung it out. With gentle, short strokes, she started to wipe the blood off his skin. "So, what kind of Child of Fire are you, Zane?"

Gunz stiffened, not sure he wanted to answer this question.

"Your secret is safe with me, boy," said the old woman without stopping what she was doing. "Knowing your true nature may help me figure out how to lift the God's snare off of you."

I am... Gunz bit his lip, turning his head to the side. Lush, green grass caressed his cheek, the fresh scent of young leaves and dirt invading his senses. As far as he could see, he was lying in a small clearing surrounded by a dense wall of forest. Somewhere in the distance, the soft song of running water blended with the songs of birds and the sound of the spring breeze playing with the trees.

This place was everything he dreamed of just a few hours ago when the process of restoration was tormenting his body and his mind. It was peaceful and quiet here. No war, no evil chasing him on his heels, no pain, and no loss.

I'm a Great Fire Salamander, he projected the thought, closing his eyes.

The woman stopped what she was doing and threw the rag into the water, respect reflecting in her eyes. "Well, you're way too small to be Kalidus, so I assume you're the young one. Word of you has spread through the nexus after the battle for the City of Gold."

Gunz nodded and swallowed, his throat dry and sore. The woman put her hand into a small hip-purse and brought out a silvery flask. Gently lifting his head, she opened the flask and pressed it to his lips. He took a few small gulps, swallowing with effort, and she pulled away, lowering him back to the ground.

"You will feel better, Child of Fire. Soon. I've sent Zara's older brother to bring some..." Her voice faded as a thoughtful expression suffused her features. Then she smirked. "He's going to bring a remedy for you. While it's not going to free your magic, it'll restore your physical strength." She put her hand on the iron cuff, rubbing one of the runes with her thumb. "Whoever cursed you into this God's snare was extremely powerful. Even my magic is not enough to break it."

A god, said Gunz.

"Really? A god?" She shook her head and rose with an exasperated grunt. "What did you do to anger this god?"

I gave him what he wanted, but not the way he wanted it...

"That makes everything so much more complicated," said the witch, looking down at her hands crossed by thin, blue veins. "Only another god can break an enchantment cast by a god."

My friend Aidan... He is a god of the Celtic Otherworld. I just need to send him a message. As the memory of his conversation with Chernobog became clear, the thoughts swirled in his mind, most of them still entangled and incoherent. He needed to get back to the human realm. He needed to talk to Kal and Mrak. They must know about the threat they were about to face. *Where the hell am I?*

Lala opened her mouth as if she was going to ask something else but then shut it and turned around, placing her hand over her eyes to shield her vision from the sun. Gunz turned his head, following the direction of her gaze. Zara was heading briskly in their direction accompanied by two tall men and a woman in ancient Russian armor.

While he'd never seen these men before, he knew the woman, and a spark of hope ignited in his heart, giving him a tiny burst of energy. As they approached him and halted, staring down at him, he lifted his head, meeting the woman's electric-blue eyes.

"Vasilisa," he croaked, barely audible, and fell back. "But how?"

Instead of an answer, she dropped to her knees and took his hand into hers, lifting it to her forehead.

Stop... what are you doing?

She lowered his arm but didn't let go, gently rubbing his knuckles with her thumb. "I owe you, Zane Burns," she said, her bright blue eyes glistening with moisture, her voice ringing with emotions.

He glanced up at her, his lips parting, but he couldn't say a word, his damaged vocal cords refusing to work. Surely, the ancient huntress and warrior, the guardian of the sacred garden wouldn't burst into tears like a little girl?

"Zane, I had a communication from my father just before Baro arrived with the message from old *shuvani*," said Vasilisa. "What you did for him..." Her voice trembled and broke. "I owe you, Child of Fire. For as long as I live, you have my loyalty."

Gunz shook his head and glanced at the old gypsy desperately. *Please tell her, I need help,* he thought, praying that the witch was listening. *Tell her to find my friends.*

"Vasilisa, my lady." The witch inclined her head respectfully. "I know you can't stay away from the sacred garden for long. The young Salamander wants me to give you a message, but since your time here is limited, I think you should take care of the healing first, before we talk."

Vasilisa pressed her hands to her eyes and stilled for a moment. Then she reached into her pocket and produced a small glass vial filled with clear liquid, its surface sparkling with the bright flares of sunlight.

"This is the Water of Life, Zane," she said softly, holding the vial in one hand while brushing his matted hair off his face with the other. "The same Water you and your undead friend tried to steal from my garden when we met the first time. It should give you your energy back and heal any damage to your body. It won't be enough to break the God's snare and free your magic, but at least physically, you'll be back to normal in a few hours."

Without waiting for his response, she uncorked the vial and lifted Gunz's head slightly, pressing the vial to his lips. As the first few drops of liquid spilled into his mouth, he felt an unusual surge of energy rushing through him. His hands clenched into trembling fists, and his body stiffened in her hands. She tilted the vial, allowing more of the liquid to run into his mouth. He swallowed, his entire body trembling as the pure energy of Life circulated through him.

Vasilisa made sure he drank the entire contents of the vial to the last drop before she let go and sat back on her heels.

"Vasilisa, find... Kal... my friends... tell them—" His voice broke, and he coughed, trying to clear his throat. Even though he felt stronger, his vocal cords were still out of order and every word he did manage to say took a serious effort.

"I'll see if I can summon the Great Salamander or the Ancient Master." A sad smile crossed her face as she put the empty vial back into her pocket. "It'll take a few hours before your voice will return, but you should start feeling better soon." She leaned forward slightly and caressed his cheek with the tips of her fingers. "I must go, Zane. Make sure to get a few hours of sleep while you can. You need some rest."

She got up to her feet and approached the old gypsy. They exchanged a few words in a soft whisper, but he couldn't make out anything they were saying. Throwing one more glance at Gunz over her shoulder, Vasilisa smiled and snapped her fingers, vanishing from the clearing.

Once she was gone, the old lady lowered down next to Gunz and waved for the two young men who came with Zara to approach her. Both tall with black hair, a mustache, and dark brown eyes, they looked like they could've been brothers. Pointing at the shorter one, she smiled fondly.

"This is my son, Baro," she said and turned to the second man, giving him a stern once-over. "And this troublemaker is the sorry excuse for a blacksmith we have since old Stevo passed away."

"Aj, Lala, why so mean?" asked the young man with a heavy hammer and an iron wedge in his hand, trying to sound hurt, not very convincingly though. But a moment later, he wrapped his arm around the old lady's shoulders, and a wide grin spread on his face, mischievous twinkles dancing in his black eyes. "Aw, I know why... You love me."

Old Lala huffed and threw his hand off her shoulder, rolling her eyes. "Just do your job, Yanko, would you?"

The young blacksmith threw an affectionate glance at Zara and squatted next to Gunz. He cocked his head and observed him, the same mischievous expression still lingering on his face.

"So, little man, who gifted you with such pretty bracelets?" He winked at him and grabbed his arm, exploring the chain attached to the cuffs. After a moment, he dropped the chain and turned to the other man, flicking his eyebrow at him. "Hey, Baro, can you lift him to his knees? Shouldn't be hard even for you, considering his size."

Size doesn't matter, you jackass.

Gunz groaned as Baro lifted him into a kneeling position, moving him closer to a large boulder. Once steady on his knees, he raised his eyes at the blacksmith and showed him the "L" sign with his thumb and index finger, a lopsided smirk curving lips.

Then giving him a pointed stare, he flipped his hand upside down, so his index finger made the lower part of the letter L.

Rising, Yanko glanced at the old gypsy, confusion written all over his face. "Is he trying to tell me I'm a loser, Lala?" he asked, suppressing laughter.

For a moment, Lala stared at Gunz and then slapped her hands on her hips and started laughing. "No, you jackass," she said to Yanko once she stopped laughing. "He just showed you that the size of the manhood doesn't depend on the height. Basically, small man—big dick. Big man—well, you do the math." She winked, showing him the upside-down "L" sign.

Zara snorted, covering her face with her flowery kerchief, her cheeks flushing bright pink. Yanko and Baro exchanged a quick look and burst out laughing. Shaking his head, the black-smith lowered to one knee and seized the chain, placing Gunz's arms atop the boulder.

"Now, don't move, *chavo*," he mumbled, quickly sobering up as he positioned the wedge into the link of the short chain between the cuffs. "You can pray if you want."

Gunz squeezed his hands into fists, turning his head away, and Yanko raised his hammer, ready to plummet it down, but Lala stopped him. Placing her hand on the hammer, she whispered something under her breath and a magical energy field spiked around her.

"Now, do it," she ordered, stepping away.

Yanko raised his hammer again and slammed it down, driving the wedge in. As soon as the face of the hammer touched the wedge, smoldering flames and a fountain of sparks erupted from under it. As the chain broke, a blast wave of magical energy swept through the clearing, throwing Yanko and Gunz into opposite directions.

Propelled a few feet back, Gunz hit the back of his head hard and blacked out.

CHAPTER 18

~ ZANE BURNS, A.K.A. GUNZ ~

A pleasantly fresh wind caressed his skin and the faint scent of smoke and burned wood touched his senses. Without opening his eyes, Gunz inhaled deeply, and the corners of his mouth lifted slightly as he sensed the presence of fire energy close by. He was warm and comfortable, and something soft was placed under his head. He felt a gentle touch as someone readjusted the blanket, pulling it tighter over him, but he refused to open his eyes, enjoying every second of peace and comfort.

"Aw, Zara, I know this look. You shouldn't look at him this way, daughter." He recognized Lala's cracked elderly voice, and his mind came to a high alert, the layer of bliss gone. "He's not a Romani, and his path is dark and perilous."

"So what?" Zara sounded annoyed. "Just because he's not one of ours doesn't mean I can't look at him, mama." She chuckled softly. "He's not that hard on the eye, you know."

"No, he's not," agreed the old gypsy, warmth returning to her voice. "He's a good man, but his heart is not free, and it's broken. I can sense the constant ache in his soul even though he would never admit it." A soft rustle of skirts and the light jingling of manisto followed Lala's words as the old witch got up with a groan. "Let's go, Zara, and let him get some rest. He needs his strength."

The sound of steps announced that both women walked away, leaving him alone. Carefully, he opened his eyes and pushed himself up to his elbows. With relief, he realized that the weakness and soreness were gone, and he felt strong enough to get up without getting sick and dizzy.

He was lying inside a large tent on top of a few blankets placed on the ground. The door was lifted, and the fresh breeze brought inside the scents of the night and the sounds of the forest. Carefully, he got to his knees and then rose to his feet, enjoying his restored strength. Looking down, he noticed that the God's snare runes glowed with a soft white light, too bright in the surrounding darkness.

Gunz shook his head, thinking that at night, the runes would give away his position to anyone who cared to look. He walked out of the tent and halted by the entrance, surveying his surroundings. A bright pyre burned in the center of a sizable clearing and a group of gypsies sat around it. The soft sound of an acoustic guitar flowed through the air as someone's fingers lazily touched the strings. A few tents were positioned at the edge of the forest, a safe distance from the fire, and everything looked nice and peaceful.

Somewhere far away, he heard a barely noticeable whisper of waves, and without thinking twice, he headed toward it, following a barely visible trail. He dipped into the dark coolness of the forest, but soon, the trees opened into a tiny lakefront beach.

He sat down on the cold sand a safe distance away from the water and pulled his legs to his chest, wrapping his arms around his knees. The surface of the small lake rippled a little with the light wind, breaking the reflection of the moon into thousands of shining flares. A fish jumped, spreading circles through the water, and he wished he had a fishing pole in his hands.

For a while, he just sat there, enjoying the view, his mind blissfully blank. When he felt a gentle touch to his shoulder, he gave a start and snapped around, his hand moving down to his pocket where he had his Swiss army knife. As he recognized Zara, he relaxed and patted the sand next to him, inviting her to sit down.

Showered by the silvery light of the moon, she looked breathtaking with that enchanting and mysterious beauty of a gypsy woman. Her long, black hair flowed down her chest and back, reflecting the ultramarine shades of the night. A thin head chain with silver coins attached to it sparkled in the moonlight and the stones of her hoop earrings shone with a deep red glow that seemed to be coming from within the jewels. Her every move was accompanied by the soft jingle of bracelets on her ankles and wrists and the manisto on her neck.

For a few minutes, she stared at the lake, saying nothing, and Gunz started to wonder why she was here. Then she turned her head slightly, gazing up at him, and her full lips opened into a light smile, displaying a set of perfectly white teeth.

"Here." She took a canvas bag he hadn't noticed before off her shoulder and offered it to him. He frowned but took it, peeking inside. "It's fresh clothes," she explained. "Yours are soaked with blood and torn. These are my younger brother's. They should fit you."

"Thank you," muttered Gunz, feeling as uncomfortable as it gets.

"Go on. Change." She waved her hand dismissively, her eyes never leaving him, mischievous twinkles in her eyes.

At first, he was going to ask her to turn around, but something in the way she cocked her head and placed her hands on her hips told him that asking that would be a waste of his breath. He sighed and headed toward the woods accompanied by her laughter, hiding behind the natural screen of shrubbery.

Once out of her sight, he pulled a white shirt, black pants, vest and a wide leather belt out, and quickly changed. After that, he moved his Swiss army knife from his old jeans into the pocket of his new pants and discarded his destroyed clothes. Just as Zara had promised, the clothes fit him perfectly. He glanced down at himself and threw his hands up. *I'm missing the riding boots and a goddamn horse.*

He walked back to the beach and halted in front of her. "How do I look?" he asked with a lopsided smirk on his lips, returning her bag.

She came closer and took something out of her pocket. Adjusting the collar of his shirt, she placed a black neckerchief around his neck and tied it upfront. For a moment, she gazed at him, her black eyes getting foggier by the moment. Then she cleared her throat and chuckled, bobbing her head approvingly.

"I've yet to make a real *chavoro* out of you, Zane," she whispered breathlessly.

Gunz sat down, stifling a sigh, the memory of Zara's conversation with her mother still fresh in his mind. She sat down next to him, her wide skirts spreading around her in a colorful waterfall of fabric.

"It's beautiful here, isn't it?" she asked at length.

He nodded without looking at her, not sure it was a good idea for him to be alone with this young woman on an empty lakeside. From what he knew, gypsies had hot blood and were quick to pull their knives out, and he didn't need a confrontation with her brothers or the young blacksmith who seemed to be infatuated with her.

"Wouldn't you want to stay here?" she asked, sounding so innocent and young that he turned to her, doing a double-take.

"Yes," he replied, his voice still raspier than normal. "I would, but I can't. I have my obligations... As much as I like it here, I'll have to leave as soon as I can."

She fell silent again, and he was glad she didn't press the issue.

"Zane..." She touched his shoulder, and he turned to face her, meeting the warm gaze of her deep, brown eyes. "Why did my mama say that your heart is broken?"

He turned away with a pained smirk. "A long story."

"Did she leave you?" she asked, ignoring his clipped reply.

"No."

He sighed, forcefully pushing the memory of Angelique to the back of his mind. He loved her, and he still hadn't given up on the idea of separating her essence from Zmey's, but right now, he needed to stay sharp and focus on the major problem at hand—the evil triad—Zlebog, the god of all evil and his two powerful allies, Skiper-Zmey and Aoife. And what was a Celtic air demon doing in the company of a Slavic dark deity and the Lord of Chaos, anyway?

"Is she dead—"

"Zara, please," he interrupted, his voice shaking as pain spiked through him. "She's not dead. She didn't leave me. It's a lot more complicated, and I don't want to talk about it."

She didn't say anything but changed her position to sit in front of him and spread her skirts wider, smoothing out the folds. Then she reached into her pocket and brought up a deck of playing cards, placing it on top of her skirts between them.

He glanced at her and smirked, his eyebrows rising. "You want to play with me?"

She chuckled, bobbing her head side-to-side in the gypsy manner. "Aj, *chavoro*, I would love to play with you. Or rather play you... I would play you like a guitar, pulling one string at the time... slowly and passionately... till you can no longer move... spent and breathless..." Her eyes sparkled and a blush of desire rose to her cheeks. "But no. Not now. You're not ready for a woman like me."

Gunz almost choked, looking away to hide his amusement. "So, what's with the cards then?"

"I want to read you, Zane," she said, touching his hand softly. "My mama is *shuvani*, and I have the gift, too. I'm the best *drabarovkinya*—fortuneteller—this land has seen in ages."

"There is nothing to read." He stared straight forward at the still surface of the lake. "My past I know already and my future…" His voice faded, and he smirked bitterly. "My destiny was set in motion, Zara. I know exactly what my future holds."

"You're not a gypsy man, but you're as stubborn as one." She grabbed his hand, pressed it over the deck and whispered something.

Slowly, Zara started to place one card at the time between them, positioning them in three rows. Once done, she stared at the cards, leaning forward slightly, her hands propped on her knees. Raising her eyes at him, she shook her head, playfulness gone from her gaze.

"What?" he asked, his voice flat and empty. "I told you, there's nothing good—"

"*Nat*," she interrupted him, gathering all the cards back into a deck. "It can't be right. It's some kind of mistake."

Zara seized his hand again and placed it over the deck, muttering something under her breath. She spread the cards again and gasped. The cards lay in the exact same pattern.

He shrugged. "I told you—my destiny was set in motion. You can repeat that"—he waved his hand at the cards—"as many times as you wish. It'll be the same every time."

"It's not only your destiny that—" She cut herself off, her face ashen, her eyes wide with fear. Quickly gathering her cards, she shoved them back into her pocket and hopped to her feet. "Let's go, Zane," she said urgently.

Seizing his arm, she pulled him up and ran into the forest

toward the gypsies' camp. He followed her at a much slower pace, not in a rush to discuss whatever the young gypsy had seen in his future. When he reached the tent, both Lala and Zara were already there, and the cards lay on the blankets in the same pattern he'd seen earlier. As soon as they noticed him, Lala nodded to her daughter.

"Zara, please give me and Zane a few minutes alone," she said in a no-nonsense tone. As the young woman left the tent, Lala turned to him and an expression of warmth suffused her features. "Sit down, boy." She gathered the cards into the deck and put them away. "Something tells me you already know what's coming."

Gunz sat down and leaned forward, resting his arms atop his bent knees. His eyes halted on the iron cuffs with the glowing white runes, and he smirked.

"Right now, my future is locked within the God's snare," he said softly. "Until the spell is broken, there is nothing I can do."

Lala patted his hand gently. "Vasilisa will find your friends. I have no doubt. I've never seen the Guardian of the sacred garden swear her loyalty to anyone." She glanced at something over Gunz's head, her eyes reflecting the distant flames of the pyre. "A terrible war is coming, Zane." She ran her fingers over the runes, and deep wrinkles materialized around her mouth, making her look tired and older than her age. "To survive it…" She closed her eyes for a moment, and a tear slipped down her wrinkled cheek. "You said to my girl that you have your obligations. I assume it's to your friends and to the human realm?"

"Yes, ma'am."

"Ma'am?" She huffed and chuckled bitterly but quickly sobered up. "The darkness is here, Zane, and to beat it at its own game, you'll have to walk through the fire."

Gunz pressed his hands to his face and exhaled, running his fingers up and through his hair. "I *am* the Fire, my lady," he said at length. "Walking through the fire is the only thing I'm good for."

The old lady got up, readjusting her kerchief. "Not that kind of fire, child," she said, gesturing for him to follow her. "Evil comes in many shapes and forms. Some of them you know and recognize. Some of them you don't see coming." She halted by the entrance, stopping him. "You *will* walk through the Fire, Zane. Even though my words don't make sense to you now, when the time comes, you'll know."

"You sound cryptic, my lady," he replied with a sad smile. "But I guess it's a part of your job description."

She patted his cheek gently and smiled back at him, but an expression of fear never left her eyes. "We'll get back to this conversation when you're free from the God's snare. I would want to read the cards again at that point. In the meantime, try to relax and have some fun. While you can, that is."

They left the tent, and Lala walked him to the pyre. Gunz lowered down next to Yanko, the blacksmith, and relaxed, enjoying the close presence of his element. An older man with a long, gray beard and an unruly mane of gray hair sat across from them with a guitar in his hands, his fingers strumming the strings gently. The music, soft and tender, weaved through the air, and Gunz's soul ached with distant memories of what his life once had been—a long time ago, before he discovered the Fire.

Someone tapped him on his shoulder, and he saw Baro sitting down on his other side. He gave Gunz a quick once-over, and a wide grin split his face.

"I see my sister put her eye on you," he said winking at him. "She is trying to make a *Rom* out of you." He laughed. "You don't know my sister, Zane. Once she has her mind made up, nothing can stop her."

Gunz chuckled, stretching his hand closer to the fire. "She's young," he murmured, touching the tips of the flames with his fingers.

The sound of the guitar became louder, and the musical voice of a young woman joined it. A few women got up, slowly moving and swaying with the music, their movements graceful and fluid. Before he knew it, one of them separated from the rest and approached him, touching his shoulder. He raised his eyes and saw Zara standing in front of him.

"Dance with me," she said, her words sounding like an order.

Baro laughed and winked at him. "What did I tell you?"

Gunz got up and inclined his head in a slight bow, throwing an apologetic gaze at Yanko. "I'm sorry, my lady, but I don't dance. I can't."

"You have two feet, as far as I can see." Zara pushed him on his shoulder, shaking her head. "Why can't you dance?"

"You're right, but unfortunately I've got two left feet." He smirked, shying away from her touch. "So, my apologies, but you'll have to choose someone else, my lady."

She stomped her foot, but before she could say anything, a loud howl sounded in the distance, and a gust of chilly wind swept through the clearing. Gunz froze in place, staring in the direction of the sound. Even with his magic suppressed by the God's snare, he could sense an evil presence, and the small hairs rose on the back of his neck.

"Baro," he said through clenched teeth, "besides your mother, anyone else has magic here?"

"Most of us do. Gypsy magic is a powerful one." The young man got up and closed his eyes, spreading his arms wide. "What kind of beasties are those? Do you know? I don't recognize the energy signature." He pointed toward the forest.

Gunz glanced in the direction he was pointing, and cold sweat beaded his forehead. "Dammit!" He put his hands into his pocket and brought up his knife. "Baro, gather everyone who can fight. Anyone who has combat magic."

"What are you planning to do with that little knife?" asked Yanko, staring at him with curiosity. "These wolves sound big enough to eat you alive."

"These are not wolves, my friend," muttered Gunz.

Praying that he could summon his sword with his magic blocked, he stepped closer to the fire, put his hand into the flames and whispered his sword's name. As he stepped away from the pyre, a long medieval blade gleaming with the reflected orange light of the fire materialized in hand.

"These are volkolaks!" yelled Gunz, raising his sword to his shoulder.

His voice got swallowed by a loud howl, and a pack of huge volkolaks charged through the forest toward them, tearing through the bushes and breaking small trees.

CHAPTER 19

~ ZANE BURNS, A.K.A. GUNZ ~

Joined by ten other men, Yanko and Baro sprung to their feet, forming a line in front of the fire. The rest of the gypsies—mostly women and elderly—stood behind them, holding whatever makeshift weapons they could find.

"Thirteen people against a bunch of monsters," muttered Gunz, stepping next to Yanko. "The fun never ends."

"Our family is small," replied the blacksmith through gritted teeth, squeezing his massive hammer in one hand and a dagger in the other. "Not all of us wield combat magic either." He gave him a quick once-over and jerked his chin in the direction of the fire. "You should step back too, little man. Without your magic, you're useless."

"Even with my magic blocked, I'm still faster, stronger, and a better swordsman than any of you." Gunz chuckled darkly, holding his sword at the ready. *Dammit! Without my magic, I'm too slow and too weak.*

Throwing a quick glance back, he locked eyes with Lala and moved his arm in a wide arch. With a curt nod, she stepped forward and whispered something, repeating his gesture. A bright yellow glow of her protective magic surrounded the people behind her.

Like a dirty, disgusting avalanche, the volkolaks invaded the clearing, destroying everything in their path. In a split second, the peaceful silence of the night was replaced by a terrible commotion. The howls of the monsters, the screams of terrified people, and the shouting of commands—all merged into one continuous pandemonium as gypsies met the monsters with their first energy blast.

Gunz watched an approaching volkolak, and as the monster came within his reach, he swung his sword, decapitating it with one precise move. The monster-wolf fell, the metallic reek of its blood polluting the air, and the pack responded with ear-splitting howls. Glancing sideways, he saw Baro and Yanko fighting by his side. They were slicing and dicing attacking monsters with one hand while striking them with energy orbs, fireballs and lightning bolts with the other.

Gypsy combat magic was powerful and didn't look like any magic he'd ever seen before, but the problem they had was in numbers. Volkolaks kept coming non-stop, more and more of them flooding the space, emerging from the woods. Even though the gypsies still stood their ground, fighting, Gunz knew without a shadow of a doubt—it was only a matter of time before they would get overrun.

The monsters surrounded the protective shield Lala was holding, throwing their fury bodies at it, clawing and biting. Even though a few more people joined her, fueling the glowing dome with their magical energy, Lala's arms started to tremble, and it looked like she wouldn't be able to hold the shield for much longer.

A massive volkolak leaped in the air, landing atop the old man next to Gunz, pushing him down with the weight of its body, his dangerous fangs snapping an inch away from the man's neck. The man's hand unlocked, and he dropped his dagger, struggling to gather enough magic to kill the monster, but to no avail.

Gunz twirled to the side and thrust his sword forward, running the volkolak through. He pulled the blade out and struck the monster again and again, until it finally swayed and fell, pinning the man to the ground. Without stopping, he swung his sword again and took its head off. Since these weren't actual wolves, killing them wasn't easy, decapitation and fire being the only sure ways to destroy them.

Gunz leaned his shoulder against the massive body of the dead monster, struggling to push it off its victim when another monstrous beast launched forward, aiming to sink its fangs into his leg. Grabbing the dagger the gypsy had dropped with his left hand, he met the second volkolak with a sharp strike, pushing the thin blade through its throat. As the monster yelped in pain and backed away, Gunz regrouped and swung his sword, decapitating it.

Turning around, he offered his hand to the old man, helping him to his feet. Surveying the clearing that turned into a bloody battlefield, he shuddered. Only eight men were still on their feet. The ground, soaked with blood, was covered in dead bodies of volkolaks and more were coming from every direction.

"I need my fire," he growled.

Raising his sword again, he tensed his shoulders, feeling that every next strike came with more and more effort, his muscles burning, and the heavy iron manacles on his wrists and ankles didn't help, slowing him down.

"Goddamnit!" he shouted, striking the next volkolak that attacked him. "I need my fire!"

The ground trembled abruptly, almost unbalancing him, and he gasped, feeling a wave of fire energy rushing through the area.

"Yeehaw!"

A familiar, high-pitched voice rang above his head, and he raised his face, unable to believe his eyes. A small wyvern, no bigger than a house cat, flew around the perimeter of the clearing at the edge of the forest, spraying the monsters with fire like a military flame thrower, setting their thick furs ablaze. The volkolaks twirled in place and rushed back toward the darkness of the woods, yelping and howling in pain.

"Mishka!" yelled Gunz.

The earth trembled again, and a powerful gust of wind swept through the clearing. Thorny vines erupted from the ground, creating an impenetrable wall, blocking all ways in and out of the clearing. The trees shook and bent down, their branches seizing monsters one by one. Raising them high in the air, the trees plummeted them down, slamming them against the rocky land, strangling them with vines, tearing them apart.

A giant man dressed in ancient Russian armor and a long cape towered over the tallest tree in the forest, unadulterated fury contorting his youthful face. He stepped over the bushes and walked out into the clearing, the earth quaking with every step he took. His eyes blazed with a bright, green light, and nature responded to his every move. He swung his arm, and roots broke the ground, wrapping around the remaining monsters, holding them in place. At his order, the trees parted, and another man, riding a beautiful stallion with a long, golden mane burst out of the darkness, his katana cutting through the monsters like they were nothing more than a piece of paper.

Gunz took a deep breath, lowering his sword. "Svyatobor? Yaroslav? How?" he mumbled, dropping his tensed shoulders.

Gypsies stopped fighting, too, observing the Slavic god of Nature in awe. A few minutes later, the fight was over. The bodies of dead volkolaks covered the land, and the fire was slowly devouring them at the edge of the clearing. The air was thick with the reek of burned fur and flesh, smoke and blood.

Baro and Yanko stood next to Gunz, breathing laboriously.

Drenched in blood from head to toe, they both had multiple bite marks on their arms and legs, but they were alive. Out of twelve gypsies, four lay dead, their throats shredded by terrible fangs. Lala let go of the protective magic and collapsed, exhausted.

Gunz stuck his blade into the ground and wiped the sweat off his brow, smearing blood all over his face. Leaning heavily on the pommel of his sword, he watched as Svyatobor returned to his normal size, heading toward him. Yaroslav got off his horse and sheathed his katana beneath his leather coat, following Svyatobor, a wide grin playing on his face.

Mishka landed on Gunz's shoulder and wrapped his wings around his neck, pressing his hot head to his cheek.

"I heard you needed some fire, boss," he said, a wide dragon-like grin showing off his fangs. "Ask and you shall receive."

Gunz laughed, joy warming his heart. "Am I glad to see you, my friend." He petted the wyvern's hot back, ignoring the flabbergasted look on Baro's face.

"Is this little dragon yours?" Yanko asked, staring at Mishka with curiosity.

"Not a dragon, dufus," grumbled Mishka, spitting a tiny fireball at him. "Mighty wyvern, thank you very much. Kneel before me, puny human."

To Gunz's shock, except for him, every person who was still standing after the battle kneeled, pressing their hands to their hearts. He looked up and saw Svyatobor and Yaroslav standing in front of him.

Without saying a word, the god of Nature pulled him into a hug, giving him a quick tap on his back as he released him. "I'm glad to see you in one piece, Fire Gecko. Aidan painted a scary picture." He chuckled, shaking his head.

"Aidan?" asked Gunz, his eyebrows rising. "How did he know?"

"A very long and boring story, but I'll try to make it short. Aidan sent us here to find you, but Vasilisa sensed my presence as soon as we walked into the Lady Gatekeeper's house. She told us what had happened to you and directed us here. All the details later," said Yaroslav, extending his hand, but as Gunz took it, he pulled him closer and quickly explored the glowing runes on his cuff. "This is what Aidan was talking about." He turned to Svyatobor. "Do you think you can remove it?"

Svyatobor touched one of the runes, sending some of his magic through it, and Gunz hissed in pain as an electric shock spiked through him, originating under the manacle.

"I have to try," said the god, frowning. Then he noticed that the gypsies were still kneeling and waved his hand. "Please rise. Thank you for helping my friend."

Lala approached them, her eyes fixed on Svyatobor. "My lord," she said, bowing to him. "My magic is strong. I can assist you in removing the God's snare."

Svyatobor frowned, his green eyes getting slightly unfocused, but then he shook his head. "Thank you, my lady, but you're tired after the fight, and it's too dangerous. I'm afraid that once I free Zane's magic, the elemental power will run wild, and he won't be able to control it. Perhaps it would be wiser for you to use your magic to conjure a protective shield over your people." He fell silent, his gaze lingering on Yaroslav for a brief moment. Then he switched his attention to the old gypsy and added, "And if you wouldn't mind taking our friend under your protection too, I would greatly appreciate it." He pointed at Yaroslav.

Lala glanced at the vampire and staggered back, color draining from her face. "Wurdulak!" she hissed, making a protective gesture with her fingers. "I don't want this disgusting monster anywhere near my family."

A pained expression shadowed Yaroslav's features, but it was gone almost immediately as he smiled, sadness lingering in his slightly glowing eyes. "Not a wurdulak, my lady," he said calmly with a ceremonious bow. "Not an upir either. I'm a vampire. I'm sure you know the difference."

"I know the difference—," started Lala, disdain curving her lips, but Gunz stopped her.

"Lala," he said quietly, putting his hand on Yaroslav's shoulder. "Yaroslav is one of the best and most honorable people I've met in my life. Vampire or not, he's my friend, and I would give my life for him. I swear you and your family are safe with him."

"Yaroslav?" Lala stared at the vampire, her gray eyebrows rising. "As in—"

"Yaroslav Potemkin, at your service," said Yaroslav, slightly inclining his head.

For another moment, she stared at him, astonished, then she waved her hand toward the other end of the clearing. "Follow me, vampire," she said and headed toward the others.

"Wait, Slavik," Gunz called, as the vampire moved to follow her. Yaroslav turned around, giving him a puzzled stare. Gunz turned his sword into the Swiss Army knife and gave it to his friend. "Hold on to it for me. I don't want to have it on me while Svyatobor does his magic. Just in case, you know?"

Yaroslav took the knife, placed it in the pocket of his coat and sped away to catch up with Lala.

GUNZ WALKED THROUGH THE FOREST, shivers running up and down his back, and he wasn't sure why he was so nervous. It had been only a couple of days since Chernobog pulled him into the Dark Nav and restrained his magic, but to him, it felt like forever. Maybe he wasn't sure if Svyatobor was powerful enough to break the enchantment placed by the god of Destruction, or maybe he was terrified of the idea of not being in control of his elemental power, but all the way to the lakeshore, he couldn't relax, his nerves on edge.

They walked out on the tiny strip of the beach, and Gunz sat down on the cold sand. Svyatobor lowered next to him and smirked, tapping him on the knee.

"Relax, Fire Gecko," he said, "I'll set you free in no time."

"I know, Sven." Gunz stared at the lake, a strange sense of vague regret spreading through him. "I don't know why I'm so nervous."

"Listen, Zane." Svyatobor glanced at him sideways, guilt reflected in his emerald eyes. "I understand that a few years ago, I put you through hell with my tricks, and we've never been close since, but trust me, there is no one else who can do it. Both Belobog and Semargl agreed that only a Slavic deity can break Chernobog's enchantment. So, it has to be me." He shrugged, looking just as apologetic as he sounded.

Gunz turned to him, observing Svyatobor as if he saw him for the first time. "Forget it, Sven," he said softly after a moment. "Let bygones be bygones. I trust you. To be honest, with all the people around, I'm just a little uncomfortable with the idea of losing control of—"

He didn't finish his statement as Mishka manifested in the air between them, making the deity gasp and jerk backward.

"Aw, boss, it must be hard for you," sang the wyvern, hopping up and down as he flapped his golden wings. "A control freak who's out of control? Sounds painful."

"Mishka!" Gunz threw his hands in the air. "I'm not a control freak, but I don't think anyone here would enjoy it if I reverted into the natural state of the Great Fire Salamander?"

"Sure, you're not a control freak at all," purred Mishka, showering him with a fountain of sparks, "you just know exactly what needs to be done and who should be doing it."

Svyatobor and Gunz exchanged a look, and both laughed, waving at Mishka like at an annoying mosquito. The wyvern snorted, sticking his tongue out at them, and then vanished in swirls of white smoke.

As soon as the wyvern was gone, Svyatobor shifted a little closer and placed his hands over the cuffs on Gunz's wrists.

"I think I know what troubles you, Zane," he said, closing his eyes as he channeled his power. "Right now, with your powers locked, you're the closest you can ever get to being human— carefree, without the constant need to stay in control. Once I break the God's snare, you're the Great Fire Salamander, the protector of the human realm with the weight of the world on your shoulders…" His voice faded, and he sighed, opening his eyes.

"I don't think I know how to be human anymore." Gunz smirked, weight settling on his heart. "I'm not sure I've ever been human. Mrak hasn't done anything to awaken the fire in me. He just told me to do what comes natural to me." He dropped his head, his mind traveling back to that day. Then he raised his eyes and shook his head. "What I did that day… and the fire… Mrak was right—it was easy, natural. Fire is what I am. What I've always been." He sighed and smiled sadly. "Just do it, Sven. I'm ready."

Svyatobor closed his eyes, and his body lit up with a faint green glow. Holding his hands on the cuffs, he started to chant, slowly pronouncing the words of an ancient language Gunz couldn't recognize. Nature froze. The surface of the lake became still like a mirror, reflecting the dark void of the sky, and even night birds silenced, stopping their endless chatter.

The powerful energy of the Slavic deity rushed through their connected hands, settling around the cuff on Gunz's wrists and ankles. As Svyatobor kept chanting, his fingers locked tighter, and his hands started to shake with strain. A burning pain originated under the manacles, and Gunz pressed his teeth together so tight they squeaked. The runes glowed brighter, but their sharp outlines became blurry, and they flickered on and off like a dying electric light bulb.

For a brief moment, Svyatobor stopped chanting. "Zane, get ready," he hissed through gritted teeth. "Now!"

He said the final words of his spell and the ground trembled. Nature came back to life, and the wind rushed across the beach, lifting sand in the air. Still glowing, the runes rose slightly over the surface of the manacles. They lingered there for a brief moment, but then slowly dimmed down and disappeared.

The iron cuffs clicked and fell off, and as soon as it happened, the magical energy of the nexus entwining with the energy of his element rushed through Gunz like a tidal wave, wiping everything in its way. The flow of the fire lifted him in the air, and he screamed, throwing his head back. The fire flooded his entire being, and as much as he tried to stay in control, the Fire Salamander in him took over.

He shifted into a giant golden lizard, flames rising around him like a smoldering wall, and an undiluted wave of elemental energy spread around him, rushing through the area. With an enormous effort, Gunz suppressed the Fire Salamander in him, reverting into his human form and fell to one knee, leaning forward with his arm braced against the cold sand of the beach. Breathing hard, he lifted his head and saw Svyatobor lying on the ground a few feet away with his arms wrapped around his head.

"Sven!" he yelled, straining to get up.

But before he managed to get to his feet, Svyatobor rose and walked up to him, a wide grin on his face. He approached Gunz and took his cape off, wrapping it around him.

"It worked," he exhaled, sounding almost shocked.

"You weren't sure when you started?" asked Gunz, readjusting the cape and wrapping it tighter around his body.

"No," admitted the god of Nature. "Chernobog is older and more powerful than I am. But from what his brother explained, he was already drained when he activated the God's snare. I was counting on his power impotency." He winked and tapped Gunz's shoulder. "How do you feel?"

"I feel whole again," whispered Gunz. He turned his hands up, slowly unlocking his fingers one at the time, and bright flames ignited in his palms. Then he punched the air with his flaming fist and shouted, "And I'm fuckin' pissed!"

CHAPTER 20

~ ZANE BURNS, A.K.A. GUNZ ~

Gunz walked out of the forest and halted at the edge of the clearing. As his eyes traveled over the battlefield, his heart twisted with grief. Dark swirls of smoke curled over the field, and the reek of burned hair and flesh permeated the air heavily, making it hard to breathe. Lala had removed her protective magic after the blast of the elemental power rushed through, and her small family was busy setting up giant pyres to burn the corpses of the volkolaks. Out of all the tents, only two had survived by some great miracle, and they placed the bodies of their fallen comrades into the smaller one, getting everything ready for the burial ceremony.

"This is all my fault," whispered Gunz, biting his lip.

"How is that?" asked Svyatobor.

"Isn't it obvious?" replied Gunz. "It's Aoife's handiwork. It has to be. I don't know anyone else who can conjure so many volkolaks and control them. She must have known I'd be here." He glanced at Svyatobor. "But how? Even I had no idea where I was. I wonder if Chernobog knew where he threw me."

Svyatobor ran his fingers through the mass of his light curls and shrugged, a vibe of uncertainty lingering over him. "I have no idea, but if you're right, we better find out. And we better do it soon."

Noticing Siv shifting from hoof to hoof by the larger tent, Gunz sighed and started on his way there. "Let's get Slavik and Siv. We need to go back home. I must talk to Kal, Gwyn and Mrak as soon as possible."

He walked inside the tent and found Yaroslav sitting on the floor with his eyes closed and his legs stretched out. Lala kneeled next to him, supporting his arm as a thin stream of his blood ran into a glass jar she was holding in her other hand.

"Gunz..." The vampire opened his eyes and smiled faintly. "As you can see, I'm not the only vampire here." He arched his brow at the old gypsy.

"Aj, *chavoro*," muttered Lala sarcastically, throwing a quick glance at Gunz. "You have a smart-ass wurdulak for a friend. How much lower can you go?" Lowering Yaroslav's hand gently, she closed the jar and got up with a strained grunt. "But you were right about him. Wurdulak or not, he's a good man." She smirked, bobbing her head side-to-side just like her daughter. "Wait for me here. I must have a word with you before you leave."

As soon as she left, Gunz lowered down next to Yaroslav, but Svyatobor remained standing, stroking his close-cropped beard absentmindedly. The vampire's eyes darted from Svyatobor to Gunz, and he frowned. Raising his arm up, he checked the incision Lala had made on his wrist. The wound already closed, and he wiped the blood on his shirt, covered in reddish-brown splatters and dirt, switching his attention back to Gunz.

"Spill it, Salamander. What's going on?" he murmured. "You have this particular look on your face that usually means nothing but trouble."

"Trouble, alright," muttered Gunz. "With a capital letter T."

He massaged his wrists where the iron manacles used to be

wearily, not sure how to start. Making a split-second decision, he decided to tell them straight and make it quick.

"Chernobog told me who the third figure in the evil triad is, and you're not going to like it." As briefly as he could, Gunz recounted everything the god of Destruction had told him about Zlebog and his powers. "So, it's only a matter of days before we have to face them. The Slavic god of all Evil, the Lord of Chaos and an indestructible Celtic air demon—one big, vicious family."

Svyatobor's eyes widened as soon as Gunz said Zlebog's name, and he clasped his hands together until his knuckles were white. "Are you sure he said it was Zlebog?" he asked.

Gunz glanced at him, feeling the small hairs rising on the back of his neck. He already knew that Zlebog was bad news, but seeing Sven's reaction, made it so much worse.

"I am sure. A hundred percent," he said quietly. "Chernobog didn't exactly try to soften the blow, you know? He told me straight. He even showed me what was left of his dungeons after Zlebog had escaped."

"He brought you to his lower dungeons? He made you cross the bridge over the river *Smorodina* into *Peklo?*" asked Svyatobor through clenched teeth, a thick blue vein pulsing on his neck. "You have a human soul… how could he…" His voice faded into a strained silence, and a deep wrinkle formed between his brows. "That asshole—"

"Hey, Sven, take it easy. Thanks to Voron, I survived with my soul intact," said Gunz, cringing inwardly at the memory of his trip to *Peklo*. "Don't get me wrong. I'm mighty pissed at Chernobog myself for everything he's done to me over the course of the last few years, but now is not the time. From what I understand, he's the only one in the entire Slavic pantheon who's equipped to deal with that primeval asshole. So, we must find a way to work together."

"It takes a primeval asshole to fight one," grumbled Svyatobor, but then raised both hands in a peaceful gesture and added through gritted teeth, "You're right. We need him." He fell silent for a moment, thinking about something. "Now that you're back in your full power, I believe I can leave you and Yaroslav on your own."

"We'll be fine. Siv can take us wherever we need to go," replied Yaroslav with a dismissive wave of his hand. "Where are you going?"

"Back to the Prav," replied the god of Nature. "I have to talk to Belobog and Veles. They must know what's going on."

"Good idea." Gunz rubbed his eyes tiredly. "Listen, Svyatobor, I wasn't joking when I said to take it easy on Chernobog, so do me a favor. When you see his twin, give him my message. Tell him that he must talk to his brother and be kind to him. Tell him that if we all stand a chance of winning this war, he must hear him out and not be a judgmental jackass. They must work together. This is our only chance for survival."

Svyatobor rolled his large eyes and pursed his lips. "How can you defend him after everything he put you through?"

"I'm not defending him," Gunz objected quietly. "When I think about Chernobog and his shady ways of doing things, I can barely contain my anger. But I promised Voron that I would do the right thing, and I intend to keep my promise."

"Fine. I'll give your message to Belobog." Svyatobor frowned, looking uncharacteristically serious. "Slavik, did you talk to Aidan? He's waiting to hear from us."

"Already did. He knows we found Gunz," replied the vampire. "We'll be on our way back to the Otherworld in a few minutes, anyway."

Svyatobor threw one more glance at Gunz, the same vibe of unease surrounding him like a stormy cloud. "See you soon," he muttered after a moment and snapped his fingers, vanishing in a fountain of green lights.

Gunz turned to Yaroslav, who sat with his eyes closed, his face—normally pale—looking almost porcelain now.

"Are you okay?" he asked, nudging him softly.

"Fine. Lala took a lot of my blood. It'll take me a few minutes to recharge." He chuckled weakly.

"Do you need to feed?"

"I do. Not on you."

"Slavik, come on. Why do you always do it?"

"Because he's ashamed of what he is." Lala's voice sounded on his right, and Gunz snapped his head to see the old gypsy standing by the entrance into the tent. She approached them and offered Yaroslav a bottle filled with blood. "I thought you may need it. It's horse blood. Not human. But it should be enough to give you some of your strength back faster."

Yaroslav turned a shade paler but took the bottle, inclining his head. "Thank you," he said quietly and put it down next to him, his eyes lighting up with a hungry scarlet glow.

Lala looked at him and sighed. Bending down, she gently brushed his golden hair off his face with her fingers. "Yaroslav, I'm sorry for what I said to you earlier," she said, straightening up, remorse lacing her words. "I truly am. You didn't deserve it… I hope you can understand my initial reaction. After all, my kind used to hunt and destroy your kind for centuries."

"You don't need to apologize, my lady." The vampire looked up at her but quickly averted his gaze. "It is what it is. I learned to live with what I've become. It's just I'm not very comfortable feeding in front of humans. I prefer not to if I can help it."

Lala didn't add anything else and switched her attention to Gunz. "Zane," she said, "I wanted to talk to you about your future."

"I have none," he replied, wrapping Svyatobor's cloak tighter around himself.

"Aj, child, don't be like that." The gypsy sat down in front of him and produced a crystal orb, placing it on top of her spread out skirts. She touched the top of the sphere and raised her other hand, calling Gunz's attention. "Look inside. Tell me what you see."

Gunz glanced at the orb. A flock of silvery sparkles swirled inside it in a continuous counterclockwise motion, and he could no longer take his eyes off of their dance, transfixed. The sparkles twisted faster and faster and suddenly disappeared, swallowed by a dark, stormy cloud. A purple lightning bolt flashed inside the orb and two glowing, yellow eyes materialized inside it.

"I s-s-see you..."

A soft hiss sounded in his mind, and Gunz flinched, his arms rising to shield his face of their own accord. "No," he whispered, or maybe he just thought it, but diabolical laughter thundered in his mind, filling him with dread. "No..."

Something flashed, and for a second, the yellow eyes got replaced by purple ones. A thin fracture cut through the image, splicing the space between the eyes. A bright ray of light broke through the crack, and the image shattered. A blinding white light flooded the orb, and Gunz's eyes watered, bright spots dancing in his vision.

When he was able to see, the orb was clear again, reflecting his own face drained of color. He raised his wide eyes at Lala, and his mouth opened, but he couldn't form words.

"What did you see?" asked the witch.

He swallowed hard, taking a breath with effort. "I'm not sure," he replied, his throat dry like old parchment. Slowly gathering his scattered thoughts, he described the strange vision he'd seen in the orb and fell silent, heaviness settling in his chest.

"As I mentioned, evil comes in all shapes and forms, but no matter how great the darkness is, there is always enough light to fight it," said Lala, hiding the magic orb in the folds on her long skirts.

Gunz leaned forward slightly, hiding his face in his hands, and the cloak slid down his shoulders, exposing his naked torso, but he didn't bother to readjust it. A moment later, he lowered his arms and looked up.

"Speak plainly, Lala," he said flatly. "Just tell me what all this means. What do I need to do?"

"I wish I knew." Lala took his hand and peered at his palm, gently tracing the lines with her fingers. "Both my daughter and I have seen the same thing—your destiny is..." Her voice faltered and a shadow of sadness crossed her face. "Your position on the Board of Destiny is set, Zane. Sooner or later, you *will* face great and terrible evil."

"I knew that already," said Gunz, cringing at how flat and indifferent he sounded even to his own ears.

"Zane, listen to me," said the old gypsy. She glanced away from him and quickly wiped her eyes with the corner of her kerchief. "What you and your friends are about to face is way above your pay grade. Nevertheless, it won't be the first time for you, so I believe you can do it." She sighed, and her eyes widened for a moment, a shadow of fear hiding in their depth. "There's something else... My daughter's destiny is somehow connected to yours, and it scares me more than I can say."

"How is that possible?" Gunz shrugged. "I'm about to leave the Land of Dreams and most likely, Zara will never see or hear from me again."

"I don't know. This is something we have both seen in the cards but neither of us can explain it. We didn't get a clear reading," replied Lala, readjusting her bracelets nervously.

Now it was Gunz's turn to look away. He swallowed, everything inside him crumbling with sadness. "You were right," he whispered, staring at his hands. "My heart is broken. I lost the woman I loved to the ultimate evil I'm about to face again." He raised his eyes at the old gypsy. "I knew that with my lifestyle, and because of who and what I am, anyone who dared to love me would be in danger. But I let myself fall in love with her, and I thought I could keep her safe." He clenched his jaw, rage rolling through him. "I was stupid, selfish, arrogant—"

"You were a man in love," said the old gypsy softly. "A young man with a loving human soul. You did nothing wrong, child."

Gunz exhaled a ragged breath, shaking his head. "Anyway, I would never allow myself to fall in love again," he said evenly. "Like I said. Yaroslav and I are leaving in a few minutes, and I will never return here. Your daughter will never see me again."

"Thank you, young Salamander," said Lala, gently touching his hand. "There is just one more thing I wanted to mention."

"What's that?"

"Don't try to imprison this evil," she said, rising heavily. "Don't punish it. Don't curse it. Destroy it, so it will never have a chance to walk this Earth again."

Gunz exchanged a look with Yaroslav and shook his head no. "I would love to do that, my lady," he said, his voice no more than a hoarse whisper, "but I don't think I can or should. There is a reason Veles didn't kill the Lord of Chaos but cursed him for all eternity." A sad, lopsided smile appeared on his face for a moment before he continued. "Anyway, I don't think it's possible to destroy an indestructible evil being of magic. I'll be happy if we all survive the battle and send them back into Chernobog's lower dungeons."

A tight-lipped smirk tugged at Lala's lips as she headed toward the exit, but then she halted by the doorway and turned around. "You know what they say, Fire Salamander." She flicked her wrist lightly. "Where there is a will, there's a way. And where there is no will, there are thousands of excuses."

"Lala, wait…" Gunz started to get up, but his cloak slid off, and he snapped his arms down, stopping it at his hips, blush coloring his cheeks.

"I like you, *chavoro*. You still remember how to blush." The old gypsy chuckled, shaking her head. "Wait, don't leave yet. I'll get you something to cover all that smoldering beauty." She moved her hand up and down. "Besides, there is still a small personal favor I wanted to ask you. Give me a moment."

Before Gunz could ask anything, she walked out the door.

"Smoldering beauty, alright," murmured Yaroslav, biting his lip to stop himself from laughing.

"Something tells me you're not gonna let me live this down, are you?" asked Gunz, wrapping the cloak around his hips tighter.

"You're probably right," agreed Yaroslav, now laughing out loud.

Gunz bit his lip, trying not to say anything that would fuel his friend's undying sarcasm. He paced the tent while the vampire uncorked the bottle, drinking the blood slowly, careful not to spill it. His fangs expanded, and the scarlet glow of his eyes became brighter, betraying the level of his thirst. But as soon as he noticed that Gunz was watching him, he lowered the bottle and averted his gaze, pressing the back of his hand to his lips.

"Slavik—," Gunz started with a light shrug, but Lala walked into the tent, interrupting him.

Zara followed her mother and halted next to her, clutching her bag in her hands. Mishka sat on her shoulder, purring something into her ear, making her giggle quietly and blush. She approached Gunz and offered him her bag.

"If you continue this way, my brother will end up without any clothes," she said, a thin layer of sarcasm in her words.

"Thank you. I don't think we'll be staying much longer. But even if we did, now that I have my magic back…" Gunz winked at her, reaching inside the bag. He took the clothes out and placed everything on the floor, whispering a quick spell to make them fireproof. Then he held out his hand and channeled his fire, igniting a small flame in his palm. Picking up his shirt, he moved it over the fire, but no matter how long he held it, it didn't burn. "You see?"

"Clever," murmured Lala. "I guess you had to learn how to live with your abilities."

"You may say so." Gunz straightened and readjusted the cloak around his hips, tucking its corner so it wouldn't unfold. "Mostly, I had to learn how to suppress my elemental energy twenty-four-seven, so I wouldn't kill every human in a mile radius. You know how it is..." He shrugged, indifferently. "It's hard to live in the world of humans when you're a walking, talking weapon of mass destruction."

"Are you suppressing it right now?" asked Zara, gazing at him with unconcealed curiosity.

"Yes, I am," replied Gunz, throwing a veiled look at the clothes, wondering how he could politely ask them to leave so he could get dressed. "Not everyone in your family has magic that would protect them from the elemental energy. I have to, or they would be dead in a matter of seconds."

"Oh..." Zara's eyes widened, and she was about to ask another question, but Lala stopped her.

"Zane, there is a personal favor I wanted to ask you," she said.

"Anything, my lady," replied Gunz, sensing a slight discomfort in the old gypsy's voice.

"It has nothing to do with your mission, and it's a really long and old story," she started from afar, looking away. Her eyes got fogged for a moment, and her shoulders sagged. "I'll have to tell you some parts of it so you would understand, but I can't tell you everything. Sorry."

Gunz nodded, and she continued.

"A long time ago..." She cleared her throat, her fingers fidgeting with the ring on her finger. "A few centuries ago actually, my great-great-great-grandmother, Vita, fell in love with a young man—a human from the human realm, or so we thought. Just like it happened with you, she found him here, at the far end of the nexus. He was badly hurt, a step away from crossing the veil. And just like we did for you, she treated him and took care of him. He was cursed by a dark sorceress, and it took my family a long time to break the enchantment and free him from it."

She fell silent, and Gunz wondered where she was going with this story. He exchanged a quick glance with Yaroslav, but the vampire just gave him a tiny shake of his head, looking just as puzzled as Gunz felt.

"You'll understand in a minute," promised Lala, noticing their silent exchange. "Yaroslav Potemkin wouldn't know anything about him since it happened before he was born, I believe." For a heartbeat, her gaze lingered on the vampire, but then she sighed and continued, "Anyway, this man wasn't one of the Romani people, but he decided to stay with us, accepting our traditions and lifestyle. I can't disclose his secret, but I can tell you that by the time Vita passed away fifty years later, he looked just the same as the day we found him in the forest."

"He wasn't human. He was one of the immortals," whispered Gunz. "A god?"

"No," said Lala, shaking her head. "He wasn't a god. His true nature has nothing to do with what I'm about to ask you. All you need to know is that he's a good man." Since Gunz didn't ask anything else, she continued, "After Vita was gone, he left our family, returning to the world of humans. Even though Vita's passing was a tragic accident, he couldn't forgive himself, blaming himself for what happened to her."

She reached into her pocket and brought up a small orb, glowing with a strange red light.

"When I took a peek at the Board of Destiny, exploring your future, besides all the darkness that I found there, I noticed that you will cross paths with this man at some point," she continued, her gaze never leaving the shimmering orb in her hand. "I want you to give him a message from Vita. Would you do it for me?"

"Of course," replied Gunz, "but how am I going to recognize him? You didn't even give me his name."

"You don't need his name," she objected, a touch of arrogance and pride reflecting in her eyes. "Besides, I'm sure he's changed his name quite a few times since then. I don't know what name he goes by nowadays, but gypsy magic is powerful. It'll help you recognize him and transfer the message when the time comes."

"Fine," said Gunz, frowning. "What's the message?"

"That's the part that I can't tell you. It's personal, but my spell will take care of it," said Lala, but then smiled and gently caressed his cheek in a motherly manner. "Trust me, Child of Fire, I wouldn't ask you to do anything dishonorable. To give you an idea... Vita wants him to move on. She wants him to know that her death wasn't his fault and that she loves him even from behind the veil. That's the gist of it. The details of her message are meant for his ears only."

"What do I need to do?" asked Gunz.

"Your hand, palm up," ordered Lala.

Gunz stifled a sigh. Holding the cloak with his left hand, he extended his right arm to her. *More magic...* He bit his lip. *Nothing except pain and suffering ever comes from it.*

The old gypsy seized his hand and placed the orb in his palm. As she covered it with her hand, muttering something under her breath, the orb dissolved into a cloud of soft red light and melted into his skin. He gasped, taking in a sharp breath as its magical energy traveled through his arm, settling somewhere in his head. It wasn't painful. The energy carried warmth, love and kindness, and he knew he was doing the right thing.

Lala removed her hand, her eyes searching Gunz's face. "Are you okay?" she asked at length.

He nodded.

"When you see him, you'll recognize him, and he'll detect the presence of gypsy magic in you," she said. "Just look at him and that will be enough for him to receive the message."

"Will do," he promised, and a lopsided grin touched his lips. "Do you mind if I get dressed now?"

"Not at all." Lala waved at her daughter. "Let's go, Zara. Give him some privacy."

"Must we?" whined the young woman, mischievous sparkles igniting in her dark eyes. "Things are just about to get interesting."

"Shameless!" grumbled the old gypsy, pulling her daughter out the door.

Gunz changed quickly and took his Swiss army knife from Yaroslav, putting it in his pocket. Together, they walked out of the tent where Siv waited for them, dancing impatiently in place.

"Well, hello, little Salamander," he neighed, nudging Gunz on his shoulder. "Glad to see you in one piece with your tail still attached."

"Siv," said Gunz warningly. "What did I say about calling me little Salamander?"

"Not to." Siv snorted and then all but hopped in place. "But why? I thought the truth was supposed to set you free."

Gunz turned to Yaroslav with an exasperated sigh. "Deal with him, Slavik," he muttered. "Because if I will, we'll have no horse to take us home, and you'll have to walk through the Fire Salamander portal."

"Fine, fine," whined Siv, backing away from Gunz as he reared behind Yaroslav. "My deepest and most sincere apologies, oh magnificent Great Fire Salamander whose head touches the sky and whose ego doesn't fit the size of his tiny body." He rotated his wide eyes exaggeratedly and added, "Oops, I shouldn't have said that."

A soft giggle sounded behind his back, and Gunz twirled

around, forgetting about the obnoxious magical stallion. Zara stood in front of him, Mishka nestled on her shoulder.

"He's right, you know?" she said, flicking her eyebrow at him.

"About?" asked Gunz.

"The size of your ego, of course," peeped Mishka, a wide grin showing off his sharp little fangs.

"Traitor," muttered Gunz, shaking his head.

"Firetwat," huffed Mishka, turning his head away from him as he folded his wings over his chest.

Zara approached him and fixed the collar of his shirt, looking up at him. Just now, Gunz noticed how tiny she was. Standing barefoot, she barely reached up to his shoulders.

"Zane, stay," she whispered. Wrapping her arms around his neck, she caressed his hair on the back of his head gently, gazing pleadingly into his eyes. "Don't go back to the realm of humans. I've seen your future. There's nothing there for you except pain, suffering and loss. Stay here... with me. I will make you happy."

She pulled up on her tiptoes, forcing his head down, and before he could object, her lips pressed against his. His heart skittered, and heat spread through his body, responding to her kiss, but he pulled away, unlocking her arms.

"I'm sorry, but I can't," he said, his voice deep with a desire he was trying to suppress. "You're a beautiful young lady, but I'm not the right man for you. Besides the age difference—"

"Screw the age difference!" Zara stomped her foot, sounding hurt. "The man my mother told you about... Vita didn't care about his age, and he didn't care about it either. He was immortal, like you. Their love was the stuff of legends. We could have it too..." Tears glistened in her eyes, and she wiped them in one angry move of her hand. "Zane, stay with me..."

Mishka flew off her shoulder, landed on Gunz's head and bent down, craning his long neck. "Come on, boss," he whispered loudly into his ear. "I like her. Let's stay in the Land of

Dreams. The human realm is boring and deprived of elemental energy."

Gunz chuckled, moving Mishka to his arm. "I must go back, my friend," he said, stroking his golden wings. "I'm afraid if I don't go back immediately, the human realm will become more *'fun'* than any of us could handle."

Giving Zara a disappointed look, Mishka shrugged his wings and vanished, merging into Gunz's tattoo. Yaroslav jumped easily into the saddle and directed Siv closer to Gunz, offering his hand. Gunz took it and rose up, sitting behind the vampire. Giving Zara a military salute, he smiled.

"Farewell, my lady," he said. "One day you'll meet someone who's truly worth your love."

Siv reared slightly and pushed off the ground, quickly rising high into the air.

"Look at you go," murmured Yaroslav, notes of laughter in his voice.

"Go where," growled Gunz.

"Girls are falling all over you—"

"Ugh, shut up, Slavik, or you'll be next to fall. And not in a good way."

"Jupiter, you are angry, therefore you are wrong," quipped Mishka, snickering in his mind.

As the magical stallion took off at full speed, Gunz closed his eyes, cursing horseback riding, evil triad, and Chernobog who forced him into this situation.

CHAPTER 21

~ ZANE BURNS, A.K.A. GUNZ ~

Siv landed next to the door out of the Land of Dreams and made a wide circle, galloping around the shiny rectangle.

"This is as far as I go, boys," he neighed. "From here, you're on your own."

Gunz dismounted but held on to the saddle for a few seconds, feeling slightly unsteady. Yaroslav jumped off with ease and walked around the stallion. Siv lowered his head, placing it on the vampire's shoulder, and Yaroslav wrapped his arms around his neck, pressing his cheek to his warm coat.

"Siv," he said softly, "why now? I thought we made a good team."

The stallion backed away and looked to the side, his gaze wandering over the endless forest of the Land of Dreams.

"I don't belong in the human realm. Sorry, Yaroslav," he said, shifting from foot to foot, and the fact that he used Yaroslav's name instead of the usual 'defective vamp' told Gunz how deeply sad the stallion felt. "City life—being surrounded by glass, concrete and pesky humans—is not for me."

"Siv, we're in the middle of something…" Gunz shrugged, searching for the right words. "I can't even call it a war, because it's something a lot scarier than any war this world has seen since the moment of creation." He brushed his hand over the stallion's golden mane. "Anyone with magic who can fight counts. Are you sure you want to leave now?"

"Aw, I'm not leaving you." Siv grinned, flashing his huge choppers. "I'm just going back to my old home for some R & R. Summon me if you need me, and I'll be with you in a jiffy."

"R & R, huh?" muttered Gunz, shaking his head. "I'm sure you need it. See yah, Siv." He lifted his hand to his temple in a military salute and then waved it, unfolding the fiery curtain of his portal.

* * *

GUNZ WALKED out of his portal in the underground labyrinth under Glastonbury Tor. He closed the portal and carefully lowered Yaroslav to his feet.

"Jeez, man, it seems like you're getting heavier by the day," he muttered, massaging his shoulder.

"I doubt that. I didn't gain an ounce of weight since Akira turned me. Are you getting weaker, little Salamander?" Yaroslav smirked, but his smile vanished almost immediately. "With all your protective magic, I can still feel your purifying energy. It's not fun for me either, you know. I wish you would start using your teleporting abilities." He shivered, rubbing his arms with his hands as if he could feel cold.

"I have to ask Father or Mrak Delar to train me on that," replied Gunz. "I still don't feel comfortable doing it on my own, let alone with a passenger."

Channeling fire, he drew a flaming rune in the air and placed his hand over it, ready to summon Gwyn ap Nudd, but before he finished the last word of the summoning spell, a blazing door opened up in front of him. He motioned for

Yaroslav to go first and followed him through the brilliant white light.

* * *

GUNZ HALTED in the middle of Gwyn's living room, and his jaw dropped. Kal and Gwyn ap Nudd sat on the couch, chatting in hushed voices. They stopped talking as soon as Gunz and Yaroslav appeared and stared at him, their faces wearing an identical strained expression.

While their look was unsettling, it wasn't the reason multiple red flags went up in his mind, setting his nerves on edge. Viggo Warrington sat in a white leather armchair with his legs crossed at the knee. His expensive business suit was wrinkled, the collar of his shirt was unbuttoned, and his tie was pulled down and slightly askew. With his hand clutching at his throat, he looked beyond nervous. All in all, these three were exuding a vibe of general anxiety and discomfort.

Gwyn ap Nudd got up and approached Yaroslav, placing his hand on his shoulder. "Prince Potemkin," he said, taking in his appearance. "I believe you wouldn't say no to a fresh set of clothes and a shower?" He pointed upstairs. "Let me show you to your room."

Yaroslav exchanged a troubled look with Gunz but followed Gwyn ap Nudd to the second floor. Gunz turned to Kal and War, an expectation of trouble squeezing his heart, and for a moment, he felt like a troublemaking child who stood in front of a stern parent, expecting to be scolded.

"Mr. Warrington, my lord," he said, bowing to him.

Then he turned to Kal and made a move to kneel, but the Great Salamander got up and crossed the distance between them in two long strides. Pulling him up, Kal wrapped his massive arms around him, pressing him to his chest. Gunz stood with his arms down, not sure what was going on or what to do next. Kal wasn't big on public display of affection, always impassive and firm when it came to him, and seeing him so emotional sent Gunz's thoughts into wild confusion.

"Gunz..." Pulling away, the Great Salamander seized his hands and quickly explored the tiny white lines on the skin of his wrist where the cuffs used to be. He rubbed the white lines with his thumb gently as if trying to wipe them off and shook his head, frowning. "Scars left by magic. Chernobog had better lock himself in his dark hole and keep his head down, for I'm coming for him," he whispered, angry flames igniting in his eyes. "My boy, I'm just glad you're back home and safe. I'll deal with this Slavic monster later."

"No, Father." Gunz pulled his hands out of his grip carefully. "I have something to tell you and Gwyn. It will change everything. Trust me. You don't want to fight Chernobog. At least not now."

Kal nodded, and the fire went off in his eyes as he threw a glance back at Viggo Warrington. He raked his fingers through his flaming hair and turned back to Gunz.

"We'll talk about it later, my child. War and I..." His voice trailed away, and a troubled expression clouded his features.

"What's going on, Father?" asked Gunz, his heart pounding in his chest.

"We need to speak with you," said Viggo Warrington, approaching them.

"Someone please tell me what's going on," Gunz repeated his question, his eyes darting from Viggo back to Kal.

"Why don't you sit down, son," said Kal, gesturing at the couch.

"Thank you, I'm fine." Gunz folded his arms over his chest resentfully. "In the last couple of days, I had more than enough bullshit. So cut the crap and tell me whatever it is you two are dancing around."

Aggravation mixed in with anxiety spiked through him and

flames broke through his skin, dancing on his arms and shoulders. But together with the elemental fire, the bloody flames of War came to life, throwing bright-red flares around him.

Viggo touched a small, scarlet flame on his shoulder and moved it to his palm, showing it to Gunz. "This is one of the things we need to talk to you about," he said calmly. He snapped his fingers and the flames of War got extinguished.

"Cease," said Kal, and the rest of the fire went off.

"Fine!" Gunz threw his hands up and headed toward the couch where he took a seat. "Sitting. I'm all ears."

Viggo moved closer but didn't sit down, his steel eyes staring down at Gunz without blinking. "Gunz," he started, shoving his hands into the pockets of his pants. "Have you asked yourself why you can still wield the power of War?"

"No, not really." Gunz glanced up at him and smirked. "I wouldn't call it wielding, sir. They come and go as they please, and I have no control over them. All I was trying to do is stay calm because they seem to be fueled by anger." He scratched the back of his head and smirked coldly. "Well... me staying calm didn't really work, and Chernobog had an interesting reaction when he saw the War flames for the first time. He said to talk to my father"—he threw a glance at Kal—"as soon as possible and do whatever I can to keep them down."

Kal sat down next to him, placing his hand on Gunz's knee. "You know that biologically speaking, I'm not your father," he said softly.

Gunz huffed, rolling his eyes. "Genetics is not the most important part of being a father, Kal," he said quietly. "Since I discovered the Fire, you were and are my father in everything that counts. I don't know if I would have survived becoming the Fire Salamander without you teaching and supporting me." He closed his eyes, channeling his fire. Then he took his Swiss army knife and made a small incision above his wrist. His blood, mixed with liquid fire, dripped from the cut. "You see? You're in my blood. You are my blood." He shook his head, looking to the side. "My biological father was killed before I could even remember him."

Kal pulled back, his lips pressed into a straight line. "Gunz, my boy," he said, his voice raspy, liquid fire gathering in his eyes. "Your biological father is alive…"

Gunz didn't move, but his chest tightened up to the point where he couldn't take a breath, his limbs filled with lead. "Kal—"

Viggo Warrington took a step closer. "Gunz, the reason you can still wield the flames of War is that they belong to you. They're part of who you are," he said softly. "The power of War is your birthright because you are my son."

"Ah-huh…" Gunz dropped his arms on his lap and remained silent, feeling hollow inside.

For a few long minutes, he sat like that, staring at the ancient being of destructive power who just claimed him as his son. All this time, anger and the adrenaline had surged through him, but now that he felt safe and calm, they were gone, and the exhaustion started to take its toll, settling in his very bones. He turned to Kal and smiled faintly.

"Father, do you think I can take a little break before we continue this conversation?" he asked, his speech a little slurred. "I just went to Hell and back. Literally. I'm exhausted. Just a couple of hours of sleep. Please."

Kal looked at Viggo and sighed. "Yes, you're right," he said, patting his hand. "Get some sleep, and we'll talk when you wake up. Hopefully, Aidan and Tessa will have returned by that time, too."

Gunz got up and headed toward the stairs, his entire body aching. Halting by the first step, he turned around and peered at War. Viggo Warrington sat next to Kal, hiding his face in his hands.

"Mr. Warrington," he called, his fingers clutching at the railings. Viggo raised his head, and a mix of emotions flashed across his normally controlled face. "If the power of War is part of who I am, I would appreciate it if you could teach me how to control it. Chernobog was terrified when he saw me using it, and I must say, the god of Destruction is not easily scared."

"Yes, of course. Gunz, do you think we could—," he started, but Gunz raised his hand, interrupting him.

"I think I'm too tired to think," he said, shaking his head. "We'll talk later, sir."

CHAPTER 22

~ ZANE BURNS, A.K.A. GUNZ ~

Gunz barely made it upstairs, each step taking more effort than the previous one. He opened the door of the room he normally used when he stayed in the Otherworld and walked inside, shutting it with his foot. Throwing a quick glance in the direction of the bathroom, he thought that a hot shower would be nice but couldn't make another move. He collapsed on the bed without taking his shoes off and was dead to the world before his head touched the pillow.

Since no one woke him up, Gunz wasn't sure how long he'd slept. Gwyn's house in the Otherworld didn't have windows, which was understandable considering it was surrounded by the everlasting darkness. He cracked his eyelids open, staring at the white ceiling for a few long moments. Then he turned to his side and closed his eyes again.

"Don't you dare fall asleep again." A familiar deep male voice sounded behind him, and Gunz turned around, narrowing his eyes to see in the dark.

The man snapped his fingers and a small flame ignited on the tip of his thumb, illuminating his face, but Gunz didn't need to see him to know who he was. As he wasn't hiding his energy signature, he was easily recognizable.

"Mrak..." Gunz sat down, lowering his feet to the floor. "You're here. But how? I thought you were supposed to remain in Kendral and help Alliandr."

"Yes, I was," replied Mrak Delar nonchalantly, making the flame run from his thumb to his fingers and back. "But then both Alliandr and I received an interesting communication from Kal, and we decided that it would be better if I returned to the human realm. Kendral will be fine with two Masters of Power, three Elementals and the mighty Phoenix protecting its border. Besides, we already reinforced every single entry. The World of Magic is all but sealed."

"Kal summoned you?" Gunz cringed inwardly.

"Yes, he did." Mrak Delar extinguished the flame and whispered a spell, conjuring the light orbs. "Gunz, you must talk to War and learn how to harness his power."

"I know."

"The power of War is just as dangerous as it is effective against the forces of evil," continued Mrak Delar. "If you don't learn how to control it, you may throw the realm of humans into doomsday, my friend."

"I figured that." Gunz chuckled, rubbing his stubbled chin. "You should've seen Chernobog's reaction."

"That jackass," mumbled Mrak Delar, a dangerous dark light igniting in his eyes. "Yaroslav filled me in on everything that happened in the Land of Dreams." He frowned, but then leaned forward and touched Gunz's arm. "Listen, Gunz, you should talk to Viggo, you know. He's a little shocked by your reaction. From what I understand, he expected pretty much anything from you, but not complete indifference."

"What did he expect?" Gunz threw his hands up. "I'm not a child. I'm a grown ass man. I grew up without a father and I think I can survive without one now that I'm an adult. Besides, why would I need a father who ignored me all my life?"

"It's not that simple," objected Mrak Delar. "War is an ancient magical being of tremendous power. He's not supposed to… you know… associate with mortals." The Master of Power got up and approached him. "Just talk to him like a grown man and don't be an ass. I understand that you're not a child, but don't you want to know a little more about who you are and your abilities?"

"You're married to a mortal," muttered Gunz, a lopsided grin playing on his lips.

"I'm not that ancient," objected Mrak Delar. "And I definitely don't hold the power to destroy the world."

"I can argue both facts, old man," said Gunz and ducked to the side, avoiding a low voltage energy ball Mrak threw at him. "Fine, fine. I'll talk to Viggo. To be honest, I was so tired, I don't think I could've reacted even if I wanted."

"Good." Mrak Delar tapped him on his shoulder, heading toward the door. "He's been waiting outside your room since I walked in."

"Wait, Mrak." Gunz got up, seizing his friend's elbow. "There's something else. I think I need your help."

"Oh?" The Master of Power halted and turned around, his hand on the door handle.

"I assume you know I'm not the Codex anymore?" asked Gunz, looking down at his tightly pressed hands.

"Kal told me," replied Mrak Delar, "and I hope you will explain to all of us what drove you to give up one of the most powerful magical artifacts at a time when we need all the power and magic we can get." He turned to him, folding his arms over his chest. "I'm sure you had a good reason to transfer the Codex to a dark deity, who happened to be the King of the Realm of demons and spirits. But let me also remind you that you swore to Master Warden Raoul de Beaumont to return it to the

Wardens Order. You broke your oath, my friend." He shook his head, his black eyebrows lowering over his blazing eyes. "You're not going to enjoy the consequences of that."

"Trust me, Mrak, I had a good reason," replied Gunz, just now realizing that he indeed broke his promise to Raoul. "I'll explain everything to everyone as soon as I get downstairs. But what I'm about to tell you, I want you to keep between us. Do I have your word, Master?"

"I don't like it already," muttered the Master of Power, leaning his back against the door. "Spill it. What's going on?"

"Do I have your word?"

"Yes, go on." Mrak Delar waved his hand impatiently. "Or do I need to kneel and swear?"

"No, your word is more than enough," replied Gunz, massaging his wrists as a nagging pain originated in the place where the cuffs used to be. "The Dark Codex used to protect my mind from the outside intrusion, and now that it's gone, I feel the presence of Skiper-Zmey again. He's not invading my dreams yet, just lingering on the outskirts, but I know he's there. Mrak, I am…" His voice shook, and he looked away. "I'm afraid that…" He grunted, biting his lip, unable to verbalize his worst fears. "Anyway, I lost the ring you made for me, and I was wondering if you could make a new one."

"Dammit, Gunz," whispered the Master of Power. "Last time, it took two Masters of Power to make that ring, and it was a torture for you every time you needed to wear it." He exhaled, staring somewhere above Gunz's head, a blue light of the magical orbs reflecting in his obsidian eyes. "I'll have to think about what to do. Just give me a little time. Are you still psychically linked with Yaroslav and Aidan?"

"Yes, sir."

"Good. I'm not going to say anything to anyone, but you realize that they will know the first time Zmey will make an appearance in your dream, right?"

"I know. I'll tell both of them once Aidan is back… wherever he is now," muttered Gunz, and then waved at the door with a deep sigh. "Let me talk to my father-dearest first. One headache at the time."

"Be nice, Fire Gecko," murmured Mrak Delar, pushing down on the door handle.

"What are you talking about? I'm always nice."

"Except when you're not." Mrak Delar chuckled and walked out of the room.

* * *

GUNZ HEARD a tentative knock on the door and pinched the bridge of his nose, letting out a harsh breath. He had met with Viggo Warrington better known as War before. He couldn't say he knew him well, but whatever he knew about him was enough to draw some conclusions about his character. Even though War was a hard man, which probably came with his age and his job description, he was reasonable and not entirely unkind.

However, he didn't know what to think about Viggo being his father. He wasn't sure he really cared about their shared genetics, but Mrak was right—he needed to know how to control the power of War, and Viggo was the only person who could teach him.

"Come in," he yelled, rising.

Viggo walked inside and halted by the entrance, a vibe of discomfort almost palpable around him.

"Are you feeling better?" he asked tentatively.

"Thank you, my lord, I'm fine," replied Gunz, slightly inclining his head in a respectful bow. "Please come in, sit down."

Viggo bit his lip and headed toward the only chair in the room, lowering down. "You don't have to address me this way," he said quietly, barely meeting Gunz's eyes. "I'm your father."

"So you said." Gunz sat down on the bed, fidgeting with the edge of his sleeve. "What do you want me to say, Viggo? I accept it. You are my biological father. It is what it is, but if you expect me to call you 'Dad' and send you Father's Day cards, then forget it." He exhaled, pressing the heels of his hands to his eyes, and then finally looked at War, feeling bad about what he just said. "I'm sorry, sir. That was uncalled for. I just really don't know what to tell you and how to react. I'm not comfortable talking about personal stuff."

"I understand. I also hate talking about my personal life." A lopsided grin split War's face, and Gunz couldn't help but admit that they had some family resemblance—the lopsided smile, the gray eyes, and when Viggo was uncomfortable, he had a habit of biting his lip.

"Dammit," murmured Gunz, looking at the door, hoping that someone would walk in and interrupt this world's most awkward family reunion.

"Son—," started Viggo but cut himself off.

"Yeah… let's not do that," said Gunz. "I believe you know all my names. Even those I'm trying to hide. Use any of them."

"Your names were never a secret to me, Zane," said Viggo, leaning back in his seat. "Even though I've never made a personal appearance until a few months ago, I've been around you all your life. I was there when your stepfather was killed. I was there when you were drafted, went to war, and when you returned, damaged and lost. I was around when you and your friends destroyed an entire branch of the Russian mob, trying to protect your friend, Captain Svetlov. I was with you when you discovered the Fire, and when Kal stepped in, moving you to Kendral. I was always there, I swear. Because of who I am, I couldn't interfere with the affairs of the human realm, but if the situation would've gotten out of hand, I swear, I would've stepped in and helped. No matter the consequences. You're my boy! My *only* son!"

"Thank you, I guess?" muttered Gunz.

"Who do you think talked my siblings into helping you and your band of misfits to find Angel?" Viggo shrugged. "We were supposed to remain neutral. You know the risk of activating the power of Four, right? Instead, we all waited for you to show up and summon us and then went with you willingly. Have you ever asked yourself why it was so easy to make us comply?"

"I've stopped questioning the ways of the Board of Destiny a long time ago," muttered Gunz.

"Well, I'll be happy to tell you that the Board of Destiny had nothing to do with all that," replied War dryly. "I knew that finding and saving Angel wouldn't be a walk in the park. I also knew you're not going to sit this one out. So, I just couldn't take a chance with you getting hurt."

"Oh, I got hurt plenty." Gunz huffed, massaging his wrists where the nagging pain was growing stronger. "What do you think about my latest trip to the Dark Nav with a guided tour to *Peklo*? Were you around, too?"

"No, I wasn't. Just like everyone else, I have no way of entering the Dark Nav." Viggo got up and closed the distance between them. He bent down and took Gunz's arm, quickly exploring his wrist. "The reason your wrists hurt is that there is some residual energy of the God's snare embedded under your skin. When Svyatobor broke the spell, he didn't remove it completely. Let me help you, please."

Gunz's knee-jerk reaction was to pull away, but he suppressed his desire to be as far away from this man as possible and sat still. "Thank you, sir. I appreciate it."

Viggo lowered to one knee before him and took both his hands into his. Placing his palms over the thin white scars on Gunz's wrists, he started to chant softly. A wave of heat expanded through Gunz, making him dizzy and weak, and his chest shuddered with short breaths as he struggled to breathe in.

"Hold on, my boy," murmured Viggo. "I know it's not pleasant, but I'm almost done."

He let go of Gunz's hands and placed his hands over his ankles, repeating the procedure. A few minutes later, everything was over, and Viggo straightened, rising.

"Better?" he asked, taking Gunz's chin and gently lifting his face.

"Yes," Gunz breathed out, his vision slowly coming back into focus. "Thank you, sir."

Viggo nodded and sat down, pulling his suit pants up slightly on his knees. "Gunz, I must train you," he said, twisting the ring on his finger. "And I must do it as soon as possible."

"Did you know it?" asked Gunz, still feeling slightly lightheaded.

"What?"

"Did you know that if I wore your ring, it would awaken the power of War in me?" he asked through gritted teeth.

"Yes."

"Then why?"

"Because I had no choice," said War quietly, a deep crease etched between his brows. "Among your friends, you were the only person who could wear my ring and survive its power."

"Mrak couldn't?"

"No. Not Mrak, not Kal, not Aidan. It had to be you." Viggo looked to the side, a thick blue vein pulsing in his neck. "Besides, the power of War would've surfaced sooner or later, anyway, so I was hoping to be there for you when it happened."

Gunz dropped his head, staring at his wrinkled pants. "When can you start training me?" he asked, barely moving his lips.

He remembered the initial Fire Salamander training Kal put him through, and it had been nothing short of torture. The thought that now he had to go through something like that again, but a lot worse, didn't give him a feeling of comfort. If the

Fire Salamander's elemental energy could kill anyone untouched by magic, the power of War could wipe out the entire world.

"Kal and I are ready to start immediately," replied Viggo, rising. "Gwyn ap Nudd prepared an area for us to train you, if you follow me."

Goddammit... Gunz stifled a sigh. *Here goes... again... From one Peklo to the next.*

He got up with a groan and headed toward the exit, but Viggo grabbed his elbow, stopping him at the door. He turned around, staring at War in puzzlement.

"Gunz," said Viggo, his cold, steel eyes not leaving his. "I'm sorry, son."

"About?"

"I should've introduced myself as soon as you discovered the World of Magic," said War quietly. "I should've trained you together with Kal just the way we're going to do now."

"Better late than never?" Gunz smirked and pushed the door open, heading downstairs. *Actually, I think I prefer another trip to Peklo after all.*

CHAPTER 23

~ ZANE BURNS, A.K.A. GUNZ ~

As soon as Gunz walked into the living room, Gwyn ap Nudd got up and flicked his wrist, opening a magical door filled with the brilliant light of his magic. The King of the Otherworld gestured at it, amusement hiding in his cat-like eyes.

"I prepared a training facility for you, young Salamander," he explained, folding his arms over his bare chest. "It's a small field, safeguarded by Mrak's and my magic. You can revert, you can use the power of War—no matter which magical or elemental power you want to use, nothing of it will escape the blocked area. So, you can relax and let go." He gestured at the door again. "After you."

"Thank you," said Gunz, passing through the threshold.

He walked out into a clearing the size of a football field and smirked, shaking his head. Only Gwyn could call it a small area. With hundreds of magical orbs lingering in the air, it was illuminated bright enough to see the surroundings clearly. The tall wall of a forest, black and gloomy, surrounded the field, and the light, white glow of Gwyn's protective magic was easily visible against the dark backdrop.

With surprise, Gunz noticed that not only Kal and Viggo followed him through the door—Mrak Delar and Gwyn ap Nudd were here too. They walked away from the center and sat down on the black grass at the far end of the designated area.

"Where is Yaroslav?" asked Gunz, shifting from foot to foot nervously.

"He's back at Gwyn's house," replied Kal. "Just in case you need to use your elemental power, I didn't want him to be anywhere next to this place." He threw a quick glance at War over Gunz's head and switched his attention back to Gunz. "Are you ready?"

"As ready as I can be," replied Gunz, shuddering inwardly. "Is it going to be as... um... complicated as my Fire Salamander training?"

Kal laughed goodheartedly, tapping him on his shoulder. "Man up, son. Something tells me it's not going to be nearly as painful or long for that matter. When I started to train you to control your elemental power, you were new to the World of Magic and controlling your elemental energy wasn't the only thing I had to teach you." He motioned for Viggo to approach. "I believe the power of War is going to be a lot easier to control now that you have a few years of experience with magic under your belt, so this training could be"—he shrugged, mischievous flames dancing on the bottom of his eyes—"fun, if you let it be."

"Fun," muttered Gunz, cringing. "In a deadly, apocalyptic kinda way."

"The Great Salamander has a point," said War, his face so calm, he looked almost serene. "Some aspects of the power of War are similar to the elemental Fire, but it's actually easier to control."

"How is that?" asked Gunz carefully, waiting for the other shoe to drop. Since the Fire Salamander in him had made an appearance, the only time he could relax was when he was in Kendral or in the Otherworld. Any place where there could've been humans, he had to control his elemental energy even while he was asleep.

"Unlike the elemental fire, the power of War is not active all the time," explained Viggo, shoving his left hand in the pocket of his pants. "The only time you have to control it is while you're using it. Just like most magical powers, it's connected to your emotions—mostly anger, but it will respond to physical pain as well as any kind of distress."

"I noticed," muttered Gunz.

"In a moment of distress, it can be hard to control it, and the power of War can easily take you over—body and mind," continued Viggo. "And this is something you don't want to happen as it would shift the fragile balance of this world toward doomsday."

"Well, enough with the small talk." Kal put his hand in his pocket and produced a small jewelry box. He threw it into Gunz's hands. "I know how much you hate jewelry, so here is another piece for you," he said, smirking. "Put it on." Then he waved at Mrak and Gwyn and they both got up, channeling their powers.

"Oh, shit," murmured Gunz as he watched the Master of Power rise off the ground slightly. The colorful waves of the quadruple power swirled around him, and the black mask materialized on Gwyn's face. "I don't like it already."

Carefully, he opened the box and gasped as the undiluted power of War washed over his senses. He touched the red stone embedded into a ring made of *Ardenium* steel, and his heart skipped a beat. The power of War rushed through him, taking his breath away, amplifying his elemental powers. He grunted, struggling to control the fire in him, and a few flames broke through his skin, flickering on his shoulders and arms. He closed his eyes and took a deep breath, getting in control of the elemental energy.

"Very good... very good, son," murmured Viggo Warrington,

showing him his right hand with the ring of War on it. "Your ring has the stone of War, just like mine. But unlike mine, it's set in *Ardenium* steal, which should minimize and keep the destructive side of my power suppressed. Now put it on. You can handle it."

Gunz glanced at Kal, and the Great Salamander gave him a curt nod. Slowly, he slipped the ring on the middle finger of his right hand. As soon as the cold steel touched his skin, the Fire Salamander in him took over. He screamed and spread his arms, engulfed in smoldering flames wide, rising a few feet in the air. As his muscles spasmed, and his body arched like a tightly stretched bow, he squeezed his hands into tight fists, fighting to get the Fire Salamander under control.

He shifted into a large, golden lizard, a wave of elemental fire spreading around him. The bright red flames of War surrounded the lizard and for a few long moments, he dropped his humanity, completely submitting to the powers rushing through his body.

"Come back to me, my boy..." He heard Kal's voice somewhere in the back of his mind, and he screamed again, forcing the Fire Salamander down as he reverted back to his human form.

The Power of War is connected to my emotions. A thought flashed through his mind and a slow, lopsided grin crossed his face. He closed his igneous eyes and dropped his arms, taking a few deep breaths to get his anxiety under control. Slowly, he lowered down to the ground and moved his arm in a wide arch.

"Cease..." he breathed out, and all fire, including the flames of War, slowly dwindled down, responding to his command. Turning to Kal, he smiled. "I'm in control, Father. I can do it—"

"You can do it?? What makes you think that?" A terrified, high-pitched voice sounded on his right. Gunz looked to the side and saw Mishka flapping his wings furiously at him. Without saying another word, the wyvern turned in the air and flew toward Mrak Delar at full speed, his wide, round eyes filled with fire. "Master, Master!" he yelled at the top of his tiny lungs. "Who gave this ignoramus the power of War? Take it back! Take it back!"

He landed on Mrak's shoulder, wrapping his wings around his neck, burying his head into the mass of his black hair.

"Mishka, relax," said Mrak Delar, barely containing his laughter. "Gunz is in control. If anyone can handle the power of War, it's him. We're going to be fine."

Mishka pulled away, and his jaw dropped. "Are you okay, Master?" He placed his wing over Mrak's forehead. "Nope, no fever. You think your age is getting to you? Dementia or whatchamacallit the other one? Oh! My! God! We're all gonna die!"

He flew toward Gwyn, screaming, "Let me out of here! Let me out!"

"What the hell is that?" asked Viggo, pointing at the wyvern, a bewildered expression on his face.

"That is—" Gunz burst out laughing and for a few seconds couldn't stop. Finally, he stopped laughing, wiping tears from his eyes. "Mr. Warrington, meet Mishka, my wyvern and a serious pain in my neck."

"Oh?" War stared at the wyvern with his mouth open. "You have a pet wyvern. Why am I not surprised?"

"Aw, you shouldn't have said that, Viggo," murmured Kal, chuckling.

Mishka turned toward Viggo, spitting furious fireballs in his direction. "I'll deal with you later, Strife almighty." He fell silent for a moment, staring at War. "Was it you who was stupid enough to give the powers of destruction to a half-witted child? Don't you know the number one safety rule of magic?"

"What safety rule?" mumbled Viggo, flabbergasted.

"Don't let your children play with powers that can destroy

the world!" yelled Mishka, flapping his wings wildly, sending Gunz into the next fit of laughter.

"Mishka." Gunz expanded his arm once he stopped laughing, inviting the wyvern to land on it. "I promise. I'm in complete control. You can relax now. Look." He lifted his other hand and snapped his fingers. Two flames ignited in his palm—the orange flame of the elemental fire and the scarlet flame of War. He gathered his fingers into a fist and when he opened it, both flames were gone. "You see? It's all good."

"Yeah, right," grumbled Mishka. "It's all good until it's bad and then who do you call to save your fireless ass? Me!" He gave Gunz an arched stare, but then sighed and merged into his tattoo.

Viggo approached him, a wicked grin playing on his lips. "I'm glad to see you can control my power while relaxed. Now let's see if you can handle it under distress."

"What distress?" muttered Gunz, raising his eyes at him.

"The one we're about to put you under." Kal laughed, an enormous, flaming hammer materializing in his hand.

Gunz glanced from Kal to Viggo, and a cold sweat covered his forehead. War had transformed into his natural state. He stood clad in heavy armor with a giant sword in his hand.

"Your sword, Salamander," yelled Viggo, swinging his enormous blade at Gunz.

"Fu-u-u-ck!" yelled Gunz, jumping back. In one fluid move, he pulled the Swiss army knife out of his pocket and transformed it into a medieval sword, mirroring Viggo's wicked smirk as he assumed a guarding stance with his sword at his shoulder. "Sorry, that's all I have. I forgot my can opener in my other pants."

Bloody flames of War wrapped around Viggo, setting his armor and his sword ablaze as he moved into a frontal attack, crashing his blade down. Gunz parried his blade, but before he could regroup, Kal's hammer connected with his temple, crashing his skull. He fell into a soft, black mush, everything melting into the darkness.

As the Fire Salamander in him took over, starting the restoration process, Gunz screamed coming back to life. Looking around wildly, he jumped to his feet and twirled around, avoiding Viggo's sword and Kal's hammer, and then staggered back, breathing hard, the elemental fire wrapping around his arms like silky ribbons.

"Father!" he yelled, reproach ringing in his voice, and both Kal and Viggo halted, looking at him. He grunted and pointed at the Great Salamander. "Kal, you told me it's not going to be painful!" Gunz regrouped, raising his sword again.

"And it's not!" Kal gave a deep guffaw, throwing his flaming hair off his face. "It doesn't hurt me in the slightest."

Feeling the movement behind his back, Gunz spun around, meeting War's sword with his. Sparks flew in the air as the blades collided, and Gunz made a circular motion with his free hand.

"*Ignius Amplio,*" he yelled, and a circle of flames surrounded War. At the same time, he ducked to the side, getting away from the powerful strike of Kal's hammer.

He knew that the circle of fire wasn't going to hold War for longer than a few seconds, but he hoped it would slow him down long enough for him to come up with a plan. Responding to the adrenalin pumping through his system, the elemental fire entwined with the energy of War skyrocketed in him, both types of flames manifesting on his arms and shoulders.

"Control your power, Salamander!" yelled Kal, moving faster than Gunz had ever seen him move, leaving a fiery trail in his wake.

"Use your power! There is more to the power of War than just fire!" shouted Viggo, dropping his sword arm lower in a forward thrust. "Call to it. Listen to it and control it!"

Quickly stepping back, Gunz blocked Viggo's strike. "I wish

245

I still had the Codex," he murmured. "I would kick both your sorry asses."

"Next time don't give a powerful weapon to a dark god," yelled Kal, lowering his hammer at Gunz's right shoulder.

Gunz cried out, dropping his sword, his arms hanging limply at a weird angle.

"Why are you standing, boy! Revert! Heal your goddamn arm!" yelled Kal without stopping.

Gunz screamed, clutching his shoulder and let go, reverting into the natural state of the Fire Salamander. Realizing that he was still under attack, he kept the Salamander form long enough to heal his wound and changed back into his human form, just to receive a formidable punch in the face as Viggo's metal glove connected with his jaw.

"Stop fighting like a Fire Salamander!" yelled Viggo. "Use the other power you have!"

Gunz howled as anger swept through him like a tidal wave. The power of War charged through him and for a moment everything stopped. Time slowed down. All sounds ceased. Kal and Viggo halted, staring up at him, and just now, he realized he was levitating a few feet in the air.

He peered down, and suddenly, he saw the flow of power and magic as he had never seen it before. Kal was wrapped into the elemental fire energy, its soft waves flowing all around him. He could see Kal's heart pulsing with the fire, just like he had seen the hearts of the wyverns a while ago in the Land of Dreams when he controlled them.

Glancing at Viggo, he gasped. His entire body was shimmering with the scarlet colors of the energy of War. He was glowing brighter and then softer, the light around him pulsing with short flares. And just like with Kal, he could see and feel his beating heart.

Mrak Delar, surrounded by a four-colored river of elemental energy, was high in the air, wielding the power of all four elements, and Gwyn stood on the ground, his magical energy interlacing with the protective shield around the area. He could see their hearts just as clearly as he could see their faces and their magic.

I know what to do now... He switched his attention back to Kal and Viggo. Channeling both his elemental fire energy and the power of War, he seized their hearts into the grip of his magic and squeezed, commanding them to obey. Kal screamed, fighting his control, and for the first time since he'd become the Fire Salamander, he knew the Fire Elemental stood no chance against him.

Viggo spread his arms, the power of War rising around him to the next level. Gunz laughed and switched his tactics. Instead of commanding them to stand down, he ordered them to attack.

Kal twirled his massive hammer, making it swoosh through the air as he charged Viggo. War met his blow with his sword, staggering back. Gunz lowered down to the ground and let go of both powers, carefully getting them under control.

"Cease..." He pointed at Kal, and all the fire surrounding him dwindled down. "Father, stop... I'm sorry, I controlled you."

Kal came to a sharp halt, his wide chest rising and falling with laborious breaths, his eyes filled with pride settling on Gunz. "You did it, my boy... You did it."

As both powers slowly abandoned his body, Gunz returned to his human form, slowly lowering down to the soft, black grass. He grabbed his sword, turned it back into the Swiss army knife and placed it in his pocket.

"You've seen it. The true power of War," said Viggo, sitting down next to him. "You can see the hearts and the minds. You can control them all—people and supernatural beings. You can make them do anything you wish." He readjusted his position, placing his sword across his lap. "It's not easy, and as you noticed, it's quite draining—especially for you. Unlike me, you're still human. It's just as deadly as it is dangerous. Don't use it unless you have no choice. But if you're forced to use it, do it wisely. The ring will help you control it and contain its destructive side, so you don't have to worry about bringing forth the Apocalypse."

"Thank you. Now I feel like I'm ready to collapse," murmured Gunz, looking sideways at Viggo.

War got up, seamlessly transforming into his human form.

"It'll get easier with time." Viggo offered him his hand, and Gunz took it, rising.

"I hope so. I feel more drained now than after a full day of wielding the fire." Gunz smirked, wiping perspiration off his brow. "A fresh meal, hot shower and some peace. Not necessarily in that order."

He turned to Kal, about to ask if he was ready to leave when he detected a strange fluctuation in the magical energy field. Expanding his Salamander senses, he stilled but since he couldn't detect anything out of the norm, he assumed his overly stretched nerves drove him to imagine something that wasn't there.

Turning to Gwyn ap Nudd, he saw him and Mrak Delar running across the field toward them. Without slowing down, Gwyn waved his hand and opened the door, allowing the Master of Power to go through first. Catching Gunz's puzzled look, he screamed, "We have to go. Now! The veil is fluctuating. Something is going on outside the Otherworld, and I want to know what it is."

So much for a moment of peace... Gunz sighed and walked through the blazing light of the door.

CHAPTER 24

~ TESSA ~

In this weird plane of existence, time didn't move at a normal speed. Nothing here was normal. The strange, multicolored sky had never changed, remaining the same no matter what time of day or night it was. Tessa could only guess that time here was moving differently than in the human realm.

It seemed that no more than a few hours had passed when she felt a sudden fluctuation in the magical energy field. She scrambled to her feet and massaged her numb leg, feeling pins and needles prickling in her muscles. Aidan was already on his feet, a light glow in his eyes revealing that he had also detected the spike.

"Aidan—," she started, but he pressed his finger to his lips, asking for silence, and the glow in his eyes became brighter.

"Something has changed," he whispered so softly that she practically had to read his lips. "Something is coming."

A light tremor ran through the ground, and a soft wave rushed through the strange emerald grass. The massive branches of the oak moved ever so slightly, making its leaves tremble, a few of them brushing Tessa's arms on their way down. With a mournful screech, a shadowy hollow opened up at the base of the tree, releasing a cloud of sparkling dust. A blast of magical energy rushed through the air, and the abnormal sky shone brighter, making Tessa's eyes water.

She blinked a few times to adjust her vision and spun around, searching for the guardians, but they were nowhere to be found. With a slight shrug, she approached the oak and peeked inside the hollow. It was dark but not black, and the air inside the tree shimmered with a soft blue glow.

"I think this is our invitation," she muttered without turning around.

The hollow wasn't wide enough for Aidan with his broad shoulders, and it was so low that she started to doubt he would be able to get in at all. Tessa with her five-foot-two height had to bend down to pass through the threshold. Once inside, she turned and waved for Aidan to follow.

"I don't think I can fit in." He bit his lip, and his forehead furrowed. "Tessa, as much as I don't want you to go alone, if I can't go through, you must complete the mission on your own."

"At least give it a try," she whispered urgently. "There is a lot more space inside. You just need to make it through the threshold. And if you can't, then I'll go alone."

"Tessa—" He grunted and channeled his power, but no matter what he tried, he couldn't make the opening wider.

"Fine, I'll go alone. Nothing is going to happen to me, anyway," she said with a half-shrug. "He's my father after all. I don't think he would hurt me." A derisive smirk crossed her face, and she winked at Aidan reassuringly, even though she felt none of it. "The old man can try."

"Dammit, wait," muttered Aidan, slamming his hand against the bark next to the hollow. "Let me try to squeeze through."

He went down to his knees and turned sideways. Moving slowly, he pushed his shoulder through the threshold. Then he bent his head lower, struggling to get through. The harder he tried, the narrower the hollow became, and in the end, he was stuck, unable to move in either direction.

"Tessa, I can't..."

"Friggin' giant," muttered Tessa.

"Oh, come on... I'm only six-two..."

"I'm not going to leave you, Aidan." She sighed, brushing his shoulder with her fingers. "We do things together, right? That was the deal. Always and together. I'd never leave you. Especially not like this."

Grabbing his upper arm, she tried to pull him through, bracing her other arm against the inside wall of the tree. Aidan grunted as the edges of the hollow squeezed his chest tighter, tearing his shirt and his skin under it, and she let go, leaving him in an awkward position. Something cracked, and Aidan cried out, his mouth opening as he struggled to breathe.

"Goddamnit!" she yelled, reaching up, and the Axe materialized in her hand. "Perun! I know you're doing this! Let him through, or I swear, I *will* diminish your oak into a pile of splinters." Lightning struck inside the tree as her power responded to her emotions, and she grabbed the handle with two hands, raising the deadly weapon above her head.

A loud laughter boomed through the oak, deep and rumbling like the sound of thunder. The tree creaked heavily, and the hollow opened up in all directions at once. Aidan collapsed to all fours, dropping his head low as he gasped for air. A moment later, he sat back to his heels, pressing his hand to his bleeding chest.

"Your father doesn't like me already," he exhaled. He started to get up, but the ground quaked violently, and he fell back down.

A shimmering blue light started to swirl around them, moving faster and faster, and soon Tessa could see nothing except a whirlpool of cerulean lights. She put her hand on Aidan's shoulder to keep herself balanced. As the ground disappeared, her stomach clenched, and she closed her eyes, suppressing the nausea. A few seconds later, the lights slowed down and dissipated, and she finally felt a hard, steady surface under her feet.

Tessa took a deep breath, observing a large room with interest. It was brightly illuminated, but the source of light wasn't obvious. She could clearly see the walls, but instead of a ceiling, a veil of soft, white clouds spread over her head. The room wasn't a living area, but rather a training facility with equipment that would make any state-of-the-art gym envious.

A tall man stood at the far end of the room with his back toward them, lifting two dumbbells that looked like they could be anywhere in the vicinity of five hundred pounds or more. He moved his arms, wrapped in tight ropes of enormous muscles, with such ease as if the dumbbells weighted nothing. His well-defined back glistened with sweat, his black tank top stretched tightly over it.

Tessa and Aidan exchanged a look, and she caught an uneven smirk on his face as he scratched the back of his head. She cleared her throat loudly, hoping that it would be enough to draw the man's attention, and tapped her foot on the floor. The man dropped the dumbbells, which made the floor shudder, and slowly turned around, running his hand through his stylishly cut short hair.

He was tall, no less than six-foot-seven, and appeared to be in his late thirties or early forties. His black t-shirt had a small picture of a lightning bolt with the words "I do it!" written under it. As the gaze of his youthful, blue eyes halted on Tessa, a warm smile graced his face, making his hard features seem kinder. But as soon as he looked at Aidan, an icy expression took over, and if he could look any colder, it would probably start snowing.

"Therasia, my darling," he rumbled, his voice even deeper

than she'd expected. "I'm so glad to finally see you so close. You grew up to be beautiful and powerful, my child."

"No thanks to you," muttered Tessa, rolling her eyes.

He either didn't hear her comment or chose to ignore it and switched his attention to Aidan.

"Aodh mac Lir," he muttered dryly, barely inclining his head.

"Perun," replied Aidan in kind.

Perun moved back to Tessa. "Darling, is he your boyfriend?" he asked without even trying to mask his disappointment, disdain curving his thin lips. "As far as I can see, it's a hopeless misalliance. Why couldn't you find yourself a nice Slavic god, sweetheart? Why do you need this Celtic half-breed?"

Tessa huffed, placing her hands on her hips. "First, none of your business. Second, who gave you the right to tell me who to date? You haven't been my father since I was born. Let me say it, so it sticks in your mind—my choices and my life are none of your business."

"Well, that's a matter of opinion, isn't it?" Perun chuckled, shaking his head. He seized a strand of Aidan's hair on the back of his head and pulled down on it, rolling his eyes. "Cut your hair, boy. Maybe you'll look like a man then."

Aidan grunted, the energy of the Otherworld magic spiking around him. "What did I do to receive this kind of attitude?" he grumbled, his hands clenching into fists at his sides.

"Nothing." Perun shrugged indifferently. "My daughter can do a lot better than you. You're just not worthy of her," he replied frostily. "That's it."

"And you are?" Aidan stepped closer, his eyes lighting up with his magic, anger contorting his handsome features. "What kind of father leaves his newborn child on the steps of a Warden's church and takes off, never to be heard from again?"

"The kind who's willing to sacrifice his fatherhood and his love for his new baby-girl to give her a few years of safety to grow up in peace!" yelled Perun, invading Aidan's personal space.

"Being one of the most powerful gods of the Slavic pantheon, I'm sure you could've figured something out that wouldn't have turned your child into an orphan, you asshole!" shouted Aidan, the room quacking as his power ran away from him.

"How dare you!" yelled Perun, thunder echoing his deep voice. "You know nothing!"

Tessa stared at both of them with her mouth open, her mind refusing to process everything that was happening. Aidan stood with his hands clenched into fists, the light of the Otherworld magic surrounding him like a glowing shield. Perun stood facing him, the air around him thick with electric discharges, the scarlet glow of his power throwing bright flares on the walls of the room. The scent of ozone permeated the air, and the fluffy clouds above his head got replaced with low, stormy ones.

Before she knew it, both Aidan and Perun manifested their swords, standing in front of each other, mutual animosity radiating between them. They swung their weapons at the same time, and the sound of clashing blades ripped Tessa out of her stupor.

"No, you don't," she grumbled, anger rising within her.

Connecting with her power, she hit them both at the same time with a low voltage energy blast. The blast wasn't strong enough to send two gods flying, but it was powerful enough to push them away from each other. Tessa stepped between them, holding her arms up.

"Aidan, stand down," she shouted, her eyes blazing furiously.

"Tessa, I was just—"

"Shut up!" She didn't let him finish, turning to Perun. "Don't you dare insult and attack the man I love!" she yelled, angry tears gathering in her eyes. "Touch a hair on his head, and I swear I will find a way to destroy you, god or no god!" She fell silent for a moment, her chest rising and falling with heavy breaths, then she glanced at Aidan, and a touch of a smile ghosted her lips before she turned back to Perun. "I will do anything for him."

"Therasia, I wasn't—," started Perun.

"Enough!" she yelled, interrupting him. "There is just too much testosterone between the two of you in this room. I can't breathe!" Her eyes darted from Perun to Aidan and back, and she took a deep breath, clutching her throat. "We have a bigger problem at hand than your disapproval of my dating choices, Perun. So, you will shake hands with Aidan and accept that him and I are together. Always and forever. And if you can't accept him, then you can go and—"

"Whoa, whoa... take it easy, sweetheart." Perun laughed, raising his hands up. "I came in peace."

"What peace?" yelled Tessa, stamping her foot. "Have you looked outside your hidey-hole? Have you seen what's going on in the real world lately?"

"Tessa, take it easy—," started Aidan, but fell silent as she scolded him with a fiery gaze, switching her attention back to Perun.

"You're sitting here, safe and sound," she continued furiously, "while your old friend, Skiper-Zmey, walks the realm of humans, accompanied by two indestructible jackasses. What do you say to that, Mr. Universe?"

She took a ragged breath, glaring at her father. He opened his mouth to say something, but then snapped it shut, and his sword vanished.

"That's right." Tessa arched her eyebrow at him. "You better keep your mouth shut." She motioned for Aidan to come closer. "You two are going to kiss and make up. And then we'll sit down like civilized, mature adults and talk about what needs to be done to save the world."

Perun grunted and a muscle in his jaw tightened as he

offered his hand to Aidan, his face a stone mask. Aidan shook his hand reluctantly and tried to pull away as soon as he could, but Perun held it, pulling him closer, a troubled expression on his face.

"Aidan, hold on," he said, his cockiness gone, his eyes fixed on Aidan's chest. "Where did you get this? Who gave you this?" He pointed at the pendant on the silver chain.

"It's the Guardians pendant," explained Tessa before Aidan could say anything. "I have a similar one. Every member of the Guardians and Wardens Orders has one of these." She pulled her pendant out and showed it to Perun.

He touched it with his fingers and closed his eyes for a brief moment, holding his breath. "It's not the same, daughter," he said softly, and his quiet voice sent shivers running down Tessa's back. "Yours is clean. His is not."

"What do you mean?" asked Aidan. "The Destiny Council gave it to me a few months ago."

"And I do feel their magical energy on your pendant," agreed Perun. "But since you received this pendant, it's been tampered with. There is another energy signature mixed in with that of the Destiny Council. I can sense it clearly, and it's a dark one. Where did you use it the last time?"

"Wardens Order." Aidan picked up the pendant, gently probing it with his magic. "I'm assigned to assist them for one year. So, I used it to enter a few of their locations. Church by the Sea is one of them—you should know that one."

"Yes, I do know that location. Father Collins runs it," murmured Perun, rubbing his chin absentmindedly.

"Father Collins is no longer in charge," said Aidan, dropping the chain. "He's the Grand Master of the entire Order now, so he moved to Paris."

"You don't say…" Perun looked up at Aidan and bright lightning flashed in the depth of his eyes. "Take it off, boy. This pendant is…" His voice trailed, and he looked up, as if searching for a better word. "How do you humans call it? A bug? It's bugged. Whoever placed a spell on it can hear anything you say."

"Impossible. I never take it off," objected Aidan.

Perun chuckled darkly. "Like I said. You're not worth my daughter," he said, shrugging his overly muscled shoulders. "For a twenty-five-hundred-year-old god, you really know very little about the Dark Arts."

"And you know an awful a lot," retorted Aidan. "Should I be worried about that?"

"No. You don't need to worry about me," replied the god of Thunder frostily. "Worry about whoever bugged your pendant, dear boy."

"Why?" whispered Tessa breathlessly.

"Because whoever was spying on your boyfriend most likely followed you here," snapped Perun. "And we're running out of time."

As if to prove his point, the entire room trembled, and the stormy clouds above their heads became darker. For a moment, Perun stilled and looked heavenward as if trying to sense something. Then he frowned and snapped his fingers. The room around them spun, transforming into something that resembled a living area. His appearance changed as well. He stood clad in ancient Russian armor with an enormous sword in his hand.

Tessa glanced at his weapon and gasped. It wasn't the same sword he used earlier against Aidan. Shining with a blinding white light, the blade was crackling with thousands of volts of electricity, lightning bolts striking along its length without stop.

"Listen to me, kids," he said quietly, but the urgency in his voice made Tessa's hair stand on end. "I was right. Whoever tempered with Aidan's pendant followed you here. I can sense the dark energy flowing all around the oak. So far, the guardians are able to hold them down. But they won't last long."

He looked around as if expecting someone to burst through the door. Bending down slightly, he whispered, "You two must go back to the human realm. I'll stay behind and give you a few minutes of a head start." He put his gloved hand on Tessa's shoulder and for a moment, an expression of warmth suffused his features. "Listen to me carefully because your lives and the future of the human realm depends on it."

"Father, come with us. We can leave together and fight whatever is coming," mumbled Tessa, not realizing that she called this man *father* for the first time.

"Don't worry, darling. I'll be fine." Perun smiled and shook his head. "Now listen. At the dawn of creation, my father, the mighty Svarog, created three powerful swords. The first one was called the Sword of Prav"—he lifted his mighty blade, showing it to them—"and I have it. The second sword he made from white gold which runs out of the Alatyr stone. It shines like the sun itself, and the ray of magical energy it produces can destroy pretty much anyone."

"Mech Kladenets," said Aidan. "Sword Kladenets I mean."

Perun glanced at him, an uneven smirk curving his lips. "That's right. I'm glad to see that you're not a stranger to the Slavic lore, Aidan."

"I've been around long enough." Aidan shrugged.

Perun nodded and continued, "The last sword Svarog created was the almighty sword of the sun—Sword-Krest." He fell silent for a long moment, thinking. "You need to find Sword Kladenets. That is the only way you can destroy Skiper-Zmey and his buddies. Unfortunately, I have no idea where to look for it. You'll have to do some digging and you'll have to do it fast."

A deep shudder ran through the walls of the room, and a deafening bang rolled through, making Tessa clasp her hands to her ears.

"Dammit," growled Perun, adding a few Russian curse words. He waved his hand and a portal swirling with bright blue light opened in front of him. "The wards have collapsed. Go now! I'll hold them for as long as I can."

As Tessa and Aidan approached the portal, he seized Aidan's elbow, stopping him.

"Aidan, you must figure out who messed with your pendant," he hissed. "None of you are safe until you find out who's spying on you all."

He let go of Aidan and put his hands on Tessa's shoulders, pulling her closer. "Be safe, my daughter. Even though you find it hard to believe, I love you..." He kissed her forehead gently and pushed her slightly toward Aidan. "Now go, and I'll join you as soon as I can."

Another bang rattled the floor of the room and the wall exploded inward, showering them with dust and debris. Perun muttered a quick protection spell and pushed Tessa and Aidan through the portal before she could say anything to him.

CHAPTER 25

~ ZANE BURNS, A.K.A. GUNZ ~

A s soon as Gunz crossed the threshold into Gwyn's
house, a low buzzing noise filled his ears. It wasn't
loud, but it was accompanied by a soft vibration, and it
seemed like everything around him was humming. Yaroslav
stood in the center of the living room with his eyes closed and
his arms spread. His mouth was opened slightly, showing his
fully expanded fangs, and for the first time since they met,
Gunz noticed that his fingernails elongated, turning into
claws. Mrak Delar stood by his side with his black sword in
his hand.

"Slavik," Gunz called the vampire, carefully touching his
shoulder. "What's going on? What is this sound?"

Yaroslav opened his glowing eyes but ignored his question,
turning to the Master of Power. "It's not in the Otherworld,
Master," he said, his claws slowly retracting. "But in the human
realm, right above us"—he pointed up—"there is something
going on. Whatever it is, it's demonic in nature, and it's getting
closer and more powerful by the second. I'm sure you sense it
too."

"Gwyn, open the door into the labyrinth," said Mrak Delar,

his fingers wrapping tighter around the grip of his sword. "I need to see what's going on."

Gwyn ap Nudd snapped his fingers and the humming noise ceased. "Not alone, Master. You're not going anywhere alone," he objected, frowning. "Did you hear that buzzing? Those were the wards Aidan and I set up in the human realm over the Otherworld. Something or someone triggered them."

Gunz probed his magic just to realize that after the beating Kal and Viggo put him through, he was nearly drained. *Dammit,* he thought. *Did Kal really have to kill me? They made me revert twice. After all they put me through, I'm too drained.*

Biting his lip, Gunz reached into his pocket and brought up his knife, turning it into the sword. "Gwyn is right," he said, cringing inwardly at how weak his voice sounded. "I'm coming with you, Mrak."

The Master of Power glanced at him and then threw a quick veiled gaze at Kal, shifting slightly. "I appreciate the offer, Gunz, but you just went through corporal punishment." He chuckled, shaking his head. "You can barely stand. I'll take Yaroslav with me."

"Su-u-u-re," murmured Gunz, a lopsided smirk lifting the corner of his lips. "And if something happens to him, his mother will bite my head off. Literally." He turned to Gwyn ap Nudd, massaging his shoulder, still aching after the blow of Kal's hammer. "Gwyn, open the door. We're wasting time."

Gwyn waved his hand and opened the door, but the troubled expression never left his face. Mrak Delar and Yaroslav walked through the light, but as Gunz approached the threshold, he seized his arm, halting him.

"Gunz," he said quietly, his fingers digging into Gunz's arm. "Listen, it's just a feeling I have... I think Aidan is out there, and he's in trouble."

"Can you sense his energy?" asked Gunz, a knot twisting in the pit of his stomach.

Gwyn ap Nudd shook his head, a deep crease crossing his forehead. "No, I don't," he replied softly. "It's just a feeling, you know?" He touched his chest over his heart and added with conviction, "He's there, Gunz. Take care of my boy…"

"I will," promised Gunz and stepped through the light.

* * *

AFTER THE BLINDING light of Gwyn's door, the labyrinth under the Glastonbury Tor seemed to be darker than usual. Gunz squeezed his eyes shut and then opened them slowly, read-justing his vision to the surroundings.

"Are you ready?" whispered Mrak Delar, putting his hands on Yaroslav's and Gunz's shoulders. "There's a maelstrom of dark energy going on right above our heads."

"As ready as I can be," muttered Gunz, and the world around him spun as Mrak teleported them out of the labyrinth.

All this time, Gunz hadn't realized how much time he'd spent training with Kal and War. To him, it had seemed like a few minutes, an hour at the most, but as they materialized next to St. Michael's tower, the cool evening air touched his face, and he took in his surroundings in shock.

It was dark, and the sky, absent of the moon and stars, was veiled by stormy clouds. The heavy wind seemingly blew from every direction, and the moisture gathered in the air, threat-ening to turn into a heavy rain. The droplets of water settled on Gunz's skin, making him wince and clench his teeth. But worse than the assault of the opposing element was the thickness of demonic essence and dark magical energy that permeated the air with its foul stench.

Gunz sharpened his senses but couldn't hear anything. Despite the silence, he could clearly detect the disturbance in the magical energy field surrounding the tower.

"*Déjà vu…*"

He heard Yaroslav's voice in his mind and nodded, knowing perfectly well what his friend was referring to. He touched Mrak's arm to attract his attention. The Ancient Master turned around and pressed his finger to his lips.

"Not a silencing spell," Mrak whispered, and since Gunz could hear him, he had no doubt his friend was right.

Moving the tips of his fingers over the rough wall of the tower, Gunz walked toward the corner and carefully peeked over it. As he surveyed the view that unfolded in front of him, he held his breath, unable to move, his hand squeezing the grip of his sword so tight, his knuckles turned white.

Just a few yards away from the entrance into the tower, a massive crowd of people surrounded a small dome of protective magic. Their eyes glowed with the poisonous yellow light of chaos, but through the malignant miasma of the demonic infection, he could still sense the warmth of a human soul in each of them.

Dark and malevolent, the infected crowd kept assaulting the protective shield with anything they could find, and those who couldn't find anything suitable, threw their bodies at it, banging their fists and heads to blood against the magical wall. Looking down, Gunz noticed dark silhouettes moving up the hill as more and more infected humans were rushing to help.

Gunz looked up, and icy shivers ran down his spine. A massive blob of dark energy surrounded by dark mist and smoke-like swirls hung in midair right above the magical shield. Black tendrils slithered out of it, wrapping around the top of the protective dome, and it looked like the darkness was feeding on its energy. Everywhere where the tendrils touched its surface, disgusting dark splatters spread through its light.

"Is that a—?" started Gunz.

"A dark spell," said Mrak Delar, confirming Gunz's suspicions. "Extremely powerful, too."

The dome flickered slightly, and Gunz knew that it was a

matter of minutes before the dark magic would break through. He turned to Mrak, staring at him with a question in his eyes.

"Mrak," he whispered as quietly as he could. "We can't kill all these humans. But if we do nothing…" His voice trailed off as his thoughts flashed back to the last words Gwyn ap Nudd had said to him, and with sudden clarity, he recognized the energy signature of the evil spell. "Aidan… Oh, God. Mrak, it's Aidan and Tessa inside this protective shield."

"How do you know—," started Mrak Delar, but Gunz wasn't listening.

"Mrak, can you purify the crowd?" he asked, interrupting him. "Yaroslav and I will deal with the rest."

"Gunz, wait," hissed the Master of Power. "You don't even know what this dark spell is. Are you going to jump in headfirst as usual?" He threw his hands up. "If you die, all these people are dead, too."

"We can't wait, Mrak. It's Aidan's and Tessa's safety at stake," objected Gunz. "The good news—I recognized the energy signature, and I have a pretty good idea of what that is. The bad news—it's not going to be easy to get rid of it. It's Aoife's handiwork, and as usual, she's after her stepson."

"If you're right, let me remind you," said Mrak Delar in a quick whisper, "Aoife is an extremely powerful, ancient demon, and you're drained. How much magic can you use before you collapse?"

"I'm not a Master of Power. I'm not gonna shut down," replied Gunz lightly, but everything inside him tightened up with worry. "Yaroslav will bring the attention to himself and lead the humans away from the dark mass, closer to you. When you see the opportunity to purify the crowd, take it and do it quick."

"If you get hurt, Kal will skin me alive. And I don't even want to think about what War would do." Mrak Delar grunted and peeked over the corner, frowning. "Fine. Let's do it. Give me a few minutes to get in position."

Gunz turned to Yaroslav with a lopsided smirk. "Slavik, as usual?"

A wide grin crossed the vampire's face, and the excitement of the upcoming confrontation lit up his blue eyes with a bright, scarlet glow. "Bring it on," he growled, turning the corner.

Gunz glanced back, watching the Master of Power running stealthily in the opposite direction, circling around the tower. Once he was sure that Mrak was on his way, he walked out in the open, following the vampire.

As they came closer to the infected people, the silence gradually got replaced by a hushed noise. Every single person in the crowd was whispering something, their soft, monotonous voices sounding as one. Even though it seemed like they were saying the same phrase over and over, Gunz couldn't distinguish the words as they blended together, becoming a continuous low hiss.

The mass of dark magical energy moved lower, its tendrils wrapping tighter around the protective shield beneath. A dark cloud of demonic essence rose around it and started to spin in a counterclockwise motion.

The people became more agitated, moving and shifting from place to place. They kept chanting while attacking the dome vigorously, and the surface of the protective magic gave the first crack. The whispers became louder, sinister excitement lacing their dull voices.

Gunz and Yaroslav stopped a few feet away from the circle of infected humans, and Gunz glanced at his friend, doubt tearing at his heart.

"Slavik, are you sure you'll be fine on your own?" he asked through their blood bond.

"Come on, Gunz, give me some credit," replied the vampire,

rolling his eyes. *"These are just humans. Pretty low on the food chain if you ask me."*

"That's the problem." Gunz sighed. *"You're gonna have to hold back. You can't kill them."*

"Can I at least have a quick snack?" whined Yaroslav, projecting heavy vibes of sarcasm through their blood bond. *"Get into position, Gunz. Trust me. I'll be fine. They'll be fine too..."* He chuckled and added with a nonchalant shrug, *"Mostly."*

Shaking his head at his friend's dark humor, Gunz channeled the elemental power and placed his hand over his tattoo.

"Mishka, are you here?" he whispered. "Wings, please?"

"Sorry, boss," the wyvern's voice sounded in his mind, making him flinch. *"I'm fresh out of wings. How about chips and a six-pack instead?"*

"Mishka!" hissed Gunz. "Not a good time for that!"

"Party pooper," grumbled Mishka. *"You never have time for fun!"*

Without giving him any warning, the wyvern began the merging process, and a sharp pain surged through Gunz's body, making his muscles spasm like from an electric shock. He clenched his teeth, stifling a scream, and a moment later, two golden-red wings unfolded behind his back. Channeling his elemental power, Gunz rose in the air, transferring as much of the purifying energy toward his hands as he could.

"Slavik, we're ready!" he said, with a shock realizing that even in his head his voice was joined with Mishka's. *"Be careful. Once we start wielding our power, stay low."*

"Don't worry, I'll get out of your way," replied Yaroslav. *"I choose life."*

"Coming from a vampire, that sounds priceless."

"Ha-ha..." Turning toward the raging crowd, Yaroslav waved his hands, trying to attract their attention. "Hey, you!" he yelled, his strong voice rising above the hissing noise of the mob.

The whispers ceased all at once, and every single person

turned to face him. Their movements were mechanical, and they all looked like puppets led by the steady hand of an invisible puppeteer. Their eyes lit up brighter, the energy of chaos rising over them to the next level. Without saying a word, they took a step toward Yaroslav, shifting forward like a mindless mass.

Yaroslav spread his arms wide and a wild grin stretched his lips, exposing his long fangs. "Come get me, guys!" he yelled, taking a step back and to the side, toward the tower.

People raised their hands, trying to reach him, but because they couldn't catch him, they quickly lost interest, turning back toward the protective dome. The vampire cursed under his breath and vanished. He materialized a split second later, a step away from the line of infected people. Before they realized what happened, he pulled one person out of the line, and once the man had turned around, he punched him out. It was just a short jab, but it knocked the large man out flat.

Showering him with profanities, the crowd responded to his assault with loud screams and growls. Nevertheless, they slowly followed him, taking another step toward the tower, shifting after him like mindless zombies. Yaroslav repeated the maneuver a few times, assaulting and egging on the crowd to keep their attention. Little by little, he managed to lead the infected mob away from the protective shield and closer to the Master of Power who was crouching in the shadows of the tower.

As Gunz watched Yaroslav playing his cat-and-mouse game, doubt reared its ugly head again. *Too easy... Why do I have a feeling that I'm missing something...*

He forced the troublesome thoughts to the back of his mind and focused on the malignant mass of the evil spell in front of him. From such close proximity, it looked gloomier and more sinister than from below. Like tentacles of a giant, menacing octopus, its tendrils wrapped tightly around the protective dome, now most of it surrounded by a dark mist and dirty, smoke-like swirls.

Gunz squinted, trying to see who was inside the dome, but could see nothing through the darkness of the spell. Opening his other sight, he checked the dome, recognizing the white light of Aidan's energy signature. It was so weak that he had a hard time detecting it, but it was enough for him to know that Aidan was there. Next to him, he noticed the reddish-golden glow of Tessa's soul, and it was loud and clear.

"Aidan, I'm here. Hang in there, my friend." He reached out to Aidan, using their psychic link, and held his breath, waiting for his answer.

"Gunz..." Aidan's voice was weak and shaky. *"Leave..."*

A wave of icy fear followed by a surge of anger shook through Gunz, and he growled, pointing his sword at the blob of the malignant spell. Gathering all the elemental fire in his blade, he blasted the spell with purifying energy. The dark magic responded with an ear-splitting howl, and for a brief moment, it loosened its grip on Aidan's protective shield. It stopped rotating and halted, bracing against the assault of the fire, and Gunz could swear it stared at him even though the mass had no visible eyes.

Channeling more elemental fire from nature, Gunz doubled the flow of purifying energy. The spell started to vibrate, sprouting more tentacles, growing bigger and bigger. It stopped attacking Aidan's shield and slowly stirred forward, its entire form progressing toward him. Gunz looked down. The crowd of infected people was encapsulated in a glowing sphere of Mrak Delar's protective magic, and he knew that the humans were safe.

Holding his sword with both hands, he flew closer to the mass of the spell, increasing the flow of his magic. The slithering tentacles increased in size and like in some terrible nightmare, he felt their icy touch to his arms and face. His skin crawled, and his stomach turned, but he didn't stop what he was doing.

The tentacles pulled him closer, wrapping around him, forcing his wings down. In a split-moment decision, he lowered his sword and let the darkness consume him. The mass of the spell surrounded him like a dense wall, immobilizing him. His skin burned from its icy touch, but he ignored the pain.

"*Slavik, run,*" Gunz yelled through their bond and let go of his control as much as he could without fully reverting into the natural state of the Fire Salamander.

Physical fire and elemental energy enveloped him, attacking the darkness from within. The spell howled and squeezed him tighter, suffocating him with its poisonous fumes. He screamed and connected with the power of War, entwining it with the elemental energy he was wielding. Mishka's wings went up in smoldering flames, breaking the hold of the dark spell. Gunz's muscles stiffened as he strained to channel more and more of his power, and the stone of War on his finger ignited with a bright red light.

With significant effort, he managed to bring his sword above his head, clutching it with both hands. A bright ray of elemental fire wrapped with the scarlet flames of War rushed through the blade, setting it ablaze. The evil spell started to vibrate, moving side to side like a disgusting, gray jelly. Gunz screamed, throwing everything he had into the last blast. With an ear-splitting bang, the spell exploded, its blast wave propelling him a few feet backward.

For a moment, a haze of gray particles hung in the air like a revolting, filthy curtain. Diabolical laughter rushed through the area, making his blood run cold, and the particles moved closer together, forming two glowing eyes. Gunz stared into the abyss of darkness hidden behind electric blue irises, and his soul twisted as if he were walking through the gates into *Peklo* again, abandoning all his hopes. The eyes rose higher and dissipated, leaving behind a soft, scarlet glow reflected on the edges of the stormy clouds and the barely noticeable stench of sulfur.

Gunz lowered down to the ground and dropped to his knees, his chest rising and falling with heavy breaths. His wings were still expanded to full length, and he could still feel the burning pain that was always there when he had to merge with the wyvern.

"Mishka," he rasped, barely able to move his lips. "Thank you, my friend. Please, let go now…"

As the wyvern separated from him, Gunz fell forward to all fours, struggling to fill his lungs with oxygen. Lifting his head, he saw with relief that Mrak Delar was done. The confused and disoriented people slowly headed down the hill, looking around wildly.

"Aidan! Tessa!" Gunz screamed, struggling to get up.

He felt Yaroslav's strong hands gently helping him to his feet and leaned heavily on his shoulder. By the time he reached the place where Aidan's shield used to be, Mrak Delar was there already. The Master of Power glanced at Gunz over his shoulder, drops of sweat running down his pale skin, and his lips pressed into a grim line, a muscle twitching in his jaw.

Tessa sat in front of Mrak Delar, looking gray with exhaustion. Tears ran down her face, leaving glistening paths in the dirt and brown splatters on her cheeks. Aidan lay on the ground, his head resting on Tessa's lap, and her fingers trailed through his matted hair absentmindedly. A long piece of rebar pierced his chest right above his heart, and his shirt, torn in a few places, was soaked with blood. A thin, red rivulet oozed from the corner of his mouth, and his hands were trembling slightly as he pressed them against the wound.

Gunz looked at his friend, his limbs filled with led. "He's a god," he whispered more to himself than to anyone else. "He can't die." He threw a quick glance at the Master of Power. "Mrak, can you heal him?"

Mrak Delar shook his head no. "Gunz, I'm too drained to perform healing magic. It took all I had to purify the crowd. We should get back to the Otherworld as soon as we can. I promise Aidan is going to be all right. Once he's in his domain, Gwyn can restore him." He rubbed his forehead, his moves slow and fatigued. "Or Yaroslav can donate some of his blood." He glanced up, pointing at the sky. "Besides, I think we have a serious problem on our hands."

Gunz glanced at the sky, and his jaw dropped. The slight scarlet glow the dark spell had left behind intensified, and now, the sky was colored in sinister crimson shades. The edges of the stormy clouds were lit up with a brighter, scarlet outline, and purple lightning bolts kept flashing in the depths of the clouds. From time to time, shining fireballs flew across the sky, emitting bright-orange sparks around them. They didn't reach the ground, quickly dissipating, but the overall scenery looked like something from a post-apocalyptic movie.

"What the hell?" muttered Gunz, rising unsteadily.

"Not yet," whispered Aidan, his lips coated with a layer of blood barely moving. "But we're getting there..." He glanced at the Master of Power. "Mrak... take me home..."

Mrak Delar got up with a strained groan and threw his long hair, soaked with sweat, off his face. "Yaroslav, I need you to lift Aidan," he said softly. "I'm too drained to teleport all of you at the same time." He glanced at Gunz, and an expression of concern flashed through his face. "Gunz, you look like you're ready to collapse, too. Can you and Tessa wait here for my return? I'll be back as soon as I can."

"I'll be fine, Mrak," replied Gunz with a faint smirk. "Go already."

He watched Yaroslav lift Aidan with his usual ease, and a chain of thoughts rushed through his mind, a heavy weight settling in his soul. Aidan's head dropped powerlessly, lolling with every move the vampire made. The rebar still protruded from his chest, and blood dripped down his side, falling to the ground in thick, red drops. The Master of Power looked just as uneasy as Gunz felt, and that just added to his overall feeling of dread, but he smiled and waved his hand, telling Mrak to leave.

Mrak Delar put his hand on Yaroslav's elbow and snapped his fingers. As they vanished from the hill, Gunz wrapped his arm around Tessa's shoulder, directing her toward the tower. Once they reached it, he lowered down and put his sword by his side, resting his back against the rough stonework of the wall. Tessa sat next to him, wrapping her arms around her bent legs. Gunz glanced at her sideways and smiled, gently pulling her closer.

"You know Aidan is going to be fine," he said softly.

She nodded, tears sliding from her wide-open eyes. "It was his stepmother," she whispered. "She sent demons after us and then attacked us here…"

"Where were you?" asked Gunz as she lowered her head to his shoulder.

"A long story," she said quietly. "When we get back to Gwyn's, I'll tell all the details to everyone, but to make it short— I found my father."

"Perun?"

"Yeah…" She readjusted her position, pushing her hand through the crook of Gunz's arm. "Interesting character…" She lifted her head, gazing up into his eyes. "Listen, Gunz, there was something Aoife said when she attacked us… Aidan was wounded already, lying on the ground, and I conjured the protective shield."

Gunz gazed into her deep brown eyes where sadness seemed to take a permanent residence. "Whatever she told you—ignore it. She lied. She's a master manipulator, Tessa. She tried to unhinge you… make you react."

Tessa nodded, averting her gaze, her finger fidgeting with the tear in the jeans on her knee. "You're probably right," she said at length. "But there was one part she said... It bothers me." She bit her lip, and a deep wrinkle appeared between her eyebrows. "She said that you, Aidan and Yaroslav are so deeply codependent that you would let this world crash and burn before you'd let anything happen to each other."

Gunz froze, and the hair on the back of his neck stood on end.

"She said," continued Tessa, her voice barely audible, "she would exploit this codependency... starting now."

"Now? How?"

"She knew you wouldn't leave Aidan stranded and under attack," said Tessa. She looked up, pointing at the sky. "This firework... Do you think it happened because you broke her spell?" She peered at him, her lips trembling. "Because you saved us, did you start the Apocalypse?"

"Thunderstorm of hail and fire," said a deep male voice from above, and Gunz sprung to his feet, grabbing his sword.

Viggo Warrington stood in front of them, his left arm in the pocket of his pants. He pointed up and smirked. "Apocalypse it is not," he said icily. "But it is a big problem." He offered his hand to Tessa, helping her to her feet. "I'm not sure what happened here. The Master of Power asked me to bring you back to Gwyn's house, so I didn't hear the entire story. But something tells me Tessa is right."

Gunz turned his sword into the knife and put it in his pocket. "You mean, I did that?"

Viggo shrugged. "The oldest trick in the book, son," he said and waved his hand, opening his portal. "My guess, she needed the elemental fire energy to start"—he waved his hand at the blood-red sky—"whatever that is. You gave her what she needed."

CHAPTER 26

~ ZANE BURNS, A.K.A. GUNZ ~

G unz sat on Gwyn's couch, struggling to stay awake while Tessa told them everything that had happened from the moment Aidan and she left the Otherworld to find her father, the Slavic god of Thunder. She was trying to stay calm, but that made her voice soft and monotonous, and he couldn't help it, his mind drifting on and off.

Sitting next to him, Yaroslav kept poking him in his side to make sure he wouldn't fall asleep. Tessa didn't tell anyone what Aoife had said to them, but she didn't have to. Somehow both Kal and Gwyn ap Nudd knew exactly what had happened on the top of Glastonbury Tor.

Mrak Delar sat on his other side, his eyes half-closed, his hands resting on his lap, but Gunz was positive the Ancient Master didn't miss a word of Tessa's story. Aidan was missing, recovering upstairs after Gwyn performed the healing magic, and Viggo stood by the wall with his hands in his pockets.

"So, Perun told you that to fight the evil triad, you need Sword Kladenets, but he gave you no directions," said Viggo, pushing himself off the wall. "How very helpful."

"He didn't know himself. He would tell me if he knew,"

objected Tessa, and Gunz chuckled at how defensive she sounded. Just a few days ago she was going on and on about how much she didn't care for her biological father, and now, she was ready to bite Viggo's head off, defending him.

"Stop! Don't say another word..."

A raspy voice, filled with urgency, sounded from the second floor, and Gunz snapped his head up, instantly awake. Aidan stood at the top of the stairs, his hand pressed to his bare chest. The rebar was gone, and the wound had healed already, but the front of his body was covered in brown stains of dried out blood, and his pants were torn and dirty.

"Aidan," gasped Tessa, taking a step toward the stairs. "You should be in bed."

Clutching the railing with his hand, Aidan took an unsteady step forward and halted, swaying on his feet. Carefully taking one step at the time, he made it all the way down and stopped, breathing laboriously as if he had just climbed Mount Everest. Gwyn ap Nudd approached him and helped him into an armchair.

"What are you doing here, son?" he said with the kind of tenderness Gunz hadn't thought the stern Lord of the Wild Hunt capable of. "You were gravely wounded. Your human body needs some rest to recover."

Aidan raised his hand asking for attention and then in one sharp move, he ripped the Guardians' pendant off his neck.

"Slavik," he said in a hoarse voice, "can you help me, please?"

Yaroslav threw a baffled gaze at Gunz, but got up and approached Aidan, halting in front of him. Aidan gestured at him to get closer, and when the vampire kneeled in front of him, he leaned forward and whispered something into his ear.

Yaroslav's eyebrows rose, and his eyes widened as he took the pendant from Aidan's hand. "Are you sure you want me to do it, my friend?" he asked quietly. "That would—"

"Not a word, Slavik," hissed Aidan. "Do it now. I'm too weak, otherwise I would do it myself."

Yaroslav nodded and squeezed the pendant in his hand. Bright sparks erupted from his fist as he crushed the medallion into a few pieces. The vampire hissed, jumping to his feet, staring down at his hand. A deep, angry burn marred his skin in the place where the pendant had been. He sat down on the couch next to Gunz, watching his wound starting to close.

"Thank you," exhaled Aidan and fell back in his armchair.

"What did you do?" asked Gwyn ap Nudd, an expression of horror imprinted on his face. He picked up the pieces of the pendant, staring at them in shock.

"You're an oath breaker once again," said Kal, a dangerous growl in his voice. "But this time you broke the oath you swore to the Destiny Council. What's wrong with you, boy?"

"Stop," said Aidan quietly, barely lifting his arm. "Please, stop talking and let me explain."

"Fine. Please explain why you just moved yourself to the top of the Destiny Council's most wanted list," said Gwyn ap Nudd, folding his arms over his chest.

Aidan sighed, shaking his head. "Because we have a traitor among us, but I'm sure they're not in this room," he said through gritted teeth, anger lighting up his eyes with a faint white glow. "Someone who's tampered with my pendant, turning it into a surveillance device, projecting everything I say and do to the evil triad." He fell silent, his chest moving with ragged breath. "We've been watched for the last six months through this pendant. And who knows? Depending on who this person is, we could have been watched for many years."

In so many words, he told them everything he had learned from Perun. A pregnant pause hung in the room, making Gunz's skin crawl. No one moved. No one said anything.

"How do you know it's not one of us?" asked Viggo Warrington, moving his hand around.

Aidan raised his eyes at War, and a tired smile touched his lips. "You're too new to our small group, Mr. Warrington. Besides, your position doesn't allow you to get involved into the affairs of the human realm or take sides. No matter what, you must remain neutral," he said dryly. "You can't be the traitor. The rest of the people in this room I trust unconditionally. Each of them would die for me. Just like I would give my life to protect them."

"That's the problem. In more ways than you know." Viggo smirked, stroking the stubble on his chin with his fingers. "You must remember one thing, my young, godly friend. Real betrayal never comes from your enemies."

"Be it as it may," objected Aidan. "I'm positive. The traitor is not in this room."

Gunz stared at Aidan, his mind traveling back to the attack of the volkolaks on the gypsies' camp. "Aidan, you sent Yaroslav and Svyatobor to the Land of Dreams to find me. You knew that I was helpless after what Chernobog had done to me, didn't you?"

"Yes. We all knew it," replied Aidan, his pale face losing whatever color it had, becoming almost translucent. "Belobog and Semargl told us about that. Why?"

"That explains it," muttered Gunz. Catching puzzled gazes directed at him, he continued, "I was attacked in the Land of Dreams. A giant pack of volkolaks." He threw an arched stare at Aidan.

"Aoife," growled Aidan, squeezing the armrests of his chair, his fingers digging deep into the white leather. "Only she can conjure so many monsters in such a short time and control them."

"My thoughts exactly," murmured Gunz. "Luckily, Slavik and Svyatobor showed up in time."

"To modify the energy of the Destiny Council's pendant," started Gwyn ap Nudd, staring at the shards of the pendant in

N. M. THORN

his palm, "the traitor must be quite powerful. I used to make these pendants, and I assure you, it's not easy to change its magical properties."

"I second that," murmured Kal, fire breaking through the skin on his shoulders and arms, betraying his emotional state. "The person who did this must be either a part of the Guardians Order, Wardens Order or a member of the Destiny Council."

"Well, that narrows it down," said Tessa, lowering on the armrest of Aidan's chair.

"Actually, it does," objected Aidan, leaning to the side to rest his head against Tessa's shoulder. "I haven't been to the Guardians Order since the Destiny Council gave me the pendant. Also, I haven't been in touch with anyone from the Destiny Council either."

"Wardens then," said Gunz, unease spreading through him as Aidan frowned and nodded. "It can't be…" His voice trailed away, and he swallowed hard, unable to say the name of the person they trusted with their lives. The only representative of the Wardens Order who had stood by his side when the Destiny Council was hunting him across his world and every magical world out there.

"Gwyn, open your door for me, please," said Mrak Delar, rising, and the glass walls of the house trembled. "Let's get to the bottom of this now."

"Mrak, what are you planning to do?" Gunz got up, grabbing Mrak's arm. "We don't even know if it's him."

"All the more reasons to find out," replied the Master of Power through clenched teeth. He turned to Gwyn ap Nudd with a light bow, and an ominous smirk crossed his face. "Keep your door open for me, my lord. I'll be right back."

As the Master of Power disappeared through the blazing light, Aidan wrapped his arm around Tessa's waist and closed his eyes faintly. "He's one step from shutting down."

"He's one step from unleashing an Armageddon." Viggo

278

Warrington chuckled, amusement not reaching his steel-gray eyes. "The dark side of your Master of Power is something to behold. I don't envy whoever is on the receiving side of his anger."

"Yeah, well," murmured Kal, "if you don't want to end up on that proverbial receiving end of his power don't remind him about his dark side. He doesn't appreciate it."

"Let me guess." Viggo tilted his head a little, tapping his fingers against his lips. "The more he tries to leave his darkness in the past, the more people keep throwing his past in his face. I can't blame him for being a little upset."

Before Kal could reply, the walls of Gwyn's house trembled again, and the Master of Power emerged through the light, carrying a man draped over his shoulder. Without slowing down, he snapped his fingers, muttering something under his breath, and a kitchen chair materialized in the middle of the living room. He dumped the man unceremoniously into the chair and snapped his fingers again, restraining him with the glowing ropes of his magic.

The man's head dropped to his chest, his long, wavy hair falling down like a curtain as he hung limply in his restraints. Gunz sucked in a sharp breath, leaning forward to see his face.

"I didn't hurt him," said the Master of Power icily. "But I had no time to deal with his questions and objections, so I put him in an enchanted sleep." He turned to Gwyn ap Nudd, his black eyes sparkling with fury. "He's all yours, my lord. Turn his soul inside out if he has one."

The Master of Power stepped away and sat down on the couch heavily, his hands still trembling with suppressed anger. He took a few deep breaths to calm down and leaned back, stretching his long legs.

Gwyn ap Nudd approached the man in the chair and seized his hair, lifting his head. He placed two fingers on his forehead and whispered a few words, breaking Mrak's enchantment. The man sucked in a sharp breath and his eyes flew opened.

"Hello, Raoul," said the King of the Otherworld in a soft whisper, and it sounded like the purr of a panther ready to pounce on its prey.

Raoul de Beaumont looked around and pushed against his restraints. "What's going on?" he asked, confusion reflected in his blue eyes.

"We're about to find out, but I promise, you're not going to enjoy it," replied Gwyn ap Nudd, the power of the Otherworld gathering around him in soft, glowing waves.

"No, my lord, please!" yelled Raoul, fear contorting his handsome features. "I swear, it's some kind of mistake!"

"Gwyn—," started Gunz but fell silent, scolded by Gwyn's angry stare.

"Let's see what you're hiding under this thin layer of modern civility, *Monsieur* de Beaumont..." Gwyn ap Nudd placed his hand on Raoul's chest and channeled his power through him, staring directly into his eyes. As the brilliant white light surrounded both of them, the Warden screamed and thrashed in the restraints of Mrak's magic, unable to break his eye contact with the King of the Otherworld.

As Gwyn kept chanting, Raoul's appearance started to change. He was still the same man—the same face and body— but a barely noticeable visage of his true form appeared around him, lingering in the air like a three-dimensional hologram.

Little by little, the image took shape and color, becoming more apparent, merging with the young man in the priest's apparel. Soon after, a medieval knight sat in the chair, a bright red cross of a knight Templar shining on his bloodied tunic. His face was swollen and covered in black and blue spots of bruises, and terrible wounds appeared on his wrists and neck.

Gwyn ap Nudd let go, and the knight Templar disappeared.

Raoul sat in the chair, gasping for air, tears running down his colorless face.

"He's not the one," said the King of the Otherworld. "His soul is pure. He doesn't have an ounce of darkness in him. He never had."

"What did you think I was? A demon?" Raoul lifted his head, his eyes filled with angry tears, darting from one face to the next, burning them with reproach. "Have I ever given you a reason to doubt my loyalty? Or my devotion to the light?"

"Master, you can release him," said Gwyn ap Nudd, dropping into one of the armchairs. "My apologies, Father de Beaumont, but we had to be sure."

"Sure of what exactly?" growled Raoul, massaging his wrists as Mrak Delar removed the restraints of his magic. "You couldn't just ask me?"

"I'm sorry, Raoul, but we couldn't ask you," said Aidan. Quickly, he explained the situation to the Warden, including everything that Perun had told him and Tessa.

"Jesus Christ Almighty," exhaled the Warden, his eyes wide. "I don't even know where to start with all that."

"Did you know about Gunz's disappearance or about Tessa's quest to find her father?" asked Aidan.

"No," replied Raoul. "I swear I had no idea. Anyway, there was only one Warden who has ever touched your pendant, Aidan. This man is the light in its purest form. There is no way—"

"His name, please," said Gwyn ap Nudd, interrupting him, suppressed fury ringing in his deep voice.

"My lord, I'm begging you." Raoul de Beaumont got up, taking a step closer to the King of the Otherworld. "Do not put another innocent man through the torture you just put me through."

"His name!" yelled Gwyn ap Nudd, the black mask flashing over his face. "Someone is spying on my son and on all of us here, reporting to the evil triad. If you didn't notice, the sky is blood-red! Someone is putting the entire world in danger of destruction! So, I will put thousands of so-called *innocent* men through my reading if I have to! Give me the name, Raoul, or I'll beat it out of you!"

Raising his arms, Raoul shied away from the infuriated King of the Otherworld, just to run into Viggo Warrington and Kal. The Warden spun around and gasped. Viggo stood with his hands folded over his chest, the icy expression on his face promising nothing good. Kal towered over him silently, the anger in his igneous eyes burning brighter than Gwyn's light.

Viggo grabbed Raoul's shoulder with his left hand and waved his right hand. Surrounded by red sparkles, a giant semi-transparent clock materialized in midair, taking the entire space between the ceiling and the floor. The clock was showing one minute to midnight.

"Do you know what this is, Warden?" hissed War, forcing Raoul closer to the clock.

"Yes, my lord," moaned Raoul, fear frozen in his wide eyes. "It's the doomsday clock."

"That's right!" yelled Viggo. He waved his hand, and the clock disappeared. "One more tick and one more tock, and my siblings and I will ride again! And you are, by concealing the name of the traitor, moving the hand of this clock!" He turned Raoul around to face him, and a sinister smile spread on his face. "Besides, whoever this man is, he put my son in harm's way, and I don't take things like that lightly. Trust me."

"Your son?" mumbled the Warden, looking around wildly.

Viggo Warrington laughed, gazing heavenward. "Is that the only thing you registered from everything I said, Templar?" He rolled his eyes and pointed at Gunz. "Zane Burns is my biological son. Now, give us the name."

Gunz and Yaroslav jumped to their feet, ready to spring into action if needed, and the Axe of Perun materialized in Tessa's hands as she got up. Only Mrak Delar remained seated, watching the unfolding drama with interest in his obsidian eyes.

"Who's the man who had access to Aidan's pendant, Raoul?" asked Kal, fire slowly dying down in his eyes. "If he's innocent, he has nothing to worry about."

"Heavenly Father, have mercy," mumbled the Warden, crossing himself. "The only other Warden who has ever touched Aidan's new pendant was our Grand Master, Father Collins." He dropped his head, his arms dangling along his sides. "Please, my lord, have mercy. You're looking for a traitor in the wrong place. It couldn't have been anyone in the Wardens Order."

"Let me be the judge of that," growled Gwyn ap Nudd.

He waved his hand, and a dark portal materialized in midair. Dark-blue sparkles spun in a continuous clockwise motion, and a few pairs of phosphoric eyes shone through the rotating void of the portal. Being used to Gwyn's shining doors, Gunz stared at it with shock. In the meantime, Gwyn's appearance started to change and soon, the Lord of the Wild Hunt stood in the middle of the room in his full regalia, his sharply angled eyes blazing through the slits of the black mask.

"Gwyn, stop!" shouted Kal, seizing Gwyn's arm. "You can't leave the Otherworld until the night of Samhain."

Gwyn laughed, and the distant barking of dogs and neighing of horses echoed his laughter. "This year, Samhain came early," he growled. "The Destiny Council can bite me. If they feel adventurous, that is." He laughed again, pulling his long, black hair into a low ponytail on the back of his head. "I'll be back within twenty-four hours. In the meantime, if anyone needs to leave the Otherworld, Kal or Gunz can open their portals through my wards."

He walked through the portal, closing it.

CHAPTER 27

~ ZANE BURNS, A.K.A. GUNZ ~

K al threw his arms up, staring at the place where Gwyn's portal had been rotating just a moment ago. Then he punched the air with his fist, and his fire energy spiked up, smoldering heat surrounding him.

"Fire Almighty!" he shouted, anger and desperation shadowing his face. "He's going to drain himself leading the Hunt through the full veil. During Samhain the veil between the world of the living and the realm of the dead is the thinnest, and he doesn't need much of his energy to cross through it." He threw his hands up again and fell into the armchair, leaning back heavily. "Reckless!"

"If I may speak, my lord," said Raoul quietly. "I think the Lord of the Wild Hunt is going to be fine."

"How is that?" asked Mrak Delar. He rubbed his face, fatigue showing in his every move, and stared at Raoul impassively as he waited for his answer.

"Just before you abducted me"—Raoul threw a reproachful glance at the Master of Power—"I received a report from the Wardens HQ. I get them on a regular basis. The last one was more troubling than any of them. The world has tilted further toward darkness, and the veil has been compromised. Now, it's almost as thin and vulnerable as during Samhain. Gwyn ap Nudd will have to use his internal energy to merge through it, but it's not going to drain him."

"The Warden is right," said Viggo, pushing himself away from the wall he was leaning on. "The balance is no more, and darkness is slowly taking over the world. I can't say anything else, but you must put your heads together and stop the evil triad."

"And if we don't?" Tessa peeped, her brown eyes double their normal size.

"Bye-bye humanity." Viggo smirked frostily and waved his hand goodbye. Then he frowned and approached Gunz, putting his hand on his shoulder. "I must leave, son. You and your friends have to figure it all out, and I can't be a part of this discussion." He looked over Gunz's head into space wistfully. "I wish it was... different, you know?" He dropped his hand, sadness overwhelming his gray eyes. "If you need my help, you can always summon me. All you have to do is touch the stone on your ring and call me."

"Thank you, sir," replied Gunz, taking a step back and offering him his hand.

Viggo looked down at his hand, and a sad smile crossed his face. He took it and squeezed it in a handshake. "Whether you believe it or not, Zane," he said softly, "I'm always here for you." He let go of Gunz's hand and turned to Kal. "Great Salamander, would you mind opening a portal into the labyrinth for me?"

Kal got up and walked to the far end of the room. With a light flick of his wrist, he unfolded the flaming curtain of his portal, gesturing for War to go through. However, before Viggo could leave, Mrak Delar got up and crossed the living room, stopping him. He waved his hand, muttering something, and a slightly yellow glow of a cloaking spell encapsulated War and the Master of Power, leaving Kal outside.

For a few seconds, they conversed about something calmly, their faces betraying no emotions. Then the Master of Power lifted his spell, and Viggo Warrington walked through the fire, disappearing behind the flaming curtain.

"What was that all about, Master?" asked Kal, folding his massive arms as he stared down at Mrak Delar.

The Master of Power blanched but quickly recovered and smiled nonchalantly. "It was personal, Great Salamander. Nothing you need to worry about."

He walked around Kal and disappeared behind the kitchen door. A few minutes later, the bitter scent of freshly brewed coffee wafted through the living room, and the Master of Power reappeared, holding a cup with a steaming beverage in his hand.

"If anyone wants coffee, I made enough." He waved over his shoulder in the direction of the kitchen. Then he walked toward the couch and sat down, careful not to spill his drink on Gwyn's white furniture.

"Good idea." Gunz got up and headed to the kitchen.

Between the events of the last few days, he felt drained, not only magically, but physically and emotionally too, and with the constant threat of Skiper-Zmey invading his mind, he couldn't sleep in peace either. He inhaled the smell of coffee and closed his eyes, rolling his sore shoulders.

Reaching up, he opened the cabinet and grabbed a coffee mug. He filled it with steaming coffee and without adding any sugar or milk, took the first sip. As the hot drink rushed down his throat, he put the mug down and leaned on top of the counter, enjoying the feeling of the liquid energy rushing through him.

"How do you do it? It's burning hot."

Gunz heard Raoul's voice and turned around. "I'm the Fire Salamander. There is no such thing as too hot for me," he replied, taking another sip of his coffee.

The Warden grabbed another mug and filled it with coffee.

He took a small packet of sugar from a box on the counter and tore it, adding its contents into his cup. Noticing a powdered coffee creamer, he added a couple of spoons into his drink and mixed everything slowly, staring thoughtfully as the dark brown liquid turned beige.

"You broke your oath, *mon ami*," he said without raising his eyes. "What happened?"

Gunz sighed. He wasn't looking forward to this conversation. "I did what I believe was the right thing to do." He turned to face the Warden, locking his fingers over the mug. "And all things considered, I still believe I've done the right thing."

"All things considered?" Raoul smirked and bit his lip, but his voice got louder as he continued, "You gave the most powerful magical artifact to a dark deity."

He threw his hands up, forgetting that he was holding his coffee. As the hot liquid spilled on his hand, he cursed quietly in French and put the cup on the counter, grabbing a piece of paper towel.

"How can it possibly be the right thing?" He wiped the small puddle off the counter and off the floor, and threw the paper into a garbage can, his moves sharp and aggravated. "The world is taking a nosedive into darkness, and what you did just propelled it farther down."

"No, Raoul," objected Gunz. "First of all, I didn't give it to Chernobog. I split it equally between him and his twin brother. So, the balance didn't suffer any changes because of that. Second, by doing it, I bound the god of Light and Creation with the god of Destruction. Only by working together can they use the power of the Codex. And third, now that we know there is a traitor in the Wardens Order, don't you think it's a good thing I didn't give the Dark Codex to your organization?"

He picked up his coffee and took a couple of long gulps.

"No, I do not believe Father Collins would betray us,"

muttered Raoul, his French accent becoming heavier by the moment. "He's the most honorable, purest soul I've ever met."

"I guess we'll find out within twenty-four hours? In the meantime, my question to you"—Gunz raised his eyes, a lopsided smirk touching his lips—"are you going to take me to the Wardens HQ and prosecute me for breaking the oath, or are you going to help us find a way to win this battle?"

The Warden chuckled. "It's always a matter of life and death with you," he muttered, shaking his head.

"Well, I'm the Great Fire Salamander, the defender of the human realm, am I not?" Gunz laughed, tapping Raoul on his shoulder. "Come on, Master Warden, let's talk."

"Defender my ass," grumbled the Warden, making a fresh cup of coffee for himself. "You're a hot mess, that's what you are."

"At least you admitted I'm hot." Gunz winked and headed out of the kitchen.

Gunz walked into the living room and found Aidan sleeping in the armchair with his head thrown back, and his mouth slightly opened. Tessa sat next to Yaroslav, and they were chatting in hush voices, trying not to wake Aidan up. But it was Mrak's and Kal's position that drew Gunz's attention. Mrak Delar stood at the opposite side of the room, cornered by Kal. The Great Salamander placed his hands on the wall on either side of the Master of Power, towering over him, and his entire demeanor exuded unconcealed threat. Whatever the Great Salamander was saying, made Mrak pale and rigid, and if Gunz didn't know any better, he would say Mrak was terrified.

Gunz approached them, his stomach twitching with an expectation of more problems. "Father," he called the Great Salamander, tapping him on his shoulder. "Whatever is going on between you two, cut it out. Not a good time to have disputes among ourselves."

Kal took a deep breath and turned around, his thin lips

squeezed into a firm line. "You're right," he growled through clenched teeth. "We'll continue this conversation later." He walked away and halted next to the TV, leaning against the wall.

Gunz threw a quizzical look at the Master of Power, but he just shook his head and mouthed, "Not now."

Gunz decided that the best course of action would be to let it go and turned around, searching for the Warden. "Hey, Raoul," he said, making his way closer to him. "Since you're with us, I wonder if I could pick your brain."

"Why not?" The Warden huffed with a half-shrug. "You lot already took my soul apart, why wouldn't you do the same with my brain?"

"This room is overflowing with poorly suppressed hostility," murmured Gunz. His eyes darted between a fuming Kal and a jittery Mrak Delar, and he rubbed his forehead, lowering down on the couch next to Yaroslav. He glanced back to the disgruntled Warden and added, raising his voice slightly, "I suggest we all drop the passive-aggressive attitude and start working together. The way we used to do it for years."

"Fine." Raoul flicked his wrist, not without some annoyance. "What did you want to ask?"

"What do you know about Zlebog?" asked Gunz. "And if you don't know anything about him, can you check the Wardens' Archives?"

"Come again?" Raoul's face lost all color, the look of annoyance replaced by anxiety. His hand shook, and he almost spilled his coffee. "Where did you hear that name?"

Kal straightened, his moves painfully slow. "Why are you asking?" he managed to say in a hoarse whisper.

"Judging by your reaction, only Kal and Raoul are familiar with this name," said Gunz, tightness settling in his chest. "I asked that because Zlebog is the one who leads the evil triad. He's the dark deity who's been behind all this mess from the very beginning."

"Impossible," exhaled Kal. "Zlebog was imprisoned many centuries ago by Svarog himself for his crimes against humanity, and any trace of his existence was wiped out." He waved at Mrak Delar. "Even the Ancient Master with his deep knowledge of history of magic is too young to know anything about him. No one does. No one except—" He cut himself off, and his eyes widened.

"Chernobog," Gunz finished the statement calmly. "No one except Chernobog knew about his existence. He was supposed to keep him locked up and powerless in his lower dungeons."

"Fire Almighty," whispered Kal. Pressing his hand over his mouth, he fell silent for a moment before continuing, "How the hell did he break free from *Peklo*?" He regarded Gunz with narrowed eyes and understanding dawned on his face. "Is that why Chernobog summoned you?"

Gunz nodded. "Mostly. He wanted the Dark Codex in his arsenal to fight Zlebog, of course, and he thought that if I would see everything with my own eyes, it would be easier to convince me."

"God damn him," muttered Raoul, his forehead creased. "He was right."

"After everything he showed me, I decided to comply with his demands and give him the Codex. Well, sort of, anyway," continued Gunz, raising his hand to stop the interruptions. "Chernobog is the only one who has a fighting chance against Zlebog. So, if he believes that his godly powers are not enough to beat this evil—you bet, I'll give him what he asks for." Trying to be as brief as possible, Gunz told everyone about his visit to the Dark Nav and almost everything Chernobog had told him, leaving out just a few personal details the god of Destruction had revealed to him.

"God save us all," said Raoul, crossing himself. "It's the worse news I've heard since I joined the Wardens Order. Zlebog is the primordial evil. I'm not sure we can fight him and live through it to tell the tale." He slammed his hand on the table, nibbling on his lip. "I'm not sure Chernobog can stop him either. Even with the Dark Codex."

"From what I've heard, you barely survived the fight with Skiper-Zmey," muttered Yaroslav. "And the last time you fought the air demon, it took two gods, Death and an Archangel to defeat her. How are we going to handle the three of them?"

"Perun is going to join us," said Tessa. "He's one of the most powerful gods in his pantheon. Hopefully, he knows how to defeat this… whatchamacallit…?"

"Zlebog," supplied Aidan, and everyone turned to him.

"Hey man, did we wake you up?" asked Yaroslav.

"No," murmured Aidan. "I feel like I'm still asleep, stuck in some horrendous nightmare." He leaned forward, rubbing his face tiredly. "Anyway, Perun told us what we need to defeat Skiper-Zmey and the triad."

"*Mech Kladenets*," said Mrak Delar, the corners of his lips quirking up in a humorless smirk. "Aidan, you do realize that he sent you on a wild goose chase, right?"

"What do you mean?" asked Aidan, straightening. "I've heard about this weapon before. All we have to do—"

Mrak Delar waved his hand impatiently, cutting him off. He moved closer to Aidan and leaned forward slightly. "Aidan, every Slavic child knows about this weapon from their fairy tales. But no one—magical or mundane—has ever seen it. Assuming it exists, how are we supposed to find it?"

"We could summon Svarog," suggested Yaroslav. "According to Slavic lore, he was the one who forged it at the time of creation. He may know where to find it."

The Master of Power laughed, a cold and dry sound that sent shivers down Gunz's back. "Gods like Svarog or Veles don't do house calls," he objected frostily.

"I could summon Belobog," said Aidan. "He said, he'll come if I need his help."

"Belobog is not going to know. And neither will Perun," said Raoul. He took a sip of his coffee and put the cup on the table. "Don't summon anyone. If what I recall is true, they won't be able to help you, anyway. Just give me a moment."

He raised his arms slightly, his palms up, and his eyes became milky white. For a while, he remained still and silent, and Gunz threw a concerned look at Mrak Delar, but the Master of Power gave him a tiny shake of his head, frowning.

Shortly after, Raoul's eyes returned to normal, and he smiled sadly, lowering himself into the chair he'd been restrained in just a short while ago.

"I was right. Except Svarog, no one can tell you how to find it," he said, slouching in the chair. "The reason no one has ever seen the Sword Kladenets is because Svarog made sure it wouldn't be easy to find it. He gave this sword a mind of its own and the power to disguise itself."

"How?" asked Gunz.

"It's rather ingenious if you ask me," said the Warden. "The sword can shape-shift into any living or inanimate object, and it'll present its true form only to the person it deems worthy."

"Ingenious, alright," mumbled Aidan. "It can be in any world, and it can be pretty much anything."

"I think I know how to find it," said the Warden, a winning smile lighting up his features. "The sword's favorite shape is"—he raised his finger, calling for attention—"an Aspid. Didn't you kill one about six-seven months ago?"

"Yes, we did," agreed Mrak Delar. "But an Aspid is not a single entity. They can be summoned or rather conjured by using some forbidden branches of the Dark Arts. I'm sure the Aspid we killed was summoned by the triad."

"So what?" Raoul shrugged. "The Aspid was conjured by the triad, but it doesn't mean the sword wouldn't hide itself in it. The Board of—"

"Oh, please... not the Board of Destiny speech," murmured

Mrak Delar. "I'm fed up with the Destiny Council and their shady ways... even if they're finally on our side."

"Master, the Destiny Council watches over the Board of Destiny. They don't command it." Raoul walked around the table and approached the Master of Power, placing his hand on his shoulder. "This is our best chance. Don't you think we should at least give it a try? You should know better than anyone else that there is no such thing as coincidences when it comes to the paths of the Board of Destiny. And this one would be a *grand* coincidence, don't you think, *mon ami?*"

"The Warden has a point," murmured Kal with a light shrug. "Besides, it's not like we have any other leads."

"I guess I'll go and check it out, then," said the Master of Power, making a move to get up. "It won't take me long."

"You stay where you are, Ancient Master," objected Kal, tilting his head slightly. "You and I have an unfinished conversation, and until I know what you're hiding, you're going nowhere."

Mrak Delar threw his hands up, sending a desperate glance to Gunz. "Kal—"

"It's not your quest, anyway, Mrak," said Kal, iron notes in his voice.

"Great Salamander, my lord," said the Master of Power as peacefully as he could. "Aidan has never been to Mount Vottovaara. He hasn't fought the Aspid with us. I have to go. He won't know what to look for."

"Nice try, Master." Kal folded his arms resentfully. "The answer is still no."

"My lord." Tessa got up awkwardly, halting by Aidan's side. "Perun said Aidan and I must find the sword, so it's our quest. However, the Ancient Master is right. Neither I nor Aidan know what to look for or where to go. We need Master Mrak Delar to teleport us there and help us find the sword."

"Take any of these two," said Kal, pointing at Gunz and Yaroslav. "They know their way around the mountain."

"Aidan doesn't know where to go." Tessa held out her hand, bending one finger at the time as she continued. "Zane is exhausted. Yaroslav can't teleport. I need the Master of Power to accompany us, my lord."

Gunz got up, struggling not to sway as the room spun around him in a slow, dizzying motion. "I'll go with you and Aidan, Tessa," he said quietly. "It started with the three of us, and we'll finish it."

He walked around the table and approached Kal. The Great Salamander looked down at him, aggravation slowly melting away in his burning eyes.

"My boy." Kal brushed Gunz's arm with his hand gently. "I'm sorry. I know you're exhausted, but it has to be you."

"I know, Father," replied Gunz, warmth expanding in his chest as he looked into the igneous eyes of the powerful being of magic who loved and cared for him more than any person had ever done. "I have to go, but not for the reason you think." He glanced at Mrak Delar, and a twinge of remorse squeezed his heart. "I believe the three of us need to have a quick word in private." He gestured for Kal and Mrak Delar to follow him, but before he could leave, Aidan got up, stopping him.

"Wait, Gunz," he said, his voice uncharacteristically strained. "I've been..." He grunted, a thick vein pulsing on his neck. "I've been summoned by..." He grasped his head with both hands, leaning forward. "Jim Andrews..."

"He's human," mumbled Gunz, shocked. "He can't summon you."

"He can... he hired wizards..." Aidan waved his hand, opening the communication window.

The window lit up with the blue, shimmering light of fluorescent lamps, and Agent Jim Andrews walked up to it. A man in a standard FBI suit stood behind him, chanting—undoubtedly Jim's newly hired wizard. Behind the man, Akira sat in an office chair, her legs crossed at the knee, a dangerous level of aggravation imprinted on her tender, oval face.

"Stop the summoning call, Jim," moaned Aidan. "You're giving me a mighty headache."

Jim glanced over his shoulder at the wizard and gave him a curt nod. As the man moved to the opposite end of the room and sat down, Akira got up and approached the communication window. Her angled eyes stopped on Yaroslav and then moved to Gunz. She pursed her lips into a tiny pink bow and placed her hands on her hips.

"My son and my pupil," she said evenly. "You must both return to the human realm. Your assistance is needed at once."

"What's going on?" asked Gunz, walking up to the window.

"Haven't you been outside lately?" asked Jim, but then frowned and continued without waiting for an answer, "Never mind. As far as I recall, Gwyn ap Nudd has a big screen TV in his house. Turn it on."

"Gwyn's TV doesn't work the same as yours," said Aidan. "You'll have to tell us."

Jim grunted, but walked to the window and opened the blinds, pointing outside. "It's past four in the morning. Look at the sky."

The sky colored with the shades of blood was veiled with dark clouds, and fireballs kept shooting through the air, dissipating before they could hit the ground, leaving dark tales of smoke in their wake.

Jim approached the TV in the conference room and turned it on to the local news. A rioting crowd moved through a wide city street, crashing and burning everything in its way. Jim switched the channel, but every channel was showing similar videos.

"It's like this everywhere," said Akira, waving over her shoulder at the TV. "In every city and every country out there.

The energy of Chaos poisoned the air, and there is no one here with purifying power. We need a Fire Salamander. Actually, both of them. And the Master of Power, too."

Mrak Delar approached the communication window, halting next to Gunz. "That's not going to help. Even if we had both Fire Salamanders, Gwyn ap Nudd, Aidan and me wielding the purifying magic day and night, it wouldn't be enough. Especially if the demonic infection has spread all over the world."

"What are you saying, Master?" asked Jim, shoving both hands into his pockets. "*Finito la commedia?*"

"No, not yet," replied Mrak Delar. "But the only way to stop the spread of Chaos is to vanquish the epicenter of it—Skiper-Zmey and the triad."

Jim scratched the back of his head, and his jaw tightened. "Gunz, I assume you and the Master are needed there, but can at least Yaroslav come back? We need everyone who can fight here."

Yaroslav got up, readjusting his coat. "I'll be back as soon as I can. I will need someone to open a portal for me."

Relief transformed Akira's face, and her tightly pursed lips relaxed, the corners of her mouth lifting a little. "Don't make us wait, son," she said and nodded for Jim's wizard to close the communication window.

As soon as the window closed, Aidan got up. Even though his moves were still weary, he looked a lot better than before. "I'll take you, Slavik." He waved his hand, opening the rectangle of his door, and then glanced at Tessa, love shining in his eyes. "I'll be back as soon as I drop Yaroslav at Jim's office."

* * *

As Yaroslav and Aidan left, Gunz got up. "I'm sorry," he said to Tessa and Raoul. "My father, the Ancient Master and I need to have a quick word. It won't take long." He headed toward the kitchen, gesturing for Kal and Mrak to follow him.

He walked into the room, pulled the chair out and sat down, propping his elbows on top of the table. The Master of Power headed to the coffeemaker and poured himself another cup of coffee. He wrapped his hands around the cup, channeling his power through it, and a moment later light steam swirled over it.

"So, what did you want to talk about?" asked Kal, leaning back against the counter. He glowered at the Master of Power and turned back to Gunz. "Once you're done, I need to have a word with Master Jackass here."

"No, you don't," objected Gunz quietly. "At least, I hope you won't have to." He turned to the Master of Power and gave him a light nod. "Go ahead, Mrak. You can tell him."

"Oh, thank God," murmured the Master of Power, gazing heavenward. "Kal, the reason I spoke with War in private was because Gunz asked me for help. I knew nothing good would come out of it, but like an idiot, I gave him my word that I wouldn't tell anyone." He sat down next to Gunz, placing his cup on the table before him and continued, "Gunz, I'm sorry, my friend, but I had to talk to Viggo since I strongly believed he was the only one who could solve your problem. I was right, by the way." He smiled, taking a sip of his drink.

"What problem?" asked Kal, immediately alert.

"Father, I'm no longer the Codex," said Gunz. "My mind is wide open for external intrusion."

"Oh," mumbled Kal. "Where is that goddamn torture device the Master had made for you a while ago?"

"I don't have it, Father—"

"He doesn't need it anymore," interrupted Mrak. "Here is what Viggo told me. The power of War allows you, Gunz, to control the minds of others. So, no one can enter yours without your consent. As long as you wear the stone of War, you're in control of your mind even when you're asleep." He chuckled and gave a quick tap on Gunz's shoulder. "So, sleep well, my friend."

Kal exhaled a short breath and looked away. "Master," he said, discomfort emanating around him.

"Yes, my lord?" asked Mrak Delar, raising his eyebrows, a thin layer of sarcasm underlying his words. A sugary smile spread on his lips, and his black eyes twinkled with amusement.

"I think I have to..." Kal's voice shook, and he cleared his throat. "Well, what I'm trying to say... I think I owe you..." He didn't say the last word and fell silent, a tortured expression on his hard face.

"Apology?" offered Mrak Delar snidely. "Is that the word you're looking for?"

Kal grunted and pushed away from the counter, ready to escape when the floor quacked. He grabbed the counter to steady himself, the fire energy fluctuating around him. A loud howling and ringing filled the house, and Gunz pressed his hands to his ears, looking around wildly. Tessa and Raoul rushed into the kitchen, screaming something, but it was impossible to hear anything they were saying over the ear-piercing pandemonium.

A blazing rectangle of a door opened right next to Gunz, making him jump off the chair, and Aidan walked through it, his face glistening with perspiration. He waved his hand, muttering something under his breath, and the noise ceased.

"This was the alarm Gwyn and I installed," he said, breathing hard. "The veil is under attack."

CHAPTER 28

~ ZANE BURNS, A.K.A. GUNZ ~

"The veil will hold," said Aidan. The slight modulation in his voice made Gunz cringe with worry. Aidan wasn't sure, and Gwyn ap Nudd wasn't here.

"Are you sure, Aidan?" asked Mrak Delar, echoing Gunz's thoughts. His eyes were swirling with the quadruple power, and he held his black sword in his hand. "I think I should go outside and see what's going on there."

"No," objected Aidan. "The veil *will* hold." He put some pressure on the word 'will', sounding more self-assured this time. "Gwyn and I expected Aoife to drop by and poke around at some point. It'll hold. At least until Gwyn gets back."

A bright flare of a brilliant light burst through the door, blinding everyone for a brief moment. Something fell with a loud thud, and a chain of curses followed by an outburst of angry laughter sounded from the living room. The massive frame of the King of the Otherworld filled the doorway, and Gunz exhaled with relief.

"At least something went right today," said Kal. "Gwyn, the veil is under attack."

"Not anymore," replied Gwyn ap Nudd airily, "but I'm sure

the air demon will be back in a few. In the meantime, we have a guest to entertain." He motioned in the direction of the living room nonchalantly.

"A guest?" echoed Raoul. "You found Father Collins, my lord?" His face turned ashen, and he collapsed into a chair, sweat glistening on his forehead.

"Yes. Of course, I found him." Gwyn ap Nudd leaned his shoulder against the door frame. "I'm Gwyn ap Nudd. The King of the Otherworld. The White Son of Night. The Lord of the Wild Hunt. No human soul can hide from me."

Listening to Gwyn counting his titles, Raoul murmured something in French quietly and crossed himself, staring at him fearfully. The King of the Otherworld laughed dryly, his blazing eyes as cold as a winter blizzard.

"Yeah, doing that"—he made an awkward gesture as if crossing himself—"is not going to help him now. I promise, I'll get to the bottom of this."

"Father," said Aidan, "can the entertainment of our guest wait a little?"

Gwyn frowned, straightening. "Is there something I need to know, Aodh?" Catching Aidan's glance in the direction of the living room, he waved his hand dismissively. "Speak freely. Our guest is resting. I put him in an enchanted sleep."

After Aidan told him everything that had happened in his absence, Gwyn ap Nudd just nodded. "You should leave now," he said softly. "The sooner we find this sword, the better our chances to survive this war."

He walked inside the kitchen and put his hand heavily on Raoul's shoulder. The Warden winced, and a visible shudder rushed through him.

"I'm actually glad these two youngsters are leaving," he said, pointing at Gunz and Tessa, a dark, uneven smirk hiding under the thin line of his mustache. "Grownups need to have a friendly chat with Father Collins in private."

"My lord," whispered Raoul, but fell silent under the heavy stare of the King of the Otherworld.

"Go now, Aidan. Time is of the essence," said Gwyn ap Nudd, opening the blazing rectangle of his door.

* * *

GUNZ OPENED his portal straight to the top plateau of the Vottovaara mountain, and as soon as he stepped through the fiery curtain, the cold air brushed his skin, making him shiver. Usually, he didn't react to low temperatures. Being a Fire Salamander, liquid fire ran through his veins, making him impervious to the touch of cold air, but something about this place sent shivers down his back.

An image of Mrak Delar in Lucan's arms—bleeding and unconscious, a step away from death—appeared in his mind, and he stiffened, unable to take another step. A feeling of dread twisted his stomach, and he wasn't sure if it was his intuition warning him, or if it was his history with this strange place that made him feel so uneasy.

"Zane, are you okay?" asked Tessa, gently touching his arm.

He flinched and glanced at her, rubbing his forehead like a person who just woke up from a long sleep. "I'm fine," he replied. "Just memories of this place, you know? I have so much terrifying crap stored in my brain, sometimes it's hard to isolate the past from the present."

"And the older you become, the more of this kind of memories you'll accumulate. The other downside of immortality... All the luggage you have to carry with you from century to century," said Aidan, looking around with interest. "What the hell is this place, anyway?"

"This is Mount Vottovaara, the place where Mrak Delar, Lucan, Slavik and I fought the Aspid a few months ago. Locals think this place is evil." Gunz shrugged. "But it's not. It's sacred, and everything here is infused with the ancient magic of Saami sorcerers." He closed his eyes, taking a deep breath. "I can actually sense it now that it's been purified and no longer polluted by the triad's dark magic. There is nothing evil about it."

Gunz turned in place, surveying the surroundings. Everything here looked the same as he remembered it. The strange rock formations—Seids—grouped around a small swamp, which the locals called *"Amphitheater",* in the center of the plateau. Twisted and lifeless trees stood by each Seid like silent guardians. Perfectly cut rocks and stone blocks were scattered all over the ground, and it was hard to believe they hadn't been produced by the sharp saws of some modern machinery.

Now, with the sky colored red and fireballs continuously hissing through the air, the stones looked like they were smeared with blood, giving the entire mountain a sinister appearance. The still surface of the swamp reflected the scarlet shades of the clouds, resembling a murky, bloody puddle.

"This place gives me the hibbie jibbies," muttered Tessa. She extended her arm, and the Axe materialized in her hand. She wrapped her fingers around its handle tightly, lowering the deadly weapon. "Let's find what we came for and get the hell out of here." She spun in place, observing it with wide-open eyes. "Where is that Aspid?"

"Luckily, the Aspid is dead. Trust me, you don't want to meet a living one," murmured Gunz, heading toward a small trench in the rocky ground.

A massive stone monolith towered next to it, and Gunz winced as the next wave of memories enveloped him. A loud screech of a bird broke his train of thoughts, and he winced, craning his neck to look up. A large, black crow sat on the top of the stone, staring down at them with its round, black eyes.

"Chernij Voron," whispered Gunz absentmindedly, a red flag rising in his mind.

"Voron? Where?" asked Aidan, slipping him a curious look.

"Sorry," mumbled Gunz, pointing at the bird. "I meant to say a black crow... there is something about it." He opened his other sight but couldn't detect anything unusual about the bird. "Anyway, this stone monolith is all that's left of the Aspid."

"Let's see what's cooking," murmured Aidan, placing his hands flat against the stone.

The soft, white light of his magical energy originated beneath his hands as he directed it through the monolith. But as soon as his magic penetrated its rough surface, the stone buzzed with vibration, and a bolt of electricity struck Aidan in his chest, sending him flying a few feet back. Tessa yelped and rushed to his side, but by the time she reached him, he already sat up, massaging the back of his head.

"I guess we're in the right place," he mumbled, bringing his hand closer to his eyes, red stains of blood on his fingers.

He got up and placed his arm around Tessa's shoulder as she moved the Axe to her left hand and wrapped her right arm around his waist.

"So, if this rock is all that's left of the Aspid, where is the sword?" asked Tessa. "Or is it the monolith itself? Raoul said it can disguise itself as anything." She made a quick circle around the stone, running her fingers over its surface. "It exudes some kind of magical energy, but it could be the residual magic of the beast."

"Possibly," murmured Gunz.

He reached forward, carefully touching the cold stone. Feeling the cracks and indentations under his fingertips, he searched for anything that could give him a clue on what to do next. A throaty "kraa" sounded from above, and he glanced up to find the bird still sitting there, glowering down at him with its head cocked. It looked almost as if it was mocking him.

I don't like this crow. A thought flashed through his mind, and he conjured a low voltage energy ball, ready to propel it at the bird, but a gust of wind rushed through the plateau, stopping him with his arm raised above his shoulder. Carried by the flow of the air, a foreign magical force touched his senses, making the small hairs rise on his arms. With his mind on high alert, he turned around and transformed the energy ball he was holding, adding more power into it, but he still could see nothing.

"Zane!" yelped Tessa and jumped back, pointing at something behind him. She let go of Aidan and grasped the Axe with both hands. Aidan's eyes widened for a split second, and his icy sword materialized in his hand.

"Oh shit," mumbled Gunz, "don't tell me... something is standing behind my back..."

CHAPTER 29

~ ZANE BURNS, A.K.A. GUNZ ~

In one fast motion, Gunz turned around and pulled out his Swiss army knife, turning it into the sword. As he stared in the direction Tessa had been pointing a moment ago, his jaw dropped. Two glowing, scarlet eyes hung in midair next to the monolith, seemingly without any body attached to them. Even though everything around them was colored in different shades of red, the eyes shone so brightly that it was hard not to notice them.

Gunz opened his other sight, but that didn't help him. He could still see nothing but these terrifying eyes with tiny, black dots for pupils. He sharpened his Salamander senses and clenched his teeth, battling the urge to recoil. A slight amount of the demonic essence and a barely noticeable odor of sulfur hung around the glowing eyes of the invisible monster.

"Something nasty this way comes," he projected to Aidan through their psychic link. *"Be ready."*

"Well, hello there," screeched a high-pitched voice, sounding as pleasant as a microphone feedback. "Found everything okay?"

Gunz cringed inwardly but remained calm as the voice

echoed loudly, bouncing from every rock and stone block of the plateau, coming from every direction at once.

"Hey, Aidan," he said without taking his eyes off the demonic entity in front of him, "I had no idea the Cheshire cat was real. Do you think he'll smile for us? I always dreamed of seeing the Cheshire cat's smile."

"Be careful, little boy," screeched the voice. "Wishes have a bad habit of coming true around me."

A wide, paper-white smile appeared under the eyes, hanging in midair unsupported. It grew wider and wider until it became grotesquely disproportionate to the size of the eyes. The teeth started to elongate, shaping into the sharp points of predatory fangs. The eyes upturned slightly at the outer corners and narrowed, glowing brighter than before, and even though Gunz couldn't see the face of the demon, goosebumps rose on his skin as uncontrollable fear clawed its way through him.

He knew it was a demon in its natural form standing before him. He also knew that as a Fire Salamander, he was an ultimate weapon against anything demonic. Nevertheless, he felt like a little boy watching a horror movie at home, repeating to himself, *it's just a movie, it's not real*, yet too scared to get up and turn the light on. It seemed as if the unknown demonic creature dealt in fear.

"What do you want?" he growled, bouncing the energy ball in his hand.

The smile grew even wider, and the eyes narrowed into two angry slits. "It's not about what I want, little Salamander," hissed the demon. "It's about what the three of you want."

"Show yourself," demanded Aidan, channeling his power through his icy blade.

The eyes widened and grew bigger, turning into two round plates. "I'm so scared. I'm shaking in my pants," screeched the voice, dripping with mockery. "Oh, mighty god of the Other-world, please don't smite me."

A loud "kraa" sounded from above, and Gunz could swear the obnoxious crow was laughing. He glanced up at the bird and sucked in a sharp breath. Even though the crow still sat on the top of the monolith, an enormous flock of black birds was flying above them high in the sky. Silent and fast, they moved in a circular motion, their dark feathers reflecting the scarlet shades of the surroundings.

As recognition dawned on him, he pulled back and dissipated the energy ball, lowering his sword. Catching Aidan's and Tessa's puzzled gaze, he frowned, giving them a short nod. As they lowered their weapons, he put his hand on his hip and tilted his head slightly, a lopsided smirk playing on his lips.

"I know what you are, and your presence here proves that we *are* in the right place," he said calmly, but beneath the calm surface, he was ready for pretty much anything. "You can show yourself, Skarbnik."

"Aw..." The red eyes narrowed slightly, moisture glistening in the corners, imitating gathering tears. "Would yah look at that? This tiny fireball knows his Slavic mythology. How sweet... Did your mommy read you fairytales every night, little sweetie?"

Gunz ignored his snide tone and continued, "Who sold their souls to get you here, Skarbnik? I didn't think anyone in the evil triad dealt in souls, all things considered."

"Evil triad? What a cute and fancy name you found for them." The glowing eyes turned into squinty arches as Skarbnik snickered. "Is that what you think of me, boy? Just because I am a demon, doesn't mean only demons can hire me. I'm an equal opportunity freelancer, you know." One of the eyes winked. "Good, evil—as long as they pay, I don't care."

"Who is this?" asked Tessa. "I've never heard of a demon with this name. I don't think he's in any demonology books I've read."

"Sweetheart, I'm wounded," whined Skarbnik.

The air around the eyes shimmered, and they vanished. A

short man, no more than five feet tall, stood in their place. He was dressed in a modern suit which didn't fit him, and it looked like something he picked up in a second-hand store. In his hand, Skarbnik held a small notepad, scribbling something on it quickly with a ballpoint pen.

"Anticlimactic," murmured Aidan, shaking his head.

The demon ripped a page from his notepad and handed it to Gunz. "If you want me to give you the treasure you're seeking, here is what I want in return." He stepped closer to Gunz and pointed at the paper, rising on his tiptoes. "I think it's a great deal!"

Gunz looked down at the paper and laughed. Crushing the notepad page into a ball, he threw it to the ground and turned to Tessa. "Skarbnik here is the demonic spirit that guards a treasure. Someone hired him to keep it safe, and they paid for his services with their immortal soul." He glanced back at the demon and shrugged. "No deal. Three souls for one sword? That's ridiculous." He lifted his own sword, rotating it fluidly, and the *Ardenium* steel sung, cutting through the air. "Besides, I already have a sword. I can wait."

"What are you talking about? It's a great deal! Limited time offer, available today only," yelled Skarbnik, throwing his hands up. "Besides, I can add two daggers on top to sweeten the deal. After all, there are three of you losers here."

"Let me give you a counteroffer," said Gunz, leaning down slightly as he placed his sword between himself and the demon. "You show us where Sword Kladenets is, and we let you leave with your life and with all limbs attached."

"Hmmm, enticing," murmured the demon. "I need to talk to my manager." He snapped his fingers and vanished. The crow on the top of the rock screamed, and again it sounded as though it was laughing.

"Why do I have a feeling we're dealing with a used car salesman?" asked Aidan.

"I doubt you've ever dealt with a used car salesman," murmured Gunz, chuckling.

"Why not? Am I not driving?" asked Aidan, trying to sound offended, but it didn't come out right, and he laughed, tapping Gunz on his shoulder.

"Exactly. You're driving the kind of car that you don't buy used, and when you buy it, you don't ask how much it costs or look for a better deal." Gunz chuckled, rolling his eyes.

"I wonder who his manager is," said Tessa, looking around with narrowed eyes.

Before Gunz could answer, the air next to him shimmered, and Skarbnik materialized, holding another page from a notepad in his hand. He handed it to Gunz with a smile that seemed to be too wide for his face.

"Since you're such valued customers, my manager authorized me to give you a very special deal," he said, raising his finger up. "If you accept the deal, he'll also throw the extended warranty on top, absolutely free of charge."

"How about tax, license and dealer's fee?" muttered Gunz, peering down at the paper. "One soul and a lifetime of servitude after the war is over. Sounds like an awesome deal, but my counteroffer still stands. Your life for the sword." He made a circular motion with his hand, and a circle of fire rose around the monster.

The little demon laughed, his red eyes glowing with a sinister hunger. "That is the last offer, Salamander. And if you're so well-schooled in Slavic lore, you should know that your threats are empty. You can't kill me, and your purifying energy doesn't work on me."

He shrugged, putting his hand into the fire. The flames licked his skin, doing him absolutely no damage. Aidan leaned down a little, squeezing Gunz's shoulder with his hand.

"Is it true?" he asked through their link. *"It can't be killed. Not even with my power?"*

Gunz nodded. *"Unfortunately, it's true."*

"Hey, hey, hey!" screeched Skarbnik, waving his hand in front of Gunz's face. "Didn't your mother teach you that it's not polite to use telepathy in front of others? So, whose soul is it going to be? Make your decision now or you will never get this sword. And let's not beat around the bush. We all know—without this sword, you can never win this war. So, today, I'm leaving with a soul, or y'all will never leave Vottovaara."

The demon stepped through the fire, an evil snarl curving his lips. He whispered something, and three circles glowing with a scarlet light materialized around Gunz, Tessa and Aidan. Gunz thrust his hand forward, and it met an invisible, hard wall. The circle wasn't the God's snare since his magic was still intact, yet he couldn't cross it. He glanced at his friends, realizing they were locked by the demon's magic as well.

"Eenie Meenie Miney Moe," sung Skarbnik, poking each of them in their chests with his finger. "Catch a lizard by the toe. If he hollers, make him pay with his soul every day." He cocked his eyebrow at Gunz and snickered, continuing his song, "Red, white, and blue... I choose you."

He stopped in front of Tessa, and she shrunk back as far as the circle of demonic magic would allow her, her eyes shadowed by fear. The demon pushed his hand through, reaching for her.

"Wait! Stop!" Aidan and Gunz yelled at the same time.

Gunz punched the wall of demonic magic, and a low growl rumbled in his throat as he fought the rising wave of anger within him.

"Oh?" The demon pulled his arm back. His eyes flashed from Aidan to Gunz, and his snarl grew wider, a grim joy making his eyes shine brighter. "Do I have two offers on the table? Two souls to choose from?"

"No," growled Gunz, stopping Aidan with a warning shake of his head. "You don't have two offers, but you have a deal. My soul for Sword Kladenets, and you let Aidan and Tessa leave with the weapon, unharmed."

"Zane, you can't possibly—," started Aidan, but Gunz raised his hand, stopping him.

"Skarbnik, do we have an understanding?" asked Gunz grimly.

"Wonderful, wonderful." Skarbnik rubbed his hands together. "Yes, we have an understanding, Salamander. You are sacrificing your soul to save your friends and for a chance to save the human realm from the triad." An evil excitement lit up his face. "How very noble of you," he added mockingly, "and may I say—so predictable."

He snapped his fingers, and a scroll materialized in his hands. He stepped next to Gunz so he could see the paper and started unfolding it. He kept unrolling it until a part of the scroll fell to the ground.

"Cut your finger and sign the sales contract with your blood here, here and right here." He pointed at a few places on the scroll.

"Before I sign anything, I want to test drive the merchandise," said Gunz frostily, turning his sword into the knife. "Who do you think I am, Skarbnik, a village idiot?"

"Yes." The demon nodded mockingly. "Why? You're not?"

"Not everyone can wield Sword Kladenets. The magical weapon chooses its owner, and the person has to be worthy," objected Gunz. "Until I know that one of us can handle it, I will sign nothing."

Skarbnik rolled the scroll back, pursing his lips. "You're driving a hard bargain, Salamander," he said, scratching the back of his head. "I need to consult with my manager first."

The demon snapped his fingers and vanished, leaving the tree of them locked within the circles of his magic. He reappeared almost immediately, still holding the scroll in his hands.

"My manager admits your demands are not baseless," he

announced, the tones of annoyance lacing his voice. "He authorized me to let you try the merchandise first."

He approached the stone monolith and placed his hand on it. As he started to chant, the air around the stone shimmered, and a dark mist rose from the ground. It started to spin slowly, rising higher and higher, and soon the massive rock was no longer visible. For a brief moment, the mist took the shape of a giant, winged serpent, and Gunz flinched, stepping back involuntarily. The mouth of the Aspid-shaped mist opened, displaying terrifying fangs, and its ominous eyes lit up with a dim, blue light.

Skarbnik said the last few words of his enchantment, and the mist rose higher, melting into the scarlet sky. Gunz looked at the place where the massive rock had been just a moment ago and gasped. The monolith was gone. A large boulder, however, remained in its place, and a beautiful sword was trapped in it. Its blade shone brightly in the dim crimson light of the early morning, making Gunz's eyes water.

The demon waved his hand, and the circles of his magic disappeared. "You're in luck today. My manager gave you an unbelievable deal, kids. Each of you can try to draw the sword out of the stone. But wait! If you do it now, I'll give you two more tries each. Absolutely free of charge," he announced, gesturing toward the stone with the best manners of a QVC host. "Who wants to try first?"

"You got to be kidding me," muttered Tessa, rolling her eyes. "What a cliché! A friggin' sword in the stone. Where is that proverbial King Arthur when you need him?" She glanced at Aidan. "Are you sure that's the sword we need? My father didn't say it was *Excalibur* we were after."

Aidan sighed, the corners of his lips twitching in a smile. "First of all, Arthur and Excalibur—not a legend."

"Excuse me?" Tessa's eyes flashed to Gunz, making him chuckle.

"Arthur is real, Tessa, and Merlin is real, too. And pretty much everything and everyone else you've heard of in Arthurian legends are real. Things are not exactly the way they are described, of course. You know how it is. People tend to romanticize things," he said, still chuckling. "And *Excalibur* is not the only sword in the stone, by the way. *Claíomh Solais* in Irish mythology or the *Dyrnwyn* in Welsh lore have a similar story." He waved his hand dismissively. "If you want, you can ask your future father-in-law for a guided tour of Avalon. Gwyn is the only one who has access to the Isle of Legends."

"Have you been there? Avalon, I mean?" asked Tessa breathlessly, the flabbergasted look on her face sending Gunz into the next fit of chuckles.

"No, I haven't," he said, shaking his head. "But the Master of Kendral has and so has Mrak. You can ask them if you want, but I doubt Mrak will be very upfront about his adventures in Camelot since he was enslaved there. Anyway... This is neither the time nor the place for this discussion." He jerked his chin in the direction of the sword. "You wanna give it a try?"

Tessa approached the boulder and halted with her hand lingering inches away from the hilt of the sword. Frowning, she regarded the sword with suspicion and lowered her arm. She glanced over her shoulder at Aidan, and her frowned deepened.

"Aidan, I don't know why, but this weapon doesn't feel right to me." She shrugged and raised the Axe, turning away from the stone. "When I first laid my eyes on the Axe of Perun, I knew right away that it was mine. I just felt it in my gut, you know? And this?" She waved her hand toward the sword. "This isn't mine."

"Try anyway," suggested Aidan, halting by her side. "If you're right, you won't be able to draw it out of the stone."

"Go on." Skarbnik gestured at the boulder nonchalantly. "You have three attempts." He walked farther back, away from the magical sword. Then he leaned his shoulder against a nearby rock, snapped his fingers, and a bowl of popcorn materialized in his hand. He popped a kernel into his mouth, staring at the three of them with amusement.

Tessa sighed, glowering at him with disgust. "I try once. You can give the other two attempts to Aidan."

"Nontransferable," objected the demon coolly.

She passed the Axe to Aidan, wrapped her fingers around the grip of the sword and pulled at it slightly. The sword didn't budge. She shrugged and gave it a good yank, almost unbalancing herself. Then she let go and turned to Aidan.

"It's all yours," she said indifferently, taking the Axe back from him. "If you ask me, I think this demon is making fun of us." She pointed at the sword. "It's not the real sword, and Zane is endangering his soul for nothing."

"I can show the Certificate of Authenticity, signed by Svarog himself," said Skarbnik, his voice trembling with indignation. "We, Skarbniks, don't deal in dark treasures. Only legit light treasures, thank you very much. No fake or stolen goods here."

Aidan touched his icy sword, making it disappear, and then approached the sword in the stone, gently running his fingers over its blade. "Oh, it's real alright," he said softly, his eyes lighting up with his magic. "But Tessa is right. It's not mine either." He glanced back at Gunz. "You're a Slav, Zane. I think it belongs to you."

Gunz shrugged. "I don't think the sword would choose its champion according to the place of their birth, but if you want me to give it a try, I'll do it."

"It's more than just your nationality, Zane," said Aidan quietly. "I'm almost twenty-five hundred years old. Over the years, I've learned to trust my intuition. You're still learning that, so trust me, my friend. I don't need to try to know without a shadow of a doubt—it's yours. You will draw it out of the stone." He smiled and tapped him on his shoulder.

"Bluh bluh bluh." The demon rolled his glowing eyes. "Just

do it already. I haven't got all day here. I have places to be, treasures to hide."

Gunz reached for the sword and gasped, staggering back. The powerful energy of the magical weapon enveloped him, taking his breath away. As the sounds around him disappeared, he pressed his hand to his chest, hearing nothing but the desperate thudding of his heart against his ribcage.

He stepped closer to the stone and wrapped his fingers around the grip of the sword. *Is that the way Arthur felt when he drew* Excalibur *out of the stone?* A thought rushed through his mind, but he chased it away. It felt right. It felt like it belonged to him.

The elemental energy rushed through him into the blade, setting it ablaze. He heard Tessa gasp but didn't turn around. Slowly, he pulled on the sword, but it didn't budge. He looked over his shoulder at Aidan, and he gave him an encouraging nod.

Turning back to the sword, Gunz channeled more of his power through the blade and pulled at it with all his strength. The magical energy of the weapon doubled as it slowly started to slide out of the stone. Gunz leaned back slightly, applying more force, but the sword stuck at the very end, refusing to move.

"Aidan!" he growled through clenched teeth. "A little help..."

"Doesn't work like that—," started Aidan, but Gunz threw an angry look back at him, and Aidan changed his mind. "Oh, the hell with the rules. Tessa?"

Both Aidan and Tessa wrapped their hands over Gunz's, and all three of them pulled. With a fountain of bright sparks, the sword slid out of the stone, its blade emitting an unbearable white light. Aidan and Tessa let go, covering their eyes with their arms, but Gunz held it tight in his hand, raising it above his head.

"You can't do that!" Skarbnik screeched, dropping his popcorn. "It's against the rules!"

The energy of the sword rushed through Gunz, and he smiled, feeling stronger than ever. "I know," he replied softly. "But if you heard anything about me, you would know I'm not big on playing by the rules."

Skarbnik howled in anger and bolted toward Tessa, his dark energy gathering around him like a poisonous cloud. He outstretched his arm, and the dark hoop of his magical energy wrapped around her neck, suffocating her. Her eyes widened for a moment, but she managed to get her panic under control and swung the Axe of Perun. The deadly weapon went through the demon doing him no harm, and the monster snickered. Tessa choked as the noose of the demonic power squeezed tighter and collapsed to her knees, struggling to inhale. Her fingers unlocked, and she dropped the Axe, grasping at her throat with both hands.

"You're not listening, kids," the demon hissed. "I can't be killed—as in no weapon, human or magical, can destroy me."

"Aidan!" yelled Gunz and tossed him the flaming sword.

Aidan caught it just as the demon reached for Tessa again. As soon as his skin came in contact with the grip, the flames got extinguished, and a thin layer of ice covered the magical blade. Aidan swung it with his full might, infusing it with his godly power. The frozen steel cut through Skarbnik like a hot knife through butter, splitting him in two.

"*Ignius*," roared Gunz. Both parts of the demon's body went up in flames, and a flock of black birds burst out from the burning remains. With loud screams, the crows circled above them, almost touching their heads, and then rose higher into the bloody sky, disappearing behind the low clouds.

Aidan stood with the sword in his hand, his chest rising and falling with heavy breaths. He raised it, staring at it in awe.

"You were right, Zane," he said, his voice hoarse. "It started with the three of us, and the three of us will finish it." He threw the weapon back to Gunz and bent down, helping Tessa to her feet. "How did you know that the sword could kill Skarbnik, anyway? He said nothing could kill him."

"I didn't." Gunz caught the sword, raising it in the air, and the blade went up in flames in his hands. "But I bet my soul on my knowledge of Slavic lore—Sword Kladenets can supposedly kill pretty much anyone. I was never going to sign that contract. You know that, right?" He winked.

"I wonder if it can kill one indestructible air demon," mumbled Aidan, staring at the sword in awe.

"Look," Gunz said, jerking his chin at the burning sword. "I think it knows us. When you held it, it looked like it was covered in ice. Now, it's on fire." He turned to Tessa. "You try it."

Tessa took the sword, and as soon as she raised it, a lightning bolt rushed through it, thousands of electrical discharges crackling around the blade.

"Looks promising," murmured Aidan. "It's time we returned to the Otherworld."

He placed his hands on Gunz's and Tessa's shoulders, ready to teleport, but then removed them and stilled, listening to something intently. Gunz sharpened his Salamander senses and opened his second sight at the same time.

The rocky plateau trembled under their feet with a low grinding noise, and a powerful wave of dark energy rushed through the area. As it passed through, the elemental powers got disrupted, and Gunz dropped to his knees, lowering his forehead to the ground as he struggled to fill his lungs with oxygen.

"Zane, are you okay? What was that?" asked Tessa, lowering next to Gunz, but at the moment, he couldn't say a word, taking short, ragged breaths.

As the elemental energy slowly started to return, Gunz scrambled to his feet and surveyed the freakish scenery. Vottovaara mountain stood silent and grim, and everything seemed to be unchanged. Yet, Gunz knew—a second ago, everything changed and there was no way out for him anymore. He glanced up and held his breath. The fireballs kept crossing the bloodied sky with a soft hiss, but now, a bright comet with a long scarlet tail hung above his head.

"Aidan," he said, barely recognizing his voice. "We're not going to the Otherworld. At least not yet. Take us to the village next to Mount Karasova."

CHAPTER 30

~ MASTER MRAK DELAR ~

The man lay sprawled on the floor, his black priest's robe stark against Gwyn's white tiles and furniture. His arms were twisted behind his back and restrained with the cuffs glowing with a bright, white light. Mrak halted by the man's side, staring down at him in horror. He knew these cuffs too well. He had tried them on his own skin, and he was well aware of how they affected the prisoner.

"Gwyn," he exhaled, feeling the blood draining from his face. "These are the Destiny cuffs. Where did you get them?"

Gwyn ap Nudd glared down at him, the anger around him almost material. "The Destiny Council is assisting us, are they not?" he growled through clenched teeth.

Bending down, he seized the prisoner by the scruff of his neck and lifted him easily, as if a short but heavyset older man weighed no more than a child. He threw him onto the chair unceremoniously and snapped his fingers, tying him to it with ropes of pure magical energy.

"My lord, please," yelped Raoul, rushing to the man's side. "He's not the person you're looking for. You'll see. Please don't hurt an innocent man."

"Mrak," said Gwyn ap Nudd without taking his eyes off the prisoner, completely ignoring the Warden. "I'm going to read his soul and after that he's all yours. Do what you must."

"What are you talking about?" Mrak Delar blanched, knowing perfectly well what the King of the Otherworld was referring to, but his mind refused to accept it.

A heavy hand lay on his shoulder, squeezing it forcefully, and he snapped around, his heart beating heavily in his throat. The Great Salamander stood next to him, his deep, fiery gaze drilling through him.

"Mrak, we must know the truth," said Kal calmly, his fingers digging into Mrak's shoulder. "The future of this realm depends on it. Hell, the future of all realms depends on it. Among us, you're the only one who has the knowledge and skill with—"

"Don't say it!" Mrak Delar hissed, yanking his shoulder out of Kal's grip. His scalp prickled painfully with shame, and he couldn't exhale, his chest shuddering with short breaths. "You all have enough"—he paused and swallowed hard—"skills! You both are thousands of years older than me. I'm sure over the course of your long lives you gained enough of these goddamn... *skills!*" He shouted the last word, staggering away from the Fire Elemental.

"Don't play coy with me, Master," growled Gwyn ap Nudd through clenched teeth, crossing the distance between them in one giant step. His angled eyes shone with the brilliance of his power as the black mask flashed over his face and disappeared. "You know perfectly well which skills Kalidus referred to! You *are* the only one among us who has used the forbidden Dark Arts to torture another person."

He pushed him on his chest, and Mrak backed away from him until his back hit the wall. Gwyn towered over him and for the first time in his life, Mrak with his height of six-foot-four felt small and insignificant.

"Gwyn, don't ask me to do it," he whispered, averting his

gaze. "Please, my lord. I didn't beg when I was a slave, but right now I *am* begging you. Please don't force me..."

His thoughts rushed through his mind in a wild disarray, and he couldn't come up with the right words to express himself clearly. The only thing he understood was that he couldn't do what they were asking of him.

"You must," said Gwyn ap Nudd, his voice void of emotions. "You have no choice, Master. It's an order."

"An order?" whispered Mrak Delar, the quadruple power flooding him, responding to his rising fury. He glared at Gwyn ap Nudd and then shouted, "An order? Screw you! You know better than everyone else. It wasn't me who kept Alliandr imprisoned and tortured him!"

He stopped talking, trying to control his power, but it ran away from him, making the walls of Gwyn's house tremble and the chandelier sway around, jingling. He squared his shoulders and met Gwyn's steady gaze.

"Yes, I used the Dark Arts, forbidden spells and incantations to torture him," he hissed through his teeth, unable to unclench them. "I remember everything as if it were yesterday, and I still can't forgive myself, even though I know I was controlled, and my will wasn't my own."

He pushed Gwyn on his chest, but it was equivalent to pushing against a brick wall.

"Heaven and Earth, Gwyn!" he yelled, his voice deep with boiling fury and excruciating pain. "I atoned for everything I put Alliandr through, don't you think? I paid with interest, and you *were* there to witness everything I went through. Why is it every chance you get, you keep reminding me of my past? Do you really hate me so deeply? Even Alliandr forgave me. Why can't you?"

"There was a time I despised you, Master. You brought Kendral to the point of poverty. You tortured the young Master to the point where he almost died in your care. You were the kind of monster that should have been vanquished without mercy," said Gwyn ap Nudd, slamming his massive fist above Mrak's head, making him flinch and close his eyes. "So, yes, there was a time I hated you deeply and profoundly, praying that one day my Wild Hunt would collect your twisted soul..."

His voice trailed away, and he lowered his arm with a sigh. Mrak Delar shuddered inwardly, his knees weakened, and the room around him spun. Everything Gwyn just threw in his face made him sick, and his stomach spasmed painfully.

"Once I learned the truth about you and about what had been done to you, everything changed. I don't hate you, Master. Not anymore," continued Gwyn ap Nudd, sounding flat and emotionless. He stepped back, giving him some breathing space and folded his arms over his chest. "However, my attitude to you doesn't change anything." He motioned at the man tied to the chair. "This man spied on my son and on all of us. He's the only person who has some information about the triad and their plan, and you are going to do whatever needs to be done to get this information from him. Am I clear, Master?"

Mrak Delar laughed, a short sound infused with so much pain and anger that Gwyn took a step back, throwing a shocked gaze at the Great Salamander. Mrak dropped his head to his chest, fighting a losing battle with anger, but as he raised his face again a moment later, fury took him over, transforming his features, and a dark smirk crossed his face.

"Beware what you wish for, my lord," he said softly, cocking his head just a little. "You may wake up a sleeping beast, and it'll be impossible to get him under control later."

Kal stepped between him and Gwyn ap Nudd, the fire in his blazing eyes dwindling down. "Mrak, we've had our fair share of disagreements, but have I ever let you down?" he asked reproachfully. "Do it, Master. I swear, no matter what happens next, I *will* bring you back." He chuckled softly, shaking his head. "My son would never forgive me if I let anything happen to his friend."

"I'm glad he's not here to see that. Make sure he doesn't..." Mrak Delar stepped to the side, moving around Kal and Gwyn ap Nudd, and then headed to the prisoner. He observed him, gently probing him with his other sight, and then turned to the King of the Otherworld. "Read his soul, my lord, and if you find this man to be guilty, I will do what you want me to do."

He stepped aside and sat down on the couch, burying his fingers into the mass of his hair, his limbs heavy and stiff. This was the second time Gwyn forced him to do something he didn't want to do—to become the evil thing he once was.

Against his will.

Against his better judgement.

* * *

"Hello, Father Collins. Or whatever you are..."

Mrak heard Gwyn's soft voice and lifted his face, dropping his arms on his lap. The man was awake, and he stared at Gwyn with so much undiluted abhorrence that if looks could kill, Gwyn would be dead by now. Mrak smirked darkly—at this point, he could almost identify to this man's hatred toward the King of the Otherworld.

"Let's see what you are really hiding under this holy attire," mumbled Gwyn ap Nudd, collecting his power in his hands.

He placed his hand on the priest's chest and channeled his energy through him. The man's eyes bulged, and he ground his teeth, struggling not to scream as the King of the Otherworld started to read his soul. He pushed against his restraints, fighting Gwyn's magic, but he couldn't break free.

A moment later, Gwyn let go and stepped back, wiping his hand on his jeans, disgust curving his full lips. Raoul rushed to

Father Collins' side but didn't dare touch him and just looked at Gwyn ap Nudd, his large blue eyes pleading for mercy.

"I think you were right, Warden. At least partially," said Gwyn ap Nudd. "Father Collins was innocent. This man is no longer Father Collins. He hasn't been himself for a while."

"What do you mean, my lord?" asked Raoul, his voice barely above a whisper.

"I can still sense the human soul in him—Father Collins' soul —and that's how I was able to find him in the first place," said Gwyn, lowering himself into an armchair. "But it's not him. A monster took over this body, leaving some scraps of the host's soul inside."

"A demonic possession?" asked Kal, regarding the man restrained in the chair.

The man lifted his head, staring at Kal with haughtiness, and a malignant smirk that looked like a snarl of a wild beast distorted his features. His eyes lit up with an ominous purple glow, and there was so much animosity there that the Fire Elemental stepped away from him involuntarily.

"It most likely is," agreed Gwyn ap Nudd, "but the monster possessing him is not your run-of-the-mill demon. It's something a lot more powerful. He was able to suppress his fealty demonic essence to a degree where even I couldn't sense it until I'd read his soul. Or absence thereof. Let's find out, shall we?" He gestured at Mrak Delar. "Master, if it's any consolation, this man is not human. Not entirely. So do your worst."

Mrak Delar got up slowly, feeling numb and dead to the world. With every move causing him almost physical pain, he replaced Gwyn ap Nudd in front of the prisoner.

"Ancient Master..." Raoul de Beaumont touched his arm, and Mrak flinched, turning to him. The Warden gasped and cowered back under his empty gaze, but then cleared his throat, composing himself. "Master, is Father Collins' soul still in his body? Is there a chance to expel the demon—"

"No." Gwyn ap Nudd cut him off with an impatient wave of his hand. "Father Collins is gone. The demon destroyed his soul, leaving only traces of it to keep his memories." He glanced at Mrak Delar. "Proceed, Master. You won't be hurting a human."

Mrak Delar nodded absentmindedly and turned back to the prisoner. The man lifted his face, drilling him with his freakish purple eyes, and his mouth opened slightly for a brief moment.

"Master Mrak Delar," he said in a screechy voice which didn't sound like the voice of Father Collins. "What an honor to finally meet you—the only Dark Master in the history of Kendral. Your skills with the Forbidden Arts and the darkness of your soul are legendary."

Mrak looked down at the demon and said slowly, carefully pronouncing one word at the time, "To understand one's soul, you must have your own first." Then he turned to Gwyn ap Nudd and smirked frostily. "My lord, you would do well to take a seat or at least hold on to something because I'm about to grant you your wish."

He channeled as much elemental power and magic as he could, entwining them together, and reached under his black shirt, pulling out a silver chain with a round, red pendant attached to it.

I never thought I would be using it again. A thought materialized in his mind, and his heart gave an agonizing jolt. He disregarded it and channeled his magical energy through the stone, touching it with his fingers. His eyes flooded with blackness, but it wasn't the darkness of elemental power. His obsidian hair fanned around his face, and his lips drew back in an angry snarl.

The room shook, the house swaying like a tiny boat during a storm, and the air swirled around him, creating a small twister. The man in the chair watched his changes with an impassive expression, a tiny, derisive smirk playing on his lips.

"Are you trying to scare me, Master?" he screeched, his voice more nasal than before. "It's not working... just to let you know."

Mrak laughed, and the floor trembled again. "I'm not trying anything, demon," he replied calmly, his voice deep with the power he was wielding. "Now, let's get started. A simple question first. Who are you?"

"Isn't it obvious?" the demon replied with a question. "I'm a demon who's way above your paygrade. I hope you're not planning to try to expel me because I don't want you to get disappointed in yourself. Self-doubts are a bitch, you know?"

"Who said anything about expelling you?" asked Mrak Delar flatly. "I like you just the way you are."

He touched his pendant and then slashed his right hand through the air. The demon's body arched, pushing against the restraints, and the shirt on his chest ripped as if it was cut by a sharp knife. Mrak Delar smiled ominously as he watched fresh blood spill from a deep laceration on the demon's chest.

"Oh, it tickles," panted the demon, "do it again, Master, but next time go slightly to the left."

Mrak Delar laughed, throwing his head back. "Please keep it up," he growled. "I haven't had this much fun in years." He touched his pendant and slashed his hand again. He repeated it a few times before he stopped. Crossing his arms, he tilted his head, watching the demon thrash in his restraints. "Your name. Who are you?"

He let go, and the demon hung, leaning forward, blood dripping from the corner of his mouth. Mrak Delar sauntered closer, his movements relaxed and lazy. Seizing the demon's hair, he yanked his head up. The monster looked up from under his gray eyebrows and smirked, his teeth smeared with a bubbling, red liquid.

"You really... want to know... my name so much... Master?" he hissed, panting, splattering blood all over Mrak's shirt. "You're not gonna like it."

"Humor me," murmured Mrak. He let go of the demon's hair and wiped his hand on his shirt with disgust.

"My name... is... Archdemon Leviathan..." The demon leaned back, and his head tilted backward, his mouth opened. "Above your pay grade... Master..."

Mrak Delar stilled, everything inside him frozen with horror. Slowly, he turned to Gwyn ap Nudd, but the King of the Otherworld motioned for him to proceed. Mrak rolled his shoulders as he returned his attention back to the monster.

"Well," he said darkly, "that was a nice little exercise for me. Shall we continue?"

"Please, enjoy yourself, Dark Master. While you can, that is," uttered the monster through clenched teeth. "You can't kill me. You can't expel me, and ex-god here"—his purple eyes darted to Gwyn ap Nudd—"won't be able to hold me down forever."

"I don't need forever to get the answers I want," murmured Mrak Delar.

Touching his pendant, he channeled more of his power through it. Turning to the demon, he muttered something under his breath, and Leviathan screamed, unbearable anguish reflected on his face. Mrak waved his hand, and the demon fell back, barely conscious.

"Wonderful," he said, rubbing his hands together. "Next question. How long have you been spying on us?"

The demon looked up, an expression of delight on his face. "Aw, Master, you didn't need to torture me to get this question answered." He cackled. "You see, the good Father here expired a few years ago, when Aoife attacked the Church by the Sea and snatched your little half-breed, Therasia. So, how long has it been? Do you need a calculator, Master?"

Mrak Delar turned away to hide the expression of horror on his face and met Kal's eyes. The Great Salamander stood engulfed in smoldering flames, anger igniting his fire brighter, the smoldering hot air around him swirling in shimmering, white tendrils.

"Anything else you'd like to know, Master?" asked the demon

snidely and when Mrak turned around, he continued talking, splattering blood and saliva around himself. "Yes, we've been watching you for years. Like idiots, you trusted the Master Warden, so we had all the information we needed. All this time, we've been ahead of you a few steps, listening to your plans, manipulating all of you to our advantage."

He shook his head, his gray hair matted with sweat and droplets of blood flying around.

"Even with me captured, you still have no chance of survival." His purple eyes darted from one person to the next, and an uneven smirk lifted a corner of his mouth. "Your righteousness, your blind obedience to the rules of magic makes you weak. It makes you predictable and slow. Being good is not that good nowadays."

"It's a matter of opinion, and yours just doesn't matter," murmured Mrak Delar, regaining his composure. "When and where is the triad planning to attack first?"

"The triad? As in three? The number three?" The demon's eyebrows climbed up, and he barked laughing, his entire heavy body moving and shifting as he went from one fit of laughter to the next. "Who told you that there are only three of them? Well, us?" He stopped laughing, and a sinister glow darkened his purple eyes. He shifted forward as far as he could within the restraints of Gwyn's magic. "As far as when..." His lips stretched wider than a human anatomy would've allowed, and his entire face distorted into a sinister mask of ominous gluttony. "You're already under attack, and you don't even know it."

Mrak muttered something and flicked his wrist. The demon stopped laughing abruptly. His mouth opened wide, and a horrible howl erupted from his black lips. As soon as the Master of Power let go, Leviathan dropped his head, breathing hard.

"We'll crash this realm like an empty eggshell," he panted without looking up. "And then we'll go to Kendral." The demon glanced up at Mrak and tonged his cheek, spitting blood on the white marble floor. "If someone like you were able to subdue the Young Master, we'll take the World of Magic in no time. He's no match for us. And guess what, Dark Master?" He snickered, his eyes rolling in and out of his skull. "The first person I kill personally while in Kendral will be your pretty... little... human... wife. But not before I have my way with her, of course."

Mrak didn't move. He didn't say a word. But the entire building shook violently. The chandelier finally crashed with a thunderous bang, and myriads of crystal slivers scattered all over the floor. Stormy clouds appeared inside the house, and a lightning bolt struck from the ceiling to the floor. Thunder rolled, and the demon screamed, and screamed, and screamed, his howls and curses louder than the pandemonium that overtook Gwyn's house.

Someone grabbed Mrak's shoulders, trying to pull him away from Leviathan, but neither Gwyn nor Kal were strong enough at the moment, or maybe they weren't trying hard enough. Mrak wasn't sure what he was doing, but one thing he knew for sure—he wasn't in control. Anger took hold of him, bringing forth the very darkness he had worked so hard to keep locked up somewhere far in the back of his mind.

Through the shrieks and screeches of the demon, he heard someone calling his name. It wasn't Gwyn's voice or Kal's. It was calming and soft. It was whispering his *True Name* into his ear, ordering to let go, and as a Master of Power he couldn't disobey the one who held his *True Name*. He felt a gentle touch to his forehead, and a wave of warmth enveloped him like a lover's embrace. Soft weakness overtook him, extinguishing the fury, and he collapsed to his knees, dropping his head to his chest, sweat running down his face and back. Someone's hands gently lowered him down, and he closed his eyes, feeling numb.

"Master, open your eyes," ordered the same voice, and someone's hand gently tapped him on his cheek.

Mrak jerked and cracked his eyes open. A blinding, golden light filled his vision, and he blinked a few times, raising his eyes. The light dwindled down, and he could finally see.

"Archangel Uriel... Uri," he whispered. "How did you get here? Did Aidan—" He didn't finish his question and pushed himself into a sitting position, looking around. "What happened? What did I... Oh, God, what have I done..."

"Not much, unfortunately," said Gwyn ap Nudd.

Uri threw a furious gaze at him, shaking his head. "You've done enough, Ancient Master," he said, turning to him. "You've managed to get Leviathan into submission. He lost his control, which allowed me to sense his presence right away. I'll take it from here."

"Uri, the demon said that it's not only Zlebog, Skiper-Zmey and the air demon working against us. There are more of them," said Mrak Delar, rising to his feet. "Do you know anything about it?"

"No," said Uri, throwing a scorching stare at Leviathan. "But I'm about to find out. In the meantime, you need to know that Veles' curse has failed, and that Mount Karasova is slowly fading away. In a few hours, Skiper-Zmey will be free to walk this realm again."

"Dammit," muttered Kal, his arms dangling powerlessly. "Where is Gunz? He needs to know that. He needs to be ready."

"Yes, where is Gunz?" asked Uri. "I know Yaroslav is assisting Agent Andrews. But where are Gunz, Aidan and Tessa?"

"Mount Vottovaara," replied Gwyn ap Nudd. "Searching for the remains of Aspid."

Uri's eyes widened, his light eyebrows rising. "I have no time to ask you for details. I'm sure it makes perfect sense to all of you. But if they're outside, they're already aware." He waved at the TV. "Turn it on, Gwyn. Any country. Any channel."

Gwyn ap Nudd touched the TV, whispering something

under his breath, and the screen lit up with a soft blue light. A moment later, the light was replaced by the Local 10 Miami news channel. The sound was down, but no one asked Gwyn to turn it up. The picture spoke louder than any words.

"What time is it in the human realm?" asked Mrak Delar, shivers running down his back.

Uri shrug. "About six o'clock in the morning or so?"

"The sky is dark and red just like it was a few hours ago," whispered the Master of Power, his eyes flooding with blackness again as fear struck through him. "And what is that?" He pointed at a giant orb of light with a long scarlet tail.

"That?" As Uri stared at the comet, his expression closed up. "And the sun became black as a sackcloth of hair, and the moon became like blood. And the stars of heaven fell to the earth... and every mountain and island was moved out of its place..."

The Archangel whispered the words of Revelation so softly that even though Mrak was straining his hearing, he could catch only some words he was saying.

"Uri, dammit!" yelled Mrak Delar, desperation twisting his soul. "Speak plainly."

"If we don't stop it, Master," started Uri, "then it's the beginning of the end—"

A loud ringing and buzzing interrupted his speech, but the Archangel didn't seem to be shocked. He looked around, and his eyes fogged, going out of focus for a brief moment. "It has begun," he whispered, his golden wings expanding behind his back to their full extent. "The world is on the brim of destruction, and you all are the last line of defense. God be with you, my friends." He frowned and then added awkwardly. "All gods."

He put his hand on the demon's shoulder and snapped his fingers. The room flooded with the golden light and both the Archangel and the Archdemon vanished.

CHAPTER 31

~ ZANE BURNS, A.K.A. GUNZ ~

Gunz ran through the empty street of the abandoned village. The houses stood dark, their windows reflecting the red colors of the never changing sky. Nothing moved behind the fences, and only winds whistled between the buildings, banging the loose shutters. He opened his other sight and sharpened all his senses—human and Salamander—but couldn't detect any presence of life.

Without slowing down, he ran into the forest, following a barely visible trail. He had visited this place a few times after the fight for Mount Karasova, and he knew his way around well. Glancing over his shoulder, he made sure that Aidan and Tessa were following him and kept running, vaulting over trunks of fallen trees and bending down to avoid low hanging branches.

He stopped a foot away from the place where he expected to find the Guardians' protective circle, breathing hard. The entire area was infused with dark magic, which didn't surprise him—the close presence of Mount Karasova, Skiper-Zmey's grave, explained that. However, he didn't detect the presence of Guardians' magic, and that set his nerves on high alert. As he moved his hand in a wide arch, the magical shield didn't light up, and his heart sank, beating somewhere in his knees.

"Jeez, man, where did you learn to run like that?" asked Aidan, breathing heavily, sweat dripping down his flushed face.

"Military training," murmured Gunz absentmindedly, struggling to find any explanation to why the shield was missing.

Aidan bent forward slightly, propping his hands on his knees, trying to equalize his breathing. He glanced at him from under the veil of his blond hair and straightened, frowning. "What's going on?"

Tessa approached them, her hand pressed over her heart. "One more run like this, and I'll cross the veil myself. And why is it so cold here?" She exhaled, the white puff of her breath forming on her lips. Rubbing her arms with her hands, she chuckled. "I feel like I'm back in Chicago." But as she glanced at Gunz, the warm twinkles in her eyes died down. "You look like you've seen a ghost, Zane. Spill it."

"The Guardians' protective shield is gone, and I can't sense them anywhere," said Gunz, cold sweat trickling down his back. Using his fire energy, he drew a flaming rune in the air and pressed his hand to it, whispering a summoning spell. No one replied to his summons. "Where are the Guardians? They should be here twenty-four-seven..."

Aidan moved his hand, repeating Gunz's gesture, and his shoulders tensed. "*Latentius revelare,*" he whispered, and a soft white light spread around him, silently moving through the woods in all directions at once.

The ground shimmered with a dark mist, and the body of a man materialized next to Gunz's feet. He lay on his back, his gray eyes wide open as if he were staring into eternity, his pupils dilated into giant black holes. Gunz kneeled next to him and pressed his fingers under his jaw, searching for a pulse, but couldn't find it. There was no blood or any visible injuries on his body, yet the Guardian was dead.

"Jasper," he whispered the man's name, his throat constricted with sorrow. "How did it happen?" He raised his face, meeting Tessa's horrified eyes.

Without saying a word, Aidan snapped his fingers and vanished. He returned a few seconds later and lowered to the ground next to Gunz, his shoulders slumped.

"They are all dead," he said quietly. "Every single Guardian who lived in that village is dead. My guess, they were all killed at once." He closed his eyes and moved his hand over Jasper's body but quickly pulled it back, locking and unlocking his fingers. "It could be one of the Forbidden spells, but my guess is they were killed by a god. I can still sense the residue of the killer's magical energy."

"Do you think it was that Zlebog-character?" asked Tessa. Her voice trembled, but not with sadness—fury shadowed her features, bolts of electricity flashing in her dark eyes.

"No," objected Gunz, rising. "I'm almost positive it's Morena. Her energy signature can't be mistaken for anything else. And that would explain the cold weather, too."

He stopped talking and held his breath as a wave of magical energy—dark and powerful—rushed through the forest.

"Guys, did you feel that?" Gunz asked, turning to them. Both nodded. "It's coming from the mountain. We should... Dammit..." He punched the air, desperate fury spiking the adrenalin and the elemental fire within him. "I know what's going on."

Without waiting for their response, he took off running again, and he didn't slow down until the woods started to get thinner, and he could see the dark silhouette of the mountain on the horizon. Keeping in the shadows behind the thick shrubbery, he halted at the edge of the forest and carefully suppressed his elemental energy.

"It's hard to breathe here." Aidan separated the thick screen of bushes and peeked down.

Gunz glanced at the mountain, and his heart wrenched as if Chernobog's dagger pierced it again. He lowered his head and pressed his fingers to his eyes, pushing the thoughts about Angelique to the back of his mind. It wasn't the right time for that, but he couldn't help it.

Another blast of dark energy spread around, and Tessa gasped, staggering back. Gunz raised his eyes, glowering at the stark rock with hatred. Colored in red shades, Mount Karasova looked like a dark omen of death and destruction.

Suddenly, the entire mountain shuddered, coming in and out of focus. The wind picked up, and a frosty blizzard burst out of the cave at the foot of the mountain. It rushed toward them, glistening with splinters of ice. In one fluid motion, Aidan grabbed Gunz by his shoulder and turned him around, covering him from the flying icicles with his body. Then he whispered a spell, encapsulating all three of them in a protective dome. The pieces of ice bombarded his shield with loud thuds but didn't break through it.

"What was that?" whispered Tessa, her hands grasping the hilt of Sword Kladenets like it was her last hope for survival.

Gunz turned around, and the small hairs on his arms rose. The mountain trembled again, spreading waves of sand and dust around like a dog shaking water off its fur. Its edges became slightly fuzzy, and it sunk into the ground, a grinding noise growing louder with each passing moment.

"This is Morena, the Slavic goddess of Winter and Death, breaking Veles' curse and raising her lover," said Gunz without taking his eyes off the slowly disappearing mountain. The blizzard slowed down and dissipated, but the heavy presence of dark magical energy just became thicker, hovering over Mount Karasova like a dirty cloak.

"Gunz, we need to get help," whispered Aidan. "Let me get in touch with Gwyn—" He didn't finish his sentence and froze with his eyes widened as if listening to something distant. Then he exhaled and smirked tiredly. "Great minds think alike. Gwyn is summoning me."

He muttered a cloaking spell and waved his hand, opening the communication window. Gwyn ap Nudd paced in front of the window, urgency making his moves sharp and jerky. Once he noticed Aidan, he turned toward him, and an expression of relief suffused his features.

"Aidan, my boy," he said, speaking fast. "You must come back home immediately. The Otherworld is under attack. The air demon is here, and she's not alone, I suspect. The veil is still holding, but if we don't do something to stop her, it won't hold for long. I need your help. I need all three of you back."

"Father, I can't," whispered Aidan. "Look!" He motioned with his hand and turned the communication window toward the fading Mount Karasova. "Someone has to be here to stop Morena and Skiper-Zmey from leaving this place."

Gwyn ap Nudd looked up, and his hands went up to his head of their own accord. "Fire and Ice," he muttered, his fingers digging into the mass of his black hair.

"Aidan." Gunz touched his friend's shoulder with a warm lopsided grin and shrugged lightly. "Why are you even thinking? You're a god of the Otherworld and your domain is under attack. It's your duty to go back and help Gwyn." He glanced at Tessa and pulled her to his chest, wrapping his arms around her shoulders as he planted a gentle kiss on the top of her head. "And Tessa's place is by your side. Go, my friend, I'll be fine."

"How are you going to be fine?" asked Aidan reproachfully, shaking his head. "Alone, against a goddess and the Lord of Chaos? And I'm sure they brought reinforcements."

"You knew that one day I would have to face Skiper-Zmey," replied Gunz, sounding hollow and even. "You said it yourself— my destiny was set in motion." He pointed toward the small hill that still remained in place of Mount Karasova. "There you go.

For once, I will do what I've been told to do." He chuckled. "Besides, I'm not going to do it alone. I think I'll summon uncle Semargl."

"One day," said Aidan, his glowing eyes narrowing into angry slits, "but this day is not today, Zane. We don't know what's going on or if Semargl is going to answer your summons. I betrayed you once. I will never do it again." He turned toward the window. "Father, I'm sorry, but I have to stay here."

Gwyn ap Nudd dropped his head, a painful crease materializing between his eyebrows. "I understand you, son, but you have no choice. You must come back, and you must do it immediately. Tessa can stay and help Gunz, but not you."

"Father, no—"

"Hold on, Aidan." Mrak Delar appeared next to Gwyn ap Nudd. His black eyes darted to Gunz, and he gave him a short nod. Then he turned to the King of the Otherworld and inclined his head in a bow that looked a little too official to be friendly. "My lord, I'm going to Mount Karasova. Kal has a lot more purifying power than I do. Between the three of you, you should have more than enough purifying energy to deal with an army of demons."

Gwyn ap Nudd turned to him, looking slightly disoriented for a brief moment. As his eyes focused on the Master of Power, he ran his fingers over his mustache and looked to the side, a muscle twitching in his jaw.

"Go, Master," Gwyn said at length. He put his hand on Mrak's shoulder, and the Master of Power visibly cringed but quickly regained his composure. However, Gwyn noticed it and dropped his hand. "Mrak, for what it worth, I'm truly sorry for everything I've put you through today. Some of the things I said to you..." His voice broke, and he shook his head, looking aside. "You didn't deserve."

"Thank you, my lord," replied Mrak Delar, and while his

voice was soft, Gunz recognized the official coldness in his friend's voice, wondering what that was all about. Mrak turned back to the window. "Aidan and Tessa, please return to the Otherworld." He flicked his eyebrow at Gunz, giving him a quick smirk. "Gunz, I'll be with you shortly." He thought for a moment and added, "And while you're alone there, don't do anything I wouldn't do."

"I doubt I can think of anything you wouldn't do, Master," replied Gunz, chuckling. Mrak Delar flashed a bright, white smile at him as Gwyn closed the communication window.

Gunz extended his hand to Aidan, and he squeezed it tightly. "Are you sure you're going to be okay," Aidan asked, doubt clearly written on his face.

"I'll be fine. Mrak is coming, and I will summon Semargl. We'll be fine. You and Tessa must go now." Gunz waved his hand dismissively, trying to sound as lightheartedly as he could muster, but he wasn't sure he succeeded.

"At least take Sword Kladenets," said Tessa, offering him the magical sword.

He took the weapon, running his fingers over the beautifully crafted blade. A wave of energy and warmth spread through him, and somehow, he knew one day he was destined to wield this sword. *But not today*, he said to himself and gave it back to Tessa.

"Take the sword, Tessa, and protect Aidan," he said to her gently. "Facing the very monster who tortured him for eight hundred years and killed his siblings is not going to be easy for him. He needs you, and the both of you need this sword a lot more than I do." He glanced up at Aidan and waved his hand. "Go already. Time is of the essence."

With a heavy heart, he glanced at the place where Mount Karasova had been and shuddered—only a tiny pile of sand still remained in its place. It was a matter of minutes before the last scraps of Veles' curse would give in.

"Godspeed, my friend," said Aidan. "We'll meet again. In this world or the Otherworld."

He wrapped his arm around Tessa's shoulder and snapped his fingers, vanishing from the forest.

CHAPTER 32

~ AIDAN ~

Aidan and Tessa materialized next to the road leading toward the Glastonbury Tor. Crouching behind thick bushes, Aidan observed the tall hill, probing it with his second sight. The entire hill glowed with a red magical energy, a bright crimson stream exiting through the roofless tower of St. Michael, melting seamlessly with the scarlet sky.

The energy fluctuated, pulsing and swaying, wrapping around the Glastonbury Tor and tower like a venomous serpent. Aidan shuddered inwardly, feeling the malignant presence of his stepmother with his very skin. He stared at the hill without blinking, unable to tear his eyes off, everything inside him twisted with fear.

"Is it Aoife's handiwork?" asked Tessa, her soft voice startling Aidan. "I mean, your stepmother's?"

He nodded, swallowing hard. "I would recognize her spell work with my eyes closed," he whispered, trying to sound as calmly as he could, but even to his ear, he sounded tense.

"She's still as powerful as I remember her," murmured Tessa. She cringed visibly and added with conviction, "We won then, and we'll win again. She stands no chance against us."

"I wish I had your confidence," he murmured, longing sagging through him. "The fight will be deadly, Tessa."

"I know," she replied, a warm smile touching her lips for the briefest of moments as she met his eyes. Sadness replaced her smile, and she averted her gaze, her fingers tearing leaves off the branch next to her. "Aidan, did we do the right thing by leaving Zane alone? It doesn't feel right to me."

"No, it doesn't feel right to me either. Especially to me..." Aidan moved slightly to the side to get a better view of the hill. "I can't believe I left him alone to face a monster." He bit his lip, shaking his head. "Again!" He slammed his fist into the ground. "I felt like a jerk doing it."

"But Zane was right," said Tessa, caressing his back and shoulder softly. "Your duty lies here. So, let's get to it. The sooner we get rid of Eve, the sooner we can return to Mount Karasova and help Zane."

Aidan didn't say anything. Throwing one more glance at the Glastonbury Tor, he put his hand on her shoulder, dread settling in the pit of his stomach. *Tessa has no idea what we're going to be dealing with,* he thought. Gazing into her deep brown eyes, he snapped his fingers, teleporting them into the labyrinth.

To his shock, the shining door was opened, and he wondered if Gwyn had detected him and opened the door, or if something was terribly wrong. He pressed his finger to his lips, gesturing for Tessa to be quiet, and walked through the door first.

* * *

Aidan walked out of the door and halted, taking in the state of destruction in the living room. The tiles were covered in thousands of pieces of glass and the shattered chandelier lay on the floor, the magical light orbs hanging in the air unsupported.

Raoul sat on the couch, leaning forward with his face hidden in his hands.

Gwyn ap Nudd and Kal got up as soon as he appeared, and Gwyn crossed the room, closing the distance between them. He halted, giving Aidan a quick once-over, his attentive eyes sliding up and down his body as he searched for any visible injuries.

"I'm fine, Father," said Aidan, his jaw set with worry. "We found the sword... and—" He cut himself off, shaking his head. "Gunz... We had to..."

"Gunz is going to be fine, Aidan," said Kal. He lowered his massive hammer, leaning on the handle heavily. "My son is more than ready to handle Skiper-Zmey. Besides, Mrak Delar left as soon as we disconnected, so Gunz is not going to be facing this evil scumbag alone."

Just two of them... A thought flashed through Aidan's mind, and all blood drained from his face. *Impossible...* Tessa's fingers squeezed his elbow, and he placed his hand over hers, exhaling a ragged breath.

"I know what you're thinking," said Gwyn dryly. "Don't. You must focus on the problem we're facing right here, right now."

As if responding to his words, the entire house shook violently, dust falling from the ceiling. The tremor passed quickly, and a powerful wave of dark energy rushed through, suffocating Aidan with the reek of demonic essence.

"Aidan, the air demon made her presence known," said Gwyn ap Nudd. He looked back at Kal and sighed, pressing his lips into a thin line. "She wants to negotiate..." He paused, and a deep crease crossed his forehead. "But only with you."

Aidan tilted his head, a dark smirk crossing his lips. "Negotiate what exactly?" He folded his arms across his chest. "I don't negotiate with terrorists."

"I don't know, Aidan," muttered Gwyn ap Nudd, throwing his hands up, "but before you take a stand, let me show you something."

He turned on his heel and headed toward the TV. Touching the screen, he muttered a few words, and the screen lit up with a soft blue light. Aidan walked to the couch and sat down, throwing a sideway glance at the Warden.

Raoul lowered his arms, showing his red-rimmed eyes. "You should see it, Aidan," he said, his voice hoarse and shaky like the voice of a person who had screamed for a few hours until his vocal cords gave up. Tessa sat down next to him, placing the sword on the coffee table.

The blue light dwindled down, and the screen darkened, a soft, hissing noise enveloping the room. Aidan looked up, and his heart skipped a beat. A dark scenery was illuminated by the dim light of the magical orbs. Once in a while, bright flares of light would cut through the darkness and die down almost immediately.

A dark silhouette of an army took the entire real estate of the screen. Composed of hundreds of bodies, the mass was moving and shifting slightly. Watching everything on TV, Aidan couldn't say if these were demons in their natural form or some other supernatural creeps. But no matter what they were, the odds were stacked against them. Even with Gwyn ap Nudd and Kal, there was no way they could fight this enormous army and live to tell the tale. His shoulders slumped, and he averted his gaze, crumbling inside.

"Oh God, Aidan," whispered Tessa, staring at the screen in horror. "How are we supposed to stop this... horde?"

"Keep watching," said Gwyn ap Nudd. "That's not the worst."

"What? There is something worse than that?" Aidan met Gwyn's blazing eyes and fell silent.

Gwyn ap Nudd made a move with his hand, as if panning an image on a digital tablet, and the view on the screen moved to the side, displaying the terrain from a different angle. He whispered something, and the side of the screen lit up slightly, emitting a soft white light.

"Watch carefully," he pointed at the glowing part of the screen.

Two large groups of people stood in front of the demonic army. The whispers became louder, and a bright flare of light blinded Aidan for a moment. He rubbed his eyes to regain his vision, but no matter how hard he tried, he couldn't see clearly what these groups were. Tessa, however, gasped, rising slowly.

"Those are reapers," she whispered, pointing at one of the groups with her trembling hand. "Hundreds of them. I think I've seen so many reapers in one place only once—when Angel was missing." She approached the screen and squinted. "What is this second group? They're not reapers, and they don't look like demons."

"Humans," said Kal, his voice deep with anger. "I don't know how many of them there are, but it presents a serious problem —I can't use the elemental energy without obliterating every single one of them."

"She accounted for everything, didn't she?" growled Aidan bitterly, anger slowly rising within him.

The bright flare of light burst out of the TV screen, and the building quaked again, this time a lot stronger. Tessa lost her balance and would've fallen if Kal hadn't caught her. Aidan dropped back to the couch, almost crushing Raoul. A powerful wave of magical energy polluted with demonic essence rushed through again.

"I don't know what she's doing," Kal said, "but it makes the veil vibrate. The tremors we all feel are the veil resisting the assault from outside."

"Aoife is trying to break the veil," replied Aidan, wiping his clammy hands on his pants. "That has always been her goal. She's hell-bent on revenge, and she's not going to stop until she gets me and Gwyn."

Kal smirked, giving Gwyn ap Nudd an arched stare. "Hell has no fury like a woman scorned, my friend," he said. "You saved Aidan by sharing your power with him, but you paid for it dearly. And now, the realm of humans is going to pay for that—"

"Aidan is *my* son, and if I had a choice, I would do the same thing again. No matter the consequences," growled Gwyn ap Nudd, interrupting him. "Wouldn't you do the same for your little Salamander or for your Phoenix, Kalidus?"

"Of course, I would," agreed Kal. "I would do anything for my boys, but that's not what I was trying to say, Gwyn." He switched his attention to Aidan, and the fire dimmed down in his ever-burning eyes. "Aidan, there are only five of us here, so we have to do whatever we have to do to stop Aoife from breaking the veil. I'm sure as a god of the Otherworld, you understand the dire consequences of that."

"Yes, my lord," replied Aidan, the realization of what Kal was about to ask him sending chilly shivers down his spine.

"You will go and negotiate with your stepmother, Aodh," continued Kal. He didn't sound forceful. If anything, tones of regret were prominent in his deep voice. "I hate to ask you to do that, child... But we need time to assess the situation in person. So, while you keep Aoife busy with these so-called negotiations, the rest of us can have a look-see."

Tessa stepped between the Great Salamander and Aidan, folding her arms. She barely reached his chest, but somehow, she managed to look strong and self-assured. "That's a wonderful plan, my lord," she said, a thin layer of mockery underlying her every word. "Aoife wants Aidan, and you're giving her exactly what she wants. On a silver platter."

Kal smiled down at her and then bent his knees, propping his hands on his lap, his burning eyes on the same level with hers. "I am doing no such thing, child," he said softly, amusement lifting the corners of his thin lips. "But did you notice that there are only five of us and... let me see... a few hundred of them." He gazed heavenward, scratching the red stubble on his chin. "Maybe thousands? We have no idea. Also, we have no clue on why all the reapers are there. Don't you think we should find out before we jump into the fight, guns blazing?"

"The only way we can do it is if Aoife will let us approach her camp," chimed in Gwyn ap Nudd. "The air demon doesn't know how many of us are here. She'll think we accompanied Aidan." He glanced at Aidan over Tessa's shoulder, a pained expression shadowing his features. "Son?"

"I'll do it," replied Aidan, rising.

"I'm coming with you," said Tessa, taking the sword off the table. "You're not going to meet with her alone."

Kal and Gwyn ap Nudd exchanged a quick look. "That's fine," said Kal. "But if Aoife objects, you'll have to stay with us."

"Deal," agreed Tessa. She turned to Aidan and took his hand into hers, her eyes emanating warmth. "Always and together."

He placed his hand on her cheek, caressing it with his thumb. Then he leaned forward and kissed her, just a brief touch of his lips to hers, fleeting and gentle. "Always and together," he whispered to her and then nodded to Gwyn ap Nudd to proceed. "Let's get it over with."

As he passed through the blazing rectangle of Gwyn's door, he reached to Gunz through their psychic link.

"Zane, please tell me you and Mrak are okay... Can you hear me?"

There was no answer.

CHAPTER 33

~ AIDAN ~

The darkness was absolute. Even though thousands of magical orbs shimmered high in the air, the blackness of the endless field seemed to swallow whatever little light they produced. The black sky seamlessly connected with the black grass under their feet. The air, polluted by the heavy odor of sulfur and the reek of demonic essence, felt stuffy, unmoved even by the lightest breeze. A single black tent stood surrounded by the mass of the demonic army, stark even in the darkness of the surroundings.

The entire scenery exuded a vibe of eminent demise and despondency. Aidan shivered, panic slowly creeping up into his soul. He swallowed and rolled his shoulders, getting in control of his fears. He knew this place. He'd been here before. Before Aoife had brought and stationed her demonic army here, that is. It had always been dark, but never had he experienced such overwhelming dread.

This place was a part of the Otherworld, or rather the "suburbs" of it where the veil was thinner than in other parts of the human realm, and that explained why the air demon chose it to position her army.

Aidan closed his eyes and let go, allowing the god of the Otherworld to take him over. As he stood clad in leather and furs with a black mask over his face, he smiled, confidence slowly coming back to him. He glanced at Tessa and found a calm smirk on her face.

"About time," she said softly, and there wasn't as much as an ounce of fear in her voice. "With you glowing like a lantern, I can finally see around."

Aidan chuckled, knowing well what she meant. He looked to the side over Tessa's head and met Gwyn ap Nudd's eyes blazing through the slits of his black mask. A few giant hounds sat by his feet, and his fingers played with their fur absentmindedly. Their eyes shone with a bright phosphoric light, and low growls rumbled in their massive chests.

Kal stood by Gwyn's side, his massive hammer resting on his shoulder. Even though flames were dancing on his arms and shoulders, Aidan could sense that the Great Salamander suppressed his elemental energy, constantly keeping it under control. Aidan stifled his laughter, thinking how much the Fire Elemental had to be fuming inwardly. Kal hated suppressing his elemental energy, and since he was forced to do it because of Aoife's gimmicks, she would definitely be on the receiving end of his fiery anger.

Raoul was dressed in the complete attire of a Knight Templar, including a shield with a red cross on it and a sword with the cross on its pommel. Aidan had seen the Warden dressed in ancient armor with chainmail and helm, but never had he seen him displaying his true nature as the Warden chose to keep his past in the past.

Raoul caught Aidan's eyes and a wide grin crossed his face. "If I have to die, I'll die kicking, *mon ami*," he said, his French accent heavier than usual.

"What are you talking about, Father Beaumont," huffed Tessa, tittering. "All of you here are immortal. You can't die."

Gwyn approached her, placing his hand on her shoulder. "There are things that are a lot worse than death, my child," he said, and his glowing eyes settled on Aidan.

He took another step, halting in front of him. For a moment, he stood silent, the glow in his eyes dwindling down, replaced by endless heartache.

"Aodh," he said gently, but the strain in his voice was unmistakable. "My boy, from the first time I laid my eyes upon you on the shore of Loch Dairbhreach, I saw you for what you were— not a scared little boy tormented by his evil stepmother, but a true warrior." His voice trembled, and he touched his mask, making it disappear. "Kal spoke the truth earlier—I sacrificed a lot for you, and I don't regret anything. I would give my life for you willingly."

"Father—," started Aidan, but Gwyn smiled, silencing him.

"I wish," he continued, every word coming to him with a visible effort. "I wish I could go into this tent and meet Aoife instead of you, but this is something you must do on your own. Not because she requested your presence, but because it's time for you to face your greatest and only fear you spent most of your long life harboring in your soul."

He raised his hand to stop Aidan from interrupting him. Aidan dropped his head, unease spreading through him. Gwyn took his chin with his gloved hand, gently lifted his face and touched Aidan's mask, making it dissipate.

"Don't hide your eyes, my boy," he said, gently patting his cheek. "There is nothing shameful about it. I'm the King of the Otherworld. I can read souls. There is nothing a human soul can hide from me, so I always knew about that." He shrugged lightly. "So, face your fears, son, and today, we fight like we've never fought before."

His glowing eyes slipped from one face to the next, and a furious smirk curved his full lips into a feral snarl.

"We fight not only against the air demon but against infinite evil and darkness the entire triad brings in their wake." Gwyn touched his face, restoring his black mask. "We fight for the people we love—our friends who stand by our side and for those who are facing their own battles elsewhere. For the World of Magic and for the realm of humans."

Gwyn ap Nudd turned around toward the ominous mass of demonic army that seemed to have no end, and he laughed, the sound of his deep, strong voice rolling through the dark field.

"Aodh mac Lir," he said without turning, "we stand behind you." He glanced over his shoulder at Aidan and Tessa. "Godspeed, kids."

"Tessa, please stay here," pleaded Aidan, taking her hand into his.

He knew her answer before she said anything, but he wanted to give it one more try. She didn't say anything, instead she pulled her hand out of his grip, seized his arm and pushed him forward, toward the tent. The distance of a few hundred yards seemed to be endless to Aidan, and once they reached it, the only thing he wanted to do was turn around and run. The only desire in his heart was to be as far away from it as possible. But he suppressed his dread and walked inside the tent.

Inside, the tent was brightly lit by hundreds of shimmering blue orbs. Aoife sat on a soft sofa, leaning back with her long legs crossed at the knee, her thick blonde hair falling over her chest in soft waves. Dressed in a flaming red gown, she looked just the way he remembered her from a few years ago. Her lips, generously colored with a bright red lipstick, stretched into a carnivorous smirk as her eyes fell on Aidan. She moved her gaze up and down, sizing him up, but to him it felt as though she was undressing him with her eyes, and he shuddered, the small hairs rising on his arms.

"Well, hello, lad," she said, cocking her head. "I thought I made it clear. I wanted to talk to my son only."

"I'm not your son," replied Aidan calmly. "What do you want,

Aoife? Spit it out. Your tent reeks of demonic essence, and I don't want to spend here any longer than absolutely necessary. It'll take me forever to wash this stench out of my hair."

"Fine," agreed the air demon, snickering. "I guess I would have to meet my future daughter-in-law sooner or later, anyway. Our first meeting wasn't fulfilling enough, you see. I need to spend more time with the young lassie to really get to know her."

A deep growl rumbled in Aidan's chest as he stepped forward, shielding Tessa from Aoife's drilling gaze, wishing with all his heart she stayed behind with Gwyn, Kal and Raoul.

"Relax, lad." Aoife swung her hand, and Tessa vanished just to reappear a moment later on the sofa. She tried to get up but couldn't move, as though she was glued to her seat. "Well, now that we got this out of the way, we can talk. Take a seat, boy."

She pointed at a chair next to a low table with bent legs. When Aidan didn't move, she rolled her eyes and sat down on the second chair across the table, readjusting the front cut on her dress to effectively underline her beautiful, long legs.

"Are you going to sit your giant ass down or should I help you?" she asked, giving him a pointed stare.

Aidan grunted but sat down, folding his arms over his chest. "Fine. I'm sitting. Start talking."

"Take you mask off, son," screeched the air demon. "I should have a word with the Hunter. How come he didn't instill etiquette rules in you? A proper gentleman should remove his hat—or a mask in your case—in the presence of a lady." She snapped her fingers and a whip with a few long tales materialized on the table. "I would teach you a few lessons, but keeping in mind that you're my stepson, it's just kinky, yah know?"

Aidan touched his face, and the mask vanished. He pursed his lips, narrowing his eyes. "I have a feeling you're wasting my time, demon," he said through gritted teeth. "Why is that?"

She laughed, her silvery laughter unfit for the disgusting,

twisted creature she was. "I'm enjoying your presence too much, Aodhán. I raised you for a while as a little boy. You were an interesting child, you know? Not like your younger brothers. More like your sister, I'd say. She was a fighter, just like you. I'm glad the Hunter couldn't bring back all four of you. That would have presented a problem."

Anger spiked within Aidan, making his blood boil, but he smiled frostily. "If I were you," he said slowly, spitting one word at the time, "I would refrain from mentioning my siblings. You may end up hurt."

"How is that? They're in the realm of the dead outside Gwyn's domain. As far as I know, that was the deal Lord Hunter made with the Destiny Council to save you. He can't bring them back, and there is nothing they can do to me," she said, picking up a strawberry from a bowl he hadn't noticed before. Slowly, she brought the berry to her mouth. Her red lips parted slightly, and she touched it with the tip of her tongue before biting off a little piece.

"They can't," agreed Aidan. He channeled his power, and the black ground trembled, sending waves through the walls of the tent. "But I can."

"Oh... scary! The mighty god of the Otherworld is angry. Somebody, please help me!" She gazed heavenward, readjusting the folds of her dress, unimpressed. Aidan let go and fell back in his chair. "Now that we got that out of the way, let's talk."

"Finally," muttered Aidan, throwing a glance at Tessa over Aoife's head. She shifted on the sofa and opened her mouth, but no sound came out and she snapped it shut. "So, what did you want to negotiate?"

"Your surrender, of course," said Aoife, lifting her elegant shoulders in a tiny shrug as if it was beyond obvious. "I know there are only five of you here and that's including your little girlfriend and the Warden. Doesn't strike me like a powerful team." She flicked her wrist dismissively. "So, here is the deal

I'm prepared to offer all of you." Her voice became colder, and her blue eyes lit up with a glacial gleam. "You and Lord Hunter surrender to me, and I'll pull my army back."

Aidan's chest tightened, but he didn't let fear take him over and smirked mockingly. "I still have this burning feeling that you're wasting my time, Aoife."

Aoife got up and seized Tessa's arm, pulling her up to her feet. "Let's go, lad," she said, heading toward the exit, dragging Tessa with her. Aidan clenched his teeth, fighting the desire to strike her with all he had, but that wouldn't be a wise move, so he got up and followed her out the door. As soon as they exited, she placed her other hand on Aidan's shoulder, and they vanished in dark swirls of smoke.

They manifested at the edge of the demonic army where the two groups of people stood motionlessly. Aidan didn't need to ask—one of the groups was the reapers and the other was humans.

Aoife smiled at Tessa, jerking her closer to the group of reapers. "Do you recognize your own kind, girl?" she hissed into Tessa's ear. "Look at them. These are all the reapers I could find in the areas nearby. All of them are under my control, so they're not going to interfere with my plan. They will do what I say when I say it."

The air demon let go of Tessa's arm, and she slowly approached the reapers. Every single one of them stood silent, their wide-opened eyes empty and lifeless. Tessa touched the hand of a reaper in front of her, sending some of her energy through him, but he didn't respond, remaining terrifyingly motionless. She glanced back at Aidan and gave him a slight shake no, biting her lip.

"Don't bother, sweet child," Aoife said to Tessa. "They can't sense you or hear you." She moved closer to Aidan. "I understand it's hard for you to admit that I've got you over the barrel. Again." She cackled carnivorously, for a moment the true features of the air demon showing through the illusion of her human beauty. "So, let me demonstrate what I'm about to do, and if after my demonstration, you and Gwyn ap Nudd don't bend your knee before me, I'd be truly shocked."

She stared in the direction where Aidan had left his friends, and her eyes lit up brighter. Then she whispered something so softly that Aidan couldn't catch her words. A large demon with two massive gorilla-like arms separated from the army. He walked to the crowd of humans and pulled a young woman forward. She didn't resist, her arms hanging limply alongside her body, her eyes hollow and emotionless.

Aoife approached her and held out her hand. In a wisp of dark smoke, a large dagger materialized in her palm.

"No," yelled Tessa, but it was too late. The air demon grabbed the woman, pulled her closer and slit her throat with the dagger.

Bright blood gushed down from the terrible wound, permeating the air with its copper scent, and the woman's eyes rolled back as she dropped to the ground dead. The golden mist of her soul rose above her body, lingering in the stuffy, still air. Aoife approached the soul and touched it with her finger, whispering an incantation. The golden gleam of the spirit dimmed down and dark splatters of the demonic infection marred it, spreading quickly like cancer. Aoife made a pushing motion, propelling the infected spirit toward the veil.

As soon as the spirit passed through the veil, a bright white flair burst out of it, blinding Aidan. A blast of demonic energy rushed through the field, and he groaned, pressing his hands to his eyes. Once the spots stopped dancing in his vision, he saw a glowing fracture in the veil slowly closing up.

"You see?" said Aoife, turning to Aidan. "Being locked inside the void was the best thing that could've happened to me. It gave me time to think about how many issues my original plan had. So, I improved it." She pointed at the crowd of humans.

"Now I can destroy all these humans in a matter of a few seconds, infecting their souls with demonic essence. To kill them all at once, I don't need the Fire Salamander anymore. I gained a few skills of my own."

She put her hand on Aidan's arm, her long fingers with well-manicured red nails probing his bicep. He pulled away, throwing her hand off, and she snickered, shaking her head. "Now that you've seen what I can do with your own eyes," she said, mockery dripping from her voice, "how soon should I expect you and Gwyn at my feet?"

Aidan glanced at Tessa, and a spark of hope ignited in his soul. She smiled, mouthing the word no. He had no idea what she had in mind, but he wasn't going to comply with the air demon's demands, anyway. He looked down at Aoife, and a frosty, crooked smile twisted his lips.

"As soon as never," he said quietly. He walked around her and took Tessa's hand, heading back.

"I will kill you all, and then I'll destroy the veil, bringing this world to an end!" shouted Aoife, rising in the air.

"Yeah, you do that," replied Aidan without turning.

Aoife squealed, her voice rising over the army of demons, and her appearance began to change. Gone were the beauty, the long, blonde hair and the elegant, sensual figure. Her spine twisted into a giant hump, sharp spikes protruding through her parchment-like skin. Her face looked like a skull, a malignant yellow light burning in its sockets. She waved her talons, shouting commands, and the army of demons moved at the same time toward Aidan and Tessa.

"Aidan, we fight," she whispered. "Thanks to Aoife's big mouth, I know what to do. Just tell Gwyn to protect the humans. I'm going to need just a few minutes."

"Tessa, what are you—," he started to ask, but the demonic army went into full attack. Shouting something in a language he didn't recognize, and brandishing their enormous axes, swords and mazes, they switched to a run.

"Go!" yelled Tessa and vanished.

"Dammit, Tessa!" shouted Aidan, worry gnawing at him. He spun around, searching for her, but she was gone.

CHAPTER 34

~ AIDAN ~

Aidan snapped his fingers and teleported back to the place where he had left his friends. Gwyn ap Nudd was still there, but both Kal and Raoul were gone. He had no time to ask questions. Running toward Gwyn, he screamed, "Father, I need you to protect humans."

"Working on it already," replied the King of the Otherworld. He grabbed Aidan's shoulder and snapped his fingers, teleporting them back to the group of humans. By the time they manifested next to them, the situation had changed.

After the demonstration Aoife had given him, Aidan expected that somehow, she would kill every single person at once, infecting their souls with her poisonous energy, but that wasn't what was happening. The air demon in its natural form levitated above the crowd, wrapped in the dark mist of her magic. Slithering, thick tendrils separated from the mist, reaching down to the heads of people while another group of tendrils reached for the demons standing nearby.

Every single person raised their face, staring at their approaching death with unblinking eyes. As the tendrils reached a few people, penetrating their skulls, they screamed and twitched, their faces contorted with unimaginable pain. The tendrils ripped their souls out of their bodies and combined them with the demonic essence Aoife was extracting from the demons. She didn't kill all the people at once but kept throwing infected souls at the veil a few at a time.

The veil shuddered and vibrated, emitting a loud, grinding noise. The brilliant white light illuminated the dark field and stayed constant as Aoife kept working with admirable persistence. A web of thin, dark fractures materialized on the surface of the veil, and a powerful surge of dark energy spread around the air demon.

Gwyn ap Nudd shouted something, but through the screeches of demons, the wailing of Aoife and the noise of the crashing veil, it was impossible to hear anything. The King of the Otherworld materialized next to the veil and pressed his palms against it, his arms bulging with muscles. He sent some of his energy through it, starting the healing process. A few seconds later, he let go and switched his attention to the air demon, his eyes lighting up brighter, shining through the angled slits of his mask.

"Kal, now!" he roared over the pandemonium, and two long daggers materialized in his hands. He raised his arms and bright beams of white light exited the blades. He slashed his daggers, holding them parallel to the ground, and the beams of light cut through the tendrils of Aoife's magic, turning them into dirty, gray ash.

A fiery curtain of the Fire Salamander portal unfolded next to the crowd of people, and the giant, flaming blacksmith walked through it, carrying a massive hammer on his shoulder. With his fiery hair, burning eyes and giant frame, Kal looked terrifying in his anger, and Aidan was almost grateful that all these people were in a magical trance, unable to see anything happening around them.

Kal swung his hammer and slammed it on the ground,

sending tremors through the field. A circle of smoldering flames surrounded the crowd of people, emitting an unbearable heat. Startled, the air demon hissed and rose higher into the air, shying away from the heat. For a split-second, she lost her focus, and her appearance flickered back to her human form.

Aoife let go for a moment shorter than a heartbeat, but it was enough for Gwyn to move forward with his plan. He shouted a spell, entwining the magic of the Otherworld with the elemental Fire Kal provided. A dome of powerful protective magic manifested around the group of people, shielding them from the air demon's influence. The circle of fire ignited brighter, sending fountains of sparks and swirls of light gray smoke in the air. It blocked the demons' way to Gwyn's protective shield, sending them into a frenzy as they hustled to retreat from the fire. Aoife squealed, her rage almost palpable as she attempted to break through, but to no avail.

A flare of light ignited within the dome, and Raoul de Beaumont materialized in the middle of the crowd. The Warden raised his arms and started to chant, the energy of his magic spreading around him in soft white waves. Slowly, people's eyes returned to normal. Dark with shock, they looked around, confusion reflecting on their terrified faces. A few of them pushed against the walls of the protective magic but couldn't break through.

As Raoul kept chanting, he spread his arms wider, and a large, pulsing vein crossed his forehead as he strained to keep up his enchantment. The radiant light of his magic accumulated within the dome, and soon, it flooded it completely, obscuring the Warden and the people surrounding him. Aidan gasped, raising his arm to shield his eyes. When the light subsided, the Warden was gone, and all the humans were gone with him.

Kal's diabolical laughter boomed over the field as the Great Salamander stopped controlling his elemental energy. "Now we play!" he shouted. "Gwyn?"

The Great Salamander raised his hammer with ease and ran toward the approaching demonic army. He crashed his terrible weapon at his enemies, and an undiluted wave of purifying fire spread around him, setting demons ablaze. The monsters howled as their essence burned out, devoured by the purifying magic. Their malformed bodies dropped to the ground, consumed by the hungry flames of the physical fire.

Aidan combined his magic with Gwyn's as they raised their swords, deflecting the forceful assault of the demonic forces. As Gwyn began to wield his purifying magic, his deep voice spreading over the battlefield, and Aidan joined him. The demons nearest to them started to fall, a small group at the time, their essence shimmering out of their bodies that were slowly dissolving into puddles of disgusting goo.

Gwyn's hounds dug into the mob of the monsters, their powerful jaws snapping at the demon's legs. Some of them jumped, ripping demons' necks with their terrible fangs, sending the enemy lines into disarray. The air was thick with the smell of blood, the reek of burned flesh and smoke, and Aidan's eyes watered as he struggled to fill his lungs with oxygen.

Aoife screamed, hovering above their heads. She twirled in the air, and the dark tendrils of her magic grew longer, reaching for Gwyn, Aidan and Kal. They had no choice but to stop what they were doing to block her attack. That gave the demonic army a moment to regroup and attack with full force.

"Father," yelled Aidan, straining to parry the massive demonic club with his sword, "we need to do something. If it'll continue this way, we won't be able to hold them for much longer."

"I know! We destroyed Aoife's plans. She has no human souls to throw at the veil, but we can't let her leave!" yelled Gwyn. He dropped to one knee and punched the ground with his massive fist. A wave of mighty tremors spread around him, unbalancing some of the demons, sending them tumbling back into the rows of monsters behind them.

"Let's send this air bitch to the hellhole she climbed out from!" responded Kal. His deep laughter rolled across the battlefield as the Great Salamander reverted into his natural state. For a brief moment, an enormous flaming lizard lingered in the air, spreading powerful blasts of purifying fire energy combined with physical fire around him.

Aidan wasn't sure how many monsters fell dead, but it seemed like no matter how hard they fought, every fallen demon was replaced by five new ones. Aoife cackled above their heads, charging her terrifying army with the malignant energy of Chaos. Ignoring the mockery and curses Aoife showered him with, Aidan kept fighting, but every next swing of his sword came with more and more effort.

Although Gwyn and Kal didn't have to deal with the limitations of a human body, their moves became slower and every next wave of their magic was weaker. They were getting drained, and Aoife knew it, doubling her efforts with sadistic pleasure gleaming in her eyes.

Another few minutes and they will subdue us... A terrible thought flashed through Aidan's mind, and the only thing he was happy about was that Tessa wasn't here. He had no idea where she went, but anywhere would be better than here.

Suddenly, a bright zigzag of lightning spliced the black sky, and thunder rumbled loudly, following it. The cacophony of the battle was replaced by complete silence. The demons froze in awkward poses, and even the air demon stilled in midair, her tendrils spread over her deadly army.

Aidan spun around and saw Tessa. She stood a few feet away from him with her arm raised above her head, holding the Axe of Perun. Her entire body shimmered with the red energy of the god of Thunder, and electric discharges made the air buzz around her. Behind her, a large group of reapers stood like a silent, dark wall. Their eyes shone with the energy of death, and their sharp scythes reflected the flares of electricity.

Tessa met his eyes, and a smile touched her lips as electricity kept flowing around her, wrapping around her arms like shining silk ribbons. Engulfed in the crimson glow of her power, she was as beautiful as she was deadly, and Aidan couldn't take his eyes off of her. She gave him a short nod and headed toward Gwyn ap Nudd. Stopping in front of the King of the Otherworld, she motioned for him to bend down. Gwyn threw a bewildered gaze at Aidan but took one knee to be closer to her.

"Are you holding a time bubble?" asked Gwyn ap Nudd, his eyebrows rising slowly.

"Yes, my lord," replied Tessa, strain in her voice. "And I can't hold it for much longer. I need your help, sir." Keeping a safe distance, she moved slightly closer to him and whispered something into his ear, rising on her tiptoes a little.

Gwyn's face lost all color as he stared at her in shock. "No, child," he muttered, horror ringing in his voice. "I'm not going to let you do it."

Tessa smiled at him, sadness making her brown eyes darker. "My lord, earlier you said that you would do anything to save your son," she said softly. "Do you believe that I love your son so much that I would do anything for him, too?"

Gwyn ap Nudd nodded and dropped his head. She reached forward and brushed a strand of his long hair off his face, tucking it behind his pointed ear. Even though a few tiny lightning bolts escaped her hand, zapping him, he didn't react, remaining still.

"My lord," she said, her voice just slightly above a whisper. "I love Aidan. He's my life, the only family I've got... I have an opportunity to save you, him, and the realm of humans, and I'm taking this opportunity. You can help me, or I can summon

Angel, which is not a good idea. You don't want any of the horsemen using their powers in the given situation, do you?"

Gwyn shook his head and raised his eyes at Aidan, a muscle working in his tightly pressed jaw.

"Father," mumbled Aidan, a feeling of dread squeezing his throat, suffocating him. "Tessa, what do you—"

She walked to him and ran her hand over his cheek without touching him, but as careful as she was, he still felt a spike of electricity rushing through his body.

"Aidan," she whispered his name, tears brimming her eyes. "My ancient god, I love you. I can't even touch you right now..." Her voice broke, and she swallowed. "When you were gone earlier today, Gwyn ap Nudd explained to me how the Board of Destiny works. I can't say I understand everything, but now I know for sure—it wasn't a coincidence that *you* found me by your school and saved me from those bullies. Nothing of it was coincidental, because my entire life lead to this very moment." She waved at the frozen demonic army and the air demon lingering over them.

"Tessa, please, whatever you cooked up in your crazy mind, we can come up—"

"No, my love, we can't. This is the only way, and Gwyn ap Nudd agreed with me," she objected quietly. "You saved me all these years ago. You gave me life, love and purpose, and now, it's my time to return the favor." Tears spilled from her eyes, running down her pale face. "You make me so incredibly happy, Aidan... I had no idea I could feel happiness or joy at all." She held out her hand, and Sword Kladenets materialized in her palm. She gave it to Aidan, and he wrapped his fingers around its grip absentmindedly. "Use it well, my ancient god. Kill them all, and I'll see you on the flip side."

She pivoted on her heel and returned to Gwyn ap Nudd, who was still kneeling with his head bowed down.

"Are you ready, my lord?" she asked, gently touching his shoulder.

He flinched from the sting of electricity and raised his face, a haunted expression frozen in his silvery eyes. "Tessa, my child, if we do what you want, I won't be able to bring you back," he whispered in a hoarse voice. "You realize that you'll lose both your humanity and the side of you that makes you the goddess of Thunder? Forever. There will be no way back."

She nodded. "Of course, I know that," she replied calmly with a tiny smirk. "And I'm willing to do it, anyway. In this case, purpose truly justifies the means. Aidan"—she threw a momentary glance infused with so much love at Aidan that his beating heart started to bleed in his constrained chest—"is worth this sacrifice and so much more. Besides, the realm of humans must be saved, and I'm the only one who can do it."

Gwyn ap Nudd got up, his moves torturously slow. "Fine," he said, channeling his power, and his entire body lit up with the blinding white light. "If you're ready, let's do it."

"No!" shouted Aidan, but Tessa waved her hand and whispered a quick spell, immobilizing him.

She channeled more of her power and let go of the time bubble. Everything came to motion at the same time, and the terrible sounds of battle overwhelmed the dark field. Kal roared a spell, and a smoldering wall of fire erupted in front of them, running in both directions for as far as Aidan could see. He spun his hammer in his hand and stepped into the veil of fire, ready to fight anyone or anything who dared pass through.

Tessa spun in place, and the dark mist of the power of Death surrounded her like an impenetrable shield. When the mist disintegrated, Tessa stood in the full appearance of a reaper, long black robes and scythe included. The Axe of Perun lay on the ground next to her feet, but she didn't bother picking it up.

Aidan moaned and dropped the sword. He glanced at her eyes and there was no recognition there, the cold emptiness of

Death in its purest form staring back at him. Wrapping his arms around his head, he bent forward as pain wrenched his heart.

Tessa glanced at the other reapers, and they bowed to her. "We're ready," she said to Gwyn ap Nudd, her voice flat and hollow.

The King of the Otherworld placed his hands on the veil and started to chant, his deep voice louder than the roar of the demons and shouts of Aoife struggling against Kal. The veil shone with a soft light and a tall, wide door opened up, nothing but darkness hiding behind it. Tessa glided through the door and disappeared on the other side.

"Father, what did you do!" yelled Aidan, his body leaden with sorrow. "Father!"

Gwyn didn't say anything. Keeping both hands planted on the veil, he kept chanting, but his tensed shoulders shuddered.

A few seconds later, Tessa came back and nodded at Gwyn ap Nudd. "Now, my lord. Do what you must."

A glowing mist emerged from the door, following Tessa. At first, it looked like an enormous, shapeless cloud, but as Gwyn closed the door in the veil, all the reapers, including Tessa, approached the mist, placing their hands on it as they whispered something softly. Slowly, the mist took shape and thousands of spirits materialized in its place. Even though they were clearly visible, their bodies were still translucent, shifting in and out of focus.

Gwyn approached them and started a complicated spell work, working his magic with his hands and his words. Gradually, the spirits turned solid, and now thousands of people dressed in clothes from different centuries and lands stood between the veil and the line of fire.

Tessa walked up to a tall woman who stood in front of the group and offered her a hand. She put her hand into hers, and Tessa lead her toward Aidan. He took in the woman's appearance, and the world spun around him, tears gathering in his eyes.

"Fionnghuala... My sister," he whispered. "My fair-shouldered sister... I missed you so... All these years... Oh God... but how? Why?"

She took one more step and wrapped her arms around his neck, placing her head on his chest. "My brother, Aodhán. The High Reaper allowed us to cross the veil so we could take a stand with you against our evil stepmother." She unlocked her arms and waved back at the two young men standing behind her. They looked absolutely the same, their young faces still carrying the softness of youth.

"My brothers," whispered Aidan. "Fiachra, Conn..."

"I wish we could spend more time with you, brother. Catch up... but we can't," said one of the twins. "Where is she? It's time we paid our dear mother back for all the kindness and love she showed us." A dark smirk crossed his handsome face.

Tessa walked into the line of the fire, flames licking her long robes, doing no harm to her. "Great Salamander," she said, her voice hollow like the voices of the other reapers, "please stand down and extinguish your flames."

Kal stepped back and moved his hand over the fire. "Cease," he muttered, and the wall of flames dwindled down, leaving only swirls of light, gray smoke in the air.

"Let's do it, brothers," said Aidan, picking up Sword Kladenets. He smiled at his sister, and she gave him a short shake of her head.

"Allow me, brother." Fionnghuala stepped forward, leading the crowd of spirits closer to the lines of demons. "Aoife!" she yelled, her sonorous voice rising above the noise.

Aoife glanced down, and her yellow, parchment-like face became green with fear. Her jaw dropped, and the tendrils of her dark magic retracted.

"I see you recognized me," said Fionnghuala calmly. "But do

you recognize any of these people?" She waved her hand at the large crowd. "Every single person here died a terrible death by your hand. They came from different death realms, from different times, and different lands with one purpose only—to see that you receive the punishment that fits all the crimes you committed over the centuries."

"It's impossible," hissed Aoife. "No one has the power to bring so many dead spirits, gathering them across different pantheons and deathly realms. No one except Death himself has that kind of power, and he's not here."

"But I am here," said Tessa, stepping next to Fionnghuala, her scythe glowing with the light of her power.

"You are—," started Aoife but cut herself off, and a malignant snarl distorted her lips. "You sacrificed yourself for your lover. Even I didn't see that coming." She cackled icily, shaking her head. "But you are too late, little girl. You forfeited your life for nothing—"

"Seems like you didn't see many things coming," replied Fionnghuala, serenely.

She waved her hand and a thick veil of mist rose behind her, leaving Aidan, Gwyn ap Nudd and Kal behind. Tessa stepped back through the veil and gestured at the other reapers to join her. Then she glanced at Aidan, slightly tilting her head.

"Stay here," she said flatly and walked back through the mist.

Aidan made a move to follow her, but Gwyn's heavy hand lay on his shoulder, holding him in place.

"Do what you've been told, son," he said softly. "It'll be over soon. There is nothing more dangerous and scarier than infuriated spirits going after a person who caused their suffering."

Aidan expected to hear screams, commands, the commotion of a battle, but there was nothing. Absolute silence enveloped the field as if someone had cast a silencing spell. He wasn't sure how long it lasted, but to him it seemed like an eternity. When the mist finally disappeared, he gasped, taking in the terrifying view.

Every single demon was dead, and the land was covered in a layer of thick, putrid goo, the black clouds of demonic essence slowly seeping through it into the dirt. Aoife in her demonic form hung limply, suspended in the air by the glowing hoops of magical energy wielded by the reapers. The yellow light in the sockets of her skull were extinguished, making her look like a skeleton wrapped in flowing, dirty rags. Aidan didn't consider the possibility of the air demon being dead since he knew she was indestructible, so he assumed she was either unconscious or asleep.

Fionnghuala approached him, taking his hand into hers. With her other hand, she caressed his face, her fingers rubbing the stubble on his chin.

"Aodhán, you're no longer that little boy," she whispered, and his heart sped up at the sight of such a familiar smile on her face. She sighed and sobered up, wistfulness gone from her voice. "It's over, Aodh. Over forever. You're truly free now, my brother."

He took her hand into his and brought it up to his lips, planting a gentle kiss on her fingers. "I doubt it," he said quietly. "Even the void couldn't keep her down, Nuala. She'll be back sooner or later. It's my destiny to live forever in her shadow."

"The void is an obvious location." Fionnghuala dropped her hand. She looked up at the ugly form of the air demon, and a deep shudder rushed through her. "Any evil bastard that still walks this world would know to look for her there. The place she's going to now is so obscured, no one will be able to find her there. Only the High Reaper and Death himself know about the location of it." She patted Aidan on his shoulder, rubbing his arm with her hand. "Trust me, my sweet brother, you *are* finally free."

Tessa approached them and glanced at Fionnghuala, her face

an emotionless mask. "It's time," she said flatly. "Say your goodbyes."

"Yes, High Reaper," replied Fionnghuala, turning back to Aidan.

"High Reaper?" repeated Aidan, his eyes glued to Tessa's back.

"Yes, brother. Only the High Reaper and Death have the power to gather so many spirits from different places and times," replied his sister. She reached up and kissed his cheek, one more time embracing him. "Farewell, my brother. I will always love you..." Her voice faded into silence, and her body slowly became translucent.

Following the reapers, the long chain of spirits flowed through the door Gwyn ap Nudd opened for them. Tessa waited by the door until the last spirit walked through it. Then she bowed to the King of the Otherworld and passed through the threshold, disappearing on the other side.

FOR A FEW LONG MINUTES, Aidan stood stupefied, staring without blinking at the place where Tessa had disappeared. His eyes burned but there were no tears, only the overwhelming torment twisting his heart. He closed his eyes and pinched the bridge of his nose, swallowing painfully. Slowly, he started on his way toward Gwyn ap Nudd, every step producing an almost physical ache.

He halted a foot away from the King of the Otherworld, giving him a cold once-over. With a low grunt, he lowered to the ground and picked up the Axe of Perun, pulling it closer to his side. Then he rested his folded arms atop his bent knees and glanced up at the man he considered his Father.

"How could you?" he asked quietly, pain seeping into his voice.

Gwyn stifled a sigh. "Tessa was right, Aidan, and I did what I had to do," he said, throwing a glance in Kal's direction as if searching for his support. "We couldn't have allowed the air demon to capture us, leaving the veil unprotected." He shook his head, exhaustion visible in his every move. "It wasn't me. There was something Aoife said during your negotiation that gave Tessa this idea."

"You turned her into the High Reaper!" hissed Aidan, slamming his hand on the ground. The sharp edge of the Axe sliced his palm, and blood trickled from the incision, but he couldn't feel the physical pain. "You knew there was no way out of this transformation, yet you still let her do it. How could you?"

Gwyn threw his hands in the air, a desperate gesture infused with heartache and misery. His image shimmered, and he reverted back to his human appearance, his naked torso glistening with sweat. Kal tapped him on his shoulder and sat down next to Aidan, throwing his hammer on the ground with a dull thud.

"First of all, Gwyn didn't turn Tessa into the High Reaper. No one could do it except her. It was her choice." He glanced sideways at Aidan and leaned forward, resting his arms on his bent knees. "Second, she did it to save you, Aidan. To give *you* a life without constant fear. Of course, she also did that for the greater good, to save the realm of humans and blah blah blah... But the truth is, she did it to save a single person—the man she loved."

"You could have stopped her, Father!" yelled Aidan, ignoring the Great Salamander, his hands clenched into tight fist. "That was in your power." He turned to Kal, regarding him with a mixture of reproach and anger. "And you, Kal... You speak all these politically correct words, but would you do the same if it was your son in my place? Would you destroy your son's life if Gunz was here instead of me, or would you look for a different solution? I'm sure we could've found some other way that wouldn't—"

Kal chuckled bitterly, shaking his head. "You're in pain, Aidan," he said, trying to sound calm, but his voice shook, betraying his true state of mind. "You're not thinking straight, so I'm going to forgive your childish outburst. You're forgetting that Gunz was in your situation, and what I did to him was a lot worse..." He swallowed, turning away for a brief moment. "Gwyn had no choice. Tessa made his choice for him. I had a choice, and I chose to control my son, removing his ability to fight for his love. I betrayed him in the worst possible way. For the greater good, I hurt my son so bad... I still see his tormented eyes in my worst nightmares."

"Just curious... What did Gunz do after he came back home?" asked Aidan absently. "I'm sure he didn't appreciate what you'd done to him either."

"No, he didn't. But he blamed himself for everything that happened. Not me." Kal shrugged heavily. "Mrak and I went to his house immediately. Gunz did what he always does when he's in pain—he got drunk to the point where he could no longer think or function." Kal chuckled bitterly. "Mrak had to carry him to his bedroom and put him in an enchanted sleep. But he forgave me. The next day we talked. After he sobered up, that is. I have no idea how or why, but this boy found it in his heart to forgive me... But I..." Kal choked on the last word and bit his lip. "I can never forgive myself..."

"I'm sorry," whispered Aidan. He got up heavily and approached Gwyn ap Nudd. "Father, I shouldn't have—"

Ignoring his words, Gwyn ap Nudd pulled Aidan into a tight embrace, burying his fingers into his hair. For a few short moments, he let himself be a normal man who just lost the woman he loved and forget that he was a god of the Otherworld with the weight of the world on his shoulders. Aidan rested his forehead against his father's chest and closed his eyes, allowing grief to take him over.

"All is not lost, my boy," Gwyn said, gently patting his back. "I don't think Tessa could be brought back as she was before all that, but maybe there is a way to bring back her memories and feelings for you. I'll have to do some research. Maybe the Master Warden can help us with that."

The moment of normality, as illusionary as it was, was gone, and reality came back crushing him under its weight.

"Come to think of it... Where is Raoul?" asked Aidan, pulling away.

"He's fine," replied Gwyn. "He teleported all the humans back to safety. Some strange spell he'd seen Gunz perform a while ago. Then he had to stay with them to make sure the Destiny Council would modify their memories."

Aidan picked up the Axe of Perun and the magical sword. Gathering some of his power, he reached out to Gunz, using their psychic link.

"Gunz, are you okay? Say something..."

There was no answer. He raised his eyes at Gwyn ap Nudd and then looked at Kal. "We need to go. Immediately. Gunz hasn't been answering my calls for a while. He and Mrak could be in way over their heads, going against the Lord of Chaos and the goddess of Winter and Death."

Kal closed his eyes, and the elemental energy swirled around him into a mini twister. A second later, he opened his eyes, filled with dancing flames, and the corner of his lips quirked up.

"I can sense him," he said softly, relief suffusing his features. "He's alive, but you're right, Aidan. They're in way over their heads. We must go at once."

Gwyn ap Nudd opened the blazing rectangle of his door, motioning for them to go through. Aidan glanced back at the dead black field and sighed.

Tessa, if there is a way to bring you back, I swear, I'll find it...

CHAPTER 35

~ ZANE BURNS, A.K.A. GUNZ ~

As soon as Aidan and Tessa were gone, Gunz channeled a minimal amount of his elemental energy and drew a flaming rune in midair. He pressed his hand to it, whispering a summoning spell as he called to the Slavic god of Fire, Semargl. He waited a while, but since the deity didn't reply to his summons, he tried again with the same outcome. For the next few minutes, he tried to summon Belobog and Svyatobor, but it seemed like none of the Slavic gods were willing to answer his call.

That can't be good... He sat down on the ground with a soft grunt and pulled his legs to his chest, wrapping his arms around them. Carefully, he opened his other sight and probed the small pile of sand that remained in place of Mount Karasova. Except for the same dark energy he had been feeling since Aidan teleported them into the village, he didn't discover anything new.

He lowered his head, his heart aching—a dull, twisting pain that hadn't stopped since he arrived here. Glancing to the side, he recognized the surroundings. This was the same hill he and Karma had used to bring down a few dark wizards Morena had positioned around the mountain. Now, Karma was dead, and Angelique was worse than dead. So much loss. So much pain.

He sighed and closed his eyes, trying to clear his mind and stop any negative thoughts from taking him over. With his combat experience—magical and human—he knew that any kind of negativity before a dangerous confrontation was a sure way to lose not only the battle but life as well. No matter what, he had to believe he could win, otherwise he was better off waving the white flag and kneeling before his enemy.

He felt a brush of cold air against his cheek, and a familiar magical energy washed over him. Opening his eyes, he glanced sideways, greeting his friend with a faint smile. Mrak Delar stood by his side, gazing at him with curiosity. His eyes were darker than usual, and bitterness was hiding in the curve of his tightly pressed lips.

"When you sit like this, you look like a sad little boy who was grounded by his father," said the Master of Power, and his gaze warmed up just a touch.

"What can I tell you? Not all of us look like a mountain of muscles," grumbled Gunz, rising. "What took you so long?"

"In a rush to get your ass kicked?" Mrak Delar smirked, arching his eyebrow.

"I'm not sure there is anyone here to do the kicking," replied Gunz, pointing at the place where Mount Karasova used to be. "I'm afraid we're too late."

"What do you mean?" Mrak Delar narrowed his eyes, staring in the direction of the mountain. Then he turned to Gunz, regarding him with concern. "Are you using your second sight, Gunz?"

"Not right now." Gunz shrugged, frowning. "But a few minutes ago I was, and I didn't see anything different from what I see with my human sight."

"And that would be?"

"Mount Karasova is gone, and a small pile of sand remains in its place." Gunz opened his other sight again and surveyed the area just to confirm he could see nothing different.

"Fire and ice," exhaled the Master of Power incredulously. "These evil bastards expected you to be here. They built an illusion specifically for those who use fire energy to see." He moved his arm, weaving a quick spell. "*Ostendium Amnia.*"

A thin layer of his magic infused with three out of the four elemental energies materialized in front of Gunz. He peered through it and gasped, unable to take his eyes off the new view that unfolded before him.

Mount Karasova, the way he remembered it, was no more. A tall rocky mountain stretched to the sky in its place, its single sharp peak piercing the dark clouds like a thick, roughly cut needle. Its top glistened with snow and ice, and at the foot of the mountain, the dark hole of the entrance into a cave gaped at him with malice.

Evil magical energy slithered out of the dark maw of the cave, spreading around the area like toxic smoke. Seemingly, no one was guarding the entrance, but his sight couldn't penetrate the walls of the mountain, and he couldn't say if anyone was waiting for them on the inside.

"Can you see inside?" asked Gunz, throwing a glance at the Master of Power.

"No," he replied. "Powerful magic. I can't break through it." Mrak Delar waved his hand, removing the spell. "I guess we'll use your favorite battle strategy."

Gunz raised his eyebrows, flashing a lopsided grin at him. "What do you have in mind, Master?"

"We jump in headfirst blindly," replied Mrak Delar with a half-shrug. "Isn't that what you do best?"

"I didn't invent this strategy, but I sure perfected it." Gunz laughed and even though the situation looked grimmer than ever, he felt a little better. "But today, I think I'll call for backup."

"Semargl?"

"No. I already tried every Slavic deity whom I knew how to summon." Gunz rubbed the back of his neck and sighed. "None of them answered my call. Not even Svyatobor."

"Dammit, why do I have a feeling we should be elsewhere?" muttered the Master of Power.

"Didn't you tell me it was my destiny to fight Skiper-Zmey?" asked Gunz. "If it's true, then I'm in the right place."

"True. Assuming Zmey is still here, that is." Mrak Delar waved at the mountain.

Using his elemental energy, Gunz drew a flaming rune in the air, and Mrak's eyes widened.

"Are you summoning the Destiny—" He didn't finish his statement and laughed darkly. "You're growing on me, boy. Or maybe you're just growing up." He winked. "Go for it."

Gunz pressed his hand against the rune and whispered the summoning spell. No one manifested on the dark hill next to him, but a large communication window suspended in midair opened up at once. A man stood in front of the window, an uneven smirk playing on his thin lips. He was dressed in gray sweatpants and a black tank top that stretched tightly over his muscled chest covered in short, black hair. Once he laid his eyes on Gunz, he crossed his massive arms over his chest and tilted his head a little.

"Well, hello, Burns," he said in a raspy voice. "Had a change of heart? Ready to join my team?"

"Over my dead body, Commander Moore," replied Gunz calmly. "But if you don't get your ass down here together with your highly overrated team, we may have a lot of dead bodies soon."

He moved his hand, turning the window toward the mountain. The Commander stared over Gunz's head and then slammed his beefy fist into the wall next to the window.

"Damn, boy," he muttered, shaking his head. "I hope you're not planning to go into this ice-and-rock fortress on your own."

"He's not alone, Commander," said Mrak Delar, stepping into view, "but the sooner you get here the better."

For a moment, the Commander remained silent, a muscle twitching in his square jaw. "Just the two of you, Master?" he said at length, his voice raspier than usual. "And you're planning to kick this hornet's nest all by your lonesome selves?"

"Haven't you heard yet? The Otherworld is under attack," replied Mrak Delar. "Gwyn ap Nudd, Kal, Aidan and Tessa took a stand there. The entire Slavic pantheon is nowhere to be found. So, yes... the two of us are all we have."

"It's a suicide mission, Master," murmured the Commander, raking his fingers through his short-cropped hair. "And you know it, don't you?"

"I do. We both know," replied Mrak Delar and smirked darkly. "But when did something like this stop us?"

"I need fifteen minutes," said the Commander, peering down at his wristwatch. He raised his eyes, drilling Gunz with his heavy gaze, and then added, "You hear me, Salamander? Don't play games. Stay put for fifteen minutes. I'll be there with my team. *Do not* go in there alone." He stressed the words 'do not', but doubt was written all over his face.

"We'll stay down for as long as we can," promised Mrak Delar. He threw a quick glance at the mountain and a vibe of unease lingered over him. "For as long as we can is the keyword here, Commander. So, don't take your time."

"Roger that, Master. See you in fifteen." He snapped his fingers and closed the communication window.

Mrak Delar glanced at Gunz, scratching the back of his head. "Gunz, why did he call me Roger?"

Gunz pressed his hand to his mouth to stop himself from laughing, his eyebrows climbing up. "No, Master," he replied, laughter ringing in his voice. "It's modern military slang. It means he acknowledged your order and will act on it."

"Modern." Mrak Delar snorted, rolling his eyes. "There's nothing modern about Moore. He's older than Aidan."

Gunz nodded. "Figures. All of you—the retirement club."

Mrak Delar averted his gaze, readjusting the cuffs of his long sleeve shirt. "Gunz, are you sure you did the right thing?" he asked quietly.

"What? By summoning Moore and his team?"

"No," replied Mrak Delar. "By giving Sword Kladenets to Aidan. What you're about to face..." He dropped his arms, looking in the direction of the mountain.

Gunz shrugged, but a heavy weight settled in his chest. "I'm sure, Mrak. Aidan needs it more than I do. Besides, you said it yourself—I use a sword like a woodsman. At least Aidan would do this weapon justice."

"That was a long time ago," murmured Mrak. "Now Akira believes you to be one of her best pupils. After her son, of course."

"But of course." Gunz chuckled, thinking about Yaroslav, wishing the vampire was here. "It doesn't matter, Mrak. Aidan was terrified of the idea of facing his stepmother again. He would never admit it, of course, but he's been harboring this fear in his soul for centuries. He needed that little extra umph to believe he could beat her and finally put this ancient fear to rest."

"True," agreed the Ancient Master. "But don't tell me you're not afraid to face the Lord of Chaos."

"Do I look like an idiot?" Gunz chuckled and raised his hand peacefully. "Wait. Don't answer that." Mrak shrugged innocently, the corners of his lips lifting just a little. "Of course, I'm afraid. Only idiots fear nothing. But I'm not afraid of Skiper-Zmey or Morena, per se. I'm afraid of what will happen to the realm of humans if we lose the battle—"

A loud, high-pitched laughter rolled through the forest,

echoing from one tree to the next. A gust of chilly wind carrying icy flurries followed it, assailing Gunz and Mrak Delar.

"So, you are saying you're not afraid of me, little Salamander?" A female voice as cold as winter itself sounded in his head, and Gunz cringed, pressing his palms to his temples. "Let's see what kind of song you're going to sing in the presence of the Lord of Chaos."

A heavy winter blizzard came from nowhere, engulfing him in its glacial embrace. He screamed as hundreds of tiny icicles penetrated the skin of his face, neck and arms, drawing blood. The wind lifted him off the ground, and he twisted, trying to control his body suspended in midair. The blizzard got heavier. Now, he could see nothing but the rotating ice and hear nothing but the howling of the wind. As he raised his arms in a fruitless attempt to shield his face, he felt Mrak's fingers seizing his arm.

"Hang in there, Salamander!" he heard Mrak's voice, and it sounded muffled and strained. "I guess that's your invitation to a private audience with Skiper-Zmey."

CHAPTER 36

~ ZANE BURNS, A.K.A. GUNZ ~

W hen the blizzard died down, Gunz found himself kneeling on the rocky floor of a dark cave. At least he assumed it was a cave since he could barely see his own hands in the surrounding darkness. The air was cold and musty, and the weak odor of dirt and stale water touched his senses.

His clothes were soaked with icy water and every move caused him a burning pain. He raised his arms and carefully brushed his fingers over his face, feeling the slippery wetness of blood. All exposed areas of his skin were covered in thousands of small paper-cut-like incisions, and blood trickled down his arms and face.

"Gunz, revert... Do it while you can."

He heard Mrak's voice somewhere on his left, but he couldn't see him. Clenching his teeth to stifle a cry of pain, he channeled as much elemental power as he could and let go, reverting into the natural state of the Fire Salamander. The fire engulfed him and for a moment he could see a shimmering layer of illusion wrapped around him. A red flag went up in his mind, setting it on high alert. He suppressed his fire energy, returning to his human form.

As soon as he felt the steady ground under his feet, a few pairs of strong hands got hold of him. Twisting his arms behind his back, they forced him down to his knees. He grunted, struggling to break their hold, but it was impossible. Someone's fingers dug into his hair, pushing his head down.

Where is Mrak? I hope he's okay...

A melodious laughter rolled through the cave, and someone clapped three times. Hundreds of light orbs ignited around the perimeter of the room, illuminating it with a shimmering blue light. The hand holding Gunz's hair let go, but not before slapping him on the back of his head. He growled as anger spiked through him but couldn't make a move with his arms twisted at a sharp angle. With an effort, he raised his head and quickly assessed the situation.

Mrak Delar was on his knees next to him. Two men held him down with his arms twisted behind his back. Another man had wrung his long hair around his arm, pulling his head back while holding a dagger under his chin. Gunz didn't need to use his other sight to know that all these men were dark wizards. The energy of their enchantments was practically visible, wrapping around the Master of Power like a disgusting net. They restrained them not only physically but magically as well.

Even though the walls of the room were made of natural rock, unpolished and rough, the place wasn't a cave. It was a giant throne room with two solid-rock thrones positioned at the far end of it. The shadows hid behind massive seats, shaking and slithering around, following the never-ending movement of the light orbs. Gunz looked up, but the tall ceiling wasn't visible behind the veil of the rotating blizzard. The rough surface of the walls was covered in tiny icicles, and they sparkled like diamonds, reflecting the blue light of the orbs.

A tall, bald man sat on one of the thrones, his yellow eyes glowing brightly in the gloomy surroundings. Leaning back in his armchair with his legs spread wide and his arms lying on the

N. M. THORN

armrests, he was a picture of relaxation and comfort, which seemed to be impossible considering how hard his seat must have been.

A woman sitting next to him could have been called beautiful if not for the overly hard set of her lips and icy gleam in her large, blue eyes. She leaned slightly to the side to place her hand on the man's arm. Her long, silvery dress reflected the flares of blue light produced by the orbs, shimmering like fresh snow in the moonlight.

The man and woman exchanged a quick look, and his lips stretched into an ugly, lipless smirk, his forked tongue coming in and out of his mouth like that of a serpent.

"Morena, darling," he said, a soft hiss accompanying his every word, "you may proceed. I think I'll just enjoy the show from here, if you don't mind."

"My pleasure, love," replied Morena, rising. She halted next to Skiper-Zmey and leaned down, kissing him while her hand landed on his crotch, her long fingers stroking him demonstratively. Zmey didn't move, but a blissful smile stretched his mouth as he closed his yellow eyes.

Gunz silently observed them, and for a brief moment, he felt sorry for Chernobog. Mrak Delar grunted, his face turning a sickening green, and he looked like he was about to vomit.

Morena tore her lips and her hands off her lover and threw an icy look at the Master. Then she laughed softly and made her way to him, swaying her shapely hips seductively.

"Master Mrak Delar." Leaning forward, she seized his chin with her fingers and lifted his face. "The natural act of physical love and pleasure makes you sick, Ancient Master? I'm positive you're not a monk. Don't you let yourself enjoy it at least once in a great while? With your looks, I'm sure any woman would love to put her hands on you."

"There is nothing natural about what you and Zmey are

doing," replied Mrak calmly. "I'm married, Morena, and unlike you, I don't stray outside my marriage."

She let go of his chin and petted his cheek a little too strong to call it gentle. "I've heard about your undying love for your wife. To be with her, you forfeited your power, gave up your throne in Kendral, then sacrificed your freedom, almost losing your life in the process. Stuff of legends, you know." Morena straightened, gazing down at him icily. "I always wondered what kind of woman she must have been to make a man like you fall in love so deeply. I guess I'll find out soon. I'll be happy to meet her in person, Master." She cackled, and a predatory look distorted her face. "Any last words you wish me to convey to her? Before I kill her, that is."

Mrak jerked in the hands restraining him and dropped his head, a low growl rumbling in his chest.

"Hey, Morena," yelled Gunz just to get her attention away from the Master of Power. "Your husband loves you just as much as Mrak Delar loves his wife. It was your choice to fornicate with this monster instead of opening your heart to the man who worships the ground you step on."

Morena turned to him, raking him with icy contempt. "Aw, little Salamander," she hissed, "I see my husband brainwashed you too. Did he tell you his scary stories about his father and brothers? Did he show you the scars on his back?"

"Not the point," replied Gunz, sounding almost bored. "As flawed as he might be, he loves you more than his own life. I can't say the same about the monster you're kissing, you winter-slut."

"How dare you!" Morena swung her arm and slapped Gunz across his face.

His head jerked to the side, and blood filled his mouth. He chuckled, spitting it on the floor. All he needed was to waste a few more minutes until Commander Moore would arrive with his team, and he was willing to take a few punches or slaps to keep Morena and Zmey occupied.

Zmey got up to his feet and stretched his arms lazily. Slowly, he made his way to Gunz and stopped next to Morena, draping his arm over her shoulder.

"You know what's interesting, young Salamander?" he asked, sounding almost friendly. "Your Angelique... She loves you just as much as Chernobog loves his beautiful wife." He cocked his head, staring down at Gunz, his face an emotionless mask. "I kept her soul intact for you, boy. Even right now, I can feel her squirming in my head. She can hear your voice, and you have no idea how much she wishes she could touch you... Just a..."

His eyes fogged and lost their yellow glimmer, replaced by such a familiar bright gaze that everything inside Gunz twisted with pain. He dropped his head to his chest to hide his true feelings, but Zmey squatted in front of him and placed his finger under his chin, gently lifting his face.

"Don't avert your gaze, Salamander," he whispered, gazing at him with Angelique's eyes. "She wants to see you. I believe after she sacrificed her life for you, she deserved this little something from you."

Zmey's image glittered with soft sparkles, and for a fleeting moment, Gunz saw Angelique replacing him. Unsteady and shimmering like a mirage, she reached for him and gently brushed his face with her fingers. Gunz closed his eyes, a tear escaping his tightly pressed eyelids. He felt someone wiping the tear off his cheek and looked up. Angelique was gone, but Zmey was now kneeling in front of him.

"It's amazing," he whispered, curiosity in his yellow eyes. "She loves you so much, it's infectious. I can't help but feel..." He shook his head and got up slowly, as if this simple move was taking too much out of him. "I hate to admit, but I can see why she loves you. In your natural state you're a sight to behold..."

"That's not why she loves me," whispered Gunz, his vocal cords painfully hoarse.

"I know," replied Zmey. "Remember? She's in my head. I know everything she knows. She's not in love with the Fire Salamander. She's in love with the man. Shocking. Truly. A woman's heart is a true mystery."

Gunz smirked faintly, shaking his head. "Can we just move on straight to torture?" he asked, winking at Morena. "I'm sure your darling ice-queen can't wait to make me bleed."

Zmey glanced at his lover over his shoulder and smirked. "You're probably right, boy," he said. "But physical torture is loud and messy. Why should I do it if you're already in pain? Right here"—he placed his hand over Gunz's heart—"you're already bleeding. No physical torture can ever inflict as much pain as the torment of one's soul."

Moore, where the hell are you? Gunz glanced sideways at the Master of Power, but his long hair fell over his face, and Gunz couldn't read his expression. For a moment, he considered trying to use the power of War, but quickly abandoned this thought, sticking to the decision he'd made earlier to keep his new power hidden from the enemy for as long as he could.

"I know why you're here, Salamander," continued Zmey, his voice soft and insinuating.

"Isn't it obvious, genius?" asked Gunz snidely, switching his attention to his enemy.

"It is." Zmey shrugged his enormous shoulders. "But did you know that to kill me, you would have to kill Angelique, too? Did you know that she's only alive for as long as I live? Our life forces are fused together. She exists only as long as I do. Are you ready to kill the only woman you've ever loved, brave Salamander?"

The next blast of pain surged through his soul, squeezing his heart in its deadly grip, and he pushed against the hands holding him down before he could stop himself.

"I'm ready to do whatever needs to be done," he said, cringing inwardly at the coldness of his own voice. "Don't count that you can use Angelique as your shield. She won't forgive me if I let you do it."

Zmey laughed—a cold, venomous sound that ended in a loud hiss. "Amazing. You two are a match made in heaven." He tapped his finger against his temple. "She just agreed with what you said, by the way."

He turned to Morena and pulled her into a tight hug, his lips crushing hers as his forked tongue slipped into her mouth. He pulled away a moment later and waved in Gunz's direction. "He's all yours, darling. Enjoy."

He started on his way back to the throne when the light orbs flickered and got extinguished all at once. As complete darkness enveloped the room, Gunz felt the touch of powerful magical energy. He strained his Salamander senses, probing the dark space around himself, but the energy signature he had noticed before was gone.

Morena clapped three times somewhere close to him, but the light didn't even flicker, the darkness remaining absolute. A strangled gasp sounded on his left side and a noise of a short struggle followed it. Whoever moved in the darkness was dangerous and extremely fast. Cold air brushed the back of Gunz's neck, sending a wave of chills down his spine, and a moment later, the hands holding him down disappeared.

Not expecting that, he fell forward on all fours, but someone seized his shoulders, yanking him to his feet. A heavy hand pressed over his mouth, and someone whispered into his ear so quietly that only his overly heightened Salamander hearing could make out the words.

"Burns, don't use your purifying fire. I have vamps with me..."

The hand that had silenced him vanished, and the next moment a blinding flair of light exploded next to him. A deep, feral roar filled with scorching fury sounded on his left and the ground trembled beneath his feet. After the darkness, the brilliance of the light was unbearable, and for a few long seconds, Gunz could see nothing, blinking and pressing his hands to his eyes. But a magical storm of terrifying proportions unfolded around him, and he didn't need to see to know what was going on.

When Gunz was finally able to adjust his vision, he turned to the side but didn't find his friend there. Mrak Delar was levitating a few feet in the air. His eyes were swirling with all the colors of his power, but his face was contorted with a fury beyond imagination. He stretched his arm up, and a lightning bolt zigzagged from the place where the ceiling was supposed to be. Collecting the electricity in his hand, the Master of Power redirected it toward Zmey. The monster reacted faster than anyone had expected, ducking to the side. The lightning struck the throne, and it exploded with a thunderous bang into thousands of pieces.

Mrak Delar raised both arms, spreading them wide, and the entire mountain shook violently, sending a shower of rocks and debris down. Morena screamed, covering her head with her arms. The Master of Power laughed, and the sound of his laughter sent a jolt of fear through Gunz. He stared up and swallowed hard. His friend was gone. The dark side had taken the Master over, and the only thing Gunz could think of was that he'd never seen Mrak give in to his dark side so fast and so easy.

The lightning struck again, and thunder boomed through the large room, bouncing loudly from one wall to the next. Mrak Delar kept shooting electricity, interchanging it with high-voltage energy balls, pushing Zmey and Morena back toward the other end of the room. The ground kept quaking, and the winds howled inside, forming multiple dark twisters.

Someone shouted a protection spell, and a powerful magical

dome manifested over him. Gunz spun around and found the Commander standing behind him. With his arms folded over his chest, he observed the Master of Power with interest. His team stood behind them, staring at Mrak in awe.

"If I can't use my power," said Gunz, frowning at the Commander, "don't you think you and your team need to step in and help Mrak Delar?"

"What? Why?" Moore shrugged. "And spoil such a wonderful show. I think the Master is doing splendidly on his own. Besides, his dark side is a lot more powerful than the light one." He tapped Gunz on his shoulder and gave a deep guffaw. "I'm just curious what set him off?"

"Morena threatened his wife," replied Gunz, his attention back on the fight.

Zmey muttered a spell, and a tight protective dome unfolded over him and Morena. His face contorted with dark excitement, and for a moment, his features changed, his face resembling the snout of a serpent with long fangs and yellow eyes with red vertical pupils.

As Gunz watched Mrak Delar lower to the ground in front of them, a feeling of dread spread over him. He didn't know what it was, but his intuition screamed bloody murder.

"Mrak, stop!" shouted Gunz. Taking a step forward, he ran into the wall of the Commander's shield and yelled, turning around, "Commander Moore, let me out!"

Moore shook his head no. "I can't endanger my team. There is too much magical energy in the air. The Master is unleashing Hell out there."

A dark smirk crossed Gunz's face. His split lip started to bleed again, and he wiped it with the back of his hand. "And I'm about to turn Hell into *Peklo*, Commander." He waved his hand, unfolding the flaming curtain of the Fire Salamander portal. "I suggest you reinforce your shield with all the power you have if you want your team to survive it."

Gunz walked through the fire and manifested on the other side of the protective shield. "Mrak, stay back!" he shouted at the top of his lungs, magnifying his voice with his magic.

He let go of any control and let the fire consume him without reverting into the natural state of the Fire Salamander. His appearance started to change, and he rose to the same height as Kal. His hair became long, flowing down his shoulders like a flaming river. He walked toward Zmey and Morena, and with each step he took, the air around him got hotter, steam swirling over him in soft, white wisps. The ice started to melt, thin rivulets of water running down the rocky walls.

Gunz approached Zmey's protective magic, and a furious smile appeared on his face. He placed his burning palms against it, and the magic vanished, devoured by the purifying energy. Zmey met his flaming gaze without so much as a blink, and his lipless mouth curved into a ferocious snarl, exposing the long fangs of a serpent.

"Wow," he hissed without a shadow of fear in his yellow eyes. "I must admit, little Salamander, you have grown up from the time we fought the first time. I respect that. Your power and your skills are impressive. But you know what's even more impressive than that?"

"What's that?" asked Gunz, tilting his head slightly. Something wasn't right, but he couldn't put his finger on what it was.

"Your blindness, Child of Fire. You have the magical sight and the heightened senses of a Fire Salamander, yet you see nothing," replied Zmey calmly, and Morena giggled like a little girl, putting her arm through the crook of his elbow. "Your friend is in so much pain that he let the darkness consume him, but you're too righteous and too self-absorbed to notice that." Zmey gave him an arched stare, but since Gunz didn't turn around, he chuckled. "I was hoping you would at least give your loyal Master of Power a quick look-see, but I guess his life is not of any importance to you."

"His life is worth the world to me," growled Gunz, staring directly into Zmey's poisonous eyes. "But I'm not going to fall for your tricks and take my attention off of you, allowing you to escape."

Zmey and Morena exchanged a look and both burst out laughing. "But you've done it already, Salamander," he said once he was able to speak again. "You all, including the Destiny Enforcers here, fell for my trick and that tells me none of you are anywhere close to me in my power and my skills. You stand no chance against me."

He stopped talking, his shape changing into the giant serpent. Slowly, he lowered his flat head closer to Gunz, and the semblance of a smile exposed his two long fangs. As his head was swinging slightly from left to right, Gunz kept following his motion. With his thoughts in complete disarray, he couldn't understand what Zmey referred to.

Finally, Skiper-Zmey pulled back and took his human form, wrapping his arm around Morena's shoulders. "Thank you for being so easy to trick. I'm sure we'll see you again pretty soon. But no matter how fast you figure out the truth, you're already too late." He snickered acidly, and both Morena and Zmey disappeared. They didn't teleport but slowly melted into the dark background, vanishing like an illusion or a mirage.

Heavily, Gunz turned around and threw his arms in the air as despair speared through him. Mrak Delar hung limply in the arms of two vampires. His head was bowed low, his black hair cascading down, concealing his face.

"I had to put him into an enchanted sleep," said Moore, approaching Gunz. "I'm truly sorry, Burns, but he's done."

"What do you mean?" Gunz whispered, unable to speak louder.

"You heard what Zmey said. He wasn't lying." Moore shrugged. "The darkness consumed him. You know the Ancient Master's past. His mind was controlled for a long period of time, and the person who controlled him, infected him with darkness. For years, he kept this darkness under control. I don't know what triggered the transformation." He waved in Mrak's direction.

Gunz glowered at the Commander and shook his head. "No."

"You can't stop me, Burns. Please don't make me do something I don't want to do," said the Commander, his voice almost pleading. "There are only two places the Ancient Master can go now—the Destiny Council prison or in Master Alliandr's care back to Kendral, if the Young Master is willing to take responsibility for him."

Gunz let him finish and smirked. "No," he repeated, dangerous tones in his voice. "Mrak would never give up on me. Unhand him now or suffer the consequences."

"Burns—"

"Do as I say, or I swear to God, I will obliterate every single one of you," shouted Gunz, the fire energy spiking around him. He put his hand over the ring, ready to activate the power of War. "I swear on my power, Moore, you touch one hair on his head..." His voice shook, and he clenched his jaw so tightly, his teeth squeaked.

"What's wrong with you, Burns!" shouted Moore, throwing his hands up. "One day your blind loyalty will be the end of you." He waved at his vampires. "Put the Ancient Master down." He approached Mrak Delar and touched his forehead with two fingers, breaking the enchanted sleep. He got up, towering over Gunz. "You have fifteen minutes to bring him back, Burns. If you can't, you can fight me if you wish, but I'm taking him. Am I clear, soldier?"

"I suggest you either get the hell out of here or cover your team with the strongest shield you have," muttered Gunz, ignoring the Commander's question. Lowering to his knees next to the Master of Power, he surrounded him with purifying energy, channeling it through his forehead and his heart. Mrak

Delar's eyelashes fluttered, and his eyeballs moved beneath his tightly shut eyelids.

"Please, Mrak," whispered Gunz, doubling the amount of purifying energy he was wielding. "Please open your eyes. Let me see your eyes, you stubborn bastard."

The Master of Power didn't move. Gunz bit his lip, pressing the heels of his hands to his eyes. He sat like this for a few seconds, rocking back and forth slightly. "I'm not losing you, Master," he whispered. "Not today." He held out his hand, and a large fireball materialized in his palm. "Forgive me..."

He thrust the fireball through his friend's chest, and Mrak's body arched, the energy of fire spreading through him in red, pulsing waves. Without giving him a break, Gunz manifested a high voltage energy orb and repeated the procedure. A terrible scream tore from Mrak's lips, and his eyes flew open as he gasped for air, staring around wildly.

"Oh, no...," Gunz exhaled. Mrak's eyes were black, flooded with darkness from corner to corner, and it wasn't the darkness of elemental power. "You stubborn, evil bastard... I said no! Not! Fucking! Today!"

He put one hand on Mrak's forehead and the other one on his chest and let go, reverting into the natural state of the Great Fire Salamander, channeling all the purifying power he could gather through his friend. The Master of Power screamed, thrashing in his hands, but he didn't let go, holding him tightly within the grip of his power.

"Gunz... Gunz... please..."

He heard Mrak panting and let go, coming back to his human form. Mrak lay on his back, staring at him without blinking, his face contorted by pain, but his eyes were clear.

"Oh God," moaned Gunz, sitting back on his heels heavily. "Oh God..."

"Sometimes, I wish I were," whispered Mrak Delar, sweat running down his pale face. He scrambled into a sitting position, bending his legs and wrapped his arms around his head, hiding his face.

Gunz looked at the Commander over his shoulder. "He's back," he said dryly. "Thank you for your help, Commander. You and your team saved us. But can you please leave now?"

"Burns, don't you think you need to find out where the *real* Lord of Chaos and the goddess of Winter and Death are?" he asked, staring at him coldly. "What you fought here earlier was nothing more than an extremely powerful illusion."

"I need a few minutes," replied Gunz. "Nothing will change in a few minutes."

"Let's agree to disagree, Salamander." Moore chuckled but twirled his hand in a circular motion, pointing up. "Let's roll out, boys. Our work here is done."

His team's wizard opened a portal, and they all jumped through it, disappearing on the other side.

Gunz sighed with relief and turned around, readjusting his position to sit next to Mrak Delar. The Master of Power didn't move and didn't say anything.

"Mrak, are you okay?" he asked, realizing the stupidity of his question as soon as it escaped his lips.

Mrak lowered his arms but barely raised his eyes. "I'm going to be. I think."

"What happened?"

"Can we not...?"

"No," objected Gunz. He glanced at his friend and shook his head. "I must understand what triggered you. I won't be able to protect you if I don't know what happened."

Mrak Delar chuckled and finally looked up, his bloodshot eyes gleaming with sadness. "You can't protect me from myself, my friend," he said quietly. "There is always going to be someone who will force me to use my dark side, and the next time it happens, there will be no way back for me."

"Mrak, what are you saying?" Gunz leaned forward to see his

face better. "There aren't too many beings of magic who are more powerful than you are. Who forced you to use dark magic? And why?"

"It doesn't matter, my friend." Mrak Delar got up with a strained groan and offered Gunz his hand. "Moore was right. If I survive what's coming—which I hope I won't—I'm going back to Kendral. I'll have to tell Master Alliandr what happened and let him decide what to do with me next."

Gunz didn't take his hand and got up, facing the Master of Power. "First of all, what the hell? What kind of mindset is that? You hope you won't survive what's coming?" Anger and pain bubbled up in him, and the flames went up in his eyes. "You go into a fight with this kind of attitude, and you'll find exactly what you're looking for, Master. Death!"

"Gunz—"

"Don't Gunz me!" Gunz yelled, slashing his hand through the air. "Unless you tell me the truth right now and deal with it, you're going back to Kendral immediately."

"You can't force me, Gunz—"

"You bet your ass I can." Gunz raised his hand, pointing at the ring of War. "You're forgetting, Master. Now, I know how to control you, and I'm not going to bring a man with suicidal thoughts into a deadly confrontation!" He took a deep breath to calm down. "Tell me, Mrak. I have to know who forced you to use dark magic against your will and why."

"I can't tell you that, because—"

A bright white light lit up inside the throne room and Gwyn ap Nudd, Kal and Aidan walked through it.

"Because I was the one who forced him to use the Dark Arts," said Gwyn.

CHAPTER 37

~ ZANE BURNS, A.K.A. GUNZ ~

Gunz shook his head bitterly. "As if it's not enough that our enemies abuse us. Do we need to start worrying about our friends doing it, too?"

"Gunz, remember whom you're addressing—," started Kal with a warning, but Gunz raised his hand impatiently, interrupting him.

"I know perfectly well whom I am addressing, Kal!" he shouted. "The man who's the most powerful among us all. The one we're supposed to trust unconditionally. But please tell me, how can I?" His hands clenched into fists at his sides.

"Gunz!" roared Kal, taking a step forward.

Gwyn ap Nudd put his hand on Kal's shoulder, stopping him. "Hold on, Kalidus. Your boy is right." He walked past Gunz and halted in front of Mrak Delar. "Master, I already apologized, but after all this is over, I'd like to make it up to you if you don't mind."

"As you wish, my lord," replied Mrak Delar calmly, inclining his head. "I believe right now it's not important. We need to find Morena and Skiper-Zmey before it's too late." As concisely as he could, he described everything that had happened in Mount Karasova. "As it is, Skiper-Zmey hinted that we're too late."

"Aoife said something to this effect, too," said Aidan.

He sounded so drained of life that Gunz raised his eyes, doing a double-take, and just now he realized that Tessa wasn't with them. *Dammit,* Gunz cursed silently. *Something happened to her. She would never let Aidan go into a deadly battle alone.* He rubbed his forehead as dread sent shivers down his back. *I can't bring it up and start asking questions now... I can't take a chance of Aidan falling apart.*

"I had a feeling we were at the wrong place," grumbled Mrak Delar, shaking his head. "All this was just a skillfully crafted illusion. A misdirection to keep our attention away from what truly matters. I'm sure the attack on the Otherworld was also a decoy. I can't believe none of us figured it out earlier."

"The attack on the Otherworld was real," said Aidan, staring at his clenched hands. "I must admit at some point I felt as if Aoife was trying to waste my time... as if she was trying to delay something... But in the end, she wasn't an illusion." He pressed his fingers to the bridge of his nose, swallowing painfully hard. "Anyway, she's gone. This time, forever."

"Good. We have one less monster to deal with," said Mrak Delar.

"At what cost?" asked Aidan without raising his eyes.

Aidan's voice faded away, and Gunz cringed inwardly, his mind drawing all sorts of worse-case-scenarios. *What happened?* He cleared his throat but didn't voice the burning question.

"It's not late, and it's not over," he said, observing the small group of men in front of him. "Just because these monsters want us to believe they won, it doesn't mean we should put down our weapons. We just have to figure out what our next step should be."

"I think I know," said Mrak Delar at length. He turned to Gunz, staring at him intently, and for a moment his eyes darkened. "You said none of the Slavic gods answered your summons, Gunz, correct?"

"Mrak—," started Gunz, noticing the Master's dark eyes.

"Yes or no, Gunz?" demanded the Master of Power.

"Yes," replied Gunz. "I tried a few of them, and no one answered my calls."

"I can bet you anything, we'll find them on the Isle Buyan," said Mrak Delar. "If Zlebog is running this show, his first act would be bringing down the Prav and the Dark Nav. And the only way to get there is through the World Tree." He looked around, but since no one said anything, he continued, "It seems Zlebog doesn't mind facing Slavic gods, but he wants to keep us away for as long as possible."

"That's interesting," murmured Kal, a thin layer of sarcasm lacing his words. "The primordial evil doesn't mind taking on the ancient gods of his pantheon, but he's scared of two Fire Salamanders, a Master of Power and a god of the Otherworld? He couldn't know that Gwyn ap Nudd would break the order by leaving his domain. Something doesn't add up."

"I guess we're about to find out." Gunz waved his hand, unfolding the fiery curtain of his portal, and stepped aside, allowing his friends to go through.

* * *

GUNZ WALKED out of his portal and checked his surroundings. Night had fallen on the Isle Buyan, and the sky, dark and starless, seemed to be covered by a strange gray smoke-like veil. The coolness of the air touched his skin, and he inhaled deeply, appreciating the freshness after the stuffiness of the throne room inside Mount Karasova. However, a barely noticeable reek of dark magical energy invaded his senses, breaking through the powerful magic of the nexus.

Even though he intentionally opened his portal at the opposite end of the isle, as far away from the World Tree as possible, he could sense the waves of magical energy spreading around it in all directions.

Mrak Delar took a deep breath to deal with the effects of the nexus. With his face relaxed, he looked slightly intoxicated. "I was right. Can you feel it?" he exhaled, pointing in the direction of the World Tree. "The problem is, I can't see anything with my other sight."

Gunz closed his eyes, probing the area with his Salamander senses and his other sight. While he felt the disturbance in the magical energy field, he couldn't identify what it was. After a moment, he let go, staring at Kal puzzled, but the Great Salamander shook his head.

"Something is blocking my sight, too," he said quietly. "Gwyn?"

The ground trembled, and a strong gust of wind rushed through the Isle Buyan, bending the tall grass down. Electric discharges illuminated the sky above the Tree, and thunder rumbled in the distance.

"I would hate to jump into this mess blindly," murmured Gwyn ap Nudd, running his fingers over his mustache. "But I don't think we have a choice. Neither Aidan nor I can see anything."

"Hold on. Maybe we do have a choice." Gunz placed his hand over his tattoo, sending a smidge of his fire through it. "Mishka, my friend, are you with me today?" He lowered his hand and looked around, but the wyvern was nowhere to be found. "Dammit, Mishka, not today... not a good time to play games..."

"Who's playing games?" Gunz heard Mishka's high-pitched voice behind and spun around. The wyvern hovered in the air in front of his face, his golden wings working at an incredible speed.

"Mishka, thank God," muttered Gunz, extending his hand

toward the wyvern, but Mishka pulled away, arching his brow at him.

"I don't know about God," he grumbled, "but there are plenty of gods there."

"Can you see what's going on around the World Tree?" asked Gunz, ignoring his grumpy mood.

Mishka flew closer and waved his wings in front of Gunz's eyes, glowering at him. "Are you blind again, boss?"

"We all are." Kal chuckled, shaking his head. "Our magical sights seem to be blocked. Can you tell us what's going on around the World Tree?"

"Yes, sir!" Mishka brought his wing to his head in a military salute and vanished.

"You are a bad influence on my wyverns, Gunz," murmured Kal, but before he could say anything else, Mishka materialized in front of his face, beating his wings vigorously. He glanced into Kal's eyes and darted back to Gunz.

Wrapping his wings around his neck, he whispered into his ear loudly, "You can't go there, boss."

"Why is that?" asked Gunz, throwing an apologetic glance at the Great Salamander.

"The World Tree is blocked by a giant shield of magical energy, and even if you manage to break through it, you are not going to fit inside," replied Mishka, peeking in the direction of the World Tree over Gunz's shoulder.

"Why is that?" Gunz sighed. Despite Mishka's usual shenanigans, his nerves were on edge, his Salamander senses stretched to the maximum.

"There are way too many gods stuffed into this tiny island," whispered Mishka, shrugging his wings. "Between them and their egos, there is no space left for any of you."

"We're in the right place," concluded Mrak Delar. "Gunz, open your portal a little closer to the World Tree."

Gunz petted Mishka's wings, whispering something back to

him. The wyvern pulled away ever so slightly. He peered into his eyes, and a wide, dragon-like smile appeared on his face. Gunz nodded to him, and the wyvern vanished. Catching Kal's quizzical stare, he shrugged and waved his hand, opening his fiery portal.

"A Plan B," he explained to the Great Salamander, allowing him to go through the portal first.

* * *

GUNZ WALKED out of the portal just a few feet away from a massive shield of magical energy that encapsulated the area around the World Tree. He tilted his head back, but the shield seamlessly melted into the dark sky, obscured by a layer of gray smoke.

The shield wasn't see-through, and the only thing he could see was the constant flashes of light. They illuminated the swirling veil of smoke with flares of different colors and intensity. He approached the shield and placed his palms against it, leaning forward slightly. The cacophony of different magical energies overpowered his senses, and he grunted, staggering back.

"This shield," he managed to say, panting. "It's made of energy the likes of which I've never sensed before..."

Gwyn ap Nudd approached it and ran his finger over the barrier, leaving traces of his glowing magic behind. "The energy of Creation," he whispered, observing it in awe. "We better be careful. We can't jeopardize the stability of this shield."

As if to prove him wrong, something impacted the shield from the inside, and a heavy vibration spread through it. The shield flickered, and ugly, dark splatters of negative energy spread over its surface. Gwyn frowned. Stepping away from it, he turned around, his glowing eyes slipping from one person to the next.

"Seems like we don't have much time. Ready?" He took a deep breath, assuming the form of the Lord of the Wild Hunt. "Kalidus, you know what needs to be done, brother. The stage is yours."

Kal approached the shield and channeled the elemental fire. Carefully, he drew a large, burning rune on the surface of the barrier, muttering something in Dragon tongue. Gunz had seen Kal opening a Fire Salamander portal enough times, but never had he seen anything like this. The Great Salamander pressed both hands against the rune, but instead of unfolding the flaming curtain, a rotating portal opened up, seemingly embedded into the shield of protective magic. Furious flames danced around the perimeter of the portal, and the elemental energy of the fire flowed freely through it.

"Go!" shouted Kal, his chest and arms bulging with massive muscles as he strained to sustain the weird portal.

Gunz waited until Gwyn, Mrak and Aidan had gone through and followed them.

* * *

GUNZ STEPPED out of the portal and froze in place, shivers running down his back. The space inside the shield seemed to be a lot larger than it looked from the outside. It wasn't the first time he visited the World Tree, and he believed he knew this place well. Now, however, the entire area looked different. The only thing that remained constant was the actual giant Tree growing in the center of it.

An enormous field unfolded in front of his eyes, expanding in every direction as far as he could see. Two terrifying armies clashed in a deadly confrontation—the army of Light and the evil horde of Darkness. Dark stormy clouds obscured the sky above the field of the battle, and lightning spliced the sky, followed by mighty thunder.

The gods of the Prav stood in front of the army of Light, wielding their mighty powers. But unlike during the original fight between the Light and the Darkness, Chernobog stood beside his brother, fighting on the side of Creation. The twins channeled the power of the Dark Codex, holding the terrible horde of Darkness back, and the Svarozhich brothers unleashed the raging elements over the deadly battlefield.

Semargl, the god of Fire, wielded his fiery power, and the air was thick with the presence of fire. Veles, Stribog and Dazhbog fought by his side, and the combined energy of their magic was so overwhelming that Gunz held his breath, unable to inhale.

As a loud noise assailed his senses from above, Gunz raised his eyes and was unable to take them off the harrowing battle unfolding in the sky. Thousands of light birds of Viraj fought the twisted, winged monsters and phantoms of Darkness, and their screams and screeches could be heard for miles around the battlefield.

Despite the mighty gods and warriors fighting on the side of Light, the monsters of the Darkness seemed to hold the upper hand. Slowly but surely, they gained more and more territory, pushing the army of Light away from the World Tree.

Leading the bone-chilling monsters stood Skiper-Zmey. In his serpent form, he towered at least seven feet tall, his terrifying fangs dripping with green poison, his yellow eyes burning with obliterating hatred. Next to him was his loyal lover, Morena, the goddess of Winter and Death. Wielding her icy power, she fought the fire of Semargl, sending one wave of winter blizzard after another. The smoldering flames collided with ice, and it started to melt, water boiling at the touch of the purest form of the elemental fire, swirls of steam rising over the battlefield.

However, the most terrifying was the monster leading them all. Zlebog in the form of a three-headed dragon stood before his army, and his magical energy permeated the air with its deadly miasmas. In its claws, he held a huge sword glistening like black ice, and every time he swung his mighty weapon, he inflicted significant damage to the army of Light.

"Brother, finally!" rumbled Semargl, his igneous eyes locking with Kal's. "We need all the help we can get."

Without waiting for the second invitation, Kal rushed to Semargl's side. Wielding his massive hammer and the elemental fire, he joined the attack. Mrak Delar connected with all four elements, and rose above the ground, assaulting the dark army from above.

"Aodh!" shouted Belobog, flashing a glance at Aidan. "I was trying to summon you, but you wouldn't reply. What happened to your Guardians' pendant?"

Aidan in his godly form and Gwyn ap Nudd joined the twin brothers, adding their purifying magic to the assault of the Dark Codex. A thunderous bang sounded from behind, and the ground trembled, tremors spreading for miles around. Gunz swayed, struggling to keep his balance, but two strong arms seized him, pulling him behind the lines of the army of Light.

A tall man he had never seen before stood in front of him. Dressed in ancient Slavic armor, he emitted such a powerful magical energy that Gunz had no doubt he was one of the gods of the Slavic pantheon. In his hands, he held a double-edged battle axe and a mighty sword glistening as bright as the sun.

"Perun," Gunz breathed out, with horror recognizing Tessa's weapon—the Axe of Perun. For a moment, his mind boiled with uncontrollable thoughts, fears and dread, but he suppressed them, getting his nerves under control.

"You're the young Fire Salamander," said Perun, and Gunz wasn't sure if it was a question or a statement.

"Yes, sir..."

Perun pointed his sword at Skiper-Zmey, and a dark smile crossed his face. "This time around, it's your destiny to put this monster to rest," he said, speaking quickly. "I will create a distraction, allowing you to get closer to him. Chernobog and the rest of my brothers will keep Morena and Zlebog busy. Use the opportunity to strike."

"Yes, sir," replied Gunz, trying to sound self-assured, but he felt none of it. "I'll do my best."

The god of Thunder put his hand on Gunz's shoulder heavily and sighed, shaking his head. "Fire and ice, young Salamander. I never realized how truly young you were." For a brief moment, he fell silent, staring in the direction of Skiper-Zmey. "Your best may not be enough... Do you have the sword? Sword Kladenets?"

"Aidan has it," replied Gunz, throwing a glance at his friend fighting alongside his powerful mentor.

"Get it from him. You must strike as soon as possible," said Perun. "I will support you, but only you can bring Zmey down. Once he's out, it'll be easier to handle Morena and Zlebog. Do you understand me, Child of Fire?"

"Yes, sir."

"Now, go, Fire Salamander!" he shouted, raising his deadly weapons. "I'm right behind you."

CHAPTER 38

~ ZANE BURNS, A.K.A. GUNZ ~

Holding his sword in his hand, Gunz conjured a protective shield around himself and ran toward Aidan, ducking energy strikes and combat spells that were cutting through the air in every direction. Luckily, the god of the Otherworld was still in the same place Gunz had last seen him, and despite the mayhem unfolding around the World Tree, finding him didn't present a problem.

An enormous monster with two grotesque heads attached to short, thick necks swung its curved blade, crushing it down on Aidan. The god of the Otherworld sidestepped it to avoid the direct impact and thrust his sword forward, penetrating the demon's side. If a demon of this size was struck by a normal sword, the injury wouldn't be fatal, but the blade of Sword Kladenets went through the monster easily, sinking into the dark flesh to the hilt. Bright light burst out of the wound, and the demon exploded, showering everyone around in dirty shreds of flesh, dust and sticky goo.

"Aidan!" yelled Gunz without taking his eyes off the approaching dark forces. "I need Sword Kladenets."

"What are you planning to do?" Aidan manifested his icy blade and threw the magical sword to Gunz.

"I'm going to do what I've been told to do." Gunz caught the sword, wrapping his fingers tightly around the grip. In response to his touch, the elemental fire rushed through the blade, setting it ablaze. "I'm going to face my destiny," he said calmly. "Perun is right. Until we disable Zmey and Morena, dealing with Zlebog will be impossible. Even for Chernobog. Together, the three of them wield too much power."

His eyes darted toward the World Tree, and he saw Zmey and Zlebog still standing there, commanding their terrifying army. Morena, however, stood by the Tree with her palms pressed against its bark. A thick, silvery layer of frost was rising from under her hands, spreading up and around the trunk, moving higher and higher toward the branches.

"She's trying to break the defensive magic Rod has built around the World Tree. Should she succeed, the path to the Prav and to the Nav will be wide open for them," yelled Aidan over the clamor of the battle, jerking his chin toward Morena. "We need to rush. I'm coming with you."

"No, you're not, Aodh." Perun's deep voice sounded next to Gunz, making him flinch. "You're coming with me. The young Salamander must face Skiper-Zmey. He has no choice, but the only way we can help him is by keeping Morena's and Zlebog's attention away from him."

He seized Aidan's elbow and snapped his fingers. Lightning struck in the place they had stood a moment ago, and Gunz had just enough time to raise his sword and block a mighty blow of a demon's axe. He swung the magical sword, trying to clear some space around himself, destroying the monsters with each touch of his blade. Then he waved his hand and opened his flaming portal, aiming closer to the World Tree.

He walked out of the portal amid enemy territory, and as

expected, the monsters of different types and forms surrounded him.

"*Ignius Amplio*," he roared, sending a blast of physical fire infused with purifying energy. As the fire set the monsters ablaze, he kept moving forward, fighting his way toward Skiper-Zmey. Glancing up, he could see Morena still casting her frosty spell, the World Tree's branches trembling in fear. Both Zmey and Zlebog turned their heads and stared in his direction, Zmey's mouth of a serpent stretching into a ferocious snarl.

Suddenly, an explosion rattled the battlefield, followed by a blinding flare of white light. Despite the ear-splitting discord of the fight, the explosion was so loud that for a moment, Gunz's ears buzzed, and he could hear nothing, feeling slightly disoriented. Morena yelped, dropping her hands for a moment, but that was enough for her frosty spell to start to thaw down. Zmey spun to her, hissing something into her ear, but Zlebog didn't react. He spread his webbed wings of a dragon, and two purple energy orbs materialized in his talons, twirling and crackling with electrical discharges.

Using the temporary confusion, Gunz rushed through the enemy lines toward Skiper-Zmey, setting as many monsters on fire in his wake as he could. He thought he kept his eyes on his adversary, but one moment he could see Zmey standing next to Morena, and the next moment he was gone. Gunz stilled, searching the battlefield intently, but couldn't find him anywhere.

The magical mayhem intensified as Aidan and Perun fought their way through to Morena and Zlebog. Despite that, Gunz detected a tiny fluctuation of a magical energy field right behind him and spun around—a moment too late. He saw Zmey's face inches away from his as the monster slammed his hand on his shoulder and snapped his fingers.

* * *

FOR A HEARTBEAT, everything went dark, and when Gunz could see again, he found himself standing by the World Tree, or at least in the area resembling it. It was quiet—no cacophony of the battle, no whistling of the wind and crackling of fire. There was no army of Light or the horde of Darkness. There was no one here, except for him and Skiper-Zmey.

Zmey stood with his arms folded and glowered at him with narrowed eyes, his head slightly tilted. "Well, hello, young Salamander," he said, sounding almost friendly, but shivers ran down Gunz's back at the sound of his voice. "As you can see, I was expecting you." He waved his hand around.

"Where are we?" asked Gunz calmly, but his every muscle tensed, ready to spring into action at any moment.

"Still on the Isle Buyan by the World Tree," replied Zmey with a slight shrug. "As I said, I was expecting you, so I created a little playground for us only—a tiny new plane of existence inside the nexus. No one ever will find us here." He scratched the back of his head with a thoughtful expression, and an ugly smirk distorted his mouth. "Unless you found a new witch with psychic abilities, of course. Only someone like that can find us here."

Gunz didn't say anything, putting all his effort into remaining calm and collected.

"Did you?" asked Zmey, cocking his eyebrow.

"Did I what?"

"Find a new seer-girlfriend to screw," replied Zmey snidely.

"And how is that any of your business?" asked Gunz with a sigh.

"Oh, Zane," he said, his voice modulating and morphing into a musical soprano of a woman. "You found a replacement for our dear Angie so quickly?"

Gunz didn't react visibly, but anger spiked within him, and it took him all the willpower he had not to show it.

"Are we going to fight, or are you going to talk me to death?"

he asked, lifting Sword Kladenets. He brushed the blade with his fingers lazily, and the cold steel went up in dancing flames.

Zmey cocked his head and chuckled. "What a fine little toothpick you have there, little Salamander," he quipped, waving at the magical sword derisively.

"Surprise-surprise."

"I'm touched," said Zmey, pressing his hand to his chest. "You know what they say—it's the thought that counts." He raised his arm and whispered a short spell. A large box wrapped in black silk materialized behind him. Slowly, he sauntered toward it and seized the corner of the cover, turning to face Gunz. "I hate to admit it, but I also thought of you. I even prepared a little something..."

That can't be good... Gunz didn't say anything, but his fingers clenched the grip of his sword as his heart pounded in his chest.

"I can hear your heartbeat, Salamander," said Zmey, snickering. "It's about to explode. I guess I better unveil my little present before you have a coronary."

He yanked the silk cover off, exposing a massive cage. A man lay on the bottom of the cage, his entire body crisscrossed by thick silver chains. His torso was unclothed, and his skin was red and raw everywhere the silver touched it. Even though he had a black bag over his head, Gunz didn't need to see his face to know who he was. His shoulders tensed, but he didn't make a move. He didn't think he could—his limbs had filled with lead.

"What?" asked Zmey innocently. "You don't like my gift? Should I exchange it for something else?" He pushed his arm between the bars of the cage and pulled the bag off his prisoner's head. Long, blond hair cascaded down, falling around Yaroslav's head like a golden waterfall. The vampire glanced at Gunz, a tortured, haunted look in his blue eyes.

Gunz took a deep breath, forcing himself to relax. *Impossible. Yaroslav is in Florida with Jim and Akira...*

"Fool me once, Zmey," he growled, shaking his head.

"Aw, sorry about the earlier misrepresentation," said Skiper-Zmey and pointed at his prisoner. "But this is real. You can test him. Someone told me you and Yaroslav Potemkin are quite close. You even have a blood bond. Who would guess that someone like you would swing both ways?" Zmey snickered, winking at Gunz as though he was his best friend. "Go ahead. If it's true, you'll have no problem using your bond to ask him anything only you two love-birds would know."

"Slavik," called Gunz. *"Is it really you? How did it happen? You were supposed to be in the human realm..."*

Yaroslav lifted his head and hissed as the silver chain pressed to the exposed skin of his arms and back. *"I'm sorry, Gunz. There were just too many of them... So many of our vampires are dead..."* He threw a look full of loathing at the Lord of Chaos. *"You'll have to let him kill me. You know that, right? You can't let him use me against you."*

"Akira? Jim?"

"I don't know... I don't remember anything from the moment they captured me until I woke up in this cage. They used some kind of spell..."

"Do you believe me now?" asked Zmey, his eyes lighting up with the sickening yellow glow of Chaos. "You know, Zane, I can almost understand your attachment to Aodh mac Lir. He's a sort of a god. But a vampire?" He waved in Yaroslav's direction, disgust distorting his face. "Abominations of this world—too strong to be humans, too weak to be real demons."

Gunz took a step forward, raising his sword, but Zmey squeezed his right hand into a fist and twisted it slightly. Yaroslav screamed, thrashing on the floor of the cage.

"Not so fast, Salamander," he roared. "Another step and I will turn your friend into a pile of ashes."

What the hell? What kind of game is he playing...?

"What do you want, Zmey?" he growled but didn't lower his sword.

"I've heard the three of you would kill for each other," said Zmey with a crooked smirk. "Don't worry, I'm not asking you to kill anyone. I know how righteous you are. I offer an exchange—Sword Kladenets for your precious vamp."

"Sure, as you wish." Gunz lowered his sword arm, slowly channeling his power closer to his hands. "The only way you will get it is with its blade through your dead heart."

Skiper-Zmey started to turn toward the cage, but Gunz waved his hand, whispering a spell. A circle of flames encircled the monster, dancing feebly around him. The Lord of Chaos chuckled, leaning forward to move his palm over the fire.

"Your elemental power is not as potent here as it is in the outside world, little Salamander," he hissed, his forked tongue flickering in and out. "I told you, I was ready for you." He straightened and folded his arms, smirking. "Besides, let's imagine for one crazy moment that you managed to kill me. How are you planning to get out of here?" He moved his hand around. "You don't even know where you are, and good luck opening the Fire Salamander portal here, by the way." He shrugged and jerked his thumb over his shoulder at Yaroslav indifferently. "You kill me—you'll doom yourself to spend an eternity dealing with a feral vamp driven by the thirst to the edge of insanity."

As the Lord of Chaos lifted his leg to step over the circle of flames, Gunz roared and swung his sword, anger setting his entire body ablaze. Zmey reacted immediately. In one swift motion, he manifested a large sword. The weapon shone with black shades as if it were forged out of obsidian. The two swords collided with a mighty bang, and a wave of their magical energy spread around the area.

Gunz took a step forward, forcing his blade down, but Zmey didn't pull back. Staring over the crossed blades, Gunz met the ominous, yellow eyes of the Lord of Chaos that were glowing just inches away from his face.

Ignius, he thought rather than said, but the sword responded to his command anyway and ignited brighter, emitting an unbearable heat. Skiper-Zmey hissed, yellow-green venom trickling from the corner of his mouth. He spun around and twisted his wrist, eliciting a terrible howl out of Yaroslav.

Gunz grunted, his hand reaching for the ring of War. He was positive that the triad didn't know about his connection with War, and that could've been his strategic advantage in the fight against Zlebog—the element of surprise. But he couldn't let the Lord of Chaos kill Yaroslav. As the vampire screamed again, struggling against the silver chains, Gunz touched the ring, ready to connect with its power.

All of a sudden, a thunderous bang rolled through the imitation of the Isle Buyan, and for the briefest of moments, Gunz saw the thin walls of magic surrounding the fake reality Skiper-Zmey had created. The monster twirled in place, staring around, genuine shock reflected on his face. The ground trembled as the second impact rattled the bubble of his magic, and a thin, shinning line materialized behind Yaroslav's cage.

"What the hell?" yelped Zmey but didn't turn around to check. Instead, he brought his sword above his shoulder and attacked Gunz, moving at considerable speed.

That wasn't something Gunz expected, but his Salamander senses reacted, and he was able to parry the strike of the obsidian blade in the last second. Zmey didn't wait for him to regroup and kept attacking him, forcing him into a defensive position as he pushed him away from the cage.

Another powerful blast rolled through the fake Isle Buyan, followed by a few more in rapid succession. The world rattled under the mighty attack from the outside, and the ground quaked under his feet. Gunz had no choice but to retreat, struggling to keep his balance. Zmey lowered his sword too, but his eyes lit up brighter, the energy of Chaos spreading around him, polluting the air with its miasma, hatred and ill-wish.

For a moment, Gunz's thoughts became murky and scrambled as the power of Chaos assailed him. But a wave of fire rushed through him, responding to the infection, and he held on to it with all he had, adding more of his magic to it. His mind cleared enough for him to realize that even with Sword Kladenets, he would have a hard time fighting against this ancient monster. Up until now, Zmey had been toying with him, not utilizing even half of his power.

Why? Another decoy? Is he trying to keep me away from whatever Zlebog is doing?

As clear as day, he remembered the fight against the Lord of Chaos a few years ago. A few gods couldn't bring the monster down until Angelique fused her soul with his, keeping him under control just long enough for Veles to apply his curse. A cold wave of fear clawed through Gunz as the realization that alone he stood no chance against the Lord of Chaos flashed through his mind. His destiny was set in motion. He was the one who was supposed to face him. But why would the Destiny Council do that if he stood no chance of winning this fight? What would happen to the realm of humans if he lost?

Doesn't make any sense. Why? Why me?

Zmey shouted something, and a dark orb crackling with deadly energy materialized in his palm. Pulling his hand back, he spun around and propelled it at Yaroslav. The vampire stopped struggling and closed his eyes, ready to die. Gunz screamed, knowing that in his position there was nothing he could do to prevent what was coming, and an uncontrollable rage rushed through him.

At the same time, one more mighty impact shook the world, and the shining fracture behind Yaroslav's cage became wider, blinding light flooding the entire area.

"Procedia Amnia!" shouted a strong, young voice, and a glowing shield materialized around the cage just in time to stop the deadly orb from obliterating the vampire.

Skiper-Zmey howled in anger but didn't bother to see who the newcomers were. Moving forward at incredible speed, he attacked Gunz, his black blade slashing through the air with deadly precision. Gunz raised his sword, but all he could do was maintain his defensive position, keeping his eyes on his enemy.

Even though he couldn't see who had saved Yaroslav, he knew he was no longer alone. His friends had found him, and this thought alone gave him a new burst of energy. A loud bang —metal colliding with metal—rushed through the area, and Gunz hoped that Zmey would slow down to take a look, giving him a chance to take a breath. But the monster wouldn't stop his vigorous attacks even for a moment.

I won't be able to keep up this speed for much longer... A troublesome thought rushed through Gunz's mind, sweat running down his neck and back.

Zmey's sword swooshed through the air, grazing Gunz's bicep, and he grunted, jumping aside, feeling the warmth of blood trickling down his arm.

"Zane, hold on! We're coming!" He heard a slightly accented voice, and as he blocked Zmey's next assault, he allowed himself to glance over the monster's shoulder.

With shock, he recognized Baro and Yanko. The young gypsies ran toward him with their weapons at the ready. Yaroslav's cage was broken, most likely by the powerful blows of Yanko's hammer, and Zara was already inside, carefully taking the chains off the vampire.

Without slowing down, Zmey spun around and met Baro's sword with his black blade, a sinister snarl curving his mouth. He cackled, deflecting the gypsies' attack, toying with them like a giant cat with little mice.

"A sword! My kingdom for a sword" roared Yaroslav, rising, a dangerous smirk crossing his bloodied face. He was silver-free, and his skin started to heal immediately. His eyes lit up with a scarlet glow, responding to his anger, and he rose in the air slightly, spreading his arms wide.

As Zmey turned to the young men, Gunz used the opportunity to pull out his Swiss army knife and manifest his sword. "Slavik," he yelled. "I have a sword for you." Before he finished his statement, Yaroslav stood next to him.

"Silence! Everyone, stop!" A bright, girlish voice rang through the air, and Zmey froze, lowering his weapon. His glowing, yellow eyes probed Zara, and he smirked, turning to face Gunz.

"So, you did find yourself another seer who's ready to die for you, Salamander?" he asked coldly.

"She's not a seer—," started Gunz but cut himself off as realization dawned on him.

Only a witch with psychic abilities can find us here. Zmey's words surfaced in his mind, and a cold sweat covered his forehead.

My mama is shuvani, and I have the gift, too. I'm the best drabarovkinya... Recalling Zara's words, he cringed, cursing himself. *Drabarovkinya—a seer, a fortuneteller... Dammit, how could I be so blind... Stupid...* He turned to Baro and Yanko, grabbing Baro's arm.

"Baro, get her out of here," he hissed, unable to speak louder than a hoarse whisper. "If you want your sister to live, get her the hell out of here..."

The young gypsies exchanged a troubled look but didn't move. Gunz seized Yanko's shirt and shook him once.

"Yanko, if you love Zara, you will get her away from here now!" he shouted, large drops of cold sweat running down his face. "If she tries to bind Skiper-Zmey, she'll die. Just the way my Angie died." He froze in place, his chest rising and falling with strenuous breaths. "Please... I'm begging you... I can't let something like this happen again!"

Whispering something under her breath, Zara approached

Skiper-Zmey and halted before him, her eyes moving up and down his body, sizing him up.

"Zara, please—," started Gunz, but she wagged her finger without taking her eyes off the monster, stopping him.

"Little witch, your lover is right," hissed Zmey, slowly morphing into his serpent form. His mouth stretched, displaying his sharp fangs, and his eyes lit up brighter. "I feel charitable today. You should take your boys and run while you can. It's between me and the Fire Salamander—"

Zara cocked her head, placing her hands on her hips. "Didn't I tell you to be quiet?" she asked softly, and the monster snapped his mouth shut. "Much better." She smirked and continued, "First of all, he's not my lover. He can dream..." She threw a glance at Gunz and bobbed her head. "And you, Zane, should know better. A man has not yet been born who can boss me around. I do what I think is right, and when I believe it's the right time to do it." She flicked her eyebrow at Gunz and switched her attention back to Zmey. "And right now, I believe I'm exactly where I need to be."

Slowly, she started to chant, weaving a strange spell in Dragon tongue, supporting it with the wide movements of her arms. Both Baro and Yanko stepped aside, giving her some space, and by the looks on their faces, they weren't concerned even in the slightest bit.

Zmey growled, a low and dangerous sound rumbling somewhere in the depth of his chest. He didn't move but went rigid, and the energy of Chaos wrapped around him as he resisted the spell the young seer was weaving. As she kept chanting, increasing the potency of her magic, Zmey fought her, disgusting poison dripping from his mouth contorted by unimaginable strain.

Zara's voice grew louder as she rose slightly above the ground, lifted by the energy of her magic. Gunz watched her in awe, a mix of emotions clawing through him at the memory of Angelique casting a similar enchantment.

As she proceeded with her spell work, now shouting her spell at the top of her lungs, Zmey slowly started to morph again. Fighting the effects of the magic, his image flickered, switching between his human form and that of a serpent. Zara didn't stop. Moving closer to the monster, she placed her hand on his chest and shouted the last words of the spell.

Zmey screamed, throwing his head back, his body shuddering and twitching. A dark mist started to rise around him, and Zara seized his wrists, holding the monster down.

"Zane!" she yelled, her voice strained. "You will have just a few minutes to kill him. When he assumes his human form, cut his head off!"

When the mist dissipated, Angelique stood in Zmey's place. She turned her head, and for a brief moment, her eyes—her normal, bright eyes—lingered on Gunz, sending a wave of fire through him. Then she turned to Zara and inclined her head.

"Thank you, sister-seer," she said, a tender smile ghosting her lips. "Thank you for giving a fighting chance to the man I love... for giving him an opportunity to free this world from a terrible monster."

As Zara let go of her wrists, Angelique turned around and took a step closer to Gunz. He reached to touch her, but she shied away from his trembling hand.

"I love you, Zane, my strong, handsome boy," she whispered, moving her long black hair to the side, exposing her neck. "Please, my love, set me free... I know it's not easy, but you have to do it..."

Her voice melted into the void of Gunz's frazzled mind. With sudden clarity, he remembered the trials Viggo Warrington made him and Lucan go through. At the time, he thought War was playing a cruel game with him, and only now he understood why his biological father had done it. He was trying to prepare him for what was coming.

He understood everything. He knew what had to be done. He also knew it had to be him. Yet, he couldn't move. He couldn't lift his arm, his sword too heavy, his muscles weak and powerless.

"Zane!" Angelique and Zara yelled at the same time. "He's coming back! We can't hold him much longer! Do It! NOW!"

Snapping back to reality, Gunz glanced around wildly, and the fire rose around him, a powerful heatwave spreading in all directions in response to his entangled emotions. Angelique's image flickered, and both young women screamed, straining to force Skiper-Zmey back under their control.

With a terrible howl tearing from his lips, Gunz swung Sword Kladenets. The blade of pure white gold that was forged on the Alatyr stone at the dawn of Creation cut through the neck of the Lord of Chaos, decapitating him in one move. For a split second, Angelique remained standing, her gaze still fixed on Gunz. Then she closed her eyes, and her head fell to the ground, rolling to his feet. Her body collapsed to her knees and then fell to the side awkwardly.

Gunz's fingers unlocked, and the magical sword dropped to the ground with a loud clatter. He staggered back until he ran into Yaroslav and then froze, unable to take his eyes off Angelique's dead body. Zara kneeled next to her and touched her shoulder, whispering something. A dark mist rose around her and when it dissipated, Angelique was gone, the dead body of a repugnant monster remaining in her place.

Zara whispered something, and a simple iron box materialized in her hand. She touched Skiper-Zmey's body, and it turned into a pile of dust. The dust lifted in the air and spun around, rotating slowly over her before settling inside the box. She closed the lid and offered the box to Gunz.

"Give it to Veles," she said faintly. "He'll know what to do."

Gunz took the box and bent down, picking up Sword Kladenets. Zara smiled at him, then her eyes rolled back, and she collapsed. She didn't hit the ground as Yaroslav with his vampire's speed managed to catch her before it happened.

Gunz froze in place, his eyes on the young woman lying limply in the vampire's arms. Yaroslav met his eyes and smiled slightly, shaking his head. "She's alive, Zane," he said, rising with Zara in his arms. "I can hear her heartbeat. She overused her magic is my guess."

Baro took his sister out of Yaroslav's arms and turned to Gunz. "Our mother will know what to do, Zane. Don't worry, she'll be all right. Zara is an extremely powerful *drabarovkinya*," he said. Then he glanced at the shining fracture in the fabric of the world Zmey had created. "You can leave through the opening we've made. I believe you still have some work to do."

"Something tells me we'll meet again, little man." Yanko winked at Gunz. Then he seized Baro's arm, snapped his fingers, and all three of them vanished.

CHAPTER 39

~ ZANE BURNS, A.K.A. GUNZ ~

For a moment, Gunz stood motionless, staring at the fracture shining with a brilliant white light. He wasn't thinking, or rather, he was forcing himself not to think.

"Are you okay, Gunz?"

Gunz turned toward Yaroslav. "Not even close," he said, lifting his shoulders in a half-shrug. "But the gypsies were right. I don't have the luxury of falling apart..."

His voice wavered, and he smirked, staring at the iron box in his hand. Slowly, anger boiled up in him, and for the first time, he didn't care about controlling it. He slammed his hand over the ring of War, and the scarlet flames broke through his skin on his arms and shoulders.

"They want a war?" he growled, and the ground responded to the terrible power he had activated, trembling beneath his feet. "They got themselves War!"

Relinquishing himself to the ancient power, he started to chant, making a circular motion with his arm. A portal swirling with scarlet flames opened up in front of him. Gunz stopped chanting and stared at the portal in awe, unable to believe that he had actually managed to do it.

"Come?" he whispered, putting his fingers into the crimson flames.

His hushed voice rolled through the fake reality, reverberating through its magical walls. The neigh of a horse sounded from within the portal, and a moment later, a giant red stallion engulfed in scarlet flames walked out and halted before Gunz, staring at him with round, flaming eyes.

"You summoned me, young master?" asked the stallion, hitting the ground with his hoof. Even though Gunz expected the stallion to speak with him telepathically, he couldn't help but flinch when his voice sounded in his mind.

"Yes," replied Gunz, projecting the images of the battle between the forces of Darkness and the army of Light.

"Your will is my command, young master," replied the stallion, inclining his head.

Gunz put the iron box into the saddlebag and mounted the horse, sheathing the magical sword into a simple leather sheath attached to the saddle. He closed his eyes, spreading his arms, and when he opened his eyes again, his body was clad in strange armor. The top of it looked like an ancient Roman legionnaire armor but was made of modern materials. Cargo pants and combat boots completed his strange hybrid outfit.

"You want to ride a horse," said Yaroslav, staring at his friend in disbelief. "You?"

"Yeah, I do," replied Gunz, patting the stallion's neck. "No more Mister Nice Gunz." He offered his hand to Yaroslav. "Are you coming?"

"I thought you'd never ask." Yaroslav took his hand and easily rose in the saddle.

The stallion reared on its hind legs, and then pushed off the ground, rising in the air and leaving through the fracture the gypsies had created.

* * *

As the stallion carried him high above the ground, Gunz looked down at the battlefield from a bird's-eye view. Just now, he realized the full grandeur and the brutality of the battle unfolding below. Two great armies stretched across the Isle Buyan, taking most of its land. Entangled in a merciless struggle, the horde of Darkness was slowly advancing, pushing the army of Light back, away from the World Tree, and it seemed like the evil army was at least three times larger than the army of good. In the sky, the birds of Viraj fought the phantoms, and there was no peace either on the ground or above.

The air was thick with the strikes of magical energy, flying energy orbs, and fireballs. Combat spells rushed through the air, leaving a faint glow behind like large tracer bullets. The sky was still blood-colored, and a blinding comet hung high above the blood-and-gore scenery.

The stench of demonic essence, the metallic smell of blood, and the nauseating reek of demonic goo and quickly decomposing bodies made the air almost unbreathable. The clamor of metal on metal, cries of pain, curses, and growls rose above the battlefield, blending into an unbearable, ear-splitting cacophony.

Observing the battle through the power of War, Gunz had no problem singling out his friends in the crowd, and with relief, he realized that all of them were still standing, fighting what seemed to be an endless battle.

The barrier surrounding the Isle Buyan still held, despite the dark splatters spreading over it here and there. Now, Gunz could see that a few Slavic deities, including Svyatobor, supported the protective shield by channeling their power through it. To his surprise, he realized that not only the Slavic gods but also Archangel Uriel, and a few more people emitting unmistakable angelic energy signatures, stood by the barrier, channeling their power through it.

Feeling a soft tap on his shoulder, he glanced back at Yaroslav.

"I'm going to dismount here," yelled the vampire, trying to raise his voice above the noise of the battle.

"Slavik, be careful!" shouted Gunz. "The air is infused with fire and combat spells. Not a good place to be a vampire."

"I'll be fine."

"I know you will be," replied Gunz. He glanced down, his eyes searching for the Master of Power in the crowd. "Mrak Delar is right there." He pointed down. "Find him and fight by his size. It's important that you do it. When the time is right, you'll understand."

"When did you become so bossy?" The vampire chuckled, sarcasm playing in his glowing eyes. "Control freak." But then he raised his hand, peacefully. "Fine, fine. I'll do as you said."

Holding Gunz's sword in one hand, Yaroslav crouched on the stallion's croup and then jumped up, seamlessly morphing into a large, white bird. Gunz followed his progress through the air and only relaxed when he saw the vampire shifting back to his human form next to the Master of Power.

He placed his hand over his tattoo, channeling his fire energy through it. "Mishka, can you hear me?" he asked.

Yes, boss, my ears are still attached to my head, replied Mishka, sarcasm flooding their telepathic connection.

Pesky little monster. Gunz chuckled, shaking his head.

"I heard that too."

Dammit!

Mishka snickered on the other side.

"Mishka, are you ready?" asked Gunz.

Yes, boss. We are all here, right outside the barrier, replied the wyvern.

"Perfect. Stand by and wait for my command."

Yes, boss, replied the wyvern and then added with tones of humor. *"Firetwat."*

Gunz lowered his arm, breaking their connection. Searching the battlefield, he found Chernobog and Belobog and directed the stallion to the twin-gods. As the massive horse touched the ground softly, Gunz swung his sword, unleashing a firestorm at the monsters around him to clear some space.

He halted the dancing stallion in front of Chernobog and inclined his head, greeting both deities.

"What the hell?" muttered Chernobog, staring at him in awe, his black eyes taking in his armor, his sword and then sliding down to the fiery stallion. "Do you even know what you are? What kind of—"

"I do know what I am, and I finally learned to fully embrace it," replied Gunz calmly. "Can you say the same, god of Destruction, King of the Dark Nav? Are you ready to embrace what you are and do what must be done?"

Chernobog and Belobog exchanged a quick look, and a tiny smile quirked up Belobog's lips.

"Yes, I am," replied Chernobog quietly and lowered his head.

Gunz touched the saddlebag. "Skiper-Zmey is dead. I fulfilled my destiny," he said flatly. "From what I understand, the Celtic air demon is gone also. Now, it's your turn to fulfill your duty, Chernobog." He glanced around and pointed at the World Tree. When your path is free, you must get Zlebog back to *Peklo* and then deal with your wife. And this time, remember that no matter how much you love her, the punishment must fit the crime."

"Oh, yeah?" Chernobog lifted his head, his eyes filled with defiance. "And what would you do if your precious Angelique was in Morena's place?"

Gunz grunted as the next wave of anger spread through him, fueling the fire and the power of War in him. The stallion responded by rearing on his hind legs, neighing angrily.

"A few minutes ago, I decapitated the woman I loved with my own sword," shouted Gunz, his entire body ablaze. "I did it to kill Skiper-Zmey and give you a fighting chance against Zlebog. So, please, think twice before throwing something like that in my face!" His hand wrapped tighter around the grip of Sword Kladenets as he raised it. "It's going to be fast, my lords. You'll know when it's time to act."

Gunz directed the stallion up, rising above the Isle Buyan. Channeling as much of the power of War as he could, he stared down at the army of Darkness. Just as easily as during training, he could see their dark magical energy flowing through their grotesque bodies. They didn't have hearts or souls, but dark blobs of energy were pulsing in each of them in the place where their hearts would have been.

Without thinking twice, he connected with all of them at once, feeling their life-forces beating within the grip of his power. For a split second, the darkness took hold of him, assailing him through his connection with the massive evil horde. But the Fire Salamander in him woke up to life immediately, quickly purifying his body and his mind of the malignant influence of dark magic.

"Obey," he commanded, squeezing his hand into a tight fist as his mind reached for the opposing army.

Every single demon and monster halted, upturning their ugly faces to see him, and a collective gasp rushed through the land. Even phantoms stopped fighting, staring at him with their empty, dead eyes. The silence enveloped the Isle as everyone—the army of Light and the horde of Darkness—looked at him, waiting for his next move.

"Now, kill," ordered Gunz, channeling all the power he had into his command.

In a heartbeat, the silence was replaced with an ear-splitting pandemonium as the monsters of the evil army attacked each other, killing and destroying everything evil within their reach.

"Aidan, I need you and Gwyn ap Nudd to unfold a powerful shield to protect the side of Light," he projected to his friend. He knew

Aidan heard him, so he didn't wait for his reply. Instead, he reached to Yaroslav through their blood bond. *"Slavik, tell Mrak to shield you. Do it now!"*

Placing his hand over his tattoo, he commanded, "Mishka, attack!"

"Yeeaaa-haaawwww!" Mishka's battle cry rose above the noise of the battle, and a large group of full-grown wyverns emerged through the protective barrier. They flew over the battlefield, blasting the dark forces with smoldering jets of fire. The monsters who were still standing, slaughtering each other, were set ablaze. They screamed and dropped their weapons, flailing their arms wildly as the fire devoured them without mercy.

Thick clouds of dark smoke filled with the reek of burnt flesh and demonic goo rose in the air as the wyverns, supported by Kal and Semargl, unfolded the smoldering inferno, quickly destroying whatever was left of the opposing army.

A few minutes later, it was over. The wyverns circled the blackened battlefield one more time and vanished. The noise dwindled down, slowly morphing into a deadly silence. Gwyn ap Nudd, Aidan and Mrak Delar let go of their protective magic, lowering to the ground tiredly.

Releasing most of the power of War, Gunz landed the stallion next to the twin-gods and dismounted, looking in the direction of the World Tree. Morena stood next to it, her back pressed against its trunk, her face contorted by terror. She stretched her arm to Chernobog, her eyes pleading for mercy. A pained look crossed Chernobog's face, but he didn't move and didn't say anything to her.

Instead, he turned to Veles, the god of the Three Realms, bowing to him. "My lord," he said softly. "You may take her and deal with her as you find fit." Then he switched his attention to his twin brother and smiled, not without affection. "Brother, I need your support."

"I got you," replied Belobog and the blinding light of the Dark Codex wrapped around both of them.

Chernobog twirled in place, shifting into a giant serpent-like dragon. He unfolded his huge, webbed wings and charged forward at full speed. Two enormous black dragons collided in the bloodied sky with a thunderous bang. It would've been hard to distinguish who was who, but Chernobog's entire body emitted the bright, white glow of the Codex, and Zlebog was surrounded with the dark, malignant mist of his power.

Their screeches and howls filled the air as they attacked each other, ripping each other's flesh without mercy. Thick, dark blood gushed from the wounds they inflicted upon each other, but they didn't stop.

Belobog rose in the air, adding the mix of his power and more energy of the Codex to support his brother. On the other side, mighty Perun joined the fight. Thunder rumbled over the ground covered in dead bodies, and a lightning bolt forked through the sky. Perun collected the electricity in his sword, redirecting it at Zlebog.

The three-headed black dragon cried out, his body twisting and shuddering. His wings folded, and he started to fall. The serpent-dragon chased him down, and when Zlebog hit the ground, glowering at his opponent with abhorrence, Chernobog shifted back into his godly form and placed his sword at the dragon's throat. As he started to chant, an iron collar materialized around the dragon's neck. Zlebog closed his glowing eyes, and his body went limp.

Chernobog lowered his sword and swayed a little. "It's not over," he whispered. "I'll be right back..." He waved his hand, and the black portal into the Dark Nav materialized before him. With a strenuous grunt, he lifted Zlebog, placing him across his shoulder. Then he nodded to Gunz and walked through his portal, disappearing on the other side.

Gunz spun around, searching for Yaroslav. He knew that

Aidan would be fine, but with the amount of fire he had unleashed just a few minutes ago, he was worried about the vampire. Noticing both of them walking toward him, accompanied by Gwyn, Kal and Mrak, he sighed with relief.

"Thank God, you are both alive," he muttered, wiping the sweat off his forehead with the back of his hand, smearing dirt and ash over his face.

Yaroslav and Aidan exchanged a look and chuckled.

"Which god?" asked Aidan.

"Take your pick," added Yaroslav, waving his hand around.

"The three of you..." Gunz heard an unfamiliar deep, male voice and spun around. An extremely tall man in Russian armor approached him. His golden blond hair fell to his shoulders in wavy strands, and he held a massive hammer glowing with the energy of his godly power. "The evil triad was right. The three of you would destroy the world to save each other."

Gunz glanced back at his friends and just now realized that every single person—gods, angels, the powerful beings of magic —was kneeling with their heads bowed.

"Svarog, my lord." Gunz took one knee as he recognized who this man was. "The evil triad was wrong."

The words the old *shuvani* had told him back in the gypsy camp surfaced in his mind, and he smiled, just now understanding her meaning. He got up and met the steady gaze of the most powerful god of the Slavic pantheon without blinking.

"The three of us are not going to destroy the world for each other," he continued calmly. "But we sure *will* walk through fire if our friends need our help." He held out his hand, and two flames—the elemental fire and the flame of War—ignited in his palm. "And I don't mean this kind of fire, my lord." He squeezed his hand, extinguishing both flames. Then he glanced at his friends and smiled. "Since I discovered the Fire, I realized one thing. It's not about how powerful I am. Not everything can be solved by magic, no matter how skilled I'm with it. It always comes down to the people who stand by my side when I need them the most. Together, we're a power to be reckoned with."

"Truer words were never spoken, young Salamander," replied Svarog.

Gunz took Sword Kladenets and offered it to the deity.

"Thank you for providing us with such a powerful weapon," he said as Svarog took the sword from his hands.

"Who said I provided you with anything?" Svarog shrugged, a smirk hiding under his golden mustache.

"Aw, my lord, please give me some credit," said Gunz, a lopsided grin making an appearance on his face. "You were the one who sent Skarbnik to Mount Vottovaara. The demon has a big mouth. When he said that not only evil can hire him, I kind of put two and two together. You were 'the manager' with whom he kept consulting."

For a brief moment, Svarog stared at Gunz with his mouth slightly opened. Then he slapped his hand on his thigh and burst out laughing. Turning to Kal, he inclined his head respectfully.

"Great Salamander, your child is a fine warrior and a clever man," he rumbled, tones of humor still ringing in his voice. "You should be proud."

"Yes, my lord," replied Kal, still keeping a kneeling position. "He is a fine warrior with the decorum of a village simpleton. Please, forgive his lack of manners." He threw a scorching gaze at Gunz.

"What?" mouthed Gunz, spreading his arms.

"He is a modern man, Great Salamander," said Svarog. "Modern people don't know how to bow and kneel properly, anyway."

He winked at Gunz and raised the magical sword toward the bloodied sky. A burst of bright energy escaped the tip of the blade. The comet vanished, and the fireballs burned out. Slowly, the sky started to clear, the ultramarine shades of early dawn quickly devouring the scarlet glow. Svarog observed his handi-work and nodded, satisfied.

"I believe my children can handle the rest," he said, his eyes moving from one face to the next. "Farewell, young Salaman-der." He glanced at Gunz one more time and snapped his fingers, vanishing from the Isle Buyan.

As soon as Svarog was gone, everyone got up. Gunz walked around his fiery stallion and pulled the iron box out of the saddlebag. Approaching Veles, he bowed, offering him the box.

"These are the remains of Skiper-Zmey," he said, straighten-ing. "Just a pile of dust, but the young gypsy-seer said that you'd know what needs to be done."

Veles nodded, taking the box from his hand carefully, as though he was expecting it to explode. "She was right," he said with a sigh. "Unfortunately, ultimate evil like the Lord of Chaos and Zlebog can never be destroyed entirely. There is always going to be a confrontation between the Light and the Dark-ness. So, I must return his remains to his grave under Mount Karasova and restore my curse, making it stronger this time." He glanced at Perun and smiled. "Would you assist me, god of Thunder?"

As Perun passed by Aidan, he tapped him on his shoulder. "We need to have a talk, Aodh," he said quickly. "I'll find you when I'm done with Veles."

CHAPTER 40

~ ZANE BURNS, A.K.A. GUNZ ~

Once Perun and Veles had left, the rest of the army of Light slowly dispersed, leaving only Gunz and the rest of his friends next to the World Tree. The frosty spell Morena cast on the Tree was gone, and it stood in its full glory, reflecting the pink rays of the rising sun.

Gunz wrapped his arms around the stallion's neck and rested his forehead against his hot coat. Now that the battle was truly over, anger and adrenalin stopped pumping through his system and debilitating exhaustion settled in. With an effort, he gathered some of the power of War and opened the portal.

"You may leave, my friend," he whispered, caressing the horse's flaming mane. "Thank you for coming to my call."

I will always come to your call, young master. The stallion bowed to him and walked through the portal.

Kal and Gwyn ap Nudd exchanged a quick look, and the Great Salamander waved his hand, opening the flaming curtain of his portal. "We'll see you back in the Otherworld, kids," he said with a smirk, and both of them left.

Noticing Mrak Delar sitting on the ground, Gunz lowered next to him. "Look at me, Master," he said softly, and as the

Master of Power raised his jet-black eyes, he sighed with relief. They were black, but their blackness was normal—not a touch of darkness.

"I'm okay," said the Master of Power. He lay down, folding his arms under his head. "Disgustingly dirty, but otherwise, I'm fine."

Aidan and Yaroslav sat down next to them. The god of the Otherworld looked drained, his gray face covered in slime, blood, and something thick and yellow. "I don't think the word 'dirty' truly describes it." He smirked and endeavored to wipe his face, making it even worse.

"I can't believe we survived it," murmured Yaroslav, struggling to untangle his hair with his fingers.

"Not all of us." Aidan's voice infused with pain beyond limits resonated with the way Gunz felt at the moment, and he raised his eyes, searching his friend's face shadowed by grief.

"Tessa? What happened?" he asked.

Aidan bit his lip and shook his head. "She..." His voice cut off, and he looked away, his eyes painfully dry and empty. "Sorry... I can't talk about it now..."

Mrak Delar sat up and muttered a short spell. A bottle of vodka and four shot glasses materialized on the ground next to him. Catching Gunz's flabbergasted look, he shrugged nonchalantly. "I borrowed it from Gwyn's kitchen. He's not going to notice," he explained with a slight wave of his hand. "I believe we all need something a little stronger than coffee." He opened the bottle and filled the glasses to the brim.

"To our severely co-dependent friendship that saved this world," said Gunz with a lopsided grin, raising his shot glass. "At least for now. Salute." He brought the glass to his lips and closed his eyes, inhaling the burning scent of alcohol. Then he held his breath and swallowed the burning liquid in one gulp.

As Mrak Delar filled the glasses again, Aidan lifted his, wrinkling his nose at the smell of vodka. "For peace," he whispered, staring at the World Tree basking in the warm rays of the morning sun. "I want to put my sword away, re-open my martial arts school and teach kids. I'm done with fighting."

"I'll drink to that," murmured Gunz.

They clinked their glasses again. Gunz placed the empty shot glass on the ground, thinking how much he wanted to join Aidan in his future school, but deep inside he knew it wasn't an option for him. He picked up the bottle and filled the glasses for the third time. Rising, he squeezed the glass in his fist, bowing his head.

"For those who are no longer with us... For the fallen," said Yaroslav. "Peyton..."

"Tessa..." Aidan's voice was no more than a whisper.

"Angelique," whispered Gunz, his heart wrenched with the grief he had been holding back all this time. "Karma, Jasper..." He glanced at his friends, biting his lip. They had all lost someone they loved. With their lifestyles and obligations to the realm, having a normal relationship was impossible. *Not without putting that person into mortal danger...*

"Grand Master Collins," added Mrak Delar, his fingers clenching the shot glass. "For all our fallen friends... Guardians, Wardens, the warriors of Light." He drank his vodka and grunted, pressing the back of his hand to his lips. "I need to go back home. I need to see my wife. Too many evil assholes have been threatening her lately. I put a bullseye on her back by marrying her."

Gunz nodded, realizing that the Master of Power just voiced his own thoughts. Mrak Delar got up and bowed slightly. Gunz smirked, thinking that despite everything that had happened and how exhausted he was, the Master of Power never lost his manners and his natural elegance.

"I'll see you all later," said Mrak Delar and vanished.

"I need to go back to Florida," murmured Yaroslav. "Most of the *EverSafe* employees are dead, and I need to check on Akira."

He stopped fidgeting with his hair, throwing his hands up. "Gunz, let me know when you're back home." He picked up the sword and offered it to Gunz.

"I will," promised Gunz. He took his sword and ran his fingers over its blade, feeling the familiar cool touch of *Ardenium* steel to his skin. Turning it into the Swiss army knife, he placed it into the pocket of his cargo pants.

Aidan got up, offering his hand to Yaroslav. "Gunz, I'll take Slavik home and then go back to the Otherworld. Perun wanted to speak with me, so I better be there when he shows up."

Gunz shook his friends' hands. "I think I'll stay here a few more minutes, and then I'll go home and get some sleep." He chuckled, thinking of Jim's uncanny ability to call him at the worst possible time, and added, "Hopefully..."

* * *

BARELY MOVING HIS FEET, Gunz made his way to the World Tree and slid down to the ground with his back pressed against its massive trunk. Lifting his face slightly, he closed his eyes, enjoying the warmth of the sun and the peacefulness of the moment. He wasn't sure how long he sat like this—motionless, with his mind blissfully blank. Even though he wanted to go home, take a hot shower and get some sleep, he wasn't sure he could make a move.

When he felt a slight fluctuation of the magical energy around him and a soft touch of wind against his skin, he opened his eyes with a deep sigh. Belobog and Chernobog stood in front of him, looking down at him with curiosity in their eyes glowing with the brilliant light of the Dark Codex.

"Now what?" asked Gunz without hiding his aggravation. He rose to his feet with a strained groan.

The twin brothers exchanged a look, and both laughed.

"He really has no fear of gods," said Chernobog to his brother, but there was no animosity in his voice.

"I can't understand why." Belobog rolled his eyes. Then he slapped Gunz on his shoulder as if he was his old friend. "We're not here to threaten you, Child of Fire. We want you to take the Dark Codex back. Can you do that?"

Gunz glanced at the gods with curiosity, his eyes lingering on Chernobog a moment longer. "Are you sure you want to give it back?"

Chernobog smirked. "Yes, I am sure," he said. "Firstly, with the Dark Codex, I can no longer bicker with my brother." He threw a glance at Belobog. "Where is the fun in that?"

"Second," continued Belobog, "the headache it gives every time it gets activated is more than I like to handle. I have no idea how you were able to tolerate it for such a long time."

"Unlike you, I had no choice," muttered Gunz. He channeled his power and magic, realizing how truly exhausted he was. "I'll try. To be honest, I'm drained, but luckily, bringing the Dark Codex back doesn't require nearly as much work and power as splitting it between the two of you."

Placing his hands on their chests, he started to chant, channeling all the magic and power he could gather into his spell. The bright energy of the Dark Codex wrapped around both deities, encapsulating them into the glowing orb of blinding light. When the light dwindled down, Gunz stood with a large, old book in his hands.

"Just curious," said Chernobog, peering down at the book. "What are you planning to do with it now?"

"I gave my word to Master Warden Raoul de Beaumont that I would return it to the Wardens Order." Gunz touched the book, whispering the spell Ivan the Terrible had used back in the City of Gold, and the book vanished. He looked at Chernobog and smirked faintly. "Is Voron okay?" he asked. "I didn't see him during the battle, and normally, he was always by your side."

Chernobog sighed. "Yeah, this is another thing I am grateful to you for," he said, not meeting Gunz's eyes. "You saved my best friend. From me." He slammed his hand on the pommel of his sword, shaking his head, an expression of regret shadowing his features. "Voron is fine. I couldn't leave the Dark Nav unprotected, so he stayed behind. He's still mad at me and talking to him is like pulling teeth, you know. But I have eternity to make it up to him. He'll come around."

"I'm sure he will, brother." Belobog slapped his godly brother on his shoulder, sarcastic twinkles dancing in his blue eyes. "After all, Voron only gave up his position as the gatekeeper of the heavenly gardens of the Prav for you. Something small like you trying to kill him surely is not going to affect his loyalty to you."

"Fire and ice, brother!" muttered Chernobog, throwing his hands up. "Thank you for your support."

Gunz laughed. "As much fun as I have talking to you two, I should get going. I can barely stand without swaying. Unlike some of us, I still need to eat and sleep."

"Temporary disadvantage." Belobog smirked and snapped his fingers, vanishing. Chernobog threw another glance at Gunz before snapping his fingers and teleporting out of the Isle Buyan.

When both deities were gone, Gunz sighed with relief and waved his hand. As the flaming curtain of his portal unfolded before him, he smiled and walked through the fire, enjoying the touch of the elemental flames to his skin.

He walked out in the middle of the backyard of his house in Coral Springs and quickly scanned it for any supernatural presence. Since everything seemed to be clear, he opened the backdoor and walked inside the kitchen. Glancing around, he checked his wards and protection spells. Everything was just the way he had left it a while ago, and it seemed like he hadn't been here for ages.

Barely moving his feet, he made his way to the second floor, ripping his dirty, half-destroyed clothes as he walked. His magical armor had vanished after he released the stallion, and his normal clothes were unsalvageable, anyway. He went straight to the bathroom and turned the hot water on in the shower.

He remembered walking inside the shower. He also remembered shutting down his cell phone and throwing it on the stand by the bed, thinking that no power, magical or mundane, would interrupt his sleep this time.

The number you have dialed—FIRE SALAMANDER—has been disconnected or is no longer in service... If it is a true emergency, please... do whatever the hell you want, just leave me alone.

Today only...

At least for a few hours...

Supernatural creeps can wait...

EPILOGUE

* * *

~ Aidan ~
The Otherworld

THE LIVING ROOM of Gwyn's house was in the kind of disarray Aidan hadn't seen since Gwyn ap Nudd brought him to the Otherworld. Pieces of the crystal chandelier were scattered all over the floor, and they cracked and slipped from under Aidan's feet with every step he took.

To his shock, he found the god of Thunder sitting on the couch, chatting with Gwyn ap Nudd and Kal. The Axe of Perun lay on the coffee table in front of him, and his fingers were tracing the shape of the golden inlays absentmindedly. As soon as Aidan walked in, all three of them turned to him, and Gwyn's face lit up with a warm smile.

"My lords," said Aidan, bowing to them stiffly. Following the latest events, he couldn't expect anything good from an assembly like this. Besides, after the way Perun treated him originally, he didn't have warm and fuzzy feelings toward the

Slavic god of Thunder.

"Aodh," said Perun, pointing at an armchair. "Please sit down. We need to talk."

Aidan sighed, but sat down, leaning forward slightly. "What can I do for you, my lord?"

"It's probably about what I can do for you, young god." Perun chuckled. "Would you like to see your beloved again? My daughter, Therasia?"

"Wait... what?" Aidan glanced at Gwyn ap Nudd, but his father just gave him a short nod. "Tessa is a full reaper now. She positioned herself above all reapers, assuming the mantle of the High Reaper, the right hand of Death. I don't think it's possible."

Perun chuckled, shaking his head. "You said it yourself. The High Reaper is the right hand of Death who is one of the four Horsemen of the Apocalypse. But let me ask you, Aodh, do you know any of the Horsemen personally?" He gave him an arched stare. "Maybe even two of them? One of them being..." He let his voice fade away, staring at Aidan pointedly.

"Angel," whispered Aidan, hope igniting in his soul. "Why didn't I think about it earlier?"

"I assume you were a little preoccupied with one insignificant thing, like the rise of the evil triad," suggested Perun with a light flick of his wrist. "Besides, with all the signs of the Apocalypse unfolding in the human realm, you couldn't have any of the Horsemen using their powers."

"Summon Angel now, son," suggested Gwyn ap Nudd.

Aidan got up, his heart beating desperately against his ribcage. With trembling fingers, he drew a glowing rune in the air and pressed his hand to it, summoning Death. A cold wind rushed through the room, and a dark, unmoving portal opened up under the tall ceiling of Gwyn's house.

A man dressed all in black with mighty black wings behind his back slowly descended from the darkness of the portal. Softly, he stepped on the marble floor and bowed to the

439

assembly. His eyes halted on Aidan, and his black eyes warmed up.

"I believe I know why you summoned me, my lords," he said, assuming his human form. He snapped his fingers, and Tessa materialized next to him. Slowly, she turned in place, her eyes gliding from one face to the next, but there was still no recognition in her cold, unemotional gaze.

"Angel," said Aidan, "can you give her back to me? Is there a way to revert what she's done?"

"Partially," replied Angel. "Her humanity is gone, Aidan. She's never going to be human again. But I believe, together with the god of Thunder, we can bring his daughter back. If he's willing to claim her as his daughter, that is."

Perun shrugged. "Of course, I claim her as my daughter," he replied. "I never rejected her in the first place. The only reason her mother and I had to give her up at birth was because of the rise of the Followers of Chaos. If they found out about her existence, even I wouldn't have been able to protect her."

Angel nodded and grabbed the Axe of Perun off the table. "Therasia," he called her, offering her the Axe as she turned to him. "Hold on to it and don't let go." Then he turned to Perun, arching his brow. "Together, my lord. You know what needs to be done."

Standing behind her, Angel placed his hands on Tessa's shoulders and started to chant softly. At the same time, Perun covered her hands with his and channeled his godly power, wrapping all three of them into it as he started to chant in his ancient language.

The energy of Death spread through the room, and the black wings opened to their full extent behind Angel's back. The lightning bolt struck through the Axe, and thunder rumbled, making the walls tremble a little. Aidan froze in place, unable to take his eyes off Tessa.

As they kept chanting, a full lightning storm unveiled inside

Gwyn's house. Angel let go, but Perun didn't stop, channeling more and more of his power through their connected hands. The blinding light of his power enveloped them, and Aidan could no longer see them, his eyes watering.

When the light subsided, Tessa and Perun stood back on the floor. With her arms wrapped tightly around his wide shoulders and her head placed on his chest, she was whispering something to him nonstop, but Aidan couldn't make out her words.

Finally, Perun kissed her on the top of her head and moved her away gently, turning her toward Aidan. Slowly, she raised her eyes, and everything inside Aidan crashed. Her eyes were no longer brown. They shone a bright blue, and tiny lightning bolts kept flashing in their depths every few seconds. Human Tessa was no more. The goddess of Thunder stood before him.

"Tessa?" he whispered her name tentatively.

She glanced at her father, and Perun nodded to her, encouraging her to proceed. Moving slowly, like in a dream, she approached Aidan and stilled just a step away from him.

He stiffened, unable to move or make a sound.

"Aidan?" she whispered, a question in her trembling voice. "Aidan, you..."

Her voice broke, and she swallowed, gazing up at him. When he didn't move, Tessa took one more step, closing the distance between them. She threw her arms around his neck, pulling him down slightly. Rising on her tiptoes, she kissed his cheek, the touch of her lips to his skin sending a wave of heat through him.

He encircled her waist with his arms, slightly lifting her off the floor. "Never..." He didn't finish what he was trying to say as his hands holding her trembled. Gently, he lowered her to the floor and kissed her, placing all the pain, happiness, relief and everything else he felt at the moment into a single kiss.

"Never. Leave me. Again," he whispered into her ear, pronouncing one word at a time.

"Never again..." She nodded, tears now gleaming in her bright eyes. "Always and together."

* * *

~ *Zane Burns, a.k.a. Gunz* ~
Coral Springs, Florida
Three months later

THE SKY WAS VEILED by low, dark clouds, and the scent of ozone hung in the air, predicting an approaching thunderstorm. Gunz shivered, feeling the presence of the opposing element with his skin. It was close to seven in the evening, and the sun was shifting toward the horizon, coloring the stormy clouds with a strange pinkish-yellow glow. He glanced at his wristwatch and shrugged, aggravation rising within him.

Feeling a touch to his shoulder, he turned around and threw a reproachful glance at a young woman standing next to him. Being a few inches shorter than him, she pulled up to her tiptoes and planted a quick kiss on his unshaven cheek. Wrinkling her nose, she rubbed her lips and chuckled.

"You should shave, Salamander," she said, giving him a slight slap on his arm.

He shrugged indifferently and glanced down at her with reproach. "Zara, did you pull me away from my training with the Scarlet Queen to give me grooming advice?"

As the wind picked up, throwing her long, black hair into her face, she brushed it off and shook her head. "Of course not. When it comes to style, you're hopeless," she replied. "And being rude doesn't become you, Zane."

"I'm not being rude, Zara," he replied with a sigh. "I'm exhausted. I spent all morning chasing some rogue vampires who vandalized a few local medical centers. Then I had to help

Aidan with his new martial arts school. After that, I had a training session with the Scarlet Queen and Yaroslav."

He scratched the back of his head, thinking about his last lesson where Akira had made it a point to prove that he still had a long way to go with his sword technique. The last session left him aching all over, and his body was still covered in black and blue blemishes and bruises.

"I haven't sat down since six o'clock in the morning," he added at length. "I just want to go home and relax. So, please, tell me why we are here."

He waved his hand at the entrance into a cemetery. It wasn't the first time he was in this place. Even though he had never recovered Angelique's body, Tessa, Aidan, Yaroslav and he decided to have a burial ceremony for her here. At least once a week, he visited her grave for a few minutes to bring some fresh flowers. He wasn't sure why but having a burial ceremony and a graveside to visit gave him the strange and unexpected closure he needed so much.

"Let's go," said Zara, pulling him inside.

He followed her, making his way to Angelique's grave. Taking one knee, he wiped the dust off the stone, brushing his fingers over her name. Zara leaned forward and touched a flower, its petals still fresh.

"Ai, Zane, don't do it to yourself. Angelique would want you to move on and be happy." She shook her head, placing her hand on his shoulder.

He straightened with a groan and glanced at the young gypsy. "I know. I'm moving on, just at my own pace." He brushed the dust off his knee and shivered as the first drops of rain touched his skin. "So, what was so urgent, anyway?"

"I don't know." Zara shrugged, smiling at him innocently. "I just had a feeling that you and I needed to be here at this time. Don't ask me stupid questions."

The rain became heavier, and Gunz threw his hands up, his

aggravation increasing proportionally to the discomfort water inflicted on him. Something moved in his peripheral vision, attracting his attention, and he stopped, narrowing his eyes.

When they had come in, the graveyard was empty. At least he hadn't noticed anyone. Now, about a hundred yards away, a man sat on the ground by a grave with a black backpack by his side. He was dressed in a simple hooded jacket and jeans, and seemingly, there was nothing special about him. Carefully, Gunz scanned him with his other sight, but except for the golden glow of the man's soul, he didn't notice any presence of magic in him.

Yet, something in his mind was triggered by this stranger, and he couldn't understand what it was. The man turned his head toward Gunz, staring directly at him. Even though the hood of his jacket partially obscured his face, Gunz was positive that the man's mouth opened up a little like in shock.

The man got up and pulled his hood down, but didn't move, remaining by the grave. He was tall. By the looks of him, at least six-foot-four if not taller, and his massive, athletically built frame betrayed many years of physical training. His dark hair was cut short on the back but fell in long strands over the left side of his face. As a gust of wind rushed through the cemetery, it brushed his hair off his face, exposing a deep scar running from under his hairline across his eyebrow to the middle of his cheek.

He frowned, but instead of hiding his face again, he met Gunz's eyes. As soon as their eyes locked, Gunz felt a wave of magical energy rush between them. The man dropped his head, breaking their eye contact, and stilled with his shoulders slumped. A moment later, he squared his shoulders and touched his chest, extending his hand to Gunz in an unmistakable gesture of gratitude. Then he picked up his backpack and walked away without saying a word.

"Well, that wasn't weird at all," mumbled Gunz, following the stranger with his eyes.

Once the man had left, Gunz approached the grave the stranger had been sitting by and gasped. There was no grave there, just an old, broken headstone with no name on it. He kneeled by the stone and ran his fingers over its rough surface. Beneath his fingertips, he felt tiny indentations, as if the name had been there at some point but was wiped out by time and the elements.

"Now I know why we're here," whispered Zara, staring wistfully in the direction the man had disappeared.

"What are you talking about?" asked Gunz, starting on his way out of the cemetery.

"You forgot? The story my mother told you?"

Gunz rubbed his forehead, trying to remember the story Lala had told him. "Yeah, the message I was supposed to pass to a man. Something about—"

"Vita and her immortal lover," supplied Zara reproachfully. "You just delivered the message to him."

Gunz smirked, suppressing the desire to roll his eyes. "This man was human. Not a touch of magic in him," he objected. "It couldn't have been him. All immortals have at least some kind of magical presence in them. I would've detected it."

Zara laughed, stopping him gently. "Your wyvern is right, you know?"

"About?"

"Your ego is a lot bigger than your height. There are so many immortals walking this realm who are a lot more powerful than you are, and they can easily hide their energy signatures." Zara chuckled, but sobered up, placing her hand over his cheek. "You have a lot to learn, Child of Fire."

She stretched up a little and kissed him, closing her eyes. He didn't answer her kiss but didn't push her away either, his arms remaining at his sides. She pulled away and exhaled, pressing her fingers to her lips.

"My offer still stands, Zane," she said after a moment, her voice slightly above a whisper. "Come with me..." She traced the deep wrinkle between his eyebrows with her finger. "I'll make you a happy man. Just like Vita and her immortal lover..."

"Yeah, he looked like a poster child of happiness." He seized her wrist, forcing her arm down. "I'm sorry, Zara, but my answer is still no," he replied, his lips pressed into a firm line. "I accepted what I am, and I fully embraced my destiny. I'm the Great Fire Salamander and the son of War. I have my obligations to the realm of humans and the World of Magic. With the kind of lifestyle I lead, it's not safe for anyone to be with me. It puts them in danger and makes me vulnerable. I can't. Sorry."

"I can take care of myself, you know?" she said, bobbing her head in that gypsy-like manner. "You've seen me handle Skiper-Zmey. I can defend myself."

He smirked, gazing down at her, sadness tightening his chest. "That's the problem, Zara. I don't want you to be in a situation where you have to defend yourself." He glanced around and since he didn't detect any human presence, he waved his hand, unfolding the flaming curtain of his portal. "Say hello to your family, Zara."

"You *will* come to me, Salamander. Sooner or later," she whispered as he headed toward the portal. "I know how to wait."

Gunz waved his hand goodbye and walked through his portal.

As HE WALKED out of the portal, a familiar magical energy touched his senses, and he smiled, recognizing the presence of his friends even before he saw them. He walked around the corner of his house and halted, observing Yaroslav sparring with Aidan, their swords colliding with a loud clatter. Since he wasn't hiding his fire energy, both detected his presence right away and stopped, turning toward him.

"Where were you all this time?" asked Yaroslav.

"Don't ask." Gunz sighed, his mind still going through his conversation with Zara. He shook his head at his thoughts and pursed his lips.

Aidan and Yaroslav exchanged a look and said in unison, "Zara."

"She knows what she wants, and she's not afraid to go for it. I can respect that." He nodded and waved his hand, dismissing the matter. "It's not like I'm not happy to see you, but what are you two doing here? I'm sure it's a lot more comfortable to spar in Aidan's dojang or Akira's dojo."

A wide grin split Yaroslav's face as he sheathed his katana under his leather coat. "It's been too quiet. Too ordinary, you know? Some light action would be a welcome change—"

"We're here for moral support," Aidan interrupted him, putting away his icy sword.

"Moral support for what—?" The shrill ring of his cell phone interrupted his speech.

"For that." Yaroslav pointed at his pocket, his grin getting wider.

Gunz pulled his phone out and sighed as Jim's photo appeared on the screen. He answered the call, expecting nothing but trouble.

"Mr. Burns?" asked Agent Jim Andrews, his voice slightly more urgent than usual. "I need you in my office stat."

"Jim, I just came home—," started Gunz but fell silent as his boss interrupted him.

"Gunz, I'll give you all the details when you arrive here," said Jim. "For right now, all you need to know is that we're officially under Code Shadow again. So, get here immediately. You can open your portal directly into my office."

"Yes, sir," replied Gunz, throwing a furious glance at Aidan and Yaroslav.

"Bring your team with you," added Jim and hung up the phone.

"What do you know?" growled Gunz, turning to his friends. "Spill it."

"Not much," replied Aidan with a shrug. "I guess Jim will have to give us all the details."

"For right now, all you need to know is," said Yaroslav, imitating Jim's deep voice, "that we're officially under the 'Fire Salamander—Go' Code again."

"I'm ready." Gunz chuckled and waved his hand, opening his portal.

Fire Salamander, go...

EXCERPT

*Read on for an excerpt from
N.M. Thorn's new book:*

The rain hadn't stopped since he left Florida, following him all the way through the not-so-sunshiny state, then into Louisiana and finally into Texas. Now, it was beating heavily on the metal roof of a tiny diner located somewhere off highway ten, just outside Houston. The steady drumming of the falling water mixed in with the monotonous chatter of a few visitors created a peaceful, relaxed atmosphere. The heavy odor of fried food and beer wafted through the room, adding to the already slow and sleepy surroundings.

Damian propped his elbows on the counter, rested his face in his hands and closed his eyes, enjoying the warmth and dryness. A gentle touch to his shoulder made him flinch and pull back. A young waitress stood in front of him, behind the bar. She smiled and placed a plate with a piece of apple pie before him.

"I didn't order—," he started, but she shook her head, interrupting him.

"Thank you," she said with a slight Texan drawl, moving the plate closer to him. She tucked a loose strand of her dark hair behind her ear and added, "For repairing that darn garbage disposal, that is. It's been broken for ages, making all those funny noises, but John is all hat, no cattle." She threw a defiant glance at a young man in a cook's attire, but he just smiled sheepishly and raised his arms.

"No problem, ma'am." Damian lowered his eyes, his hand rising to readjust his hair automatically. He raked his fingers through the longer strands on the front, covering the left side of his face where an old scar cut through his eyebrow down to the middle of his cheek and then shrugged. "But I'll take the pie. Thank you." He thought a moment and added, "And the receipt, please."

She moved her hand to her pocket but then changed her mind. "On the house." She waved her hand dismissively as she walked away, disappearing behind the door into the kitchen.

Damian smirked, thinking about asking her for directions to the nearest motel, but then changed his mind. It was only five in the evening, and he hoped to hitch a ride to the next town before nightfall. He finished his pie quickly and got up, reaching into his pocket for his wallet. He pulled out a twenty-dollar bill and placed it under his empty plate.

Glancing outside the window, Damian cursed under his breath at the never-ending rain and grabbed his backpack from the floor. As he approached the door, he pulled out his half-broken umbrella from the side pocket of his backpack and was ready to walk out when the waitress called him. He turned around and looked at her with curiosity, not sure what to expect. Standing a foot away, she gazed up at him, craning her neck as if he were the Empire State Building. Then she cleared her throat and smiled shyly.

"Forgive me for asking... but how far are you traveling, sir?" she asked, fidgeting with a large black umbrella in her hand.

"Phoenix," he replied, wondering what this was all about.

"On foot?" The arches of her dark brows rose slightly.

"I hope not." He chuckled. "That would be an awfully long trip."

She nodded, and a shy smile graced her pleasantly round face again. "Well, anyway," she continued, offering him the umbrella. "I saw you arriving here on foot, and with this nasty weather, I thought you could use a better one. Yours is good for nothing."

"Thank you, ma'am," he said, inclining his head slightly. He took the umbrella and threw his into the garbage can.

She smiled one more time and waved goodbye before heading back into the kitchen.

DAMIAN WALKED out of the parking lot, taking a street leading back toward highway ten. The rain almost stopped, but the net of small droplets hung in the air, amplifying the cool freshness of the evening air. Since the sky was overcast by low, gray clouds, he didn't doubt that the reprieve was temporary and hoped to find a ride before the next wave of a downpour would start.

The small street was empty, and for a while, he kept walking in complete silence, deep in thoughts. So, when he heard the sound of a horn, he flinched and spun around. A twelve-foot rental truck passed him and came to a stop a few yards ahead of him, pulling slightly to the side of the road. The passenger door opened, and an unfamiliar man in his sixties with a thick mop of graying hair stuck his head out and waved to him.

"Hey, son!" he yelled, his voice deep and raspy. "I heard you're looking for a ride to Phoenix?"

Damian froze for a moment, but as realization dawned on him, his lips quirked up at the corners, and he sped up toward the truck, switching to a light jog. The man gestured for him to get in and scooted back to the driver's seat. Damian threw his umbrella and his backpack on the floor of the truck, and then climbed inside, shutting the door with a loud bang.

The man pulled the vehicle back on the empty road and cast him a sideway glance, a smile crossing his lips.

"Big fellow, aren't yah," he muttered, his open-hearted smile growing wider, and since Damian didn't reply, he added, "How tall are you, kid?"

Damian shrugged, feeling tiredness settling in his muscles. "Six-four."

The man nodded appreciatively and offered his hand. "I'm Sam. Sam Vetrov."

Slightly turning in Sam's direction, Damian shook his hand. "Damian Blake. Thanks for the ride, sir."

"It's nothing." Sam waved his hand dismissively. "For some reason, Sophie took a fancy to you. She told me you were *walking*"—he stressed the word 'walking' and shook his head, twinkles of amusement dancing in his steel-gray eyes—"to Phoenix, and since I was traveling in the same direction, she asked me to give you a ride."

"Sophie?" Damian asked but put two and two together before Sam could answer and added, "She's very kind."

"Yeah, that she is. I've been traveling this road for a few years now, and every time, I make a point to stop at her diner. The best apple pie in the entire state." Sam leaned forward, reaching for a cigarette pack in the small tray between the seats, but then changed his mind and grunted, placing his hand back on the steering wheel. "I'm going to Blue Creek, Arizona to visit my daughter. It's not far from Phoenix. You can take a bus from there to wherever it is you're going. I think if we drive through the night, by tomorrow evening, we should be in Blue Creek."

"Perfect. Thank you," Damian mumbled, folding his arms on his lap as a wave of weakness spread through him.

He closed his eyes, his eyelids getting too heavy to keep them open. It had been a few days since he left Florida, and the trip had been nothing but trouble from day one, starting with the raw weather and finishing with a few unwanted encounters.

"Get some sleep, son. I'll wake you up when I stop to get gas and grab something to eat."

Damian heard Sam's voice and nodded faintly. He was asleep before he could reply, and when Sam shook him awake a few hours later, he found the truck parked at one of the gas pumps at a gas station that looked like it had been built during the time of the great depression.

Following his traveling companion, Damian opened the door and walked outside. As soon as his feet touched the steady ground, a powerful wave of energy surged through him, and he stretched his shoulders and arms, enjoying his quickly returning strength. He took a deep breath, relishing the freshness of the evening air and the absence of rain.

"Feeling better?" muttered Sam without taking his eyes off the questionably looking credit card machine embedded into the prehistoric gas pump, doubt written all over his face. "Use your credit card at your own peril." He scratched the back of his head and turned to Damian, a lopsided smirk curving his lips. "I guess I better pay inside." He waved toward a building at the other end of the plaza.

The building was designed in the old western style with a few large wagon wheels decorating the entrance. A sign stating "The Eternity House and Grill" hung above the saloon-style double door, squeaking slightly with each gust of wind. The windows were lit with a dim, yellow light that resembled the flickering candlelight, and a few vehicles and bikes were parked on the parking lot in front of it.

Damian gave the building a quick once-over and stilled as

shivers ran down his spine, setting his mind on high alert. He caught up with Sam and held him back, grabbing his arm. "Have you ever been to this place before?" he asked, realizing how strained his voice sounded.

Sam halted, giving him a puzzled stare. "No, have you?" he replied with a half-shrug. "Why? It looks like any of those tiny mom-and-pop joints by the main highway."

"No, I haven't been here before," replied Damian, frowning. "Why don't you let me take care of the gas. That is the least I can do to repay your kindness."

Sam tilted his head and then slapped him on the shoulder slightly. "Listen, son. If you are traveling from God knows where to Arizona by hitchhiking your ride, obviously, you're short on cash. So, it's okay. You don't owe me anything, and you don't have to pay for anything. It's all good." He winked at him, his kindhearted smile bringing forth the net of wrinkles around his eyes.

As Sam opened the door, a small brass bell rang, its melodious sound seeming too loud for Damian's stretched nerves. He walked inside first and halted by the entrance, quickly observing the area, taking in even the smallest details. The lobby of the restaurant wasn't large, and since it was stuffed to the brim with shelves full of merchandise, it appeared even smaller than it was. Despite it being a restaurant, the air was cold, and the only smell present was the barely noticeable odor of dust.

A low counter was located by the wall on the left next to the entrance into the seating area, and a young woman dressed in a black T-shirt with the restaurant's logo on it sat behind it, flipping the pages of a magazine lazily. Even though she looked absolutely normal, unmistakable vampiric energy permeated the air around her. Damian exhaled with a quiet groan of aggravation and stopped shielding his magical energy.

Slowly, she lifted her head, threw the magazine on the counter and got up, a welcoming smile stretching her lips. But as soon as her eyes moved from Sam to Damian, her smile disappeared. Her lips parted a little, forming the letter 'O', and a faint red glow lit up her eyes for a heartbeat, disappearing almost immediately.

Dammit, that's what I thought. Damian seized Sam's elbow, and Sam glanced at him, his eyebrows rising in shock.

"Sam, I need you to go back to the truck," Damian said, speaking urgently, his eyes never leaving the woman standing behind the counter. "Don't argue with me. Go back to your truck and lock the doors. Keep it running. I'll be back soon."

"Damian, what in the world—"

"Go," hissed Damian as he opened the entrance door and pushed him out.

The bell rang again. Damian winced, wishing to rip the bell off the wall. Instead, he headed toward the woman. Leaning forward a little, she braced her fists against the countertop, and a carnivorous sneer stretched her lips, exposing her long, sharp fangs.

"Would yah look at that?" she purred, the well-manicured nails of her small hands elongating, turning into sharp claws. "A meal on wheels. Supersized, too."

"I've heard supersizing meals is bad for your health." Damian chuckled frostily. "Trust me, you're trying to bite off a lot more than you can chew, vamp."

The vampire hissed and hopped atop the counter, crouching there like a predator ready to pounce. Damian stilled, gathering his magic in his hands as he watched the vampire leap off the counter toward him, aiming to sink her fangs into his jugular.

Before she reached him, he took a tiny step back, and two long daggers shining with the silvery light of his magic materialized in his hands. With speed rivaling that of a vamp, he moved his arms in a cross-motion, cutting the vampire's head clear off her shoulders. For a moment, he stood, staring down as her body disintegrated into a pile of ash. Then he turned on his heels and headed toward the entrance into the seating area.

"One down...," he muttered under his breath, crossing the threshold with the bloodied daggers in his hands.

The seating area was a single large room with a tall ceiling and windows covered with thick wooden shutters. Tables were spread evenly throughout the floor, and a group of men sat around a large table, discussing something in hushed tones. They weren't eating, but each of them had a glass filled with dark red liquid in their hands. The heavy, metallic odor of blood hung in the air, leaving no questions about the contents of their drinks.

As soon as Damian walked inside, they turned around and got up slowly. Their eyes lit up with a sinister red glow, and their lips pulled back in feral snarls.

Only six of them. No big deal. Damian turned his hands with the daggers slightly forward to expose the shiny blades and said with a frosty smirk, "Yeah, I know. Meal on wheels. Supersized."

"Aw, look what the cat dragged in," one of them grumbled, sarcasm dripping out. "A wizard who decided to play a hunter. How refreshing." His scarlet eyes slid down to the daggers in Damian's hands, and he jerked his thumb at them. "Where did you buy those? Local flee market?"

"Wanna check them out closer?" Damian raised his left hand, taking a step forward.

The vampire hissed and was suddenly gone. He didn't disappear or teleport, but he was moving with such speed that he became nothing more than a blur. Expecting it, Damian stepped aside and swung his arm, meeting the approaching monster with a deadly strike of his dagger. The blade cut through the vampire's neck like it was nothing but a piece of paper but didn't decapitate him.

The vamp fell to the floor, clutching his throat with his hands, heavy dark blood gushing between his hooked fingers. The scarlet glow slowly vanished from his eyes as he stared at Damian in shock.

There were only a few known ways to kill a vampire—decapitation, a wooden stake through the heart, and fire. Silver through their hearts was also effective, and in general, any contact with silver made them weaker. However, garlic, crosses and sunlight—all these were just urban legends the vampires spread around to deceive humans who didn't know any better.

Damian didn't wait for the vampire to recover and thrust his dagger through the monster's chest.

"*Illucious*," he whispered, and the blade ignited with a brilliant white light, turning the large vampire into a pile of ashes in a heartbeat.

The rest of the vampires stared at the blazing daggers in his hands with shock.

"The Light of Creation," offered Damian calmly. "Anyone else care to try?"

The vampires howled, anger making their glowing eyes brighter, their hands turning into claws. They charged him all at once, knocking the tables over as they approached at full speed. He spun around, the daggers in his hands cutting through the air with a soft whistle. A moment later, all five vampires lay on the floor in heaps of ashes.

"I hate vamps..." Damian straightened and took a deep breath, lowering his arms. But he had no time to relax as, all of a sudden, the presence of vampiric energy in the room tripled. He sharpened his vision, staring into the dark hallway leading toward the kitchen. He didn't see them moving. He sensed their ominous presence with his every cell. Soundless and deadly like any nocturnal predators, they weren't in a rush. Hiding in the shadows, they were observing him, making an effort to conceal their presence and intentions for as long as possible.

Even though Damian couldn't say how many vampires were quietly creeping up at him, he knew there were enough of them to make it dangerous. He threw a quick glance over his shoulder and noticed that the door into the lobby was closed and most likely locked.

He hissed a quick spell and touched his belt. The daggers disappeared and were replaced by a long whip that looked almost like a stockwhip. It was made out of a flexible metal-like material, and three sharp, silver blades with long silver chains were attached to the end of it. Hoping that the whip would help him keep the mass of monsters at a distance for a while, he assumed a fighting stance, ready to spring into action. The vampires growled and charged him, coming from the shady hallway like an ominous avalanche. There were so many of them, he had no time to count.

Damian took a step back, giving himself a bit more space, and his whip split the air with a soft hiss. The silver blades cut into the vampires' bodies, slicing and dicing them. Infused with the energy of his magic, the whip left behind piles of steaming ash. The screams of anger and curses in different languages filled the air. Despite his efforts, the circle of enemies grew tighter around him, pushing him toward the wall and away from the exit door.

So far, the whip was doing its job, but he knew it was a matter of time before at least one of them would manage to slice him with their claws or sink their teeth into his body, weakening him. Besides, the constant use of his magic was taking a toll on him, too, draining his energy and physical strength.

As his back finally hit the wall, Damian swung his whip one more time, destroying a few more of his attackers. But the vampires kept coming, replacing the fallen, and in such close combat, his whip became obsolete. He cursed quietly, dropped the whip, and his daggers materialized in his hands again.

He growled, taking a defensive position, and his blades went up with the blinding white light when, with a loud bang, the entrance door exploded inward, showering all of them with splinters of wood.

The vampires gasped, and for a moment, they shifted their attention away from Damian. He didn't care to find out what it was and used the opportunity to regroup. Fighting his way through, he attacked the vampires with all he had. Another loud bang of a gunshot bounced through the room. And then one more.

As Damian cut through the monsters, he saw Sam standing on the threshold, a shotgun in his hands. To his shock, every shot of his weapon reached a target, leaving a pile of ash at the old man's feet as he slowly progressed forward. A few minutes later, the vampires were gone—most of them dead, but a few of them retreated before either Damian or Sam could get to them.

Damian glanced at Sam in shock, his chest rising and falling with heavy breaths. The old man looked angry but not shocked, so Damian had no doubt he wasn't new to the World of Magic.

"How can you kill a vampire with a shotgun?" he asked, lowering his arms as the daggers vanished from his hands.

"Argentum NO3," growled Sam, struggling to equalize his breathing. "Silver Nitrate and a big enough caliber bullet can vanquish any monster."

Damian nodded and lowered down to one knee, moving his hand through a thick layer of ash as he tried to find his whip. He found it almost right away and raised his head, ready to get up. To his shock, he found Sam's shotgun trained at his face.

"Sam, wait—," started Damian. He dropped his whip and raised his hands in a peaceful gesture.

"Stay where you are, kid, and don't move if you know what's good for you," muttered Sam, placing the hot barrel against Damian's forehead.

"Sam, listen—"

"You're not human. What kind of monster are you?" the old man demanded, his eyes sparkling with anger, sweat running down his face.

DEAR READER

Thank you so much for reading The Burns Destiny. I hope you enjoyed the Fire Salamander Chronicles series.

If you would like to stay up-to-date on the latest information about new releases, special offers, and more, sign up for my mailing list and get a FREE novella. Click here to join.

For more information follow me on Facebook and Instagram.

www.facebook.com/nmthornauthor
www.instagram.com/nmthornauthor/

Join N.M. Thorn's Facebook Fan Group to meet other readers, discuss the novels and the characters, get updates and do anything else related to the series.

BEFORE YOU GO...

Your reviews mean the world to me and are greatly appreciated. If you enjoyed the Burns Destiny, please take a few minutes to leave a review. It doesn't have to be long. It can be just a few words or stars rating.

Please help spread the word by taking this small extra step and leave your review on Amazon and/or Goodreads.

ALSO BY N. M. THORN

The Fire Salamander Chronicles

The Burns Path (Prequel Novella Book 0 - for my subscribers)

The Burns Fire - Book 1

The Burns War - Book 2

The Burns Defiance - Book 3

The Burns Codex - Book 4

The Burns Enigma - Book 5

ABOUT THE AUTHOR

N.M. Thorn currently lives in South Florida with her husband and son. Owner of a digital marketing agency by day and a writer by night, she loves spending her times creating new worlds, paranormal planes of existence and anything that could be described as supernatural.

When she is not busy working with everything digital or exploring fantasy worlds, she enjoys spending time with her family, reading, painting and practicing martial arts.

If you would like to share your thoughts, ideas or just send N.M. Thorn a message about the Fire Salamander world, feel free to contact her at: nmthornauthor@gmail.com

Printed in Great Britain
by Amazon

21803513R00264